"You Must Accept Your Fate. . . .

"The gods have brought you to me, and when we reach Norge, you will remain as slaves in my household."

Gwendolyn's head snapped back, hatred and defiance burning in her eyes. Any hopes she had of receiving fair treatment from this man had been cruelly dashed. "I know naught of your gods," she said disdainfully. "But if it is slaves Anora and I shall be, then know this, Viking, you are no different from the two you punished earlier."

Hakon turned away. Even if he had wanted to, he knew he could not let them go. He felt drawn to the beautiful Anora as he had never felt drawn to any woman.

Gwendolyn allowed herself only a moment of self-pity before she turned to her sister. Anora's face was deadly pale in the moonlight, her eyes fixed and devoid of emotion.

"Anora, listen to me!" Gwendolyn whispered, suddenly afraid. "Anora, I vow I will find a way for us to return to our homeland."

A flicker of response lighted Anora's eyes. "Promise me, Gwendolyn?" she murmured plaintively.

"Aye, on my life . . . I promise."

TWIN PASSIONS

Twin Passions

MIRIAM
MINGER

PaperJacks LTD.

TORONTO NEW YORK

AN ORIGINAL

PaperJacks

TWIN PASSIONS

PaperJacks LTD.

330 STEELCASE RD. E., MARKHAM, ONT. L3R 2M1
210 FIFTH AVE., NEW YORK, N.Y. 10010

First edition published November 1988

This is a work of fiction in its entirety. Any resemblance to actual people, places or events is purely coincidental.

10 9 8 7 6 5 4 3 2 1

ISBN 0-7701-1000-2

To Kari, Ken and Deborah,
who helped me realize a dream;

To Stephen,
who shares it with me.

England, 973 A.D.

Chapter One

" 'Tis not safe for you to venture out alone, my lady," murmured the shy young stableboy, almost to himself. Biting his lower lip, he fumbled nervously with the leather girths of the saddle. Surely Earl Godric would not allow one of his daughters to ride out of the stronghold without a guard to protect her. Perhaps he should offer to ride along with her? That thought made him flush bright red from his neck to the roots of his scalp. He shifted his feet uncomfortably, sensing her impatience, but for some reason he could not fasten the last buckle properly.

"Here, let me do that," Gwendolyn said in exasperation. She knelt down beside him, her expert fingers deftly threading the leather strap through the metal buckle. "There, now," she muttered, satisfied. Rising to her feet, she brushed the straw from the knees of her buckskin trousers. She looked steadily at the startled stableboy, her emerald eyes searching his ruddy face. "You must be new to the stables," she said. "What is your name, lad?"

"G-Garric, m-mistress," he stammered, awestruck by her fair beauty. For the life of him he could not understand why such a fine lady was dressed in men's clothing almost as simple as his own. He looked down at his feet, fearful that she would think his gaze far too bold. " 'T-tis my first day in the stables, my lady."

"Well, Garric, look over there," Gwendolyn said, lifting the stableboy's trembling chin. She nodded toward the far end of the darkened stable.

His eyes widened as he recognized two of Earl Godric's most trusted thanes. The men were quickly saddling their horses, taking care to glance over at Gwendolyn every so often to make sure she had not yet left the stable.

"Though I am quite capable of watching out for myself," she stated, her emerald eyes flashing defiantly, "my father insists that those two thanes ride along with me whenever I leave the stronghold." She lowered her voice, her tone softening as she smiled at the boy. "So, you see, Garric, your fears are for naught. But I thank you for your kind concern."

A slow, creeping blush burned the stableboy's freckled cheeks as he stared at her, his heart beating hard against his narrow chest. He had never been gifted with such a smile before! A look of embarrassment crossed his face. Suddenly he turned and fled from the stable, the hearty laughter of the two thanes ringing in his ears.

"Lady Gwendolyn has power over us all." The burlier thane grinned at his companion.

"Aye. Just like her sister," agreed the other, chuckling to himself. With a sharp yank on the reins, he urged his steed forward and followed Gwendolyn, who was leading her dappled mare into the stable yard.

Once out in the open, the frisky mare nudged her mistress with her velvety nose. She whinnied expectantly, as if to speed them on their way. The cool autumn afternoon seemed to beckon to them. Without even a backward glance at the two thanes, Gwendolyn slid easily onto the mare's back.

"We'll soon be free, my Arrow," she whispered softly, spurring the mare gently with her heel.

Passing through the protective walls that surrounded the stronghold of her father, Earl Godric of Cheshire, Gwendolyn reined in just outside the heavy, timbered gate. The main road before her led through open fields, rich with the bountiful autumn harvest. To her right lay a smaller path that wound toward the river through dense, forested woodlands. With little hesitation, she chose the less traveled path to the river. She had not been for a ride in several days, and yearned for nothing more than to be alone for a while. Well, almost alone, she thought darkly, remembering the two silent thanes who were riding not far behind her. Clucking her tongue to her mare, she set off at a lively canter.

The late-afternoon sun was just beginning to settle into the gnarled oak trees. The brisk air was tinged with the sharp, pungent scents of autumn—damp earth, smoky wood fires—and Gwendolyn took in great breaths, filling her lungs. She loved this time of year, when the entire landscape was awash in vivid hues of crimson, orange, and russet.

Suddenly she sighed. It would not be a long ride today, for the hour was later than she had thought. She glanced over her shoulder at the two thanes wending their way along the leaf-strewn path not far behind her. They reminded her of great, hulking shadows. No doubt they would soon ride up and urge her to turn back.

She shivered, turning up the collar of her woolen shirt against the brisk north wind. She was grateful for the added warmth of her fur-lined leather jerkin, which she had donned only as an afterthought in her haste to get to the stable. She reached up and pulled her woolen cap down over her ears. Her short, silver-blond curls peered out from beneath the narrow brim, softly framing her delicate features.

Gwendolyn's emerald green eyes darkened as she reflected on the events of the past few months. Overtaken by her thoughts, she unwittingly relaxed her firm grip on the reins. The dappled mare nickered softly, tossing her head at this new freedom, and slowed her pace to a meandering walk along the familiar path.

God's blood! Why must everything change? she asked herself, a frown creasing her forehead. As if in reply, a sudden gust of wind rustled through the trees. Dry leaves, tugged from their branches, whirled silently to the ground below. Gazing at the half-naked limbs that until a few weeks ago had been green and full, Gwendolyn cursed herself for a fool.

If only Father had not made that agreement with King Edgar, she thought fiercely. As if it had been yesterday, she recalled all too well the furtive conversation she had overheard in the chapel between the family priest, Father Leofwine, and Grimbald, her father's steward, late last spring. She had been sitting on a far bench in the back of the small sanctuary, as was her wont when she wished to be alone, when the two men entered from the side door. Apparently they had not seen her, for they had not bothered to lower their voices. She listened, unbelieving, to their words, scarcely able to breathe.

"Is it true, then, Grimbald, that a marriage is being arranged?" Father Leofwine had asked, his wheezing cough echoing about the empty chapel.

"Aye, Holy Father," Grimbald replied, nodding his balding head, "but the news is yet a secret. Lady Anora has not been told."

"Hardly a well-kept secret. The very walls have ears," the stooped priest said wryly. "Well, then, why the secrecy? Is it an ogre she will wed?"

Grimbald's eyes narrowed as he leaned closer to the priest. "He is a Danish prince, Holy Father, and one of the most powerful men in the Danelaw! King Edgar himself has proposed the match as a reward, one could say, for the Dane's recent oath of allegiance to an English king."

Masking his initial surprise at the steward's outburst, the old priest nodded his head solemnly. "So, our king is seeking an alliance with the Danelaw," he murmured, rubbing his stubbled chin. "Perhaps this marriage is part of a larger plan . . . aye, a great plan—one that might end the bloodshed and hate between our two people, and further King Edgar's quest for unity. . . . " His voice trailed off, and Gwendolyn strained to hear his next words. "And Earl Godric has agreed to this?"

"Aye, Your Holiness, but not without some misgivings. You know as well as I that Anora is very dear to his heart. He is not convinced that this is the best match for her." He paused, catching his breath. "The king also asked about Lady Gwendolyn! But Earl Godric insisted that as the elder of his twin daughters, Anora was the first to be wed."

Shaking his head, Father Leofwine sighed heavily. "Pity that the child must play a pawn in a king's game, even for so great a cause. Perhaps she will go to him willingly." He was suddenly seized by another fit of coughing. "Go now, Grimbald. I am weary of this intrigue."

Gwendolyn watched furtively through lowered lashes as the priest turned toward the gilded altar, abruptly dismissing the steward. Then, wheeling around suddenly, he reached out his gnarled hand and caught Grimbald's sleeve. "Wait! One more question before you go. What is the name of this mighty prince of the Danelaw?"

"Wulfgar Ragnarson, Holy Father."

Gwendolyn had not noticed that her hands had tightened on the reins until the dappled mare snorted loudly at the rough treatment, tossing her head in protest. Gwendolyn quickly loosened her fierce grip. "Forgive me, Arrow," she soothed, stroking the rough gray hairs on the mare's neck. Her voice was calm, belying the bitter turmoil that raged within her.

He is a Dane, an enemy of our people, Gwendolyn thought angrily. *How could Father ever have agreed to such a proposal?* Yet, she knew the answer. A king's pawn . . . a reward . . . The words echoed in her mind, over and over. After that day in the chapel, she had known that her life would never be the same. The grim realization that she and Anora could be used as barter at the whim of a king, their fates so easily decided by others, had shaken her to the very depths of her being.

And now, not only had her father betrayed her, but Anora, too. Gwendolyn raged silently. Though her sister had been given the right to refuse this Wulfgar Ragnarson if she so desired, she had fallen in love with him, agreeing to be his wife! *How could Anora let herself be used so?* Gwendolyn wondered, shaking her head in dismay.

Yet Gwendolyn had to admit that it wasn't just that Anora was to marry a Dane that upset her so. Nay, there was something else, something even more painful. She had watched in silence while her sister underwent a mysterious transformation during the summer months. Where she and Anora had once been inseparable, sharing laughter and tears, secret dreams and hopes, and hiding nothing from each other, Gwendolyn now found herself alone. From their first meeting, Anora and Wulfgar had seemed as if they were in a world that only two could share. Aye, perhaps it was this that had hurt her most of all.

Gwendolyn shook her head fiercely. Nay, she didn't want to think of the wedding, of Wulfgar Ragnarson, or of Anora's betrayal anymore! But suddenly an odd thought struck her. She laughed ruefully, startling her mare. *It could have been* my *fate that was decided by the king, except for an accident of birth.* She wondered if her own betrothal was being planned to follow shortly after Anora's marriage, now just three days away. The thought of being subject to any man made her stomach knot angrily. Why, she could ride a horse and wield a weapon as well as any of her father's thanes, if not better!

"A king's pawn!" Gwendolyn snorted derisively. "Nay, I will not settle for any man unless it is by my own choosing!" Urging the mare into a full gallop, she looked mischievously over her shoulder. She could barely make out the two thanes through the thick trees. They were riding hard and fast, yet she had the advantage of distance as she rebelliously spurred her mare onward.

Spying a path that led away from the river, Gwendolyn veered down the steep side of a hill. She hid behind some low branches, watching breathlessly as the two thanes thundered past her, their steeds flecked with sweat and foam. Confident that she had eluded them, she left the shelter of the trees and urged the mare once again into a gallop.

"Faster, Arrow, faster!" Gwendolyn laughed with joyful exhilaration. She rode through the woods with wild abandon, her painful thoughts forgotten, at least for now. The brisk air enlivened her senses. Aye, it had been a long time since she had felt so lighthearted and free!

Chapter Two

Damp evening mists parted before the mare's flashing hooves as she galloped through a clearing in the densely wooded forest. At Gwendolyn's urging, the mare plunged back into the woods nimbly dodging the shadowed trees that loomed all around them. A loud clap of thunder suddenly exploded in the distance, startling the spirited animal. She reared in fright, nearly throwing Gwendolyn off her back.

"Whoa, Arrow!" she shouted, pulling firmly on the reins. Another clap of thunder echoed through the strangely silent woods, startling a flock of resting blackbirds into flight. Their raucous cries shattered the growing stillness as lightning was etched against the sky. Looking up at the dark, menacing clouds, Gwendolyn realized she had not noticed the approaching storm. She had been riding for hours, and knew it was long past the time when she should have returned to the stronghold.

She twisted around in the saddle, peering about her, but she could not make out any familiar landmarks in the gathering darkness. *Now you've done it, my girl,* she thought, cursing her foolhardiness. She had never ridden so far from the stronghold before, and doubted she was even on her father's lands.

Stifling a twinge of apprehension, Gwendolyn decided to ride toward the river. Aye, surely from there she would find a path leading back to the stronghold. She wheeled her frightened mare around, and set out the way she had come.

Riding hard through the woods, the storm surging and shrieking about her, Gwendolyn finally reached the churning river. Wracked by shivering spasms, she felt chilled to the bone. Cold, stinging rain lashed at her body through her soaking clothes. Her numbed hands could barely grasp the reins. Shielding her eyes from the rain, she searched anxiously for any signs of a path, but there was none. Desperately she plunged the mare into the heavy underbrush that choked the muddy banks of the river.

A bright bolt of lightning suddenly flashed across the sky and dashed into an ancient oak right in front of them. Orange flames leaped from the ground where the bolt pierced the earth, as if shooting up from the very depths of hell. Rearing and snorting in fright, the mare frantically pawed the air, the whites of her eyes gleaming in the dark. Another veined streak of lightning lit the sky, illuminating the swollen waters of the river.

Suddenly, Gwendolyn's face constricted in terror, her breath tearing raggedly at her throat, at the apparition before her. Before her very eyes, a demon creature, dragon-like, floated across the rushing torrents of water, leering at her with devilish glee. Then just as suddenly as it had appeared, it was gone.

"Holy Mother Mary, protect me!" she screamed, crossing herself frantically. Hot tears streaked her cheeks as she clung desperately to her mare's wet mane. She felt herself slipping from the saddle as unconsciousness drew her deeper and deeper into a frightening maelstrom of darkness.

The sound of hooves thundering toward her flooded her with relief, and revived her failing senses. Peering into the surrounding trees, Gwendolyn recognized the familiar shapes of the two thanes as they rode up beside her.

"Lady Gwendolyn, are you all right?" questioned the burly thane, his voice filled with concern. Receiving no response, he gazed fearfully at her pale, stricken face. Her emerald eyes were glazed and overbright.

Acting quickly, the thane lifted her onto his saddle and covered her with his woolen cloak. Although sodden, it would offer her some protection from the cold rain. Cursing to himself, he knew there would be hell to pay for this misadventure. "Outwitted by a chit of a girl," he muttered darkly. The Lady Gwendolyn was well known for her willful exploits, but this time he feared she had gone too far. Signaling to his companion to grab the reins of her mare, he kicked the heaving sides of his steed and headed for the stronghold at a full gallop.

Nestled within the heavy cloak, Gwendolyn could feel the warmth slowly returning to her aching limbs. The burly thane's arms about her were reassuring, and she attempted to dispel the memory of the nightmare vision from her mind. *I can tell no one*, she thought dazedly, *or they will think I am mad*. Yet, in her heart, she knew her vision had been real, though she could not explain it.

Reining in their horses at the timbered gate of the stronghold, the thanes waited impatiently for the heavy doors to swing open. Great torches, sputtering in the rain, lit up the night as loud shouts heralded their entrance into the main yard.

Gwendolyn felt herself being taken into the waiting arms of another thane. Then she was carried across the yard into the great hall. Blinking from the brightness, she felt a twinge of guilt at the anxious faces of those gathered around her. Her eyes came to rest on the figure of her mother rushing toward her.

"Quickly, we must get her warm at once," Lady Bronwen ordered, taking immediate charge of the situation. She gestured for the thane to follow her, and a serving maid who also stood nearby. Holding a thick tallow candle in front of her, she led the way up a wooden staircase to Gwendolyn's chamber.

"Lay her down on the bed," she said evenly, setting the candle in a large brass holder. The thane hastily obeyed, then stood aside, not knowing what to do next. His eyes widened as Lady Bronwen began unceremoniously to strip the drenched clothes from Gwendolyn's shivering body. She looked up at him, a faint smile curving her lips. "You may go now."

"Aye, my lady." He nodded, red-faced. Without a backward glance, the sheepish thane beat a hasty retreat down the stairs.

"Go to the kitchen and fetch some meat broth and herbs," Lady Bronwen said softly to the young serving maid. The girl bobbed her head and scurried out of the room, close on the heels of the departing thane. Lady Bronwen turned back to Gwendolyn and helped her into the bed, gently pulling the warm blankets up over her delicate shoulders. She looked kindly at her daughter, her gentle eyes speaking a message of concern, yet also a mild reproach.

Overcome by her mother's tenderness, Gwendolyn felt hot tears burn her cheeks. "Mother, I . . ." she began hesitantly, but the words stumbled on her tongue.

"Hush, lamb, we can talk of this later," soothed Lady Bronwen. She moved away from the bed and lit several small oil lamps about the chamber. The faint rustling of her linen tunic and mantle was the only sound in the room.

"Here are the herbs and the broth, my lady!" the serving maid whispered breathlessly as she entered the bedchamber. She had run all the way to the kitchen and back, anxious to please her kind mistress.

Lady Bronwen nodded her thanks, then took the bowls from the girl and set them on a small wooden table by the bed. "Go now and find Leah. I have need of her," she said over her shoulder.

"Aye, mistress," the serving maid replied, hurrying out the door once again.

Stirring the herbs into the steaming meat broth, Lady Bronwen offered one of the bowls to Gwendolyn. "Here, lamb, but drink it slowly."

Gwendolyn cupped the bowl in her hands, bringing it shakily to her lips. She took a sip, savoring the richness of the beef broth. After several more sips a gradual warmth began to spread through her, stilling at last the shivering spasms that wracked her slender body. Feeling her eyelids growing heavy, she handed the empty bowl to her mother. Lying back against the soft down pillow, she could no longer keep her eyes open. Gradually she felt herself drift into a comforting sleep.

Tucking in the soft woolen blanket, Lady Bronwen gazed down at her sleeping daughter. How could such an angelic-looking young woman cause so much trouble? she wondered, shaking her head. Indeed, Gwendolyn's fair features shone with almost unearthly beauty. Her brows arched delicately, her nose was straight and slender, her cheekbones high and graceful. Her lips, lush and rosy, were curved in the faintest of smiles, and her emerald green eyes, closed in sleep, were thickly fringed with dark lashes that fluttered ever so slightly against her creamy skin. The only feature that gave a hint of her true temperament was the stubborn set of her chin.

Lady Bronwen sighed as she smoothed an unruly curl from Gwendolyn's forehead, remembering the many times she had tried to convince her daughter to grow her hair long. Yet all her pleas had been for naught. Strong-minded like her father, Gwendolyn had insisted since childhood that long hair was a nuisance. Besides, she had not wanted to be an exact replica of her twin sister, Anora. A bright smile at her father had always ended the argument, and Gwendolyn once again managed to have her way. Lady Bronwen shook her head. She truly feared that perhaps Godric had spoiled this daughter overmuch. Her wild escapade tonight was proof of that!

'Tis hard to believe so many years have passed . . . and so quickly, she thought, reflecting on her eighteen years of marriage to Earl Godric. Their union had produced twin daughters, just turned seventeen, and one son who had died at childbirth. A flicker of sorrow passed across Lady Bronwen's lovely face. Her heart still ached at the thought of the lost child, a pain she had carried since his death.

Yet it was her husband, deprived of his only son, who had thrilled at the early interest displayed by Gwendolyn in such masculine pursuits as riding, hunting, and archery. He had encouraged her, and before long she had become proficient at all of them. Her skill and accuracy with all manner of small weapons, especially the knife, were well known. She had even accompanied her father on his twice-yearly hunts for wild boar, and had taken great delight in the dangerous sport. Never once had she shown the least bit of fear.

Ever the doting parent, Earl Godric had even allowed Gwendolyn to wear a boy's clothing, specially made to fit her slender form. She had taken to them happily, relishing the ease of movement the woolen shirts and breeches afforded her. From then on, Lady Bronwen had always been hard pressed to get Gwendolyn to wear a proper lady's tunic and mantle.

" 'Tis no wonder Gwendolyn has such a rebellious nature," Lady Bronwen murmured resignedly. Finding a husband for her tempestuous daughter would indeed be a task. He would have to be a strong man to tame her, yet wise enough not to break her courageous spirit. She wondered if there was such a man. . . .

A soft knock at the door broke into her thoughts. Glancing over her shoulder, she saw Anora waiting expectantly. "Come in, love," she whispered, beckoning to her.

Anora walked quietly across the room, her eyes wide with apprehension. "Is she well?" she asked fearfully.

"Aye," Lady Bronwen answered, noting the anxious concern radiating from her daughter's emerald eyes.

Anora's delicate shoulders slumped with relief. "Could I stay with her awhile, Mother?"

"Nay, Anora, I think 'tis best that Leah stay with her this night," Lady Bronwen replied gently. "I have already sent for her." Seeing the disappointment on her daughter's face, she continued gently. "Tomorrow will be a long day for you, Anora, and you must rest well tonight. I am sure you would want to look your best for Wulfgar's arrival."

Lady Bronwen smiled at the sudden blush in Anora's cheeks. She had no doubt that her daughter would be the fairest woman at the betrothal feast—well, save for one, she amended quickly, gazing at Anora's mirror image sleeping peacefully in her bed. Together her twin daughters made a radiant pair, neither surpassing the other in beauty, but equal in loveliness of face and form.

"Aye, Mother, you are right," Anora murmured. "Good night, then." She bent and kissed Lady Bronwen's cheek, then turned just as Leah walked into the candlelit room. "Good night, Leah," she said softly. With one last look at her sister, Anora left as quietly as she had come.

" 'Tis time you also rested, my lady," Leah admonished gently, having overheard their conversation. She clucked her tongue disapprovingly as she walked to the bed. What kind of trouble had the lass gotten herself into *this* time?

Lady Bronwen seemed to read her thoughts. "Now, Leah, let us not judge too harshly," she murmured, trying, unsuccessfully, to suppress a smile. The faithful maid had been with the family for many years, and had no qualms about speaking her mind, especially when it came to Gwendolyn.

"Would you sit with her this night? I would remain myself, but there is still so much to be done before the betrothal feast tomorrow."

"Go on with ye, my lady. I will see to the lass," Leah reassured her. Aye, she had seen both Anora and Gwendolyn through many a fever, but from what she could tell so far, there was no illness this night. "And mind you, get some rest yourself, my lady," she repeated, noting with concern the faint circles under her mistress's eyes.

Lady Bronwen nodded, then rose from her chair. She leaned over and lightly kissed Gwendolyn's cool forehead. "She seems to be fine now, but if she should call out for me, or grow feverish—"

"I will wake you if there is need, my lady," Leah murmured.

"Very well. Good night, Leah and my thanks." She looked gratefully at her maid, unspoken words of comfort passing between them.

Turning toward the door, she was not surprised to see the shadowed figure of Earl Godric standing inside the threshold. She walked over to him and took his proffered arm, the look in her luminous eyes telling him all he needed to know. Relief surged through his body, and with a last backward glance at their sleeping daughter, they descended the stairs together.

Chapter Three

"Will there be anything else, my lady?" the maid questioned softly as she poured a generous amount of perfumed lavender oil into the steaming bath water.

"Nay, everything is fine," Anora murmured contentedly, settling deeper into the large brass tub. Reaching for a small cake of lavendar-scented soap, she began to hum softly.

What a luxury! she thought, soaping a silky leg. The perfumed soaps and oils, gifts from the household of the king, delighted her beyond measure. Breathing in the fragrant steam, she giggled as she flicked scented droplets of water at the gray kitten curled up asleep on the soft towel at the foot of the tub. The kitten stretched, its little pink mouth yawning widely, then snuggled deeper into the towel.

Anora leaned her head against the rim of the tub, the smile fading from her lips as her thoughts drifted back to the night before. A troubled look crossed her brow, startling the maid, who was laying out fresh garments on the bed.

"My lady, are you not feeling well?" the maid asked, voicing her concern. With only two more days until the wedding, she could think of nothing worse than Anora's becoming ill.

"Have you any news of Gwendolyn this morning?"

Taken aback, the maid realized Anora had not even heard her question. "Aye, she is fine, but still sleeping," she replied, clucking her tongue and shaking her head. "She had a fitful night, Leah says, tossing and turning and mumbling about dragons, demons, and such." She would have continued to recite what she had heard earlier that morning in the kitchen, but thought better of it at the sight of Anora's stricken face. "Don't you worry now, my lady, she'll be just fine," she soothed, seeking to allay any needless fears. "I'll be back shortly to help you dress." With a reassuring glance, she left the room.

Hardly feeling reassured, Anora sighed as she recalled the frantic scene in the great hall the night before. It had been like a bad dream. When Gwendolyn had not returned with her guards in time for the evening meal, their father sent half his men out into the raging storm to search for them. He had then called loudly for a stable hand to saddle his own mighty steed, but had been stayed by the shouts from outside the hall. A drenched thane entered with the news that Gwendolyn had been found.

Anora shuddered. She remembered all too painfully her feelings of dread when Gwendolyn was carried into the hall, shivering and bedraggled. Her own body had felt chilled at the sight of her sister, and a feeling of helplessness had welled up deep within her. Shivering in empathy, she had experienced a strange sense of sharing in a frightening vision, but the feeling had quickly passed. Only later, after visiting Gwendolyn's chamber, had she felt reassured. Her mother's presence had lent an air of calm, and she returned to her own chamber much relieved.

But what was this talk of dragons and nightmares? Anora wondered. A shiver suddenly ran through her body, recalling her sense of foreboding from the night before. Feeling the water in her bath growing tepid, she realized she had lingered overlong. She stepped out of the tub so quickly that water sloshed onto the sleeping kitten. With a startled yowl it streaked from the room, leaving wet paw prints across the floor. Smiling once again, Anora took a towel from the table near the tub and dried herself quickly.

Wulfgar. She could hardly believe her future husband was now within the stronghold. She had heard the commotion of his arrival earlier that morning. The thought of him made her senses reel with excitement and longing. *Do all young women feel this way*, she wondered, *on the eve of their marriage?* Her fingers trembled as she loosened the ivory pins from the thick coil of hair at her nape. It tumbled about her shoulders and down her back in a riot of silvery-blond waves. Standing in a stream of sunshine from the window, she luxuriated for a moment in the golden warmth.

Returning from the kitchen with a light breakfast, the maid paused just inside the door. *Aye, here is one that was made for the love of a man*, she thought approvingly, proud of her mistress's beauty.

An air of innocence surrounded Anora as she stood lost in some private thought, a smile playing about her lips. Her lustrous hair framed her long, graceful throat and delicate shoulders, falling like a gossamer cloud about her narrow waist. Her breasts, high and firm, were small, yet perfectly rounded, the nipples pale roseates that peeked out from beneath her long tresses. Walking over to the bed, she picked up a white silken camise and drew it up over the slender curve of her hips, then slipped her slim arms through the embroidered straps.

"Here, let me help you, my lady," the maid offered, setting the breakfast trencher on a low table near the bed. She straightened the camise about Anora's body, smoothing the myriad soft folds that fell almost to the floor. "May I suggest the blue tunic for the betrothal feast?" she asked, glancing over at the array of garments spread out on the bed. Lady Bronwen's seamstresses had worked many hours preparing the fine clothes for the wedding festivities, each seeking to outdo the other in their choice of fabric and decorative stitching.

Anora nodded her approval, sighing appreciatively as the silken fabric of the tunic was slipped over her head. The rich, sapphire blue silk felt cool to the touch, caressing her creamy skin. The neck, wrists, and hem of the tunic were stitched with fine embroidery of silver threads. After the tunic went a gray silk mantle fastened at the shoulders by two filigree silver brooches.

"Mistress, you are truly beautiful!" exclaimed the maid, clapping her hands together as she surveyed her handiwork. The gray silk of the mantle enhanced the emerald depths of Anora's eyes, which were dancing with anticipation.

Seating her on a cushioned chair, the maid brushed the few tangles from Anora's lovely hair. As a final touch she placed a finely etched silver circlet on her head, as a symbol of her maidenhood. After marriage, the circlet would be worn with a transparent veil to cover her hair. The maid then handed Anora a small metal mirror, holding her breath as she anxiously awaited a response.

A radiant smile lit Anora's face as she gazed at her reflection in the mirror. "Aye, I truly feel beautiful today." She blushed, secretly hoping that Wulfgar would also find her appearance pleasing. Thanking the maid for her assistance, she gently dismissed her, wishing to be alone for a while.

As the maid shut the door behind her, Anora stepped over to the small window and gazed out into the courtyard at the busy scene below. Servants were bustling to and fro from the great hall on their varied tasks, some carrying great rounds of cheese, others laden with piles of fine table linens, and still others hurrying toward the kitchen clutching squawking chickens. Large barrels of ale and mead were being wheeled into the hall from the brewing house, guests were beginning to arrive, and the sounds of boisterous laughter could be heard all around.

Anora spied one of Wulfgar's men crossing the yard and her heart leaped to her throat. How she had yearned for this day! Wulfgar had left her for his lands near York a few weeks ago to make preparations for her arrival after their marriage. Knowing that he would soon return for her was consolation enough, but the days had passed achingly slow. The thought of him—his handsome face, and the memory of his strong arms around her—had filled her every waking hour. But it had been her dreams—veiled, breathless images of passion she had never before experienced—that had caused her to awaken trembling and flushed in the night, calling out his name.

How different she felt now, as if she had never known life without him, she mused, remembering with some chagrin the day her father had told her of his agreement with King Edgar concerning her marriage. Shocked by the abruptness of his announcement, she had retreated to her chamber in a flood of tears. Earl Godric, who had been at a loss as how best to present the news, realized he had failed miserably as he watched his daughter flee the hall. With a reproachful glance at her startled husband, Lady Bronwen rushed out after her. Shaking his head at the strange ways of women, he had slumped resignedly into his chair before the fireplace.

Sobbing miserably into her down pillow, Anora had felt that her childhood dreams were shattered forever. With her mother's comforting arms about her, she tearfully poured out her secret wish that she would one day marry for love. She knew the marriage of her parents had been decreed by others, but fortunately a great love had grown between them. Grasping a glimmer of hope that her mother would be able to make her father understand her feelings, she had watched through tear-dimmed eyes as Lady Bronwen hurriedly left the room.

Anora shuddered as she vividly recalled the loud voices she had heard resounding from the great hall. Never before had her parents raised their voices to each other! Feeling fresh tears burning her cheeks, she had rushed dazedly back to the hall to tell her father she would accept the proposal —anything to restore harmony. To her amazement she found her parents no longer embroiled in a heated argument, but wrapped in a tender embrace.

Her father had asked her to be seated, then explained the king's reasoning behind the marriage and his hopes for a continued peace in England. Glancing briefly at Lady Bronwen, he continued in a low, solemn voice. She remembered his words as if they had been spoken only yesterday: "Anora, 'tis my hope that you will honor the agreement between myself and King Edgar, and accept Wulfgar Ragnarson as your husband. But as your mother and I do not wish for you to be unhappy, we have agreed to allow you to decide for yourself if such a marriage would please you."

Aye, it pleases me, Anora thought happily. *It pleases me very much*. The sudden creaking of the door startled her, and she whirled around.

"You have not touched your breakfast, my lady," admonished the maid as she bustled in the door. "It is almost midday, and your lady mother wishes to see you in the solar."

"I will try to eat something later," Anora replied, eyeing the buttered bread and honeyed wine with little appetite. Truly, she did not feel hungry at all, what with butterflies of excitement fluttering in her stomach!

Hurrying down the steps and into the corridor, Anora wondered how she would fill the long hours before the feast that evening. As she reached the solar, she heard laughter filtering through the heavy wooden door, and the voice of Edythe, her mother's lady-in-waiting, rising above the din.

"Aye, if I had a man such as Wulfgar to warm my bed, I might even marry again!"

"But he is a Dane!" a dissenting voice replied indignantly.

"It matters naught to me. He fits his trousers better than many a man, be he Dane or Anglo-Saxon!"

Blushing heatedly, Anora pushed open the door, interrupting the merry conversation as the ladies-in-waiting sought to suppress their giggles. Lady Bronwen rose gracefully from her chair and quickly crossed the room to her daughter.

"You look lovely, Anora," she said approvingly, kissing her daughter's burning cheek. Taking Anora's hand, Lady Bronwen led her to an empty chair beside Edythe, who was suddenly very intent on the needlework before her.

A short, stout woman with a kindly face, Edythe had been married as a girl to an elderly, wealthy landowner who died shortly after the wedding. Vowing never to marry again, the rich young widow retired to her new estates, where it was rumored she amused herself over the years with many lovers. Now well past middle age, the thought of her dallying with a handsome warrior seemed unlikely, but one could never be sure. The twinkle in her eye and her flirtatious manner belied her advancing years.

Peering out of the corner of her eye, Edythe caught a ghost of a smile curving Anora's lips and seized the opportunity to make amends. "Pay no mind to an old widow, my lady, I meant you no harm. We are glad of your marriage to such a fine, handsome man!"

The other ladies nodded in agreement, including the one sour-faced dissenter, after receiving a sharp elbow in the ribs. Soon the room was once again filled with lighthearted talk of the wedding festivities as the women stitched at a magnificent tapestry that would one day grace the timbered walls of the great hall. Depicting a lively hunting scene, the tapestry told the tale of the giant boar that had been killed the past year by Earl Godric and his thanes. And, at her father's side, the small figure of Gwendolyn seated bravely on her dappled mare was immortalized in threads of every hue.

Lady Bronwen left the room quietly, assured that Anora would be kept busy the rest of the afternoon. Tradition demanded that she not see Wulfgar until the betrothal feast. Closing the door firmly, she turned her thoughts to the frenzied preparations taking place throughout the stronghold. "There is so much yet to do," she murmured to herself, as she walked down the wooden stairs that led to the kitchen.

Chapter Four

Locked in the throes of a vivid nightmare, Gwendolyn shook her head wildly from side to side. Dark, menacing trees were reaching out to snatch her from her mare, and their trunks were etched with leering faces that grinned demoniacally. She tried to fend off the grasping branches that scratched and tore at her, but she lost her balance and slipped off her mare's back. Rolling over and over down a steep embankment, she tumbled into icy, swirling water. The dark waves closed over her head for a moment. Then she surfaced, struggling and gasping for breath. Suddenly, rising up from the center of a giant whirlpool, a dragon creature loomed above her. She screamed as the apparition coiled its scaly tail about her body, but her voice made no sound. Once again she was dragged beneath the murky water. She felt herself sinking, sinking . . . surrounded by raucous laughter that rang in her ears.

"Nay!" Gwendolyn awoke with a start, her defiant cry echoing about the small room. Wide-eyed with terror, she felt her heart beating wildly in her breast. For a moment she could not remember where she was. Then a long, shuddering sigh escaped her throat as she recognized her surroundings. She shaded her eyes from the bright sunlight streaming into her room from the high, narrow windows.

How long had she been asleep? she wondered dazedly, sitting up in her bed. Faint memories of her nightmare, its twisted images blurred and foggy, still tortured her thoughts. Rubbing her aching temples, she swung her legs over the side of the bed and rose shakily to her feet. Swaying unsteadily, she felt her legs suddenly buckle beneath her and she crumpled to the floor.

"Lady Gwendolyn!" Just returning from the kitchen, Leah rushed over to her young mistress's side. She gently lifted her from the wooden floor and helped her back into bed. " 'Tis the sleeping herbs, my lady. They make a body feel all wobbly for a while," she murmured. Turning to the small table at the side of the bed, she poured cool water into a goblet, then handed it to Gwendolyn. "It will soon pass," she added. "Just give it a moment."

Leah's startled cry had pierced the gray mist in Gwendolyn's mind, painfully reviving her dulled senses. Sipping the water, she could feel a tingling in her limbs as the numbness gradually disappeared. She handed the goblet back to Leah, then stretched her slender arms above her head, yawning.

"There, now, that's better," said Leah. The color was slowly returning to Gwendolyn's cheeks, and her eyes had regained a hint of their sparkle. Satisfied that her charge was feeling more like herself, Leah patted her mistress's hand. "The hour is growing late, my lady. You slept way past the midday meal, and now you must bathe and dress for the feast. If you are feeling better we should begin, for there is little time."

Gwendolyn groaned inwardly. So, the day she had

dreaded had come at last. Tonight Wulfgar would present his marriage gift to Anora. If her sister accepted, as Gwendolyn had no doubts she would, the wedding ceremony could proceed as planned. She threw back the fur coverlet. "Very well, Leah, I suppose we had better hurry."

Leah frowned at Gwendolyn's obvious lack of enthusiasm. Surely the lass could show some joy on such a day, she thought irritably, but for once she held her tongue. Nay, there simply was not enough time to lecture her today!

Soon the room was a flurry of activity. Servants quickly filled the large brass tub in the corner of the room with buckets of warm water, while Leah began to pull silken garments from the large chest at the foot of the bed.

Gwendolyn rolled her eyes at the sight of the various tunics from which she must choose. She knew this was one occasion when a shirt and breeches would *not* be allowed. Stepping gingerly into the tub, she bathed herself quickly, ignoring the disapproving glance from Leah as she dunked her head under the water to wet her hair. Her method made much more sense than standing over a small basin while someone poured water over her head. It was far quicker, and required a lot less fuss! Shaking her wet curls, she stepped out of the tub and toweled herself dry.

"Where can I find Anora?" she asked impatiently, squirming as Leah slipped a cream silk tunic over her head.

"She has been in the solar this afternoon, no doubt working on that fine tapestry with your mother's ladies-in-waiting," Leah replied gruffly. "Please stand still, my lady!" Her attempts to smooth the many folds and pleats in the tunic were being frustrated by Gwendolyn's constant wriggling. Next came a mauve mantle of fine linen embroidered with golden threads, which she managed to get over her young mistress's tousled head with slightly less trouble.

Lastly, Leah handed Gwendolyn an ivory comb to smooth her unruly curls. But she threw up her hands in despair when Gwendolyn chose instead simply to run her fingers through her damp hair. Sliding her feet into a pair of gray kidskin slippers, the girl was out the door and hurrying down the stairs before Leah had even set the comb back on the table.

"My lady, you forgot the circlet for your hair!" Leah called out after her, running to the door. Receiving no response, she turned back into the room, grimacing at the mess. Towels were flung every which way, water sat in puddles on the floor, and clothes lay in scattered disarray upon the bed. " 'Twill be a fine day when that lass is finally wed," she muttered, picking up a sodden towel. "And I hope her man, God help him, can tame her manners!"

Reaching the door of the solar, Gwendolyn paused a moment to catch her breath. She felt guilty at leaving such a mess in her chamber, but she did not turn back. It was far more important to speak with Anora before they went to the great hall for the betrothal feast, she thought wildly. There just *had* to be something she could do to convince her sister to change her mind!

Gwendolyn gently pushed open the door to the solar. The room was empty but for her sister, who was bent over the tapestry, absorbed in her fine needlework. "Anora?" she said softly.

Whirling around in her chair, Anora had a look of startled surprise on her face. "Gwendolyn, I've been so worried about you!" she exclaimed, rushing across the room. Embracing her sister warmly, she drew her into the room. *She looks none for the worse for her misadventure*, Anora thought with no small amount of relief, quickly noting the healthy glow of Gwendolyn's cheeks. "If I'd known you were awake, I would have come to your chamber," she said apologetically.

" 'Tis no matter," Gwendolyn replied. "Leah told me I would find you here." She walked over to the tapestry, stretched across a large wooden frame, and inspected the fine embroidery. "It appears they have kept you busy this afternoon."

"Aye, and Edythe kept us well entertained!" Anora laughed. "I would have thought it impossible to keep my mind on other things besides Wulfgar, but Mother saw to it that I had plenty to do. The hours have flown."

At the mention of Wulfgar's name, Gwendolyn felt her body tense. She pulled absently at a stray thread on the tapestry, barely listening as Anora happily recounted one of Edythe's bawdy tales.

An uncomfortable silence settled over the room. With a start, Gwendolyn realized Anora had stopped talking and was gazing at her with questioning eyes.

"What is troubling you, Gwendolyn?" Anora asked gently, clasping her sister's arm. "You have not heard a single word I said." Concern touched her delicate features. "Does it have aught to do with what happened last night?"

Pulling away from her sister, Gwendolyn turned aside. "Aye," she muttered tersely.

"Then tell me, Gwendolyn. What happened?" Anora walked around to face her sister, her gaze searching.

"I went for a ride and . . . and lost my way in the dark," Gwendolyn stated defensively, staring down at the floor.

"But how could that be?" Anora asked, puzzled. "Surely Father's thanes knew the way. . . ." She paused, her eyes widening in stunned surprise. "Unless you were no longer with them!" Receiving no response, Anora shook her head in bewilderment. "Gwendolyn, I cannot believe you would have ridden off without a guard. Why, anything could have happened! We were all so worried about you, and now to find out that it was just a willful prank—"

" 'Twas not a prank!" Gwendolyn cut her off sharply, her voice strained. Tears glistened on her lashes as she fought to hold back the torrent of emotions that had raged within her for so long, but it was too late. "How can you marry an enemy of our people . . . and . . . and so willingly?" she blurted angrily, her flashing eyes mirroring her deep sense of betrayal.

Not surprised by Gwendolyn's sudden outburst, Anora sighed unhappily. *So, it has finally been said*, she thought, gazing at her proud sister. Gwendolyn had not been herself for many weeks, and Anora had long suspected it was due to her impending marriage. Yet she also sensed there was some deeper, greater hurt hanging like a palpable presence in the small room.

For a long moment Anora was at a loss for words. How could she make her sister understand what it was like to be truly in love? "You judge too harshly, Gwendolyn," she finally murmured, taking her sister's hand in her own. "I love him."

"Love is but a word, Anora!" Gwendolyn retorted vehemently. "He is a Dane. Does that not matter to you?" She spat out the words, her hands clenching into small fists.

"Aye, it mattered before I met him," Anora agreed. "Wulfgar Ragnarson is a Dane, that cannot be denied, but I see him first as a man, Gwendolyn—a courageous man who is seeking peace for his people *and* ours."

"Aye, that may be so," Gwendolyn said angrily. "But can you not see that you are being used as a king's pawn?"

Anora nodded. "Aye, but I now consider it an honor, Gwendolyn. It is through this match that I have found my greatest happiness." She paused, choosing her words carefully. "I could have denied Wulfgar, Gwendolyn. I was given a choice. And as Father's favored daughter, I am sure you will one day be granted the same freedom."

Gwendolyn opened her mouth to protest, but she was silenced as Anora rushed on. "You know that to be true, but I do not begrudge that you have always held Father's heart. So you see, you have naught to fear that you will be forced into a miserable marriage."

Anora sighed heavily as the room fell silent once again. She could not tell if her words had served to convince her sister, or had made matters worse. Well, she could think of only one other thing that could possibly have upset her so. "Look at me, Gwendolyn . . . please," she murmured. "If you are angry that I have spent most of my time with Wulfgar these past months, then I am sorry for that."

Gwendolyn suddenly turned her head away. Her lower lip trembled with emotion, hot tears streaking unchecked down her face. She quickly wiped them away with the back of her hand, but it did little good. Her fair cheeks simply grew wet again.

So, it has been that all along, Anora thought, tears welling up in her own eyes. She knew her sister's pain must be great, for she had rarely seen Gwendolyn cry. She only hoped it was not too late to make amends.

Anora again took her sister's hands in her own, her emerald eyes soft and pleading. "Gwendolyn, listen to me. 'Tis true that I love Wulfgar more than life itself, but that does not mean you hold any lesser place in my heart." Her voice caught with emotion. "Please . . . please share in my happiness, Gwendolyn."

Gwendolyn swallowed hard, overwhelmed with remorse at her sister's words. She had been so selfishly concerned with her own feelings that she had never even spared a thought for Anora's. She could feel the sense of betrayal that had gripped her these past months melting away, replaced by an even deeper humility. Somewhat wistfully, she wondered if she would ever find a love as strong as that which shone from her sister's eyes. Aye, she could only hope. . . . She met her sister's gaze unflinchingly. "Forgive me, Anora," she murmured. "Truly, I do wish you well."

Smiling through her tears, Anora hugged her sister. They both began to giggle, out of relief at first, but then with a joyful hilarity that echoed about the small room. A soft rap on the door went unanswered, until finally it grew into a loud, insistent knock. "Come in!" Anora managed to choke out, wiping the tears from her eyes.

Edythe's graying head peeked around the door. Her tone was gruff, but her eyes were twinkling. "If my ladies will only regain their composure, so I may speak," she said with feigned exasperation. When at last they had suppressed their laughter, she went on. "Lady Anora, your mother has requested your presence in the great hall. All is in readiness and your betrothed awaits!" With a wink and a merry smile, she closed the door behind her, then suddenly opened it again. "And that goes for you as well, Lady Gwendolyn!" Then she was gone, the sound of her footsteps echoing down the corridor.

"Oh, Gwendolyn, I cannot believe this moment has finally arrived!" Anora exclaimed breathlessly, her eyes wide with excitement. "Do you think he will be pleased with how I look?" she asked nervously, smoothing the fine pleats of her sapphire tunic.

"You are only the fairest maiden in the land!" Gwendolyn laughed and squeezed her sister's arm reassuringly. "Come, we must not keep the guests—or Wulfgar—waiting."

Hesitating at the door, Anora turned suddenly to look at Gwendolyn. "Tomorrow morning, before the games begin, would you like to visit the grotto?" she asked excitedly. "It would be nice to see it together for one last time, and we would have another chance to talk." She knew how much their secret place meant to Gwendolyn, and she could not think of a more meaningful gift for her sister.

Startled, Gwendolyn smiled in agreement, a warm glow of happiness spreading through her at Anora's thoughtfulness. "Aye, we could leave before sunrise, and be there and back before anyone even notices we have been gone!" she exclaimed.

Giggling brightly at the thought of their adventure, they walked quickly down the corridor, arm in arm.

Chapter Five

"My Lord Godric and Lady Bronwen, you do me a great honor to prepare such a banquet," Wulfgar stated graciously, taking his seat to the right of the earl, at the main table. Situated at one end of the great hall and raised on a dais, the main table overlooked the vast expanse of the hall and the four long tables that stretched across its length.

"The honor is indeed ours," returned Earl Godric diplomatically, grasping Wulfgar's wrist firmly in a gesture of goodwill. Having dispensed with the initial amenities, he nodded for the several hundred guests in the hall to be seated.

Conversation and eager laughter resumed as the lords and ladies, seated at separate tables in the Anglo-Saxon style, made themselves comfortable. The evening promised to be quite a memorable one. The very fact that King Edgar had arranged the marriage of an English noblewoman to a prince of the Danelaw lent a heightened air of excitement to the evening.

The magnitude of the wedding festivities was also a choice topic of furtive discussion. It was clear to the guests that no expense had been spared, fueling the rumors that Wulfgar Ragnarson was as wealthy as he was powerful. The night's feast would be followed on the morrow with a tournament of games and wrestling matches, and would culminate in the wedding ceremony and celebratory feast on the third day.

The festive scene in the large hall was illuminated by great blazing torches and thick tallow candles set in candlesticks of beaten gold and silver. Magnificent tapestries graced the massive timbered walls, depicting fierce battles and deeds of bravery from days gone by. The earthen floor had been swept and then strewn with fresh rushes. Bunches of lavender and sage hung drying from the rafters, their sweet fragrance melding with the pungent smells of roasting venison and fowl that wafted from the kitchen.

Servants rushed to and fro, endlessly filling and refilling goblets from the huge kegs of ale and mead set against the walls. Even a few of Earl Godric's favorite hunting dogs had been allowed to join in the celebration. They lay in wait under the linen-clothed tables, their tails wagging playfully, eager for any stray morsels that might be tossed their way.

Earl Godric looked out over the teeming hall, his expression growing increasingly impatient. "It seems our daughters have seen fit to keep us waiting," he whispered gruffly in an aside to his wife. "By God, Bronwen, if Anora has changed her mind at this late hour . . . !" Unable even to consider the possibility, he quickly turned his attention to Wulfgar, who was inscrutably observing the crowd of guests.

Aware of the flirtatious glances being cast his way by several bold ladies at a nearby table, Wulfgar averted his gaze to find the earl regarding him closely.

"Humph! Lord Wulfgar, I take it your needs and those of your men have been seen to adequately?" Slightly embarrassed, Earl Godric wondered if he would ever become used to the fact that his daughter's soon-to-be husband was a Dane, and a powerful one at that.

Surmising the earl's thoughts, Wulfgar smiled faintly. His features relaxed. "Aye, more than adequately, my lord," he replied, a twinkle in his eye. *What an understatement!* he thought fleetingly. Eager to please, the earl's lusty servant girls had amply seen to his men's needs all afternoon!

Wulfgar looked at his men, who sat at their own table warily watching the festivities. He was glad there would be entertainment during the feast. Somewhat uncomfortable himself amid all these Anglo-Saxons, he could well imagine the thoughts of his battle-hardened warriors as they sat among the people who had been their enemies for the last hundred years. Yet his oath of allegiance to King Edgar was their oath as well, and they were foresworn to maintain the peace. Wulfgar smiled grimly. He hoped that tonight the musicians and jugglers would be enough for a diversion to prevent any provocations or insults between his men and Earl Godric's thanes.

Earl Godric chuckled heartily at Wulfgar's answer, and slapped him approvingly on the shoulder. "More ale!" he shouted.

Lady Bronwen glanced down the length of the hall, but there was still no sign of her daughters. Growing somewhat nervous herself at Anora's delay, she wondered if Gwendolyn might have something to do with it. As much as she loved her daughter, she was very aware of her willful and mischievous nature. She started to rise from her chair to go look for them, when a roar of approval went up from the guests. Spying her daughters at the foot of the stairs, she breathed a sigh of relief. She turned to Wulfgar. "My lord, your betrothed awaits her escort," she announced softly.

Gwendolyn and Anora stood for a moment at the end of the vast hall, blushing at the obvious stir they were causing among the guests. Resplendent in their silken tunics, they were bathed in an ethereal glow from the myriad candles, their silver-blond hair shimmering and catching the light.

Many of the guests, first-time visitors to the earl's stronghold and having only heard of his daughters' legendary beauty, stared awestruck as the sisters began to walk toward the dais. Truly, they made a dazzling pair!

Anora could not tear her eyes away from Wulfgar's tall figure as he made his way toward them. His steel blue eyes, boldly taking in every aspect of her appearance, seemed to devour her. Feeling suddenly as if her heart would stop, she forced herself to breathe steadily. Her memories of him had not done him justice. *Sweet Jesu!* she whispered to herself. She had never seen him look more strikingly handsome!

His tall, lean body was clothed in a forest green tunic richly embroidered with gold threads. Stretched tautly across his broad shoulders and muscular chest, the tunic fell to his knees, meeting the tops of fine leather boots. Wide gold bands glinted brightly at his wrists, and a heavy gold chain and medallion hung around his neck. At the center of the medallion was a blood-red ruby that sparkled in the candlelight. A wide, metal-studded belt encircled his waist, from which hung the scabbard of his dress sword. Resting one hand on the silver-engraved pommel, Wulfgar looked every inch the virile warrior as he walked toward his betrothed with agile grace.

"Lady Anora . . . Lady Gwendolyn," he stated formally in a low, resonant voice, bowing slightly as he stood in front of them. Gwendolyn acknowledged him with a nod and a faint smile, then passed by him to take her seat beside Lady Bronwen.

"Welcome, my lord," Anora murmured, overtaken by a sudden shyness. Trembling, she felt rooted to the ground. Wulfgar was standing so close to her that she could feel the warmth emanating from his strong body. His clean, male scent enveloped her senses.

Wulfgar took her small hand and lifted it to his lips, gently kissing the delicate fingers. Anora's breath caught in her throat. She looked up at him, her emerald eyes locking with his steely gaze in an unspoken embrace.

"Come, Anora," he whispered huskily, offering her his arm.

The assembled guests had been silent while they watched this interchange with great interest, but they quickly resumed their hearty shouts of good wishes as the handsome couple walked to the dais and took their places side by side at the main table.

With a subtle wave of her hand, Lady Bronwen signalled to the servants to bring in the food. Soon the long tables were groaning under the weight of huge, steaming platters of roasted meat and smoked salmon. The ravenous guests, amazed at the endless parade of dishes from the kitchen, soon had their trenchers of thick, crusty bread piled high with succulent slices of beef and fowl. All this and much more was to be washed down with ample quantities of ale and honeyed mead. Savory side dishes of eggs with herbs and roasted potatoes also accompanied the meal, as well as bowls of autumn vegetables. And for dessert there were steaming puddings studded with choice bits of dried fruits and nuts.

As the guests settled down in earnest to enjoy the fine repast, their contented sounds of eating mingled with the merry conversation, occasional belches, and boisterous laughter. Once in a while a loud yelp was heard from under a table, where a well-placed kick to a growling hound would settle a dispute over discarded food.

Musicians strolled among the tables strumming stringed instruments, often stopping here and there to play a favored tune. Acrobats and jugglers performed their daring feats for the astonished guests, while lively jesters, clothed in multicolored costumes, teased and entertained with their lusty tales and ribald jokes. Countless toasts were offered for the happiness of the betrothed couple, and more than one red-faced guest collapsed into his trencher in a drunken stupor.

Gazing at Anora, still blushing prettily from the last bawdy toast, Wulfgar had all he could do not to draw her into his arms and taste the sweetness of her lush lips. He regretted that such little conversation had passed between them during the meal, but Earl Godric had kept him occupied with a long discourse on the year's political events. He had listened with half an ear, unable to concentrate fully on the heated talk of strategy. Anora's slender beauty and the occasional innocent touch of her leg against his sinewy thigh had been wrecking havoc on his senses all night.

Wulfgar took a long draft of ale from his silver goblet, steeling himself to be patient. He had eaten well of the hearty fare placed before him, but had drunk very little thus far. The warrior in him was always on guard, and he preferred to keep his wits about him while in the household of the earl. He leaned over toward Anora. "You have not eaten very much tonight," he commented gently, looking at her untouched trencher.

The sound of Wulfgar's voice, deep and resonant, sent a thrill racing through Anora. "I am not very hungry, my lord," she murmured. She looked down at her hands, folded in her lap, unable to think of anything further to say. She must appear a tongue-tied simpleton to him, she thought, chiding herself. Hearing her father launch into another political tale, she glanced up just as Wulfgar reluctantly turned his attention once again toward his host.

She studied him unabashedly, drinking in the sight of his ruggedly handsome features. His dark hair, almost black, fell in soft waves to the collar of his tunic, while his steel blue eyes were framed by arching black brows and a strong forehead. His commanding profile, strong jawline, and the high-boned cheeks of his tanned face were a testimony to his Danish heritage.

Resting her gaze on his chiseled lips, Anora wondered vaguely what it would be like to feel them possess hers in a lingering kiss. Wulfgar had kissed her lightly several times during their brief courtship, but always in the presence of her maid-in-waiting. She recalled the sense of restraint she had felt in his arms, as if he were holding something back. Gazing at him now, imagining his hands caressing her skin, she was shocked at the boldness of her thoughts. Never before had she felt this way about any man. He alone had awakened in her a mysterious longing that she knew only he could fulfill. Mesmerized by her thoughts, Anora was startled out of her reverie by Wulfgar's sudden flashing grin.

"I trust my appearance meets with your approval," Wulfgar laughed rakishly. He had finished his conversation with Earl Godric, and had turned to find Anora studying him with desirous intensity, much to his delight.

"Do not mock me, my lord!" Anora blurted, sudden tears glistening in her eyes. Flustered and embarrassed that she had been caught staring at him in such a wanton fashion, she rose suddenly from her chair, upsetting it.

Catching her quickly about the waist, Wulfgar gently sat her on his lap, much to the amusement of several guests who had overheard their exchange. He locked her within his strong embrace. "Do not try to run from me, Anora," he whispered in her ear, his breath warm against her neck. His voice was soothing as he stroked her long, silken hair. "It was not my intent to mock . . . I simply spoke in jest. Your beautiful eyes have betrayed you, Anora. They reflect a desire as strong as my own." He nuzzled her neck for a moment, breathing in the lavender-scented fragrance of her hair. "Soon, my love . . ."

By the blood of Odin, Wulfgar thought fiercely, *would that this were our wedding night!* He had wanted Anora for his own since the first day he had seen her . . . more than he had ever desired any woman. Her innocence had beguiled him, her beauty had bewitched him, yet it was the smoldering passion, reflected in the emerald depths of her eyes, that had captured his soul. He could feel her trembling within his arms, and the nearness of her threatened to overwhelm him. Willing himself to release her, he leaned over and righted her chair, and lifted her to her seat.

"Well, Lord Wulfgar, you have certainly given them something to talk about!" Earl Godric laughed, gesturing toward the many guests now watching the couple with great interest. He turned to Lady Bronwen, his voice low. "I believe 'tis a good time to sign those documents. We should summon the priest." She nodded in agreement.

"Grimbald, fetch Father Leofwine. I believe he is sitting at the far end of that table over there," Lady Bronwen murmured to the steward standing close by.

"Aye, my lady," Grimbald replied, hurrying off to do her bidding.

Anora blushed heatedly. She felt as if all eyes in the hall were upon her. She looked over at Gwendolyn. Her sister flashed her a warm smile of encouragement, but she could only nod numbly in reply. Dazed by the tumultuous whirl of emotions raging within her, she raised her goblet to her lips and took a sip of the honeyed mead. The spicy liquid spread a warm fire through her body as she drank, and she quickly drained the goblet. Feeling suddenly light-headed, she realized too late the effects of the potent drink on her empty stomach. Her vision grew fuzzy, and she could barely make out the stooped figure of the priest as he made his way toward the dais.

"My lord, may I present the betrothal agreements," Father Leofwine stated loudly. He handed the two rolled parchment documents to Earl Godric. He had spent many long hours hunched over his writing desk, meticulously inscribing the elaborate text with inks of different hues, and he was exceedingly proud of his contribution to this joyous occasion.

"My thanks, Holy Father," Earl Godric said warmly. The old priest nodded, then took his place behind Anora, where he would witness the signing. Earl Godric pulled the silken cord tied around each document. Unrolling them carefully, he placed one in front of his daughter and the other before Wulfgar.

Rising from his chair, Wulfgar motioned for one of his men to bring forth the carved-ivory chest he had brought from his homeland. The warrior set it up on the main table, then stood on guard before the dais. The air of speculation heightened in the hall, and many guests stood to get a better view.

Wulfgar opened the intricately carved lid, his voice resounding throughout the hushed hall. "I, Wulfgar Ragnarson, prince of the Danelaw, having sworn fealty to King Edgar, my liege lord, do hereby present to Anora, daughter of Godric, Earl of Cheshire, a marriage gift, in hopes that she will accept it willingly and look upon me with favor." Reaching into the chest, he lifted out a small wrapped bundle and set it carefully before Anora. Her fingers shook as she fumbled with the silken ribbon that securely tied the bundle. It seemed like an eternity passed before she was able to untie the knot, but at last the linen folds fell open to reveal the contents.

"Oh!" Anora gasped. She stared in awe at the glittering brooch that sparkled at her in the bright candlelight. She had never seen anything like it before! Made of shimmering, beaten gold, the oval brooch was encrusted with emeralds and creamy-white pearls. She could feel Wulfgar's heated gaze upon her as she shakily held it up for all to see, and she started when he laid another bundle before her. Larger than the first, it contained a set of perfectly matched earrings and two gold filigree arm rings inlaid with ivory and precious stones.

"The jewels are beautiful, my lord," Anora murmured,

her eyes wide with wonder as she looked up at him.

"No more beautiful than the woman who will wear them," Wulfgar replied softly, his voice a whispered caress. Smiling at her pleasure, he lifted a small, rolled parchment from the chest. Unrolling it gingerly, he read aloud: "I, Wulfgar Ragnarson, present to Anora, daughter of Godric, ten thousand acres of land adjacent to my own estate. Henceforth, this land is her own property, to do with as she sees fit." This announcement brought great shouts of approval from the stunned guests, with the realization that Anora was now one of the richest women of the Danelaw.

Earl Godric, slightly overcome by his daughter's good fortune, addressed her gently. "Anora, do you accept the marriage gift of Wulfgar Ragnarson, and agree to go with him willingly as his wife?" The great hall suddenly grew hushed, all awaiting her answer.

Anora rose gracefully from her chair and turned to face Wulfgar. His handsome features were inscrutable, yet the steely blue depths of his gaze were searching. His hand reached out to her, and she grasped it with trembling fingers. It was warm and strong, and reassured her. "I do willingly accept, and look upon Wulfgar Ragnarson with great favor," she answered in a clear voice, loud enough for all to hear.

The words had barely escaped her lips when a great roar went up from the guests. Servants rushed to fill empty goblets as the rounds of toasts began anew. The great beams of the hall echoed with the revelry that would no doubt continue far into the night. Oblivious to the merriment, Wulfgar bent his head and kissed Anora's lips, lingering for a moment as he savored their tender warmth.

"Ahem!" Coughing sharply, Father Leofwine gestured toward the documents still lying unsigned on the table.

A deep chuckle rumbled from Wulfgar, and, turning to Earl Godric, he laughed. "Your priest truly has your interests at heart, my lord." Dipping the pen into a small jar of ink, he made his mark on each document, then handed the pen to Anora, who did the same. Content that all formalities had been observed, the aged priest bowed before the couple and took his leave.

"We are in agreement, then," Earl Godric said, offering his silver goblet to Wulfgar.

"Aye, my lord." Wulfgar nodded, his eyes upon Anora. Taking the goblet, he drained it with one draft.

Chapter Six

Anora sipped slowly from her goblet as she watched the celebration around her. The revelry showed no signs of abating, even though the hour was growing late. She glanced at Gwendolyn, unable to suppress a smile at the sight of her tempestuous sister surrounded by anxious suitors. Gwendolyn was smiling prettily, but her eyes flashed dangerously —a strong indication of what she truly thought of their unwanted attentions. Anora sighed. She only hoped her sister would one day find the same happiness she felt this night. Wulfgar's kiss still burned upon her lips, and she closed her eyes for a moment, remembering his embrace. A wave of dizziness suddenly washed over her. Shaking her head, she opened her eyes to find him gazing at her with concern.

" 'Tis the honeyed mead, I fear, my lord," Anora murmured, rubbing her temples to ease the dull ache in her head. Accustomed to drinking only small quantities of the potent brew, she could not recall how many times her goblet had been refilled. She knew only that she had never felt so light-headed before. Chiding herself for her foolishness, she rose unsteadily to make her excuses.

"Wait, Anora," Wulfgar bade her gently. He turned to Earl Godric, his voice low. "My lord, I beg leave to escort Lady Anora to her chamber. It seems the drink and excitement have proved too much for her this evening."

Caught off guard by Wulfgar's request, Earl Godric leaned back in his chair, shrewdly appraising the younger man. *God's blood, he's impetuous,* he thought. Then he chuckled. He could still vividly recall his own haste to bed the beautiful Bronwen eighteen years ago, and gazing on his radiant wife this night he was not surprised that he felt the same even now. Yet, he pondered, sobering, propriety must be maintained. Without the proof of Anora's bloodstain of innocence on the marriage bed, the marriage agreement would be annuled.

Sensing Earl Godric's thoughts, Wulfgar stated bluntly, "No harm shall befall her, my lord. She will be on her wedding day as she is this night . . . a virgin. You have my word."

"You may escort her, then, Wulfgar," Earl Godric consented, a look of firm understanding passing between them.

Wulfgar only hoped that Anora had not heard that rather indelicate exchange. Offering her his arm, they descended the stairs from the dais. Engrossed in their revelry, very few guests noticed the couple's departure as they slipped through a side door that led to the family quarters.

The darkened corridors, dimly lit by sputtering torches, were a relief to Anora from the brightness and smoke-filled air of the great hall. Pausing for a moment to get a breath of fresh air from an open door, she looked up at Wulfgar. "Forgive me, my lord," she began, but he hushed her words with a gentle finger to her lips.

"Come, my love, the hour is late." Leading her by the elbow, Wulfgar carefully guided her through the narrow, winding halls. Grateful for his assistance, Anora doubted that she would have been able to walk to her chamber alone. Her head was pounding incessantly, and another wave of dizziness caused her to stumble on the first step that led up to her chamber.

Suddenly she felt herself lifted by Wulfgar's strong arms, and he took the wooden stairs two at a time as if she weighed no more than a feather. Crushed against his broad chest, she could hear the steady beat of his heart. The rhythmic sound sent an odd thrill coursing through her body, and she tensed within his arms. The day's past events seemed a jumbled confusion to her now, and she struggled to clear her clouded mind.

At the top of the stairs, Wulfgar swung open the door and set Anora down just inside the threshold. A copper brazier, glowing brightly in the corner, was the only light in the darkened room. "It is far too warm," Wulfgar announced. Crossing over to the small window, he pushed aside the tanned leather that served as a covering. Cool night air swept into the chamber.

Wulfgar took a deep breath of the bracing air. *You are a fool to have brought her here*, he thought distractedly, fighting to control his senses. He had never seen Anora look lovelier, or more vulnerable, than she did this night. He longed to hold her in his arms and caress her delicate curves, to awaken the smoldering passion that lay dormant within her. Leaning against the window, he tried to reason with himself that she would be his completely . . . forever . . . in only two days' time.

Anora swayed unsteadily as she stood by the door. Soft moonlight was streaming in from the window, and she could see Wulfgar's tall form illuminated against the indigo sky. "Wulfgar?" she questioned softly, fearful she had displeased him. She had never meant to drink so much mead, and she wondered if that was why he was so silent. Perhaps he had changed his mind, and there would be no wedding. The thought of being without him was more than she could imagine. A low, anguished cry tore from her throat, shattering the stillness of the room.

Suddenly she felt Wulfgar's arms around her, drawing her firmly to him. His lips, warm and hard, possessed her mouth and seemed to draw the very breath from her body. He held her so tightly she could feel the muscled hardness of his chest through her clothing. Returning his kiss with a passion born of innocence, Anora felt an urgent core of longing begin to surge within her and she trembled uncontrollably.

"Anora . . . my Anora," Wulfgar said softly against her ear. He nibbled a tender earlobe, sending shivers of hitherto unknown passion racing through her. By the blood of Odin, he could take her now but for his promise to her father, he thought wildly. Her very nearness threatened to overwhelm his resolve. Parting her lips, he deepened his kiss, his tongue gently probing the honeyed recesses of her mouth.

A soft moan broke from Anora's throat. Wulfgar hesitated a moment, holding her away from him while he gazed at her delicate features in the moonlight. Her eyes, deep emerald pools veiled by lush lashes, reflected her innocent desire. Reaching a decision, he gathered her into his arms and carried her to the bed. He laid her gently upon the thick fur coverlet, then stepped away and loosened the silver-studded belt from around his waist. Placing his sword, arm bands, and medallion on the chest at the foot of the bed, he kicked off his leather boots and hurriedly stripped off his tunic.

In the moonlight, Wulfgar's lean, battle-hardened form was illuminated in all its male glory. Anora gasped at the sight of his sculpted chest, thickly covered with dark curls, and the dark line of hair that trailed down his taut belly and narrow hips to end in another mass of curls between sinewy thighs. She stared at him openly; surprisingly, she felt little shyness. Her interest pleased him, and he laughed with pleasure at her wide-eyed admiration. Lying down on the bed beside her, he stretched his hard length against her and enfolded her in his steely embrace.

"There is much to learn of love, Anora," he whispered, tracing a path of fiery kisses along her throat. "Tonight I will give you just a taste of the pleasure we will find in each other's arms."

Murmuring gentle, soothing words, he unpinned the silver brooches from her mantle and slowly drew the garment over her head, and there followed shortly by her silken tunic. As the beauty of her form was revealed to him, Wulfgar drew in his breath sharply. His large hands trembled as he slid the lace straps of her camise from her delicate shoulders, then gently pulled the sheer garment from her body. Stunned by her beauty, he knew he had never before beheld such perfection in a woman.

"Anora," he whispered huskily, raking her body with his heated gaze, "you are truly a vision of the gods." Her satiny skin, pale as alabaster, gleamed in the moonlight. Pink nipples, hardened by the cool night breeze, seemed to cry out for his touch. Leaning over, Wulfgar captured one of the rosy peaks within his mouth, his tongue flicking gently. Startled by the new sensation, Anora tensed suddenly in his arms, moaning softly.

"Do not be afraid, my love," he murmured reassuringly, caressing the arch of her back. "It is my only wish to give you pleasure this night." Gently, and ever so slowly, he began to caress her silky skin with a feather-light touch. Anora shivered, her mind reeling with the delicate sensations. Wulfgar's lips, warm, searching, trailed a burning path across a delicate shoulder and once again found her breast. He traced a circle of molten fire around the raised nipple with his tongue, suckling gently. His strong hands moved over her body, caressing and stroking her flat abdomen and the slender curve of her hips, only to linger teasingly at the silky mound between her thighs.

Writhing under his touch, Anora gave herself over to the heady waves of passion that rippled through her body. All conscious thought fled from her mind, and she was overwhelmed by a burning ache of desire as old as love itself. She moaned in wild delight. Her slender hips moved instinctively against the pressure of Wulfgar's hand, betraying her inner desires all too clearly.

"That will have to wait for another night, my love." Wulfgar gasped, fighting to control the searing flames of desire in his loins. Encircling Anora in his strong arms, he sought her mouth in a crushing kiss, stifling her cries as his fingers explored the soft, moist core of her. Gently he probed the satiny folds, searching for her most sensitive point.

Suddenly Anora arched against his hand, her body trembling uncontrollably. Wrapping her arms about Wulfgar's muscled back, she pulled him to her, entwining her delicate fingers in his black curls. He deepened his kiss, all the while stroking and teasing the delicate bud of her desire, exulting in her passionate abandon.

Bathed in a fine sheen of perspiration, Anora felt a mounting tension of pure, unbridled ecstasy building within her, spiraling upward and upward until it reached a pinnacle of burning desire. Crying out Wulfgar's name, she felt a roaring wave of molten pleasure explode in shimmering lights and piercing sensation.

Wulfgar held her close within his arms for long time, savoring the warmth of her slender body against his own. He gazed down at the perfection of her delicate features. She had fallen asleep almost immediately, but he was loath to leave her side. She was so beautiful. . . .

Aye, there will be many more nights like this, he thought, consoling himself. *Nights when we will* both *find release in each other's arms.* Lingeringly and ever so gently, he kissed her love-bruised lips. "Sleep well, my only love," he whispered, covering her with the coverlet. He stepped out of the bed and quietly pulled on his clothes. Then, after one last, tender kiss, he silently left her room.

Chapter Seven

"Anora, wake up!" Gwendolyn whispered urgently, shaking her sister's shoulder. Deep in the midst of a dream, Anora merely yawned and rolled over onto her side. Her long hair lay in wild disarray on the eiderdown pillow, and her delicate features lay in peaceful repose, a gentle smile curving her lips as she slept.

Gwendolyn felt a twinge of guilt at disturbing her sister's sound slumber, but the feeling was short-lived. Realizing that drastic measures were needed to awaken her, she climbed onto the wide bed and began to jump up and down on the mattress.

Rudely awakened by the sudden jarring, Anora opened her eyes, a startled look on her face. "Gwendolyn, what are you doing?" she asked dazedly, her mind clouded from sleep and faint memories of her dream.

Gwendolyn plopped down beside her sister. "Forgive me for waking you so, Anora," she whispered apologetically, "but you promised we would go to the grotto this morning. Have you forgotten?"

Sorting through her jumbled thoughts, Anora groaned inwardly. Aye, she remembered all too well the promise she had made the day before, and how much it had meant to Gwendolyn. If only she weren't so sleepy . . .

But one glance at Gwendolyn's hopeful expression was all she needed to rouse herself. Anora knew she could not refuse her sister—it had been her idea to visit the grotto in the first place. Besides, if they left right away they would surely be there and back before the morning meal. Yawning, she threw back the coverlet and swung her legs over the side of the bed. "Well, we'd best be going if we want to see the sunrise," she said, stretching her arms above her head. She smiled warmly. She felt such a great sense of well-being and contentment this morning.

Gwendolyn squealed delightedly at Anora's announcement, then quickly clapped her hand over her mouth. She jumped off the bed, grabbed the silken camise lying crumpled on the floor, and handed it to her sister. Shivering, Anora pulled the garment over her head, then hurried over to the chest at the foot of the bed.

Suddenly she gasped. On top of the chest, glinting at her in the glow of the candle held aloft for her by Gwendolyn, lay one of Wulfgar's gold arm bands. Memories of the previous night came flooding back to her, and she flushed heatedly. Those memories had seemed only a dream when she had awakened . . . a breathless, swirling vision of passion and moonlight. Yet now, holding the arm band in the palm of her hand, the bright gold warming from her touch, she knew the dream had been real.

Gwendolyn's eyes widened in surprise. "Was Wulfgar with you last night?" she questioned softly, although Anora's blushing cheeks told her all she needed to know.

"Aye," Anora answered simply, ignoring her sister's startled look. She lifted the heavy lid of the chest and set the arm band inside, covering it with clothing. Pulling out a plain linen tunic and a heavy woolen mantle, she dressed quickly. At last she turned to Gwendolyn, who was still standing by the chest dumbfounded. "We will speak of this later, Gwendolyn, but for now, we must hurry." She grabbed her fur cloak from a wooden hook by the door and wrapped it about her shoulders, fastening it with a silver brooch. "Ouch!" she exclaimed suddenly.

"What happened?"

"The pin on the brooch pierced my finger," Anora winced painfully, examining the tiny drop of blood on her fingertip.

"Perhaps trousers would be a more suitable attire for a walk in the woods!" Gwendolyn suggested, chuckling softly. Dressed in a woolen shirt and trousers, a wide leather belt, sturdy leather boots, and a fur-lined jerkin, she looked every inch a young huntsman. Her short hair was covered by a fur cap, and her hand rested on the engraved handle of a large hunting knife strapped to her belt.

"Aye, maybe if I had more daring like you," replied Anora, somewhat wistfully. She quickly wrapped her wound with a small piece of linen. The thought of herself in men's trousers made her giggle, her sore finger forgotten.

"Are you almost ready?" Gwendolyn asked impatiently. It was at least an hour before dawn, yet soon the servants would be up and about their morning duties.

"Aye, just one more moment," Anora said, running an ivory comb through her tangled hair. She hastily donned a pair of sturdy leather-soled slippers. "There, I am ready."

Opening the door, Gwendolyn moved stealthily down the wooden stairs with Anora close behind her. At the foot of the stairs they stopped and peered down the darkened corridor. All was silent and still. With Gwendolyn's candle lighting the way, they hurried along the corridor, their footsteps making little sound.

Pausing for a moment at the top of another flight of stairs that led to the kitchen area, Gwendolyn listened for any noise. Hearing nothing but the snores of sleeping servants in the room adjacent to the kitchen, she beckoned to Anora and they ran quietly down the stairs.

"Do you have the key?" Anora whispered as they tiptoed through the large kitchen. The room was lit by the smoldering embers in the stone hearth. Gwendolyn nodded, holding up a heavy iron key.

When they reached the door of the root cellar, they found it slightly ajar. "Let me go first," Gwendolyn whispered, holding her candle in front of her. Squeezing through the narrow opening, she was assailed by the dank, musty smell of the earthen cellar. "Come on!" she hissed. Once her sister was through the door, Gwendolyn shut it firmly behind them. The iron hinges creaked in protest, and they froze in their steps, listening. But to their relief they heard nothing.

Gwendolyn swiped away the spider webs draped from the low, wooden beams of the cellar and stepped over to several large kegs resting against the far side of the room. She pushed aside one of the empty kegs, revealing a narrow wooden door that barely reached her waist. She fit the key into the rusty lock and turned it sharply. The little door swung open and a strong gust of fresh air surged into the cellar.

Coughing from the dust, Anora gingerly crawled through the open door on her hands and knees. When it was her turn, Gwendolyn blew out her candle, plunging the cellar into pitch-darkness. A chill went down her spine and she quickly followed on Anora's heels. Once outside, she firmly shut and locked the little door. Hewn from the same logs as the high walls of the stronghold, the door fit so snugly that it matched exactly the grain of the surrounding timber. Invisible to even the keenest eye, only Gwendolyn's familiarity with the door's location would enable her to find it again.

Pocketing the key, Gwendolyn stood up and brushed the

dirt from her trousers. "We will have to run to the trees," she whispered.

Anora nodded. She took her sister's hand and with the other held up her long tunic and mantle. She felt like giggling as they sprinted across the barren field, knowing how ridiculous she must look with her cloak flying in the wind.

"We did it!" Gwendolyn laughed excitedly when they reached the cover of the trees. She leaned on a gnarled oak while she caught her breath.

"Aye, just like always," Anora agreed happily. It did feel wonderful to be out in the woods, she thought, breathing in the brisk morning air. Reflecting on the many times she and Gwendolyn had managed to sneak away in the past, she was amazed they had never been caught.

Only their father and a few trusted servants were to have known about the secret door. But Gwendolyn had found the door years ago while playing in the cellar, and before long had learned where her father kept the key. Sneaking out of the stronghold and visiting the grotto had been the sisters' private game all these years, and it had never lost its thrill or sense of intrigue. Yet this morning Anora felt a bittersweet ache, knowing that this would be their last visit to the grotto for a long time.

Sensing Anora's thoughts, Gwendolyn suddenly grabbed her sister's hands and whirled her about in a circle until they were both laughing so hard they tumbled to the cold ground, exhausted. "There shall . . . be no more sad . . . thoughts today," she panted, smiling broadly. "Agreed?"

"Very . . . well, Gwendolyn." Anora gasped, trying to catch her breath. She wiped the tears of laughter from her eyes. "Do you think we should be on our way?"

"Aye, Anora, always the practical one," agreed Gwendolyn. She stood up and helped her sister to her feet. She could see that the shadows in the forest were fast receding with the first tentative rays of light peeking above the horizon. "We will have to hurry if we want to see the sunrise from the grotto," she said over her shoulder as she set off through the dense trees along an almost hidden path.

Scrambling to keep up with Gwendolyn, Anora held her tunic and mantle above her knees to keep them from snagging in the brambles that choked the path.

Fallen leaves and broken twigs crackled under their feet as they made their way in companionable silence through the woods. An owl, hooting its final night cry in the distance, was echoed by the melodies of mourning doves and tiny sparrows. A light layer of frost had fallen during the night, blanketing the forest in a pearly sheen of white.

Anora hugged her fur cloak tightly about her, grateful for its warmth and protection. Rubbing her cheek against the softness of the fur-lined hood, she smiled. Wulfgar had given her the luxurious cloak shortly after their first meeting. She remembered how he had wrapped it about her shoulders, gently, yet possessively. She had felt too shy to look up at him, so he had lifted her chin to meet his gaze. She would never forget the searing intensity of his blue eyes, and her whispered name upon his lips. . . .

She leaned against a tree for a moment and closed her eyes. The memory was alive and vibrant, as if it had been only yesterday. Suddenly she heard her name shouted aloud, breaking rudely into her thoughts. Her eyes flew open to find Gwendolyn looking at her quizzically.

"I said, we are almost to the stream bed," Gwendolyn repeated impatiently, shaking her head. Not hearing Anora's footsteps behind her, she had turned around to find her sister resting against a tree, her eyes closed dreamily, a secretive smile upon her lips. *God's blood! She thinks of him all the time! Men!*

Giggling sheepishly, Anora ran toward Gwendolyn and took her hand. "Come on!" She laughed, a flash of apology in her eyes. They dashed together down a steep hill, their gay laughter echoing in the narrow ravine.

At the foot of the hill, a clear stream surged through the ravine on its way to the river. Gwendolyn once again took the lead as they walked along the stream's grassy banks. The grotto lay just ahead, hidden beneath a large outcropping of rock.

Gwendolyn finally spied their secret hideaway from the bend in the stream. She whooped with delight and stepped eagerly across a natural bridge of jagged rocks that stretched across the stream bed.

"Gwendolyn, please wait!" Anora had tried to follow her, only to find herself balanced precariously on a large rock in the middle of the stream. She looked dubiously at her sister. This was the only part of their adventure she disliked. The rushing waters of the stream never failed to make her feel nervous and unsure of herself. She did not move until Gwendolyn stepped back out onto the rocks and grabbed her outstretched hand, guiding her safely to the far bank.

Hollowed out years ago by an ancient river, the grotto was set into the side of the ravine a short distance from the stream. A pool of tranquil water, glistening with the first early rays of sunlight, rested at the mouth of the grotto. A soft haze hung over the pool, lending an almost ethereal air to the quiet scene.

Gwendolyn stretched out on one of the flat rocks that surrounded the pool, breathing a sigh of contentment. Anora unfastened her cloak and spread it across her favorite rock, then knelt down along the edge. Flushed and warm from the exertion of their walk, she cupped her hand and took a drink of icy-cold water, then delicately splashed some on her face. Refreshed, she settled comfortably onto the rock and gazed about her.

"I will miss this place," she murmured softly, a hint of sadness in her voice.

"Aye, it will not be the same without you," Gwendolyn

agreed, sighing. Turning over onto her side, she propped her head on her hand. The early morning sun felt warm upon her face, and she squinted against its brightness. The sky was gradually lightening to a vivid blue as the sun inched higher above the horizon.

Trailing her hand in the water, Anora watched the gentle ripples float on the surface of the pool in ever-widening circles. The stillness of the grotto was like a calming herb, lulling her into a strange sense of detachment. Childhood memories came flooding back to her, and she recalled the many happy hours spent with Gwendolyn in this mystical place. Suddenly she laughed.

"Do you remember the time you tried to spear that huge fish with your hunting knife, and you fell headlong into the pool?" Anora asked, her eyes sparkling with mirth as she recalled the image of a very wet and bedraggled Gwendolyn sputtering indignantly in water up to her waist.

"Not without a helpful shove from you!" Gwendolyn countered, laughing. Stretching languidly on the rock, she leaned over the edge and gazed at her reflection in the pool. Hesitantly, she touched her lips, and the image staring at her from the water mirrored the movement. "Anora," she asked softly, "does a man's kiss burn like fire . . . or ice?"

Blushing, Anora looked incredulously at Gwendolyn. " 'Tis a strange question you ask, Gwendolyn! You have never been one to concern yourself with the ways of men . . . I mean, in other pursuits besides hunting or riding . . . with women, that is . . ." she stammered, her voice trailing off as she stared at her sister.

"Leah once told me that if a man's kiss burns like fire, his love will be true, but if his kiss burns like ice . . ."—she paused, a faraway look in her emerald eyes—". . . his love will bring pain and ruin." She looked up and gazed searchingly at Anora. "Last night, was Wulfgar's kiss like fire?"

Anora shivered suddenly. She had never liked Leah's

superstitious notions. "Aye," she answered softly, drawing her knees up to her chin.

" 'Twas as I thought," Gwendolyn replied. She tugged absently at a tuft of dried grass sticking up between the rocks. Lost in their own thoughts, neither spoke for several moments.

Anora finally broke the melancholy silence, understanding in her voice. "One day, Gwendolyn, you will know such a kiss." She reached out and squeezed her sister's hand.

"Perhaps," Gwendolyn said faintly, looking away. Suddenly she whispered, "Look, over there!"

A young doe stepped silently from the cover of the trees and walked toward the far side of the pool. Stopping to sniff the air, the beautiful animal stood motionless for a moment, its soft, brown eyes watchful and alert.

Gwendolyn and Anora gazed at the doe in awed silence, scarcely breathing, as the graceful creature bent its head to drink. Its pink tongue scarcely disturbed the surface of the pool. Several times the doe lifted its head and looked about cautiously, then quickly took another drink.

Suddenly a loud, crackling sound, like the snapping of a tree branch, startled the animal. It froze momentarily, its nostrils flared and muscles twitching. Then, with a bound, the doe disappeared into the dense trees.

"Gwendolyn, what was that?" Anora asked fearfully, looking beyond the pool into the forest.

"Shh!" Gwendolyn whispered, holding her finger to her lips. She rose to her feet. Listening for any sounds, her hand went to the hilt of her hunting knife, strapped to her waist. "We must get back to the stronghold!" she hissed urgently.

Anora stood and hastily wrapped her cloak about her shoulders. She had no reason to doubt Gwendolyn's instincts, honed as they were by years of hunting and training with their father.

They left the shelter of the grotto and quickly ran to the

stream. Gwendolyn stepped gingerly over the rocks to the other bank, then turned and beckoned to Anora. "Come on!" she urged, looking about them.

Lifting up her skirts with one hand, Anora held out her arm to balance herself. When she had crossed almost to the other side, she lost her footing and slid off the slippery rocks into the cold, surging water. "Gwendolyn!" she shrieked, her feet sinking into the thick mud, the heavy currents of the stream dragging at her skirts.

"Here, take my hand!" Gwendolyn yelled, stepping back onto the rocks. Pushing the wet hair out of her eyes, Anora lunged for her sister's hand and just barely caught it. She hung on desperately as Gwendolyn dragged her from the stream and helped her to her feet. "Are you all right?"

Nodding reassuredly as she fought to catch her breath, Anora managed a faint smile. "I will be fine, but I fear my tunic will never be the same." Holding up her muddy skirts, she followed close behind Gwendolyn as they quickly made their way along the steep hill.

Scanning the dense trees ahead, Gwendolyn's wary eyes spotted a flash of movement. She drew her hunting knife from its sheath and held it poised in front of her. "Anora?" she whispered, reaching behind her for her sister's hand. She felt only empty air.

Wheeling around, she was not prepared for the sight that greeted her. Anora, her eyes wide with fright, was wrapped within the huge, bronzed arm of a giant of a man, his massive hand covering her mouth. His other arm brandished a long, pointed spear, which he had trained directly on Gwendolyn's throat. Towering over them both, the bearded giant was grinning from ear to ear, but his eyes glinted dangerously. He uttered some words in a foreign tongue, motioning for Gwendolyn to drop her knife.

Hesitating for a moment, Gwendolyn understood true fear for the first time in her life. Trained expertly by her father in all manner of weaponry, she knew none of her training could have prepared her for this encounter. Licking her dry lips, she shifted her feet to better her stance.

"I would na' try anything foolish, lad. Torvald has been known to skewer larger men wi'out blinking an eye!"

Startled by the guttural voice, Gwendolyn turned slowly around to face her new opponent. Her heart sank as another man, shorter than the blond giant but stockily built and well muscled, stepped out from behind a tree. He stood with his feet spread wide and arms folded across his broad chest, eyeing her shrewdly. A jagged scar, slashing down the left side of his face and ending at the corner of his thin lips, had marred what might have once been a handsome face.

Speaking again in his strangely accented English, the man took a menacing step toward Gwendolyn. "Drop the weapon, lad. 'Twould na' do for your fair sister to see your blood spilled out upon the ground."

Ignoring his words, Gwendolyn suddenly lunged at the man. She caught him off guard by her quick movement, and was on him before he could reach for the sword at his belt. Hitting him with the full force of her slender weight, she raised her arm to plunge her knife into his chest. A sharp, sickening blow to the side of her head stopped her, and she fell heavily to her knees. Through a maze of pain she could hear Anora screaming. Then all was blackness as she slumped to the ground.

Chapter Eight

Anora's screams died to a whimper as she stared in disbelief at Gwendolyn's crumpled form lying on the cold ground. She longed to rush to her sister's side, but the bearded giant held her fast, his massive arms gripping her like bands of iron. She watched fearfully as the other man knelt down beside Gwendolyn.

" 'Twould seem your brother has little fear of death," he muttered wryly, "or else his foolishness has made him bold." He shook his head grimly. He did not relish the thought that a beardless youth had almost sent him to Valhalla! He rolled Gwendolyn roughly over onto her back, then took a leather thong from his belt and bound her hands tightly.

A large, angry welt on the side of Gwendolyn's forehead and the ashen pallor of her skin caused Anora to wince painfully. Gwendolyn was lying so still that the shallow rise and fall of her chest could barely be seen through the thickness of her fur-lined jerkin. *He thinks she is a boy,* Anora thought dazedly, her mind reeling from the sudden twist of events.

Following only a few steps behind Gwendolyn, Anora had not even heard the huge man steal up behind her. He had grabbed her so suddenly that the breath was knocked from her body, her scream stifled by his hand clapped over her mouth. Unable to voice a warning, she had watched in horror as Gwendolyn attacked the scar-faced man, only to be felled by a glancing blow from the butt of the giant's spear. Biting into her captor's hand, Anora's agonized screams had torn from her throat, echoing through the sunlit woods until a filthy rag had been stuffed in her mouth.

"There, now, that should hold the lad for a while," the scar-faced man muttered, rising to his feet. Licking his lips, his pale, blue eyes moved lustfully over Anora. Her wet tunic and mantle clung to her shivering body, accentuating her delicate curves. " 'Tis strange that a beautiful lass such as yourself would have a mere lad for her protector," he said thickly, walking toward her.

As he drew closer, Anora was assailed by the man's rank odor of sweat and grime. She longed to strike out at his leering face, but the grinning giant held her arms pinned cruelly behind her. Feeling as if she would retch, she cringed and turned her face away.

"You look to be a fine, highborn lady," he sneered, wrapping a strand of Anora's long, silky hair about his finger. The disgust reflected in her emerald eyes incensed him. "Na' good enough for the likes of you, eh, lass?" Jerking her chin around sharply to face him, he pulled the rag from her mouth and brought his lips down upon hers in a crushing kiss. His tongue, hot and insistent, forced apart her bruised lips, while his hands brutally squeezed her breasts through her wet clothing. Sickened by his foul breath, Anora suddenly bit down hard on his tongue.

Jumping back in stunned surprise, the man stared furiously at Anora for a moment in disbelief. His scarred face was distorted in rage, and a trickle of blood ran from the corner of his mouth. "English slut!" he hissed, slapping her harshly across the face. The force of the blow numbed Anora's senses, and she felt her body go limp.

Laughing crudely at the sight of his wily companion momentarily bested by a slip of a girl, the bearded giant spoke gruffly in his own language. "By the blood of Thor, Svein, if you want the girl, take her!" Ripping the sodden cloak from Anora's shoulders, he threw it on the ground and pushed her down upon it. "Just be quick about it so I can have a turn. I've never sampled so fine a wench before, and from the looks of her she's probably never been ridden!"

Looking up at their leering faces, Anora felt a terrible dread wash over her. She did not have to know their language to read the lustful intent burning in their eyes. Looking desperately about her for any chance of escape, she knew it was futile. Gwendolyn was her only hope, but glancing at the unconscious form of her sister, she knew she could expect no help from her now. *If they think she is a boy, at least she will be spared my fate*, Anora thought fleetingly. Then suddenly Svein was upon her.

Shoved roughly onto her back, Anora felt his weight covering her body as one hand frantically lifted the skirt of her tunic and the other savagely squeezed her breast. Hot tears flowed silently down her ashen cheeks as all hope fled from her mind, the serenity of her world shattered forever. Wishing for death to save her, she stared blankly into the blue depths of the morning sky.

Suddenly Svein's thick body rolled off her and he jumped to his feet. Turning to his bearded companion, he spoke raggedly, his breathing labored. "Did you hear the signal, Torvald?"

Nodding, the huge man pointed in the direction of the river. Once again the long, drawn-out sound of a horn could be heard in the distance, carried high upon the wind.

"Damn!" Svein spat angrily, fumbling with the leather

belt at his waist. Of all times to be signaled back to the ship! Groaning painfully at the heated ache in his groin, Svein narrowly eyed the trembling woman at his feet. Thor! His blood boiled just at the sight of her! Yet he knew now he would have to wait to taste her charms. The signal could mean only one thing—the longship was repaired and ready to sail. There was no time to spare, or they might be left behind. Muttering curses to himself, he bent to pick up his sword.

" 'Tis a shame to leave such a comely wench," Torvald stated regretfully, looking at Anora lying huddled at their feet.

"Who said aught of leaving her?" Without hesitation, Svein bound Anora's wrists and wrapped her in his fur cloak. Swinging her up in his arms, he hoisted her over his broad shoulder like a sack of meal.

"Have you forgotten Hakon's orders, then?" Torvald queried, shifting his feet nervously. A hint of fear glinted in his eyes that seemed oddly out of place with his massive size. "A harmless tumble with a wench is one thing—out here, no one would ever know. But to bring her aboard the ship—"

"You fret more than a weaned babe!" Svein cut him off sharply. "Are you daft, man? The gods did na' put these two in our path for us to leave them here!"

"So you also plan to bring the lad?"

"Listen, man!" Svein spoke hurriedly. "We can hide them in the cargo well during the voyage. Then, when we land, we can get them off the ship under cover of night! Think of the silver, Torvald! 'Tis rich men we'll be once we sell these two!"

"But what of Hakon, Svein?" Torvald asked doubtfully. " 'Twill not set well with him that we disobeyed his orders."

Svein peered at Torvald, his pale eyes reflecting the depth of his greed. "Look at them, man! They'll fetch the highest price for slaves—of that you can be sure!" Pausing for a moment, his voice fell to an anxious whisper. "Torvald, we'll have enough silver to buy our own ship. Aye, think of it! We can sail home to Dublin on the first tides of spring!"

The big man's eyes widened, his reluctance quickly fading. *Our own longship,* he thought shrewdly, a slow grin spreading across his bearded face. In his mind's eye he could see himself at the helm of a mighty dragon of the sea with the northern wind catching the brightly colored sail. Grunting, he nodded his massive head in assent.

"Good!" Svein exclaimed, flashing a sly, toothy grin. "Throw your fur clock over the lad's head and let's be off. 'Tis my thought the ship is ready to sail!"

Torvald lumbered over to where Gwendolyn lay. He sat down on his haunches and wrapped her in his heavy fur cloak, then tossed her over his shoulder. As he rose to his feet, a low moan broke from her throat.

"Is the lad awake?" Svein asked nervously. Hurrying over to Torvald's side, he pulled Gwendolyn's head up by her close-cropped curls and peered at her bruised face. Her eyelids fluttered ever so slightly, but she had not regained consciousness. Relieved, Svein let her head drop. Then, in a low, threatening voice, he turned his head and muttered to Anora, "Any noise from you, lass, and your brother will not live to see the morrow!"

Chapter Nine

"Sound the once horn again, Bjorn, and Loki help them if they cannot hear it!" Hakon shouted. He turned back to the men at his side, conferring with them in low tones as they stood near the stern of the longship. "You have done fine work," he murmured appreciatively, running a large, tanned hand along the oaken planks of the ship. *Truly, they have worked wonders*, Hakon marveled, thanking the gods for the skill of his crew.

He had thought their journey was ended two nights ago when a sudden, vicious storm had blown them off course, the angry seas forcing them to seek refuge along the west coast of England. Sighting a winding river that would serve as a haven until the worst of the storm had passed, he had commanded his men to row toward it for all they were worth. But the turbulent waters at its mouth had hidden the treacherous rocks below the surface. Standing at the prow, the wind and rain slashing at his face, Hakon had seen the jagged rocks too late. The loud sound of splintering wood had rent the night, the impact violently throwing the men from their rowing benches.

Hakon had yelled himself hoarse that night shouting orders over the howling wind. Yea, it was surely the will of Thor, protector of seafarers, that had gotten them safely to the banks of the river. In another few moments the mighty longship would have taken on enough water to send all of them to an early grave! Shaking his head, Hakon knelt at the side of the ship to get a closer view of the repaired hull.

"We will make it to Norge, my lord. I stake my life on it!" blustered Olav, the burly helmsman. Rising to his feet, Hakon slapped the older man affectionately on the shoulder.

"No need to stake your life, Olav," he said, grinning broadly. "After all, I need you to steer my ship!" Olav had sailed with him as his helmsman these past ten years, ever since Hakon had set off from Norway to seek his fortune as a young man of eighteen. The older man had been not only a worthy seaman over the years, but a loyal friend and brother-in-arms as well.

Hakon laughed out loud, a rich, deep sound that echoed about the surrounding woods. Why, if not for Olav he would surely have succumbed to the wiles of some comely wench and be settled on a farm in Ireland by now! There had been many an Irishman who would gladly have given their daughter's hand to a rich Viking merchant to buy themselves some peace and protection. But Olav had always been there to remind him of his love for the sea . . . and his freedom!

Shaking his head, Olav eyed Hakon shrewdly. "Yea, and who will you be thinking of now, my lord—the buxom redhead or the brunette with the flashing brown eyes?"

"I think only of home, my friend!" Hakon called out over his shoulder. He strode along the bank, admiring the curved length of his merchant longship. The sight of the tall, dragon-headed prow, carved by the finest masters in Dublin, sent a jolt of fierce pride coursing through his body. By the blood of Odin, it had been too long since he had seen his beloved homeland!

For the past six years during the winter months, he had lived in Dublin when not off trading. It had been easy for his brother Eirik's messenger to find him there. Hakon had lived well in the land of the Irish, and his fairness in trade was known throughout the land. The messenger had no difficulty finding the home of "Hakon the Fair."

Striding into the main hall, Hakon had immediately recognized the face of his late-night guest. Gnarr, his brother's faithful steward, stood before him heavily cloaked and anxious to speak. Sparing no time for the drink or meal offered him, the words fairly tumbled from his mouth. "Lord Hakon, I have awaited your return for many days." Pausing for a moment, as if to summon strength, he sighed. "I bear sad tidings from Norge, my lord."

The news of Eirik's grave illness brought great pain to Hakon's heart, for he dearly loved his elder brother. But it was the rest of the message that would change the course of Hakon's life forever. " 'Tis the fervent wish of your brother, Eirik, Jarl of Sogn, that you return at once to your homeland. Upon his death, you shall inherit his lands and wealth, as is your right of birth."

Hakon stood stunned for a moment. The ten years since he had left Norway seemed to fade away suddenly, and he recalled the death of their father, the great Magnus Haardrad, as if it were only yesterday.

According to Viking law, Eirik, as the elder brother, inherited their father's vast wealth. Hakon shared the fate of other second sons in Norway with no land—a life on the sea, trading. He had stayed just long enough to witness the marriage of Eirik to Bodvild, a beautiful woman of the Hardanger. As she would no doubt bear his brother many sons, there had been little reason for Hakon to linger. He bid his homeland farewell for what he thought would be forever.

"There are no sons?" Hakon asked Gnarr, somewhat incredulously.

"None," the messenger answered. "Bodvild has borne two daughters, one who died at birth, the other who is six years of age." Gnarr paused for a moment, then continued softly. "My lord Eirik's great love for Bodvild has kept him from taking others to wife, and he has no concubines. Nay, my lord, there are no heirs."

Gnarr waited several moments for a reply, but there had been no sound besides their breathing. And as the hour was very late, his efforts to read Hakon's face were frustrated by the shadows in the dimly lit hall. *Could it be that Lord Hakon will not return?* he wondered anxiously, in sudden terror that he might fail at his mission. Misreading Hakon's silence for indecision, Gnarr finally blurted, "My lord, Rhoar Bloodaxe lies in wait for Eirik Jarl's death!"

At these words, Hakon suddenly snapped out of his deep reverie and turned a piercing blue gaze upon the smaller man. "What is that you say?" he queried, his voice low and fierce.

Standing his ground, yet inwardly quailing at the venom in Hakon's voice, Gnarr answered quickly. "My lord, your bastard brother, Rhoar, plots at this very moment to seize your inheritance."

Rhoar Bloodaxe! Hakon stood staring at the glowing embers in the hearth, his face grim and expressionless. Every single muscle in his tall, lean frame tensed at that name, his large fists clenching in silent rage. So, his hated brother had not died after all!

Once again the years fell away as Hakon recalled the fierce battle that had raged on the day after his father's death. Rhoar, born of a beautiful, foreign slave, had always claimed to be the rightful first born of Magnus Jarl, bastard son or not. Favored by the Jarl and brought up in his household, he had truly believed he would one day inherit his father's wealth. Even the legitimate births of his younger half brothers, Eirik and Hakon, for whom he had been scarcely able to conceal a boiling hatred, had not daunted his belief. Yet his claim had come to naught at Magnus's deathbed. Turning sorrowful eyes upon Rhoar, the dying Jarl, with his last breath, had proclaimed Eirik as heir.

Swearing blood vengeance upon the Haardrad household, Rhoar had attacked the following morning with a hoard of renegade warriors. Fighting with the fury of men who had nothing to lose and everything to gain, Rhoar and his warriors at first seemed to have a victory in their grasp. But the tide of battle soon changed when he was gravely wounded by the swipe of a broadsword across his chest.

With his lifeblood pouring from the gaping wound and his face distorted in pain and rage, Rhoar was indeed an awful sight as he screamed for his men to continue to fight. Yet their spirit had been broken. They ran from the field of battle, dragging Rhoar's bloodied body with them.

"Lord Hakon!" The sound of Olav's voice interrupted Hakon's dark thoughts. He turned as the helmsman hurried to his side. "My lord, we must make haste and sail!"

Hakon noted the tension etched on Olav's face. "Is aught amiss?"

"Yea, my lord. I fear we may have been sighted by a landsman! One of the men spied a rider through the woods only moments ago."

Hakon swore under his breath. "Are those two fools back from the hunt?"

"Yea. All are aboard and at their oars."

"Then let us sail, before we must do battle," Hakon replied grimly. "There are enough battles that await us in Norge."

As if reading Hakon's mind, Olav vowed fiercely, "The wind will be at our backs. It will not be long 'til we reach our homeland, my lord!"

"Yea, if the gods are willing," Hakon answered darkly. He strode up the narrow wooden gangplank and jumped onto the deck. He did not believe in omens, but after the storm the other night, any other mishaps would seem suspicious indeed. His keen eyes scanned the thick trees that had hidden them so well these past two days. Yea, they had been lucky thus far, but if they had been sighted it would not be long before the Anglo-Saxons would be down upon them.

Following closely behind Hakon, Olav looked about him as he boarded the ship. Muttering fierce oaths, he heaved the gangplank up over the railing and secured it along the curved side of the ship, then quickly took his place at the helm.

Hakon made his way between the rowing benches toward the prow, glancing from side to side in acknowledgment of his men. All thirty-six were accounted for, including the wayward two who had been out hunting since before dawn.

Cursing silently to himself, Hakon cast a sideways glance toward Svein and Torvald. Those two had been trouble from the moment they signed on with his ship in Dublin, he thought irritably. He'd had his doubts about them from the beginning, but he had needed two more men to replace the crewmen who had died of fever during the last trading voyage. His better instincts had told him to beware, but he had found no others willing to travel the seas so close to winter.

Recalling the morning several days ago when his longship had set sail from Dublin, Hakon frowned impatiently. Not only had Svein and Torvald demanded twice the normal wage for such a journey, but they had been too drunk from their wenching the night before to man their oars. They spent the entire first day retching over the side of the ship, and then collapsed over their oars in a drunken sleep. Watching them in disgust, Hakon had vowed to leave them ashore as soon as they reached Norway, whether in sight of a settlement or not!

Hakon felt his heated ire rise even more at the sullen look thrown his way by Svein. He stopped abruptly beside his rowing bench. "Did you not hear the horn, man, or were the deer so plentiful as to make you forget the signal?" Receiving no answer, he spat, "Had you tarried any longer, you might have made your home with the Anglo-Saxons! I am sure they would have made you welcome—with an arrow between your eyes!"

"Indeed, my lord, the hunting was very good," Svein muttered churlishly, his eyes on his feet. "But in our haste to return to the ship we had to leave our kill behind." He looked up, meeting Hakon's steady gaze insolently. "Alas, we brought back many furs for the journey, my lord, but no meat," he sneered.

Without hesitation, Hakon drew his long-bladed knife from his belt. Poising the pointed tip under Svein's chin, he lifted his head so high the terror-stricken man thought fleetingly that his neck would surely snap. "You will do well to keep silent the rest of the journey, else you find yourself in the sea," Hakon murmured, his soft-spoken words belying their deadly intent.

His pale eyes wide with fear, Svein could feel a trickle of blood ooze down the side of his neck as Hakon held him on the point of his blade. "Aye, m-my lord," he rasped through clenched teeth.

Grimly satisfied, Hakon suddenly removed the blade. He watched in disgust as Svein slumped onto his bench. Aware that the rest of the crew had been watching with interest, his stern command left no doubt who was in command of the ship. "Man your oars!" he shouted. Striding to the dragon-headed prow, he stood with his long, sinewed legs spread wide and muscled arms folded across his broad chest.

"What could you have been thinking, man?" Torvald whispered fiercely to Svein, who was rubbing the side of his neck. He knew that his wily companion had a great hatred for the wealthy and highborn, but he had never seen him go so far before. And to defy Lord Hakon aboard his own ship . . .!

With a sinking feeling Torvald thought of the two captives in the cargo well. He and Svein had managed to board the ship almost unnoticed, having returned long before the final signal. Hakon had been checking the repairs to the longship with several of the men, while the others were skinning their own kill beneath the trees. Thankfully, no questions had been asked of their burdens, since it looked as if they were carrying bundles of furs.

If only our luck holds, Torvald thought desperately, hoping that the wench had been frightened enough not to make any sound in the cargo well. By the fire of Odin, he had no desire to find himself tossed into the sea!

Svein licked the blood from his hand, ignoring Torvald's incredulous look. He could still feel Hakon's eyes upon him, and he did not wish to provoke him further. Bringing his oar down from its vertical position, he slipped it through the oar hole and awaited the next command.

"Push off the shore!"

The crewmen on the port side of the ship pushed off the bank of the river with their narrow-bladed oars, setting to the task with unbridled enthusiasm. Whoops and shouts filled the air as their bulging muscles rippled against wood, the exhilaration of sailing once again coursing through their blood. With his calloused hand on the helm off the starboard side, Olav accurately guided the longship into the surging currents of the river.

"Oars to water!" Hakon shouted. In unison the eighteen pairs of oars dipped into the murky water, the men striking up a rhythm in their rowing that was as natural to them as breathing. The longship cut a swath through the water as cleanly as a sea snake, leaving scarcely a ripple behind it.

Chapter Ten

Huddled in a corner of the pitch-dark cargo well, Anora gasped at the abrupt motion of the ship as it was pushed off the shore. Suddenly she clapped her hand over her mouth, her eyes round with fear. She had not forgotten Svein's threat earlier that morning. Making no further sounds, she listened as the oars hit the water with a resounding smack. She could hear one voice shouting orders above the din of benches scraping and oars creaking, but the words were muffled by the wooden hatch above her head.

Fresh tears started anew as she realized that the ship was under way. Sweet Jesu! Why was this happening? Every muscle of her body ached from Svein's rough treatment, and she shivered uncontrollably. Her wrists chafed and burned from the leather thong binding them. Her tunic and mantle, still damp from her fall in the stream, offered her no warmth. Grabbing at one of the soft furs piled high along the side of the cargo well, she pulled it over herself and Gwendolyn, who was still unconscious from the blow to her head.

Clutching the fur desperately to her chin, she could feel her shivering slowly begin to subside.

Anora had never felt so alone in all her life. Her sister had not uttered a sound since they had been so rudely thrown into the well. *What if she never wakes?* Anora thought, her mind racing irrationally. *What if she dies?* That last thought was more than she could bear. Biting her hand to keep from screaming, she sobbed as if her heart would rend in two

Surely we would have been missed by now. . . . Leah would have sounded an alarm. *Surely Wulfgar is looking for us. . . .* The thoughts chased through her mind like frightened rabbits, tumbling and twisting over one another. Maybe, just maybe, if she closed her eyes for a moment, she would open them to find this had all been a terrible dream. Closing her eyes, Anora felt a wave of exhaustion wash over her. Lulled by the gentle motion of the ship, she drifted into a numbing sleep.

A low moan, breaking from Gwendolyn's parched throat, woke Anora with a start. *How long have I been asleep?* she wondered dazedly, rubbing her forehead. Another moan from her sister, louder than the first, brought Anora suddenly back to reality. "Gwendolyn?" she whispered, groping blindly in the dark.

Suddenly she was pitched forward and thrown against the side of a wooden cask as the floor of the cargo well moved out from under her. Wincing, she realized all too painfully that while she had slept, the ship must have passed the mouth of the river and was now sailing the open seas. Gwendolyn, who had been lying next to her, must have been rolled across the floor to the other side of the cargo well by the bucking of the waves. Reaching out her hands once again, Anora pleaded, "Gwendolyn, can you hear me?"

"Aye, Anora, but where are you?" Rolling over onto her side, Gwendolyn felt a sharp pain pierce through her head, and white lights flashed before her eyes. "God's blood, what did that blond giant hit me with?" she swore softly. Her attempts to sit up were being thwarted by the leather thong tied around her wrists, but she finally managed to prop herself up on what felt to be a sack of grain. Holding her head in her hands, she tried to get her bearings, but the rolling motion of the floor was making that virtually impossible.

Anora tentatively crawled in the direction of her sister's voice. Before Svein had closed the hatch earlier that day she had seen the dimensions of the cargo well. It was a small area, crammed full with provisions and furs, so Gwendolyn could not be far off.

She reached out in front of her, at last catching hold of a trousered leg. "Gwendolyn!" she cried out in relief, her voice wracked by pitiful sobs. She pulled herself up beside her sister. "I thought for sure you would never wake!" She lifted her bound wrists over Gwendolyn's head and enveloped her in a frantic embrace.

"If you do not let go of my neck, Anora, I may still never see the light of day," Gwendolyn murmured weakly, with a small laugh.

"Oh . . . forgive me!" Anora hiccoughed. Relaxing her hold, she removed her arms but stayed close by Gwendolyn's side. "What are we going to do?" she asked miserably, her voice trembling.

"First, tell me what has happened," Gwendolyn replied softly, furtively touching the bump on her forehead. Grimacing in pain, she already knew from the roll and pitch of the floor that they were in a ship of some kind. That certainly did not bode well for their situation!

"Oh, Gwendolyn." Anora sighed raggedly, shuddering. Pouring out the horrible tale was like reliving it, and she alternately found herself weeping or benumbed with shock.

Gwendolyn felt a great anger boiling within her at what her sister had suffered. At least she was spared a rape, she thought gratefully, knowing that Anora could never have survived such abuse.

"And Gwendolyn," Anora paused, her voice a whisper, "they think you are my brother!"

Not totally surprised by this revelation, Gwendolyn felt a glimmer of hope suddenly spark within her. She had been mistaken for a lad on other occasions, probably due to her dress and boyish mannerisms. Always seeing it as a lark before, she realized that perhaps this might be the one time when the guise could prove useful to her. How, she did not know, but she felt in time the answer would reveal itself to her.

"Anora, I want you to promise me something," Gwendolyn spoke firmly, despite the awful pounding in her head. "I want you to promise that from now on you will address me, and think of me, only as your brother."

"But, why?"

"Listen to me. Somehow we must find a way to escape, and if one of us is seen as a boy I think it will improve our chances." The more Gwendolyn thought of the idea, the more it made sense to her, yet she had to convince Anora. "You must trust me in this, Anora. If one of us is somewhat less vulnerable . . ." She paused, thinking out loud. "Well . . . I cannot say how it may help, but if you promise me, perhaps I can work out a plan."

Anora had always trusted her sister's judgment, and now she needed to more than ever. But could Gwendolyn carry it off? she wondered frantically. The idea seemed farfetched . . . but if there was even a chance it could help them to escape, certainly it was worth a try. "Aye, Gwendolyn, you have my promise!" she whispered fiercely. "You are now a brother to me!"

"Good! Now, I shall need a boy's name. Let me think . . . Eadric, Gawain, no . . . uh, Garric! Aye, Garric!" she exclaimed softly, remembering the name of the new stable-boy.

Caught up in the soaring hope of the moment, Anora suddenly laughed out loud, a joyous sound. Yet, no sooner had the laughter escaped her throat than she regretted it with all her heart. A noise, something like scraping, was heard above their heads. Then the wooden hatch swung open and hit the deck with a thud.

" 'Tis Svein, Gwendolyn, come to kill you!" Anora cried out, cringing in fear. If anything happened to her sister, she thought wildly, truly she would want to die herself.

Bright sunshine streamed into the cargo well, blinding them. Loud voices were heard overhead. Then a bearded face peered down at them. Shielding their eyes from the light, Gwendolyn and Anora squinted up at the man as he gaped back at them in total astonishment.

"What is it, Egil?" a deep voice called from beyond the open hatch.

"My lord, it seems we have some unwitting guests aboard!" the man shouted, not taking his eyes from the two huddled near a fresh-water cask. *Thor! The wench is a pretty piece!* he thought admiringly. But how did they come to be in the cargo well? Shaking his head, he knew the future did not bode well for some foolish man on the ship. Thanking the gods he had no hand in the matter, he got up from his knees and came face to face with Lord Hakon.

"What do you mean—unwitting guests?" Hakon questioned, a dark scowl clouding his features.

"Well, my lord, 'tis a fair wench and a lad in the well, and from the looks of them I'd say they've been a bit ill-used." Quickly Egil stepped out of Hakon's way.

Standing at the edge of the open hatch, Hakon looked down into the well. *By the fire of Loki, what omen is this?* he wondered, as his gaze was met by two pairs of emerald green eyes fixed warily upon him. Though the well was dark, he could tell the captives were bound, and their soiled and disheveled appearance did not speak well for their treatment. After taking a deep breath of the bracing sea air, he dropped into the well. The low ceiling prevented him from standing to his full height, which was well over six feet, so he knelt down on one knee not too far from them.

Gwendolyn instinctively moved in front of Anora, placing herself between her sister and the Viking. Aye, for now she knew the origin of their captors. She had heard enough tales of the Norsemen from her father to recognize the man before her as one of those fierce raiders of the sea.

Dressed in a richly embroidered tunic that reached to his thighs, tightly gartered leggings, and high boots trimmed in fur, the Viking looked to be highborn and very wealthy. But what fascinated Gwendolyn most, although she tried not to show it, was the large, silver amulet in the shape of a hammer that hung from his neck on a finely wrought chain, and the polished hilt of his sword that rested above a fine leather scabbard slung from his belt. He was clean-shaven, unlike the other man she had seen. Around his head was wrapped an ornamental headband that held back his hair, which was shoulder length.

Gwendolyn had never before seen such thick, white-blond hair on a man. And the startling blue of his eyes set against the tanned bronze of his skin was quite striking. His fair brows, knitted in thought, softened his somewhat hawkish features. She found herself thinking many a woman would find him an extremely handsome man, with his straight nose, chiseled mouth, and strong, square-cut jawline. Yet the glitter in his eyes was hard, and she could not read his expression.

"Come forward into the light," Hakon commanded softly, speaking the Celtic tongue. He was answered by only a blank stare. He tried again, this time in the language of the Saxons. Seeing a flicker of surprise in the lad's eyes, he could barely suppress a smile. *So, they are Anglo-Saxon,* he thought. Then his expression once again hardened. Obviously some on board the ship had seen fit to disobey his orders, and he had a strong suspicion of who the culprits might be.

Watching the angry tic in the Viking's jaw, Gwendolyn only hoped his anger was not directed at them. He had spoken their language almost without an accent, and that amazed her greatly. How had a Viking come to know their language, and speak it so well? she wondered fleetingly.

"Now, lad, I know you understand me. Come forward where I can see you better, and bring the girl with you," Hakon stated patiently in a low voice. It would serve no purpose to frighten them, he thought, although he had no delusions of winning their trust. Right now, he only needed to know who had brought them aboard his ship.

Gwendolyn hesitated for a moment, assessing their position. From the commanding look of this Viking and the richness of his garb, he could be the captain of this ship, she considered, and therefore the master of their fate. Perhaps if they cooperated with him, he might consider returning them to their homeland. He certainly did not have the same evil look as the two men who had abducted them. Daring to hope just a little, she turned to Anora, who was huddled behind her. "Remember your promise," she whispered just loud enough for her sister to hear. Struggling awkwardly to her feet, she pulled Anora up beside her.

For a moment the pounding pain in her head drowned out all else, and her knees wobbled unsteadily on the verge of collapse. Suddenly a strong arm reached out and grabbed her by the shoulder, steadying her. She looked up, her emerald eyes meeting the Viking's blue gaze as he held her against him until she regained her balance.

"There, now, lad, you will get your sea legs in a moment," Hakon assured her, reaching out to steady Anora as well. Cringing at his touch, she jerked away from him and fell heavily against a wooden cask. Hakon shook his head. He could see that the wench was as frightened as a skittish doe. Before she could dodge him again, he picked her up in his arms, then carried her struggling and kicking to the open hatch. "Take the wench, Egil, but watch your eyes!" he shouted. "She might be in the mood to scratch them out!"

With a small heave Hakon tossed Anora gently into Egil's waiting arms. Then he turned back to Gwendolyn.

"Now it is your turn, lad. You may have your choice. Climb out like a man, or I will have to toss you out as well."

"I would prefer to climb out, my lord," Gwendolyn answered with no hesitation, trying to keep her womanish voice low, "but my wrists are bound." Trying not to let him see her face too closely in the light from the open hatch, she kept her head down.

Hakon started in surprise at the lilting quality of her voice. *The lad looks to be sixteen winters, but perhaps he is even younger*, he thought. He pulled his long-bladed knife from his belt. With one quick movement he cut the leather thong binding Gwendolyn's wrists. "There, now, off with you," he commanded gruffly.

Gwendolyn stepped on one of the casks near the open hatch and pulled herself up and out of the cargo well, followed shortly by the Viking. The daylight, although beginning to fade into dusk, was still intensely bright compared to the pitch-darkness of the well. Blinded temporarily, she opened her eyes slowly to adjust to the change. Suddenly she spied Anora sitting forlornly on the deck, her pale cheeks dirty and stained with tears. She rushed over to her sister's side and sat down beside her.

"I am here now, Anora," Gwendolyn whispered reassuringly, throwing her arm protectively around her sister's delicate shoulders. Her eyes, now accustomed to the light, were wide-eyed as she looked about the Viking ship. It was just as her father had told her in his stories, she thought in awe, remembering his vivid description of a fleet of Viking vessels he had seen in the London harbor while a young man in the king's army.

She was amazed at the swiftness of the ship as it cut through the ocean swells. The large, rectangular sail, white with bold red stripes, was stretched taut by the stiff wind. A gilded bronze vane, etched with strange designs and hung with metal pendants that rattled and jangled in the breeze, was fitted to the masthead. And at its top, a proud, gilded beast was mounted, as if to keep watch over the horizon.

Letting her eyes roam, she looked toward the bow. Suddenly she gasped, her breath caught in her throat. A fierce dragon head, carved into the strongly curved prow, leered back at her with its sharp, grinning teeth. A flash of memory coursed through her mind—a bright bolt of lightning, crashing thunder, her mare rearing and pawing the air, then a demon rising from the rushing water—and with the memory came the cold shock of realization.

Her nightmare vision during the storm two nights ago had not been an evil apparition from the depths of hell, but the carved prow of the Viking ship!

"God help us! I could have prevented this," she murmured numbly, her mind racing. If only she had tried to think of an explanation for her vision that night, or had at least told one of her father's thanes about it . . . perhaps one of them might have recognized her vision for what it was and could have been alerted to the Viking threat. Then, none of this would have happened. . . .

The finality of her last thought caused Gwendolyn to curse her weakness of judgment. Heatedly she swore to herself it would never, *never* happen again. The flash of defiance was still burning in her eyes when she looked up to find the Viking regarding Anora intently.

Chapter Eleven

Hakon drew in his breath sharply. Now that the captives were in the light, he was able to study them more closely. He liked what he saw huddled on the deck before him. The wench was truly a beauty, despite her soiled appearance and tangled hair. Nay, not just a beauty, but probably the most enchantingly lovely young woman he had ever seen.

As for the lad, he obviously was her brother, for their resemblance to each other was remarkable. In fact, he thought as his sharp eyes took in every detail, their features were virtually identical. Twins were indeed a rare sight, and oddly enough Hakon found himself thinking their presence on his ship was a good omen.

Yet the lad's defiant glance served as a reminder to Hakon, and he turned his mind somewhat reluctantly to the grim task yet at hand. He turned first to the oarsmen seated in the stern. All eyes were focused upon him, their interest obviously piqued by the sight of the beautiful wench on board. Their faces revealed no knowledge of the captives, however, so Hakon turned to the oarsmen seated forward of the well in the bow section of the ship.

Again all eyes were upon him, except for those of the very two men he had suspected. With their shoulders hunched and their backs to him, Svein and Torvald were the picture of guilt.

Hakon strove to check the cold fury in his voice. "Escort those two men amidships!"

Rushing to obey, Egil noted that he had never before seen Lord Hakon so angry. He strode over to where Svein and Torvald were sitting. "All right, you two, you heard Lord Hakon. On your feet!"

With a sinking feeling in the pit of his stomach, Svein rose slowly from his bench, his face a pasty white. Surely the captain would not make good his threat of throwing him overboard, he thought nervously, but he could not be sure. Torvald also rose, his massive size somehow diminished by his apparent fear. Walking in front of Egil, the two men approached the cargo well.

Hakon's face was inscrutable as he addressed them. "I am sure you men recall my orders when we landed in England. There was to be no disruption of any kind upon the inhabitants of that land during our brief stay—no raping, no pillaging, and no killing unless we were attacked. Do you remember?" Receiving short nods, he demanded, "How did these captives come to be on my ship, then?" Another question plagued him, but he did not ask it . . . not yet. He only knew that if the wench had been raped, the two men would not live to see a new day.

Torvald looked at his feet, unable to find his voice to answer. Speaking for both of them, Svein kept his tone ingratiating and servile. "My lord Hakon, we found those two during our hunt, and thinkin' you would be pleased to possess so lovely a wench, and the lad thrown in for good measure, we could na' resist bringing them to the ship as an offering to our fine captain." His pale eyes shifted over to the captives, their watery blue depths sending an undeniable threat of violence in their direction. Shuddering, Anora hid her face in her hands.

Hakon could have struck him down at that moment for his bald-faced lie. But first he needed to hear from the captives themselves the extent of Svein and Torvald's crimes. He walked over to Anora, bent down, and tilted up her chin to face him. Staring into her eyes, so lushly fringed with gold-tipped lashes, he felt for a moment as if he would lose himself in the deep emerald pools gazing back at him. Strangely enough for a man who so dearly loved his freedom, the thought did not displease him.

"Tell me, little one," he murmured gently, "were you hurt in any way by either of those two men?" Hakon dreaded to hear her answer, fearing the worst, but he had to know.

Anora felt cold fear clutching at her throat. For the life of her she could not speak. Stark terror lit her eyes when she glanced over at Svein's evil face, remembering all too well his threat. Frightened for Gwendolyn's life, she shook her head slowly from side to side. At her answer, Hakon felt an immense surge of relief.

"Aye, if an attempted rape is not hurt enough!" Gwendolyn blurted furiously, her eyes flashing. If Anora was too afraid to speak, she certainly was not! Though unable to understand the Norse language, she could tell Hakon was indeed the captain of the ship, and a feared and respected one at that. Never had she seen men so ready to obey another's command.

Only he has the power to punish those two curs, she thought fiercely. Svein's fawning and silky tones had not fooled her. She did not have to speak their language to know a sniveling liar when she saw one. Damned if she wouldn't let the Viking know exactly what had happened!

Startled by her vehement words, Hakon felt a white-hot

stab of rage course through his body. The thought of Svein pressing his crude body against the girl's fragile beauty was more than he could bear. He grabbed Gwendolyn by the shoulders. "Tell me what you know, lad, and be quick about it," he demanded.

"My sister and I were in the woods when these two"—she pointed at Svein and Torvald—"jumped out at us from behind some trees. I was hit on the head and remember naught else. The rest I know from Anora."

Anora. So that was the beauty's name. Rolling it over his tongue like the finest honey, Hakon glanced at the girl. Even Freyja, the goddess of love and beauty, could not have fashioned a more perfect name for her. Ever so gently, he reached out and touched the purplish bruise on her fair cheek. Anora started from his hand as if stung.

"I will not hurt you," Hakon said softly, oddly distressed that she would shrink from his touch. "Just tell me who struck you, or at least, if you will not speak, point to the man."

Emboldened by Gwendolyn's outburst, Anora's hand trembled as she pointed at Svein.

"You would take the word of an English slut against one of your own?" Svein screamed, his voice an ugly snarl. Before anyone could grab him, he suddenly rushed at the captives, his eyes red with rage. Gwendolyn quickly moved in front of Anora, taking the full force of Svein's weight as he fell upon her.

Yet no sooner had Svein knocked the breath from Gwendolyn's body than he found himself hurled violently across the deck of the ship. "Seize his arms!" Hakon yelled. Several oarsmen rushed to obey. Hoisting Svein to his feet, they pinned his arms behind his back, subduing him. He struggled in vain, all the while screaming foul curses and oaths until Hakon doubled up his first and slammed it into his face. Silenced at last, Svein slumped limply amid his captors.

"Tie him to the mast!" Hakon ordered. "And Egil, prepare the lash." Striding over to the captives, he helped Gwendolyn to her feet. "You are indeed a brave lad," he said, a hint of admiration in his eyes. But his expression remained cold. Speaking to both of them, his voice was grim. "Those men brought you aboard this ship against my orders, most likely for their own gain. When we reach shore, their punishment will be far more severe. But for now, they will feel the kiss of the lash for their greed."

When we reach shore. . . . Had she heard correctly? Gwendolyn wondered excitedly. Aye, those had been the Viking's words. A feeling of elation surged within her, bringing a smile to her lips. So she had been right, she thought, proud of her intuition. They had cooperated with the Viking, and now he would return them to their homeland!

The high-pitched whine of the lash through the air interrupted Gwendolyn's thoughts, and the ship soon echoed with Svein's terrible screams for mercy. Anora, unable to watch the awful scene, leaned against the railing and looked out over the sea. But Gwendolyn counted every stroke of the lash until there had been thirty, and did not blink once when Svein, his back torn and bloodied, was finally cut down from the mast. She watched in the same manner as Torvald received his punishment, not feeling vindicated until he, too, crumpled moaning to the deck. Dragged back to their benches, the two men were left to lie in their own blood.

" 'Tis done, Anora," she whispered to her sister. For a moment they both stared off into the distance at the faint outline of land along the horizon. Aye, soon they would be home. . . . Hearing footsteps crossing the deck toward them, Gwendolyn turned to face Hakon. Squaring her shoulders, she opened her mouth to speak.

"What is your name, lad?" Hakon spoke first, catching Gwendolyn off guard.

"Uh . . . Ga-Garric, my lord," she stammered. God's blood, she winced, how could she be convincing as a boy if she did not even know her own name? Hoping Hakon had not seen her confusion in the gathering dusk, she ran her hand through her short curls and rushed on boldly. "It is good of you to return us to our homeland, my lord. Our father will reward you greatly."

Hakon sighed. If he had hoped earlier he might win their trust, he knew now that in the next few minutes he would earn only their hatred. "We sail for Norge, lad. There will be no turning back."

Stunned, Gwendolyn could not speak. *No turning back.* The finality of those words echoed in her mind, and she shook her head in disbelief. Anora had also heard them. Whirling around, she stood numbly beside Gwendolyn.

"But you said earlier . . . you said when we reach shore—"

"Yea, that I did, lad. But I did not mean your homeland."

Wrenching pain lit Anora's eyes, causing Hakon to swear softly. *You are growing soft, man,* he chided himself. Hardening his heart, he continued. "I am not usually in the habit of making excuses for myself, but in this situation I feel I must. I had no hand in your capture. My ship needed repairs, and we took refuge along the river these past three days."

Nodding toward Svein and Torvald lying on the deck, he added, "Those men acted against my orders, and for this they have been punished. But I cannot return you to your homeland. We have almost a full day of sailing behind us already, and we must make haste to Norge on a matter of grave importance to me." Feeling he had offered enough explanation, Hakon heard his voice grow hard. "The gods have brought you to me, and you must accept your fate. I offer you my protection, and when we reach Norge you will remain with me as slaves in my household."

Gwendolyn's head snapped back, hatred and defiance burning in her eyes. Any hopes she had of fair treatment by this man had been cruelly dashed. "I know naught of your gods," she said disdainfully. "But if it is slaves we shall be, then know this, Viking. You are no different from the two you punished earlier. Aye, even worse, if you hold us against our will!"

"Think what you must, lad, it makes no difference. Slaves you will be—you have no choice." Sighing wearily, Hakon turned from them. "I will bring you furs to sleep on tonight, and some food." He walked away slowly, feeling their eyes upon him. Yea, life could be cruel, he thought, understanding their feelings. Yet he also understood his own.

Anora. Whispering her name, Hakon stood alone at the prow of the ship, gazing into the darkened sky. He was drawn to her as he had never felt drawn to any woman. It was as if her emerald eyes had cast a spell upon him, and he could do nothing to dispel his attraction for her. Yea, even if he had wanted to, he knew now he could not let her go.

Gwendolyn allowed herself only a moment of self-pity before she turned to Anora. Her sister's face was deadly pale in the moonlight, her eyes fixed and devoid of emotion.

"Anora, listen to me!" she whispered, suddenly afraid. She had never seen her sister like this before and it frightened her. Shaking her roughly by the shoulders, Gwendolyn forced her to meet her eyes. "Anora, I vow we will return to our homeland, and you to Wulfgar. You must trust me in this. I will find a way for us to escape!"

A flicker of response lighted Anora's eyes. "Promise me, Gwendolyn?" she murmured plaintively, clutching her sister's hand.

"Aye, on my life . . . I promise."

Chapter Twelve

Gwendolyn rested her head against the side of the ship. If only her stomach would stop its churning, she thought miserably, staring out onto the rolling waves. Nausea swept over her again, and she quickly leaned over the side, retching. A sharp slap on her backside did not ease her condition.

"A fine sailor you would make, Garric!" Hakon shouted at her over the roar of the waves. Gwendolyn felt too ill to retort, her hate tempered by her seasickness. Wiping her mouth on her sleeve, she stumbled back to the tent that Hakon had erected for Anora near the prow of the ship, trying her best to ignore the grinning, bearded faces of his crew.

Lying on her side and covered by a thick fur to keep out the chill of the wind, Anora had moved little these past two days. Mercifully spared the seasickness, she still had been unable to eat despite Gwendolyn's coaxing and pleading. She had spoken very little, her eyes fixed out on the sea as if searching for something.

"Anora, why do you stare out at the sea?" Gwendolyn asked gently, noting once again that Anora had not touched the food Hakon had brought for her. Feeling her stomach growing queasy at the sight of the salted fish and sour milk, she pushed the wooden platter out of the tent. *With only food like that to eat, no wonder she has no appetite*, Gwendolyn thought in disgust.

A heavy sigh broke from Anora's throat. *That's enough*, Gwendolyn decided firmly, concern etched on her face. If Anora did not face up to their situation, she would no more make it to Norge than back to their homeland again! Suddenly she slapped Anora's face.

"Oh!" Anora's hand flew up to her cheek, a startled look lighting her wan features.

"Aye, there, now!" Gwendolyn cried, feeling somewhat guilty for hurting her sister, but glad that she had received some response from her. "Forgive me, Anora, but if I am to make good on my vow, then you must be with me when we reach our home again. I do not wish to face Wulfgar without you!"

"Wulfgar . . ." Anora murmured, tears welling up in her eyes.

"Aye, Wulfgar, the man you will wed one day." Taking Anora's hands, Gwendolyn met her eyes. "Anora, you must be strong, not only for yourself, but for him as well." Gwendolyn had already imagined many times what the scene must have been back at the stronghold when they had not returned. She did not doubt for a moment that Wulfgar and her father would set out to find them, yet how long it would take she could not be sure. Perhaps the Viking ship had been sighted, at least giving them a clue as to their fate.

"You must eat, Anora. You must keep up your strength for whatever lies ahead." Gwendolyn paused, hoping the fear she felt at that moment did not show in her eyes. What would lie ahead for them? she wondered anxiously. She had seen the desire written in the Viking's eyes when he looked upon Anora. *Aye, she will have to be strong*, Gwendolyn thought grimly, for if Anora could not deny him her body, then she would have to defy him with her spirit. "Do you understand?" she pleaded.

As if reading her mind, Anora nodded her head slowly. "Aye, Gwendolyn, I will try to be strong, no matter what lies ahead." Suddenly a shout went out from high up on the mast, startling them. Whatever the oarsman had said, it increased the commotion aboard the ship tenfold, for there were shouts of excitement and the clatter of feet on the deck as men rushed to and fro.

Stepping out of the tent, Gwendolyn was nearly knocked over by Hakon as he rushed by, yelling orders to his crew. The great sail was being lowered and furled, and the men were readying their oars.

"Stay out of the way, lad, if you do not wish to be knocked overboard!" he said irritably. Suddenly his tone softened as Anora stepped out from behind the leather flap of the tent and stood beside Gwendolyn. "We have reached Sumburgh Voe, in the Shetland Islands. We will stay here for the night, and sail again at dawn."

Thor! She is truly a temptation, Hakon thought appreciatively, the very sight of her stirring his blood. He was glad that she had confined herself to the tent these past days. His men had been without women since they left Dublin, and they were growing increasingly restless. He only hoped there would be enough willing women on the island to satisfy his men's needs before they sailed again on the morrow!

Not missing the heated desire in Hakon's startling blue eyes, Anora glanced sideways at Gwendolyn, meeting her sister's gaze. Aye, she could be strong, if it would bring her back to Wulfgar, she told herself grimly. Nodding, Gwendolyn gave her a faint smile.

With the oarsmen all rowing in unison, it was not long

before the longship moved into the well-protected harbor. From this distance it appeared to Gwendolyn that the settlement was quite a large one. She could count at least eight longhouses, and numerous outbuildings scattered about the larger buildings. Leaning along the railing with Anora, she was amazed at the hoards of people lining the shore to greet the Viking ship. Men, women, and children all crowded to get a better view, their faces lighted with excitement and welcome.

Climbing onto the dragon-headed prow, Hakon waved his arm and hailed an exuberant greeting.

Obviously the Viking has been here before, Gwendolyn decided, as she watched him jump from the ship into knee-deep water and wade ashore. A huge, black-bearded man stepped out from the crowd and enveloped him in a massive embrace.

"Hakon, my boy, so you visit us again at last!" the man shouted warmly, giving Hakon a hearty slap on the back.

"You look well, Cousin Einar!" Hakon laughed. "Have you room for some weary travelers?"

"Ha! What a question!" Einar roared. "Call your men ashore, and we'll break out the ale!" Winking lewdly, he lowered his voice. "I'm sure there are several lasses here who will fight like she-cats for the chance to warm such a noble Viking's bed as yours! Ha! Now, *that* will be a sight to see! Come on, my boy, the air out here is cold, while a warm hall awaits us yonder!"

Hakon smiled broadly at his huge cousin, then turned back to the ship. "Egil, take several of the men and see that Svein and Torvald are chained securely to their benches for the night."

"Yea, my lord," Egil called out. He disappeared beyond the railing.

"As for the rest," Hakon shouted, waving his arm, "over the side with you! Your welcome awaits with open arms!"

Jumping into the water with excited whoops, the men quickly waded to shore and lost themselves in the crowds.

"What is this, then, Hakon? Prisoners aboard your ship?" Einar asked, curiosity lighting his eyes.

"More than prisoners, cousin," he replied, gesturing toward Gwendolyn and Anora, who stood along the railing near the prow. "I will need lodging for two others this night." Wading back out to the ship, Hakon reached out his arms to Anora. "Come, little one, do not be afraid. I will catch you." She looked at him incredulously, and stepped away from the railing.

"Go on, Anora. Best not to make him look the fool in front of his friends," Gwendolyn whispered reassuringly. "I will be right behind you." Still somewhat dubious, Anora stepped up on a rowing bench and sat down on the narrow railing. Holding her tunic and mantle demurely in one hand, she swung her legs over the side of the ship. Then, closing her eyes tight, she pushed herself off the ledge.

Hakon caught her securely in his outstretched arms. "There, now, Anora." He smiled gently. "We Vikings can be trusted." Ignoring his soft-spoken words, she tensed in his arms. *That day will never come*, she vowed silently.

A sudden splash beside them caused Hakon to laugh wryly. *The lad follows her like a shadow*, he thought, then shrugged. More than likely he would, too, if he had a sister as beautiful as Anora.

"There will be many jealous women crying in their beds this night," Einar muttered, shaking his head. He watched with great interest as Hakon carried ashore what looked to him to be a foreign wench.

"It has been a hard journey, Einar," Hakon stated, amused by the unspoken questions in his cousin's eyes. "This woman needs a warm bath and a place to rest."

"She will be well tended to, my boy," Einar replied. Over his shoulder, he called out to a stout, red-haired woman standing nearby. "Greta, see that this wench gets a bath and a good meal." Turning back to Hakon, he threw his head back and laughed uproariously. His young cousin had never failed to surprise him, but this time he had outdone himself. "I see there are many things for us to talk of this night!" he said, grinning broadly.

Hakon set Anora down on the sandy beach. "Go with her. She will see to your needs." Anora hesitated for a moment, then resignedly allowed the woman to lead her away. Seeing Gwendolyn start to follow them, he called out sharply, "Nay, Garric, you will stay with me."

Gwendolyn stopped abruptly in her tracks, then reluctantly turned back toward Hakon. A protest was on her lips, but Hakon's expression boded no resistance. "Do not worry, lad, your sister will be well cared for."

That's just what I am afraid of, Viking, Gwendolyn thought warily, trudging behind him along the sandy beach toward the well-lighted hall.

Chapter Thirteen

"So, what has it been, Hakon—two years since you passed this way?" Einar asked between long drafts of ale from his drinking horn. Some of the frothy liquid spilled out over his thick beard and down the front of his leather tunic, but he did not seem to mind. He wiped his mouth with the back of his hand, his eyes widening lustily at the sight of a serving girl's ample breasts as she leaned over to refill his drinking horn.

Suddenly he pulled her onto his lap, his large hands roaming freely over her well-rounded body. The girl's startled squeal brought a roar of delight from the grizzled Viking. She struggled in mock resistance, giggling all the while. "Go on with you, wench, but mind you do not stray too far," Einar chortled, releasing her reluctantly. Planting a rough kiss on her smiling red lips, he followed her with his eyes as she sauntered away.

Hakon laughed heartily. "Yea, cousin, at least two. And I can see that you have not changed in the least during that time!" And he hoped Einar would never change, for he was truly fond of his unruly cousin.

Einar had sailed with him when he left Norway ten years ago, only to decide to homestead on the Shetlands after they had stopped there for several days on their journey south. At that time there had been plenty of land for the taking: lush, green, and well suited for raising sheep. And since Einar had never really been a sailor at heart, he had opted to stay.

Hakon reluctantly bade his cousin farewell, but had promised to return whenever his trading voyages brought him near the islands. He had since made many visits to Sumburgh Voe, for the Viking settlement was always in need of provisions, trade goods, and news from other lands. Yet his most recent trading voyages had all been to the south, and Hakon had been unable to sail to the Shetlands for these past two years.

"This journey is different from the others, is it not?" Einar shouted, leaning forward to hear Hakon's answer. The carousing in the hall had reached a near fever pitch, and it was proving difficult to converse over the drunken rabble and coarse laughter. He had perceived there was a great weight upon Hakon's mind, for his young cousin had been slightly subdued all evening. And for him to be immune to the provocative glances thrown his way by several comely wenches was more than Einar could comprehend.

"It seems my trading days are past, cousin. I have received word that my brother Eirik lies on his deathbed, gravely ill. And as he has no heirs, he wishes to leave his lands and wealth to me—that is, if I get to Norge before Rhoar makes his play for the inheritance."

Suddenly Einar jumped from his chair and brought his huge fist down upon the wooden table. "Rhoar lives?" he roared, his swarthy face livid with anger. The hall suddenly grew still at the chieftain's outburst, all eyes upon him.

"Yea, he lives, cousin. I am afraid your sword, though

mighty, did not end his life." It had been Einar, fighting at Hakon and Eirik's side those ten years past, who had plunged his sword into Rhoar Bloodaxe. Believing the chest wound would provide a slow and painful death to the traitor, as Einar believed Rhoar to be, he had not dealt him a final deathblow. Instead, he watched as Rhoar's men dragged their leader from the battlefield, confident that he would breathe his last before the night had fallen.

"Would that I had run that spawn of Midgard, serpent of the underworld, clean through his black heart with my sword, rather than let him wreak further havoc upon your house!" Einar blustered fiercely. Drawing his broadsword from its scabbard, he thrust it with great vengeance at an imaginary opponent, just barely missing several of Hakon's men, who dove beneath the table to escape the flashing blade.

"Yea, cousin, I would that he had died that day, also. But the gods have let him live for some purpose, if not just to try me," Hakon replied grimly. "Come, Einar, sheathe your sword, and let us walk outside for a moment. My men have a hard sail before them, and they are in dire need of merriment tonight."

Catching Hakon's meaning, Einar returned his sword to the scabbard at his wide belt. "Very well, my boy," he agreed. The cold night air would no doubt help to quench his ire, and he had no wish to spoil the evening's promise for Hakon's crew. Turning to the still-silent revelers, he shouted, "There is more ale to be had, men, so drink up, and remember the wenches are willing!"

At his words the walls once again resounded with laughter and merriment. Grinning, Einar glanced at Hakon. "But what of that scrawny lad, cousin? Will you have him accompany us, or may we walk alone? He has not left your side since you entered the hall an hour ago, but remains near you like some pup who has lost its mother!"

Hakon's gaze fell on Gwendolyn, sitting huddled on the floor near his chair. The lad had been so quiet Hakon had almost forgotten he was there. "Garric, stay here with Egil. He will show you where to sleep tonight if I do not return." With that curt command, he strode out of the hall after Einar.

Gwendolyn stood up suddenly from the ground as if to follow after him, but Egil grabbed her by the shoulder, thwarting her escape. He gestured for her to sit back down, his stern expression threatening certain punishment if she disobeyed. Sliding back down to the floor, she slumped in utter frustration.

Sweet Jesu! Gwendolyn agonized. *What if he seeks out Anora?* Once again her feeling of helplessness was almost more than she could bear. She muttered every curse she could think of upon Hakon and his kind.

Outside the hall, Hakon took a bracing breath of the sea air. The sound of the waves crashing against the shoreline enlivened his senses, and his step was light. For several moments he and Einar walked in silence, each occupied by his own thoughts. The sounds of revelry from the hall gradually receded into the distance, drowned out by the wind and the sea.

"So Hakon, tell me of these prisoners . . . and the wench," Einar said, his voice low. "From what little I have seen of her, her eyes alone could cast a spell over many a lesser man. Have you been bewitched by this silver-haired beauty?"

Hakon did not answer. Had he been bewitched? Yea, it seemed so. He had known many women in the past, and had even loved a few of them. Or so he had thought at the time. But he had never felt stranger than when he had looked into the emerald depths of this woman's eyes.

"So 'tis true, then." Einar threw back his shaggy head and laughed out loud, the hearty sound carrying over the roar of the waves. "I never thought I would live to see you taken by any one woman!"

"Her name is Anora. She and her brother, Garric, the scrawny lad in the hall"—Hakon chuckled—"were taken captive by two of my men . . . against my orders." He sobered quickly at the thought of Svein and Torvald's deceit. He continued, relating the entire story to Einar, who listened with great interest.

"Those are the men chained to their benches this night?"

"Yea. They have been more trouble than their lives are worth, but I cannot help thinking I would not have the girl now if it had not been for them," Hakon replied, recalling how it had felt to hold her in his arms when he carried her ashore. She had trembled against his broad chest, reminding him of a fightened doe.

"It sounds like the mischief of Loki is afoot, my boy, or perhaps the goddess Freyja has seen fit to turn your head with a sea nymph instead of a woman!"

"Nay, Einar, she is a woman of flesh and blood . . . and she is mine."

"Then, my boy, perhaps you would like to seek out this woman?" Einar queried slyly, glancing sideways at Hakon. "I believe you will find her in the bathing house beyond that hall over there." He pointed, a lewd grin on his bearded face. "I myself feel a call to return to where the women no doubt are more willing!" With a crude laugh, he slapped Hakon on the back. Then he turned around and was gone.

"You old bear," Hakon muttered fondly, watching Einar's huge form lumber off along the shore. Why should he feel strange that Einar knew him so well? he wondered. The man had practically raised him along with his brother Eirik. Laughing to himself, he began to walk slowly toward the bathing house.

Hakon had barely reached the small stone building when the door opened suddenly. Greta, in a great hurry and with her head down, ran right into him as he stood along the path.

"Oh . . . my lord Hakon, forgive me," she blurted apologetically, wringing her hands. "I was just coming to speak with you." Her face was flushed from the steam in the bathing house, and her massive breasts heaved from obvious frustration. "The wench refuses to bathe, my lord. She would barely eat—like a bird she picked at her meal. And now she will not let me near her to remove her clothing. She does not understand that I mean her no harm—"

" 'Tis all right, Greta," Hakon cut her off gently. "My thanks for your trouble, but I will see to the wench now."

"Very well, my lord." She smiled broadly, her eyes following Hakon's tall form as he disappeared into the bathing house. What she would give to be in that wench's place! she thought wistfully. Lord Hakon was by far the finest-looking man she had ever seen, and he no doubt knew how to please a woman!

Closing the wooden door softly behind him, Hakon stood silent for a moment. Anora was facing away from the door, her slender back proud and straight.

"For the last time, woman, I do not wish to bathe," she said clearly, yet firmly, caring naught if the woman could understand her words.

"But it is my wish that you do so," Hakon murmured in a deep, husky voice.

Startled, Anora whirled around, her hands clutching her mantle tightly to her body. Her eyes widened at the sight of the Viking looming in the doorway. He looked so much taller and broader than she remembered from the ship. Suddenly the bathing house seemed suffocatingly small to her as she stared at him across the room.

By the blood of Odin, Hakon thought, his blood hammering in his veins, *only the gods could have created a woman as beautiful as this*. His piercing blue eyes took in every inch of her. The steam, rising from the surface of the warm water in the large wooden tub, had flushed her fair cheeks with a rosy hue, and tendrils of her long, silver-blond hair curled damply about her delicate features. The curves of her slender body, accentuated by the clinging lines of her clothing, seemed to cry out to him for his touch.

Taking a step toward her, Hakon felt an inner sense of dismay as Anora edged away from him until she could go no farther, her back against the rough stone wall. He could see the pulse point at her slender throat beating rapidly, her fear of him an almost palpable presence in the small room. "Why do you fear me so, Anora?" he questioned softly, his eyes not leaving her face.

" 'Tis not you I fear, m-my lord," she murmured shakily, "only what you will do with me." Her emerald eyes met his, an unmistakable plea for mercy reflected in their depths.

But Hakon could no longer deny the powerful attraction drawing him to her. He had known from the moment he saw her on the deck of his ship that this moment would come. His arms ached to hold her, his mouth longed to taste the sweetness of her lips.

"Do you not understand that you belong to me now? I have the right to do with you as I wish." Moving slowly toward her, he stopped by the side of the tub. His voice was low, commanding. "You will do as I ask, Anora. Take off your clothes, or I shall have to do it for you."

She stared at him in horror, unable to reconcile herself to the inevitable. "Nay . . . please," she whispered desperately, her eyes looking past him to the door. Suddenly she darted across the room past the other side of the tub.

But Hakon was quicker than she had expected. Catching her about the waist, he crushed her against the hard length of his body and brought his lips fiercely down upon hers. Anora frantically pommeled his broad chest with her small fists as she tried to twist free of his arms, but to no avail.

Her slender arms were no match for Hakon's well-muscled strength. Catching both of her wrists behind her back with one hand, he entwined his other hand in her long, silky hair and deepened his kiss.

Sweet Mother Mary, protect me! Anora thought wildly. She could scarcely breathe. A stifled cry broke from her throat, shattering the stillness of the room.

The wrenching, agonized sound suddenly pierced the cloud of lust and raging desire in Hakon's mind. He pulled back from her lips, his passion subsiding at the paleness of her tear-stained cheeks and the stark fear reflected in her eyes. She stood limply against his chest, her heartrending sobs tearing through her slender body.

Stunned, Hakon angrily cursed his crude callousness. Thor, what had come over him? He had never before forced himself on any woman, preferring instead the pleasures of a willing partner in his bed. Yet, blinded by his desire, he had chosen to treat Anora like the lowliest of whores . . . and even they were well paid for their favors! Gathering her in his arms, he strode to the door and kicked it open violently.

"Greta!" he roared into the night. "Greta!" After a few moments the stout woman appeared from a longhouse nearby, clutching a woolen cloak about her shoulders and carrying a small oil lamp.

"My lord?" she asked, surprised at Hakon's obvious ill temper. He had been in such a fine mood only a short time ago.

"Show me to my sleeping room," he said curtly, a dark scowl on his handsome face.

He must truly be in a hurry to bed the wench, she thought somewhat jealously. Holding up her lamp, she hastily led the way along a dirt path until she reached Einar's hall at the far end of the settlement. As an honored guest, it was only befitting that Hakon have a room in the chieftain's longhouse.

Entering the hall with Hakon close behind her, Greta turned into an adjoining room and placed the oil lamp on a wooden table beside the large bed. "On the morrow, shall I bring a morning meal for you and the lady?" she asked, crossing the room to stand by the entrance.

"Nay, only for the lady," Hakon replied. "I sleep in the hall with my men tonight."

Greta started in surprise. "Very well, my lord," she muttered. Shrugging, she quickly left the room.

Hakon lay Anora gently on the bed and covered her with one of the warm furs. The sight of her long lashes, glistening with tears in the dim lamplight, caused him to curse himself again for his rough treatment of her. He tenderly traced the trail of a tear with his finger, marveling at the silky softness of her skin. Thor, he had only to touch her to feel the rekindling of his desire! He knew he could tarry no longer.

"Greta will prepare a meal for you on the morrow, then bring you to the ship. We will sail at first light," he murmured. "Sleep well, little one."

Anora watched in disbelief as he turned and abruptly left the room. Her thoughts whirled in dizzying confusion. Had she seen a flicker of tenderness in the Viking's eyes, where moments before there had been only a burning lust? Sighing raggedly, she only knew that for the moment she had been spared. Rolling over on her side, she clutched the soft fur to her chin and fell into a deep sleep.

Once outside the hall, Hakon leaned against the turf wall and looked up at the clear night sky. The sparkling stars, winking brightly in the heavens as if they were the eyes of the gods, seemed to be laughing at him. A trial of fire would have been no worse than what he had experienced this night.

Never before had he felt such overwhelming desire for a woman. Every fiber in his body had cried out for him to take her in the bathing house, to plunge himself into her, to feel her writhe in passionate abandon beneath him. Hakon knew it was his right—she belonged to him as his slave. But for some inexplicable reason, he would not—*could not*—take her by force.

Why am I being so sorely tempted? he raged silently, throwing his arms up to the glittering heavens. Yet even as the question tormented him, he knew the answer. It was the memory of her eyes, full of fear, that haunted him. Perhaps, with time, he thought, there would be longing and desire reflected in those emerald pools instead of fear. Perhaps, one day, she would come to him willingly.

Walking back to the main hall, Hakon breathed a fervent prayer to his gods that he would not have to wait for long.

Chapter Fourteen

Gwendolyn drew her legs up to her chin, watching wide-eyed as the lusty festivities going on about her heightened to a fever pitch. From where she was sitting she could look down the length of the low-ceilinged room, crowded as it was by Hakon's men and a dozen scantily clad serving-women. The hall was a long, wide one, its massive walls a mixture of turf and stone, with a central hearth at one end that blazed with a roaring fire. A hole was cut in the roof above the hearth to let the smoke escape, but much of it still hung in the air. She coughed, her eyes smarting.

She had thought herself no stranger to the ways of men . . . until this night. Aye, 'twas true she had practically been raised by her father, and had always been surrounded by his thanes while hunting or training in weaponry. And she had heard plenty of bawdy tales from Edythe, her mother's lady-in-waiting. Why, once when she had gone to the stable to saddle her mare, she had seen a stable hand groping wildly at the bare breasts of a serving wench, their bodies melded into one as they writhed in a dark corner. The sight had strangely excited her, yet she had run from the stable, flushed and embarrassed.

But all that could not have prepared her for what was going on only a few feet away from where she sat. Now Gwendolyn realized she really knew nothing of men. Everywhere she looked, Hakon's men were falling upon the servant women, who screamed with wild delight. On the floor, on the tables, backed up against the wall—it did not seem to matter where the men took them. Holding her head in her hands, she closed her eyes to the lurid sight. God's blood, if this was the way Vikings were with their women . . .

Suddenly Gwendolyn's emerald eyes flew open. Sweet Jesu! Anora! A cold sense of foreboding settled over her as she recalled what the Viking had said before he left the hall. "If I do not return . . ." Aye, those had been his parting words. Angrily she tried to dispel from her mind the vision of her sister struggling desperately beneath the bronzed weight of the Viking, but she could not.

Gwendolyn looked frantically about her for a way to escape. She could see that Egil was enjoying himself with a buxom woman on a nearby bench, his broad back to her. He obviously had forgotten his orders from Hakon, for he was deeply involved in his own pleasure.

Seizing her chance, she jumped up from the ground and made a dash for the entrance of the hall. Nimbly dodging flailing limbs and sweating bodies, she was almost to the door when a glint of silver caught her eye.

On a table against a nearby wall, a small cutting knife lay beside a half-eaten portion of roasted meat. Gwendolyn quickly snatched the knife from the table and slid it into her leather belt. Looking furtively about her, she breathed a sigh of relief that she had not been seen. The drunken orgy showed no signs of abating, and Egil was still preoccupied with the blond serving girl. She slipped stealthily through the main door, then ran to a nearby building and crouched down low in the shadows.

Even though the hour was late, Gwendolyn could see by the dim light of the quarter moon that several people were still walking about the settlement. Hugging the turf-and-stone wall to keep from being seen, she began to inch slowly around the corner of the building.

Suddenly a huge man ambled by her in the dark, so close that the edge of his fur cloak brushed against her leg. Holding her breath, Gwendolyn's eyes widened as she recognized Einar. God's blood, he was alone! She watched in grim silence as he stopped before the door of the main hall and leaned upon it for a moment, swaying unsteadily. The sound of coarse, raucous laughter from within the hall caused him to chuckle at first. Then with a great laugh he pushed open the door and staggered inside.

Gwendolyn swore softly under her breath. Einar and Hakon had left the hall together, but only one had returned. Where, then, was Hakon? Forcing herself to remain calm, she scanned the surrounding buildings. There were so many. How could she ever find Anora?

Hugging her jerkin tightly to her chest, Gwendolyn rubbed her arms for warmth. There was no wind, but even so, the air was cold and tinged with the sharp scent of the sea. *Nay, you will not find Anora standing here*, she chided herself. Taking the small knife from her belt, she held it poised in front of her as she ran along the side of the building.

The figure of a woman hurrying along a path not far from her caught her eye. With a start Gwendolyn realized it was the same red-haired woman who had led Anora away earlier that evening. Looking down the path beyond the woman, she saw that it led to a very large longhouse near the edge of the settlement. Perhaps . . .

Daring to hope, yet fearing what she might find, Gwendolyn crouched behind a pile of wood as the woman passed by her, mumbling to herself. She waited until the sound of the woman's footsteps had died away, then ran swiftly up the path until she reached the ornately carved entrance.

Gwendolyn hesitated. Nay, 'twould be sheer folly to walk inside the longhouse, she thought, her mind racing. Keeping her head low, she crept along the curved sides of the wall until she came to a small window. It was covered by a fur pelt to keep out the cold, but a thin shaft of light shone between the edge of the pelt and the sod ledge. With her heart beating wildly against her chest, she pushed aside the lower corner of the pelt and peered inside the room.

"Out for a breath of fresh air, lad?" Rudely jerked back by the collar of her woolen shirt and grabbed by the shoulders, Gwendolyn's feet dangled off the ground as she was spun around to meet Hakon's narrowed gaze. As he lifted her up to within several inches of his face, his eyes glinted dangerously in the pale moonlight. "It appears to me you have seen fit to disobey my orders," he snarled, his strong hands gripping her shoulders like a vise.

Wincing painfully, Gwendolyn's first thought was to plunge her small knife into Hakon's side and twist it cruelly. But her hand lost its hold on the knife and it dropped to the ground with a thud.

"So, I see you have come well armed, Garric," Hakon said tersely.

He set her down so abruptly that she staggered back against the turf-and-stone wall, almost losing her balance. Then he bent and picked up the knife. A grim smile crossed his lips as he studied the meager weapon. *Aye, Garric, you would have wasted no time in using it, if given half a chance*, he thought. He glanced at her, catching the look of pure hatred flashing at him from her emerald eyes.

Strange, Hakon thought. In the moonlight he could have sworn he was looking at Anora's face. Shrugging, his voice was stern. "I see I shall have to watch you more closely in the future, Garric."

"Do what you must, Viking, it matters naught to me!" Gwendolyn said defiantly. "What have you done with Anora?"

Hakon stepped back to get a better look at the brazen lad. Yea, what the boy lacked in size, he more than made up for in courage. Garric was dressed simply, yet his proud bearing bespoke a high birth. *That will only make it harder for him to accept his fate*, Hakon noted. He did not want to break the lad's spirit, but the sooner he accepted his status as a slave, the better.

"Your sister is no longer your concern, Garric. She belongs to me, just as you do," Hakon stated evenly. He paused, not missing her clenched fists, then went on ruthlessly. "Your efforts to protect your sister are in vain. If—or I should say *when?*—I choose to take her, it will no doubt be without your consent. Do not forget you are now slaves, Garric. There is naught you can do."

"Nay!" Gwendolyn screamed, the rage and frustration of the last several days finally overwhelming her. Lunging at Hakon, she threw her slender weight against him, striking him with her clenched fists.

Hakon had expected this outburst, but was taken by surprise at the ferocity of the lad's attack. Not a man who relished the idea of striking a mere boy, he quickly thought of another plan. Catching Gwendolyn by the wrists with one hand, he threw her kicking and struggling over his shoulder. A well-placed kick hit him in the stomach, and he grunted painfully.

"My patience is wearing thin, Garric," he said with a grimace, thinking maybe a sharp jab to the lad's chin would not have been a bad idea. "Perhaps a taste of the lash would serve to persuade you that I mean what I say."

Gwendolyn suddenly lay still across his broad shoulder,

except for her labored breathing. She had seen what the lash had done to Svein and Torvald, and would not put it past the Viking to do the same to her. And to be stripped to the waist, her slender back laid bare, would put a sudden end to her disguise as a boy. Nay, better to let the Viking think he has won this battle, she thought. Dropping her head against Hakon's back, she sighed in resignation.

"I will let you down on one condition, Garric," Hakon said firmly. "You will obey my orders henceforth without question. Is that understood?"

"Aye, my lord," Gwendolyn lied, gritting her teeth. *And may you live to rue this day, Viking*, she thought bitterly.

"I will hold you to your word, lad, so do not force me to deal harshly with you," Hakon said grimly. "Many slaves have died for less offense than attacking their master." Setting her feet down upon the ground, he towered over her. "Come, we will sleep on the ship. I doubt Einar and my men have yet had their fill of ale and women this night."

Startled by his words, Gwendolyn felt a great sense of relief. So, her effort had not been in vain. At least this night Anora would be spared a rape.

Following quickly behind Hakon as he strode along the path toward the shore, Gwendolyn looked up at the stars. Aye, she and Anora would have their chance for escape, she vowed silently. They would simply have to wait until the time was right. . . .

Chapter Fifteen

" 'Tis time to wake, lad," Hakon said. He nudged Gwendolyn's shoulder with the toe of his leather boot. Yawning sleepily, she merely turned over onto her side and snuggled deeper into the warm fur. "Very well, then," he muttered, "if that is the way you will have it." He reached down and grabbed the ends of her pallet with both hands. Then, with a sharp tug, he pulled it out from under her. Gwendolyn went rolling across the deck, stopping only after she'd tumbled into a nearby rowing bench.

"Oh!" she groaned, flat on her back, her eyes wide open now. She stared blankly into the early morning sky, just beginning to lighten in faint hues of pink and lavender. Stunned, for a moment she could not remember where she was. But Hakon's hearty laugh behind her was all it took to jog her memory. She propped herself up on one elbow and ran her fingers through her short curls.

"A good morning to you, Garric!" Hakon chuckled, his eyes alight with mirth. Holding out his hand, he bent down to help her to her feet.

"Hardly a good morning," Gwendolyn replied heatedly, ignoring his proffered hand. She rose shakily to her feet and eyed him warily.

"Forgive my rude method of waking you, Garric," he said somewhat apologetically, chiding himself for perhaps being a bit rough on the lad. "But if I had not done so, you would have slept 'til noon." He shrugged. Thor, but this lad was a delicate one, he thought, noting the swelling on Gwendolyn's lower lip. "Here, let me look at that," he said, with some measure of concern.

But Gwendolyn jerked away from his hand. " 'Tis naught," she muttered resentfully. She stepped back a few paces from him and furtively touched her lip. She winced, her expression betraying her pain.

"Well, then, at least have some bread," Hakon offered, not unkindly. He reached into a cloth bag and pulled out a dark, crusty loaf. Tearing off a large hunk, he handed it to her. "You will have to put some meat and muscle on those bones, Garric, else you will be of little use to me. I need strong workers, and it looks to me as if you have spent your life in book-learning and the like."

His observation caused Gwendolyn to bristle angrily. Better to let him know what she was capable of than to have him think she was weak and useless! "I can wield a weapon as well as any of your men, Viking, though perhaps not quite as large as your sword," she retorted hotly. "And I have killed many a wild boar with bow and arrow—while riding a horse at full gallop!"

Hakon stared in amazement at Gwendolyn for a moment, then threw back his head and laughed, a full, rich sound that echoed about the ship. By the blood of Odin, he had never seen such brazenness in a lad before! What a boast! 'Twas as if, despite his small size, Garric thought he could prevail over the mightiest of warriors without any fear of death or defeat.

Perhaps I have underestimated this smooth-faced boy, Hakon mused, rubbing his chin. He decided he would have to watch him even more carefully from now on, or run the risk of taking a sword blow in the back when he wasn't looking!

Gwendolyn watched the play of emotions across the bronzed planes of the Viking's face. *So, he laughs at me*, she thought irritably, her ire rising again. Biting into the coarse bread, she chewed angrily, nearly choking as she tried to swallow.

"Slow down, lad," Hakon muttered, slapping her hard in the middle of her back. Gwendolyn fell forward from the force of his blow, losing her balance. She put out her hands to cushion her fall, yet she landed hard against the side of the ship.

"What are you trying to do, Viking, kill me before we even reach your homeland?" she sputtered indignantly. "What use will I be to you then?"

But Hakon was given no chance to reply, for suddenly two large hands appeared at the railing. Grunting, Egil heaved himself up and over the side of the ship.

"Lord Hakon, the boy . . . he has disappeared!" Egil blurted anxiously. He leaned against the railing as he tried to catch his breath. "He must have run from the hall during the night. I . . . uh . . . I only turned my back for a short while . . . uh, the wench . . ." he faltered, his voice dying away. He looked down at his feet, red-faced. Loki take him for a fool, he berated himself. He would probably be lashed for this offense!

"He is here with me, man," Hakon said. He gestured toward Gwendolyn, who was still sprawled out awkwardly on the deck.

"Damned Viking," she muttered fiercely under her breath. She reached up and grabbed the railing, then struggled to her feet.

Hakon tried to suppress a grin at the comical sight she made, but he could not. He turned back to Egil. "I found the lad near Einar's longhouse last night, on his way to rescue his sister, no doubt." Sensing the oarsman's discomfort at having failed in his orders to watch Garric, he added, " 'Tis only an island, Egil. We would have found them had they strayed too far."

Egil looked up, astonished by his good fortune. His broad shoulders slumped with relief. Yea, Lord Hakon could be a hard man, he thought, and sometimes quick to anger, but let no one say he was not fair.

"I trust the wench was well worth the tumble?" Hakon asked, smiling broadly.

"Yea, my lord, indeed she was!" Egil laughed lustily. "And I've the scratches to prove it!"

"Good." Hakon chuckled. "I only hope the others fared as well." But he sobered as his thoughts turned abruptly to the matter at hand. "Return to the hall and rouse the men, Egil. We must sail within the hour or risk losing the tide."

Egil nodded, then scrambled over the side of the ship and waded back to shore.

Hakon glanced at Gwendolyn. His tone was stern, forbidding. "You will stay aboard the ship while I bid farewell to my cousin and fetch your sister. Is that understood?" His startling blue eyes, like the color of a cloudless, midsummer sky, seemed to burn right through her, daring any thought of resistance.

"Aye, my lord," she mumbled grudgingly, watching him as he walked over to the side of the ship.

"And while I am gone, stay away from those two," he cautioned sharply, just before jumping from the railing to the shallow water below.

Gwendolyn's emerald eyes narrowed as she looked over at Svein and Torvald, chained by their hands and feet to the rowing benches. Torvald was still fast asleep, slumped against the side of the ship and snoring loudly. But Svein was awake, his pale eyes staring viciously at her. Naked from the waist up, his back was crisscrossed with angry red stripes and oozing welts from the lash. He and Torvald had been forced to row along with the others, despite their festering wounds.

Seating herself on a nearby bench, Gwendolyn hugged her legs to her body and rested her chin on her knees. She could only hope that Hakon and his men would not be gone for long. She didn't like the idea of being alone on the ship with those two curs. She took a deep breath of the salty sea air and closed her eyes, listening to the sound of the waves as they crashed onto the shore.

Her stomach suddenly grumbled angrily, reminding her that she had eaten little since the day before. She reached out and grabbed the loaf of bread lying on top of the cask where Hakon had left it. *He must have gone to the cooking house earlier this morning*, she thought, while she had been sleeping. Aye, at least she could thank him for that! She ravenously bit into the crusty loaf, savoring the fresh-baked flavor.

"How about sharin' a bit o' that bread with me, lad?" Svein called out, his forced smile strangely distorted into a grimace by the scar slashing down the left side of his face. He looked at the bread hungrily, licking his parched lips.

Gwendolyn nearly choked, her throat constricting at the sound of his evil voice. Deep-seated feelings of hate and rage welled up within her. She could barely keep herself from running over and striking the grin from his face. "You must truly be a fool, Viking dog, to think that I would do aught to sustain your miserable life," she snapped, her fists clenched in anger.

Enraged by Gwendolyn's reply, Svein's face turned a livid purple. He jerked up from his bench, furiously tugging at the chains binding him. "Do na' think I am done with you yet, lad!" he screamed, thrashing madly. "Nor with your fine sister! If you think Lord Hakon will be able to protect you from me, think again. I swear by the blood of Odin I will have my revenge!"

Awakened by the loud commotion, Torvald gaped at his raving companion. "Svein, do you want to bring Lord Hakon down upon us again?" he questioned worriedly. His back ached from the earlier lashing, and he did not want to suffer another one.

But Svein ignored Torvald and continued his taunts. His pale eyes glittered wildly as he lowered his voice to a raspy whisper. "I have tasted your sister's lips once, lad, like honey they were, and I have na' forgotten the feel of her breasts or the heat of her body as she writhed beneath me. Do na' think I will rest 'til she is mine again!"

Sickened with revulsion by his words, Gwendolyn had only one thought. She would silence the bastard, once and for all. Her eyes fell on a sword lying under a rowing bench. With grim purpose she walked over and picked up the heavy weapon, testing it in her hand. It was larger than anything she had wielded before, but she had no doubt it would serve her well. She turned on her heel and strode across the deck toward Svein, holding the sword in a firm hand.

"Put the weapon down, Garric." Hakon's voice was firm as he quickly hoisted himself over the railing near the bow of the ship. Halfway to Einar's hall, he had realized the folly of leaving the lad alone with Svein and Torvald. Sending two of the men he had met along the path to collect Anora, he had run swiftly back to the ship, hoping he would not be too late. He knew any amount of goading on Svein's part would surely force Garric to take some action. The lad's hate ran too deep for it to be otherwise. "Garric, do not be a fool. Put down your weapon," he muttered once again, slowly walking toward Gwendolyn.

But Hakon's words seemed to have no effect on her. She scarcely blinked at his voice. Her eyes were cold, ruthless, as she stared at Svein with deadly intent. Grasping the hilt of the sword with both hands, she lifted it high into the air. *So, this is what it is like to kill a man*, she thought fleetingly, surprised at her lack of feeling. It mattered naught to her that he was chained and defenseless.

Svein cringed before her, his mouth gaping in disbelief. His eyes darted pleadingly from the sword above his head to Hakon, then back again. *Odin, help me*, he prayed wildly, sweat beading on his forehead despite the cold morning air.

Hakon waited no longer for a response to his command. Moving silently behind Gwendolyn, he grabbed the blade end of the sword. The sharpened metal cut into the palm of his hand, stinging painfully, yet he did not let go. Twisting the sword easily from her grasp, he threw it on the deck, then angrily grabbed her by the shoulders.

"You are proving more trouble than you are worth, Garric," he said angrily. Reaching for some rope atop a nearby cask, he yanked her arms roughly behind her back and deftly tied her wrists together. Gwendolyn did not resist. Her eyes were vacant, and she stared blankly at Hakon; as if in a trance. Her only thought was that she had failed . . . and that Svein still lived.

Hakon dragged her over to the makeshift tent where Anora had slept and shoved her to the deck. "You have sorely tried my patience this day, Garric," he muttered darkly. "Had your sword found its mark, I would have been forced to kill you. Any slave who takes the life of a freeman—for whatever reason—forfeits his own."

He kneeled beside her, taking hold of her chin and forcing her to look at him. "I understand your feelings, Garric. I, too, would see him dead. But it cannot be by your hand." Receiving only a sullen glance from her, Hakon hardened his voice. "You are valued property to me, and I want you alive. 'Tis not my wish to bind you, but as you cannot be trusted, you will remain so 'til we reach Norge."

He rose to his feet, wiping his bloodied hand on his tunic.

Striding across the deck toward Svein, he could almost feel the lad's defiant eyes piercing his back like poisoned arrows. Yea, 'twas true he wanted Garric alive, but for another reason as well. Should anything happen to him, Hakon thought grimly, any hopes he might have of winning Anora's favor would be dashed forever. He did not want to see the same hate reflected in her eyes that he had seen in Garric's from the moment he had found them on his ship. 'Twas strange, he mused. He had never before cared so much what a wench thought of him . . . until now.

Svein's sneering voice broke rudely into his thoughts. "My thanks to you, Lord Hakon. 'Tis the second time that cursed Anglo-Saxon has raised a weapon to me. Perhaps it would be better to throw him over the side and be done with him."

The blow came so suddenly and with such lightning speed that Svein hardly knew what hit him. Knocked to the deck, he felt as if his jaw had become unhinged from his skull. He spat out several teeth into his hand, then looked up incredulously. Hakon towered above him.

"Say another word to the lad . . . or the wench . . . and you will lose your tongue." With that, Hakon strode to the railing as his men began climbing aboard the ship. Though some of them staggered unsteadily, and all were bleary-eyed from lack of sleep, they quickly took their places at the rowing benches.

"Hail, Hakon! Reach over and lend your cousin a hand!"

Hakon could not help but laugh as he leaned over the side of the ship and grabbed Einar's thick forearms. Grunting with exertion, he pulled his cousin aboard, while several men heaved him up on their shoulders from below.

"Whoa! My boy, it seems I am growing too old for this." Einar wheezed breathlessly once he stood on the deck. "Or else the ale has grown more potent!"

"Nay, Einar, you are as fit as ever," Hakon reassured his grizzled cousin. " 'Tis the ale, I am sure." *But truly*, he thought to himself, *he does look the worse for the past evening's festivities*. He shook his head, chuckling.

Einar looked curiously about the ship. His eyes widened as he spied Svein lying in a crumpled heap on the deck. "I thought 'twas you walking toward my hall a short while ago. Then all of a sudden you turned and ran back to the ship. Is aught amiss, my boy?"

"Nay, cousin. Whatever trouble there was has been dealt with," Hakon replied evenly.

"So I see. Well, no doubt he deserved it, eh, Hakon?" He laughed, then shrugged his great shoulders. "Ah, here is the wench. Thor's hammer! If I was a younger man, I might feel the need to fight you for this beauty, my boy!"

Hakon leaned over the side once again as one of his crewmen lifted Anora into his waiting arms. "I see the rest has done you some good, little one," he murmured, noting the clearness of her emerald eyes and the rosy color of her cheeks. But she turned her head away and would not look at him.

Distressed at her lack of response, though he tried hard not to show it, Hakon hugged her against his broad chest and carried her over to the tent. He could see that she had bathed, though she still wore the same torn clothing. Her long, silver-blond hair was damp and freshly combed, the fresh, clean scent of her skin enveloping his senses. He set her down gently, but she stepped abruptly away from him. She gasped with alarm at the sight of Gwendolyn's arms bound tightly behind her back, then looked up at him, her eyes full of questions.

"Garric's hands must remain tied for the rest of the journey, if only for his own protection," Hakon muttered tersely. He angrily turned his back to them as Anora threw her arms around Gwendolyn's neck. Thor! The wench made him feel as if he should doubt his own orders!

Einar laughed out loud at the dark scowl on Hakon's face.

Yea, his young cousin had indeed been smitten by the Anglo-Saxon wench! Slapping him heartily on the back, he had to admit that he did not envy Hakon. Women were such trouble. His three wives were proof enough of that!

"Well, my boy, I had your men bring aboard a good supply of ale that should last you through the voyage, along with some salted meat and goat cheese," Einar said loudly. Not one for good-byes, he enveloped Hakon in a massive embrace, then was over the side of the ship and wading back to shore before his cousin had uttered a word. "May the gods protect you during your journey!" he called out, his hand cupped to his mouth. "And remember!" he shouted at the top of his lungs as the longship pulled away from the shoreline. "Send word if you need me! 'Twould be an honor to send that bastard Rhoar to his grave!"

Hakon waved his arm in a final salute, then turned back to his crewmen. The sun, a great glowing ball of orange, was already well above the horizon. "Hoist the sail!" he shouted with exhilaration. Though he would miss Einar, he was glad to be under way again.

Raised on a yard nearly forty feet long, the great sail flapped and crackled as it billowed out with the gusting wind. Breathing a silent prayer to Odin for a safe, swift journey, Hakon turned his eyes to the north.

Chapter Sixteen

Gwendolyn leaned on her oar for a moment and wiped her face with the sleeve of her light woolen shirt. God's blood, she was sore! Her slender back ached miserably, and the palms of her hands were blistered and raw. She stood up from the bench and stretched her arms wide above her head.

"I gave you no permission to stop rowing, Garric," Hakon said sternly, walking up beside her.

Dropping her arms to her sides, Gwendolyn turned flashing eyes upon him. "I am tired, Viking. Does that mean naught to you? I have been rowing for several hours now, and you have not once given me a chance to rest!" she retorted hotly.

Hakon pushed her back down onto the bench and set her hands upon the narrow wooden oar. "Row."

Gwendolyn bit her lower lip in anger. Very well, if the Viking wanted her to row, then so she would! Heaving with all her strength, she dropped her oar back into the water and began rowing at twice the speed of the other oarsmen. A loud crack was heard as her oar hit the one next to it, causing the man seated on the bench in front of her to turn and curse loudly at her.

Hakon smiled faintly, stifling the chuckle in his throat. Thor, if this lad wasn't a stubborn one! He gripped her firmly by the shoulder, his voice allowing no argument. "If you continue to disrupt the oarsmen and slow us down, lad, you will only row the longer. We shall soon be at my brother's settlement, so any further delay will be of your own doing. Now, row!"

Gwendolyn watched him stride to the front of the longship, where he took his accustomed place near the dragon-headed prow. Matching her stroke to that of the other oarsmen, she gritted her teeth and rowed, knowing his vivid blue eyes were upon her.

It had been a long journey. She had counted a total of seven days since they left Einar's settlement in the Shetlands; four days since they had sighted land, and another three as they had sailed farther north along the rocky coastline of Norway.

Hakon had cut her bonds one day out of Sumburgh Voe, not so much out of concern for her chafed wrists, but due to Anora's repeated pleas for him to do so. He had ignored them much of the time except to bring them food and water, and to see that Anora was granted the privacy she required for her personal needs. Gwendolyn had been forced to make do as best she could, always waiting until cover of night to take care of her own. Her guise as a boy had been sorely tested; fortunately, no one had bid her to change her clothes as yet, dirty as they were.

After only two days of sailing, the ship had encountered a vicious storm, the ferocity of which Gwendolyn had never seen before. An oarsman seated in the stern had been washed overboard at the height of the squall, disappearing beneath the angry black waves before anyone could reach out to save him. Only Hakon's knowledge of the sea and his skill at commanding his longship had saved them all from perishing, earning him Gwendolyn's grudging respect.

It wasn't until the ship had reached the mouth of the great Sogn fjord that she was forced to replace the lost oarsman. No amount of protest could dissuade Hakon, and after a few simple instructions she had been seated at the bench and ordered to row.

Gwendolyn looked up over her shoulder at the sheer sides of the snowcapped mountains towering above the fjord. Some of the sparcely wooded slopes plunged right into the deep, blue water, while others were more gently rolling, the green hillsides dotted with farmsteads and herds of grazing sheep. She had to admit that she had never seen such wild beauty as in this rugged land of the Vikings.

They had traveled west for some distance along the Sogn, then had turned sharply northward into a more narrow fjord. Gwendolyn had seen several large settlements along the way, and she had smiled softly at the fair-haired children who had lined the grassy banks to wave at the passing longship. These settlements appeared to her to be trading towns, for there were all shapes and sizes of boats lined up along the shore and scores of people milling about the clustered buildings. She heard the shouts of men, no doubt arguing over their wares, and the gay laughter of women, carrying out over the surface of the water.

Gwendolyn's eyes widened as the longship passed near a roaring waterfall, the cascading water sending a fine mist of spray into the air as it plummeted into the deep waters of the fjord. The cool moisture on her face enlivened her weary senses, and she truly smiled for the first time since she and Anora had been abducted from their homeland.

"So, Garric, you can smile after all," Hakon said amiably, stopping by her bench after conferring with Olav at the helm. " 'Tis good to know you are capable of more than angry scowls and fierce glances." The fleeting smile disappeared from Gwendolyn's face just as quickly as it had come, but not before Hakon wondered how a lad could be so pretty. He had seen such beauty in a boy only once before, several years past, in a marketplace in Byzantium.

Hakon had heard of those men who had a taste for young boys rather than women, but he could not have been more amazed at the lively slave trade this perversion encouraged. A large crowd had gathered in the marketplace around a raised pallet, upon which stood the most beautiful boy Hakon had ever seen. Young and slender, with smooth, olive skin, the boy had been stripped of his ragged clothing and was being slowly turned around for all to see.

A fat, leering merchant had pushed his way to the front of the crowd, and had bought him for several pieces of gold. Hakon would never forget the terror he had seen written on the boy's delicate features at the loathsome sight of his new owner, or the sheer desperation reflected in his dark, almond-shaped eyes. Repulsed, Hakon had turned away, when a sudden roar from the crowd caused him to wheel around. The boy had grabbed the curved knife from the merchant's belt and had plunged it into his own breast, his lifeblood splattering the merchant's fine clothes and spilling out upon the ground.

"Why do you stare at me so, Viking?" Gwendolyn asked guardedly. Hakon's eyes had not moved from her face for several moments, his forehead creased in thought. It was making her extremely uncomfortable. She would have to remember not to smile from now on. Obviously it drew too much attention to her face, and could possibly threaten her disguise.

Hakon blinked, her question suddenly thrusting him back to the present. "You reminded me of someone, 'tis all," he muttered, his mouth grim.

"And who would that be?" she queried testily, wondering what dark thoughts had chased the earlier amusement from his eyes.

"Ask me no further questions, Garric. Tend to your oar," he said abruptly, dismissing her. Without another word, he turned and walked away.

Gwendolyn opened her mouth to retort, but then thought better of it. God's blood, one minute the Viking was good-natured, the next a tyrant again! She sighed heavily, shaking her tousled head. If she and Anora were ever to escape, she would have to learn to gauge his moods. Only then would she be able to know when his guard was down, and perhaps use it to their advantage.

Hakon did not stop until he was between the benches where Svein and Torvold were sitting. "Get up," he muttered tersely.

Svein looked up at him in surprise. "My-my lord?" he stammered, a hint of fear in his pale eyes.

"You and Torvald, get up," Hakon repeated, his voice low, expressionless. "Egil, unlock their chains."

"Yea, my lord," Egil murmured, hastening to obey. He took a bunch of keys from his pocket, then bent over and unlocked the metal shackles binding Torvald's feet and those around his thick wrists. The heavy shackles fell to the deck with a clanking thud.

Torvald rose to his feet. As he stretched his massive arms and shoulders, his eyes never left Hakon's face.

Egil hurried over to Svein's bench and did the same with his chains. He could tell from Hakon's tone that something was brewing, and thanked the gods it was not directed toward him. "Is there aught else, my lord?"

"Yea. See that the men do not slacken their pace," Hakon said. He had noticed that a few of the oarsmen were no longer rowing, but were watching the proceedings with great interest.

"As you say, Lord Hakon." Egil nodded. He strode along the narrow aisle between the rowing benches. "All right, men, keep to your oars!" he shouted. The oarsmen obliged him by leaning into their oars, their muscles bulging and straining with exertion.

"Move to the side of the ship," Hakon told the two men, drawing his heavy broadsword from its scabbard in one swift movement. The polished steel blade glinted brightly in the late afternoon sun.

Torvald obeyed instantly, his quick movements belying his huge bulk. But Svein stood his ground, though he trembled visibly.

"You are a hard man, Lord Hakon, to treat us so!" he blurted incredulously, stepping back as Hakon pointed the sword at his heaving chest. "Our backs still bleed from your lashin', and the skin on our wrists and ankles has been rubbed raw from those damned shackles! Have you na' punished us enough?" he asked, his face white but for the glaring red scar. "You surely canna' mean to kill us?"

"Question my orders once again, Svein, and you will most certainly feel the sting of my blade," Hakon growled. He walked forward with slow, measured steps.

Svein did not hesitate any longer. Scurrying behind Torvald, he furtively peered out from behind his giant companion.

Hakon stopped just a few feet from them, his blue eyes flashing fire. "I can no longer bear the sight of you two aboard my ship," he said evenly. "I should have killed you for disobeying my orders in England, yet I have spared your worthless lives. We will let Njord, the god of the sea, determine your fate. Perhaps if you are lucky he will not want you either, and will spit you out upon the shore! Over the side with you . . . now!"

Svein glanced quickly over his shoulder at the deep, dark water. "B-but, my lord, I canna' swim!" he cried, gripping the railing with whitened knuckles.

"I care naught," Hakon said dispassionately. "Over the side, else I will grease the blade of my sword with your blood!"

Torvald did not wait to hear any more. He jumped over the railing, landing in the cold water with a huge splash. For a minute his blond head disappeared beneath the surface, but then he bobbed up, sputtering and coughing.

But Svein did not follow Torvald's lead. Instead, he sank miserably to his knees and hugged the splintery legs of a nearby rowing bench. "Nay, Lord Hakon!" he screamed, his voice a sickening whine. "Surely there must be somethin' I can do to make amends!"

Disgusted by Svein's cowardice, Hakon returned his sword to its scabbard. "Egil!" he shouted. Together the two men pried Svein's arms from around the bench, grimly ignoring his pitiful cries for mercy. Lifting him up by his arms and legs, they threw him over the side of the ship with a mighty heave. He immediately went under, his arms flailing wildly about, his hands clutching frantically at the air.

Though the longship had left him far behind in its wake, Torvald managed to swim over to his drowning companion with measured, though choppy strokes. He quickly plunged his arm deep down beneath the surface and pulled Svein up by the hair.

"Damn . . . you . . . damn you to Hell!" Svein screamed out, all the while choking and gasping for breath.

"If you manage to make it to shore, consider yourselves absolved of your crimes!" Hakon shouted as the longship moved farther away from the floundering pair. "But if I ever see you near my brother's settlement, rest assured your lives are forfeit!"

Grimly satisfied, he turned from the railing. His eyes fell upon Anora, standing near the tent. Though she quickly looked down, she had been watching him. He walked over to her side. "You are safe now, little one," he said softly, standing close enough to reach out and touch her. But instead of responding, she ducked behind the leather flap of the tent.

Thor, when would she not run from him like a frightened rabbit? he wondered, cursing under his breath. He could have sworn he had seen a flash of gratitude in those bewitching emerald depths . . . or had he just imagined it? He shrugged his broad shoulders, a scowl darkening his face. "All right, men, put your backs into it!" he shouted, striding between the rowing benches. "The faster you row, the faster we will make land!"

Gwendolyn pulled angrily at her oar. Why had he not killed those two curs? she wondered furiously. Had he not said he would also like to see them dead? "You are a liar as well, Viking," she whispered fiercely, wincing from the pain of her blistered hands. Perhaps she and Anora were now safe from Svein and Torvald, but her sister still had much to fear. . . .

Chapter Seventeen

It was nearing dusk when the longship finally reached Eirik's settlement at the northernmost end of the fjord. Hakon stood tall and straight near the dragon-headed prow, his piercing blue eyes taking in every long-remembered detail of the familiar rugged hills and deep valleys surrounding the settlement. He looked every inch the proud Viking warrior as the wind blew through his blond hair, his hand resting easily on the silver hilt of his broadsword. The ship had been sighted by those on land, for the deep, rich tones of a horn welcomed them as they moved closer to the shoreline.

"Return the signal, Bjorn!" Hakon called out to his hornsman. A thrill of excitement coursed through his blood as the swelling sounds moved out across the water. Yea, he was home at last! Drawing in a deep breath of the bracing night air, he marveled that the settlement had changed little in the ten years since he had last seen it. There were perhaps a few more longhouses and outbuildings built alongside the fjord, and the docking at the shoreline appeared to be far more extensive, but other than that it was largely the same. He did notice that there were several longships tied at the moorings, but this did not strike him as strange. Eirik had always talked of enlarging his fleet.

"Oars up!" he shouted. The men quickly pulled their oars through the oar holes, creating quite a din of scraping and loud thuds as they brought them up vertically in salute. Gwendolyn bit her lower lip with the effort, almost dropping her oar onto the men sitting in front of her. A rough-looking Viking caught it just in time. He grabbed the oar from her hand and set it aright, scowling all the while.

"My thanks," she muttered irritably in Norwegian, for during the sea journey she had gradually picked up some common phrases and words. The Viking merely grunted, though his eyes glinted with amusement at her foreign accent.

Gwendolyn stood up and looked curiously over the railing. She could see a growing crowd of people gathering at the wooden dock, some holding lighted torches that chased away the gathering shadows. It seemed to her that most of those waiting for the longship were men. They were all extremely well armed with spears, broadaxes, and various other weapons, and many of them held brightly painted shields with central iron bosses in the centers that glinted in the torchlight. Some of them were wearing what appeared to be shirts of shiny mail over their tunics, while others wore conical silver helmets on their heads.

"Hail, Hakon!" The deafening cry, loud and fierce, went up as a single shout from the gathered warriors, resounding and echoing against the surrounding mountainsides. The longship, now also ablaze with light as great torches were lit by the oarsmen, slid like a sea serpent alongside the dock, coming to rest with a gentle bump.

Hakon raised his arm in solemn salute. He recognized the faces of several uncles and cousins in the crowd, and a feeling of foreboding settled over him. There could be only one reason why so many of his relatives were gathered together at the settlement. He shook his head fiercely. Nay, he would not think of it, he chided himself, until he knew for sure.

He watched silently as the assembled warriors parted to make a path for a tall, dark-haired woman. She walked gracefully toward the ship, her head held high, looking neither to the right nor to the left but straight at him. Hakon recognized her immediately. It was Bodvild, his brother's wife. He could see she had changed little since he had last seen her . . . she was as beautiful as ever. He jumped with agile ease from the ship to the wooden dock, then strode to meet her where the docking met the land.

"Welcome, my brother," she stated in clear tones for all to hear. "We have long awaited your return." She took Hakon's hands in her own and grasped them firmly. Her steady gray eyes searched his handsome face. *So, he has already guessed the truth*, she thought fleetingly. She squared her slender shoulders. "I fear it is as you suspect, Hakon. Your brother Eirik is dead," she murmured. A pang of intense grief flitted across the high-boned beauty of her face, but quickly passed.

A stab of almost physical pain swept through Hakon, though he did his best not to show it. Any sign of weakness in a Viking was despised by all, and was especially abhorrent in a chieftain. "When, Bodvild?" he asked gravely, greatly impressed by her courage.

"Yester morn," she stated simply. "Come, I will take you to him." With that, she turned and walked proudly back through the crowd. All heads bowed as she passed.

Hakon followed close behind Bodvild, and as he passed, the men brought their clenched fists hard against their chests in salute. Almost a full head taller than those gathered around him, he could see that there were many others standing near the longhouses and along the wide path to the main hall. All were well armed, and again he knew the reason. If Eirik was dead, the threat of Rhoar Bloodaxe's vengeance was very real and possibly close at hand.

Bodvild and Hakon walked silently together, each in deep thought, until they reached the entrance of the hall. Two armed guards, their spears crossed before the massive wooden doors, stood on each side of the entrance.

" 'Tis I, Bodvild, and Eirik Jarl's brother, Hakon, who seek to pass," she stated. Bringing their spears to their sides, the guards pushed open the heavy doors and quickly stepped aside. Bodvild glanced up at Hakon. "Come, he lies in here." She led the way into the darkened hall.

It took Hakon's eyes a moment to adjust to the dim lighting. There were only four small torches placed around the raised bier in the middle of the large main room. The hall was silent but for the sputtering of the torches and the sound of their footsteps across the rush-strewn dirt floor. At the sight of his brother lying on the shrouded platform, Hakon's breath caught painfully in his throat.

Eirik lay in full battle armor upon the bier, his right hand resting on the jewel-inlaid hilt of his mighty broadsword. Underneath the shining silver coat of mail he was dressed in a gold-embroidered tunic made of the finest scarlet cloth. In the crook of his left arm was placed a fine gilt helmet engraved with stylized animal designs. His fingers bore rings made of plaited strands of gold, while around his neck lay a heavy gold neck ring. His expression was one of a man at peace, yet from the deeply etched lines in his face and the translucence of his skin, Hakon could see he had suffered greatly during his illness.

Bodvild reached out and gently smoothed an unruly copper curl on Eirik's head. "Do you wish to be alone with him?" she asked softly, her voice catching with emotion. The unshed tears in her eyes only now reflected the true depth of her grief.

"Nay, Bodvild, please stay with me," Hakon murmured. They stood together in silence for a long moment, their shared sorrow a palpable presence in the dark hall. But suddenly a burning question came to his mind. "Did Eirik die with a sword in his hand?" he asked, turning to face her.

"Yea, Hakon. I myself placed it in his hand before he died," she answered, her gray eyes meeting his.

Hakon breathed a sigh of relief, the admiration he felt for his brother's wife increasing tenfold. Thor, he only hoped that one day he would find a woman who could match the fearless devotion Bodvild had shown for the man she loved! Despite the strength of her own Christian beliefs, she had not denied her pagan husband his right to immortality by refusing him his sword.

Christian or no, Bodvild knew it was believed by the Vikings that if a warrior died with his sword in hand he would be carried on the winged steeds of Odin's daughters, the Valkyries, to the celestial home of the gods, Asgard. Once there, he would feast opulently forever on the flesh of the divine boar and drink streams of honey mead at Odin's table in Valhalla, the warrior's hall with its ceiling of golden shields.

"Then all is as it should be," Hakon said. "When will the feast begin?" According to Viking custom a wake was held for the honored dead, during which feasting and drinking would continue for several days and nights before the burial.

"It has been decided by the clan that there will be no feast," she stated evenly. "Eirik's burial will be this very night." At Hakon's startled expression, she continued. "The men of the clan believe that to have a feast now will leave the settlement vulnerable to attack. It is known that Rhoar has a force of many men prepared to do battle, and that he has been waiting for Eirik's death to make his move. The clan does not want the same to happen here as did in Trondheim not long ago."

"Was there a battle for a chieftain's throne?" Hakon asked. He knew of that region, though it was far to the north. He had been there with his father several times as a boy.

"Nay, not a battle . . . far worse," Bodvild replied softly. "A great chieftain of the region, Horik Skallgrimsson, was killed in a hunting accident. During the wake all the clan, including women and children, were gathered in the great hall for the feast. There had been drinking and song for many hours, when suddenly one of Horik's most hated enemies attacked the hall under cover of night." She paused for a moment, her eyes reflecting the horror she felt at reciting the awful tale. "The doors were barred from the outside so no one could escape. Then the hall was put to the torch and burned to the ground. All who were inside perished. 'Tis said their screams could be heard many miles down the fjord."

She was trembling as she took Hakon's hand in her own. "The clan was prepared to protect your inheritance until you arrived, Hakon. They see you as their chieftain, as Eirik had wanted. Yet Rhoar's threat was not one to be taken lightly. Perhaps now that you are here, they would see the matter differently . . . and welcome a feast." She looked with sorrowful eyes upon her husband. "I only regret that he did not live to see your return." A single tear trailed down her pale cheek, glistening in the golden torchlight.

Hakon nodded his head gravely. "Yea, would that I had heard his voice only once again," he said with a heavy sigh. "But 'twas not to be. The gods saw fit to delay my journey." He did not say that he thought perhaps his late arrival was a bad omen. Grasping the silver amulet of Thor's hammer hanging on a chain around his neck, he breathed a silent prayer that it was not.

Bodvild's reply startled him, for it was as if she had read his mind. "If I were not Christian, Hakon, I would say your arrival tonight is a good omen. Eirik's power and influence were great, and the territories he ruled stretch far beyond the Sogn region. Not only the clan are gathered here tonight for his burial, but other chieftains and freemen as well. Yea, 'tis true that those who know and remember you have no doubts as to your strength and ability to rule. But there are those who must see and hear for themselves."

She gazed once more on her husband's beloved face, strikingly handsome even in death. She sighed raggedly. *Yea, there will be plenty of time to grieve later, my only love*, she thought mournfully. But for now, there were other matters at hand. She tore her eyes away at last. Her voice was calm, disguising the aching torment in her heart. "Come, my brother. Now is the time for you to prove to the clan that Eirik's choice for his successor was a good one . . . the only one."

They walked back to the entrance together in silence. When they were almost at the door, she stopped suddenly and looked up at him.

"From the moment you walk through these doors your life will be changed, Hakon," she said, her eyes bright. "You are a chieftain now. Go forward, Hakon Jarl, and greet your people!"

With that, she knocked twice on the massive doors. As they slowly swung open, she and Hakon stepped out into the blazing light of hundreds of torches. A great clamor went up from the warriors gathered in front of the hall, their voices merging into one thunderous voice, all shouting the same name, "Hakon Jarl! Hakon Jarl!" The great horn that had welcomed them earlier was sounded again, over and over, while the men beat vigorously on their wooden shields with spears and axes.

Gwendolyn watched from the ship. She had never heard such a din before in all her life. Even the throngs who had rushed to greet King Edgar during his coronation visit to

Chester only months ago had not yelled as loud. Anora stood by her side, her small hands clapped over her ears. They had remained on the ship while all the others had disembarked, for it seemed that Lord Hakon had forgotten them . . . at least for now. Yet Gwendolyn knew Egil still watched them closely from where he stood on the dock lending his own voice to the melee. He was obviously not about to let her escape again while in his care.

So, this was the matter of grave importance that the Viking had mentioned on the day of their capture when he told them they would not be returned to their homeland and that she and Anora would be his slaves. Gwendolyn frowned, shaking her head. It was still so confusing. He had told them little else during the journey.

Gwendolyn could see him standing beside the same woman who had met him when the ship docked. She was very beautiful. A wife, perhaps? And why was everyone shouting the Viking's name? Could it be that he was indeed a king, returning in triumph from faraway lands? Frustrated by her questions, she shrugged her delicate shoulders, giving up. No doubt the Viking would tell them in his own good time!

Hakon raised his hand for silence, but it was several moments before the enthusiastic shouting died away. "I stand before you this night in answer to the summons of Eirik, Jarl of Sogn, my true brother, not as your overlord, but as your equal!" he stated for all to hear. This declaration brought a great roar of approval from the gathered Vikings, for though they honored their leaders, and would fight to the death for them, they considered themselves to be equals first, followers second. If a man rose to authority among them, it was only by their choice and consent.

Hakon drew his broadsword from its scabbard and held it high above his head. "I swear to you that my rule will be fair and just, as was Eirik's and my father's, Magnus Haardrad, before me! If any man doubts my word, let him come forward and try his sword against mine!"

A great rumbling raced through the gathered warriors. Yea, here was a man who was fit to rule the Sogn! Greatly impressed by Hakon's fierce presence and courage, one by one the assembled Vikings kneeled in homage and offered him their sworn allegiance. Bodvild looked on in silence, her gray eyes shining as Eirik's dying wish was at last fulfilled.

Hakon sheathed his mighty sword, his bronzed face flushed with exhilaration. "We will not allow the bastard Rhoar's threat to deny Eirik Jarl the homage that is his right. Come! Let us share a feast in honor of a fallen warrior!" he shouted. Amid the thunderous pounding of weapons against wooden shields, he strode back into the hall with Bodvild at his side.

Chapter Eighteen

Gwendolyn and Anora watched wide-eyed from the prow of the ship as the Vikings warriors surged into the hall after Hakon. That so many could all fit into one building was amazing, Gwendolyn thought, though even from this distance the hall appeared quite large. Suddenly Egil rushed along the dock to where they stood and gestured sharply for them to climb out beside him. Anora backed away in fear.

"Where do you think he means to take us, Gwendolyn?" she asked nervously.

"Perhaps to where we shall sleep for the night," Gwendolyn replied reassuringly, though she felt a twinge of unease. She trusted Egil no more than she believed a wild boar could be tamed for a pet! She looked around the darkened ship, then shrugged. "Anything would be better than spending another night aboard this wretched ship. Come on, I will help you." She held Anora's hand as she stepped up on a rowing bench and then sat down on the railing. Grinning broadly, Egil grabbed her sister by the waist and swung her over to the dock. Gwendolyn did the same, but before he could catch her she jumped to the dock by herself. "Keep your filthy hands to yourself, Viking!" she muttered, her eyes flashing defiantly.

Gesturing for them to walk in front of him, Egil nudged them along the dock and out onto the path that led to the great hall. So that was it, Gwendolyn thought irritably, bridling at his rough pushing as they made their way up the steep hill. He was taking them to the hall so as not to miss out on whatever festivities were taking place there. She grimly recalled the frenzied revelry she had seen in Einar's hall, and hoped for Anora's sake it would not be the same in this one.

Suddenly Anora tripped on the edge of her torn skirt and fell to her knees. Her startled cry caught the attention of three bearded Vikings standing near the entrance to the hall. They blocked the path, their leering faces illuminated by the light of the torch one of them held aloft.

"Thor! Will you look at that beauty!" the tallest one exclaimed. "How about sharing some of that with us, man," he said menacingly to Egil. He walked toward them with his companions not far behind. "Surely you don't mean to have her all to yourself?"

Egil quickly drew his sword from his belt and pushed Gwendolyn and Anora behind him. "Stay back, man, else I will be forced to blacken this night with the spilling of your blood!" he stated grimly. "The wench belongs to Hakon Jarl."

At those words the three men instantly fell back, their mouths gaping in surprise. Egil helped Anora to her feet, his eyes not straying once from the men as they stepped away from the path to let them pass. On such a night as this, when emotions were running high, he knew that anything could happen, kinsmen or not. Keeping his two charges close at his side, Egil walked cautiously by the men, his sword poised and at the ready.

Gwendolyn cursed under her breath. Were all Vikings barbarians such as these? She could see the unshed tears in Anora's eyes, and her heart went out to her. This episode had only served to frighten her sister further. Damn them all to hell's fire! she thought fiercely.

Finally reaching the entrance to the hall, Gwendolyn looked up at the massive log structure. She had seen a building as large as this only once before, when she had traveled to London with her father. The blazing glow of the torchlight eerily illuminated the gable above the entrance, and she gasped at the intricately carved dragon heads that seemed to leer down at her. The massive wooden doors were also richly carved, the stylized animal designs strangely twisted and contorted.

Egil sheathed his sword and pushed his two charges through the open doors. All three blinked, their eyes slowly growing accustomed to the bright light thrown off by the many torches set in sconces upon the roughhewn log walls.

Gwendolyn peered about her. She was astounded by the length and breadth of the hall. A row of stout, elaborately carved pillars supported the roof on both sides, while down the middle ran several fireplaces, a warming blaze burning in each one. The timbered walls were hung with painted shields, brightly polished weapons, and fine woven tapestries, while the dirt floor was strewn with fresh rushes and dried herbs that lent a pungent scent to the air.

But what really drew her attention was the raised bier set in the very center of the hall. The dead man looked strikingly similar to Hakon, except for the copper color of his hair. "Look over there, Anora," Gwendolyn whispered to her sister.

But her words were rewarded by a sharp cuff on the ear from Egil. He pushed Anora along in front of him, then grabbed Gwendolyn roughly by the shoulder, dragging her alongside him.

They walked hurriedly across the hall, their presence

causing quite a stir among the Vikings sitting at the long tables lining the walls. Several of them reached out to touch Anora's silky hair as she passed by their benches, their eyes hungrily following her lithe form. Fearful for her safety, Egil did not stop until he had reached the middle of the hall, where Lord Hakon sat upon the high seat. Engrossed in whispered conversation with Bodvild, who was seated at his right, he had obviously not seen them enter the hall.

Bodvild laid her hand on Hakon's arm, interrupting his words. "I believe this man has a matter of import to discuss with you, brother," she murmured gently, nodding toward Egil, who stood nervously before them.

Turning his head, Hakon looked startled for a moment. He had forgotten all about Anora and Garric, still aboard the ship. "Thor's hammer, Egil! Why have you brought them here?" he thundered, a scowl darkening his features as he noticed the lust-filled glances of several of his kinsmen raking Anora's slender figure.

Egil stepped closer to the high seat. "Forgive me, Lord Hakon, but I fear that a safer place than the ship must be found for the wench to sleep this night. She fires the blood of all who see her," he muttered softly, loud enough for only Hakon to hear. "I have already drawn my sword once to protect her."

"So you bring her here, man? Surely you can see that this place is no better!" Hakon gritted angrily.

"Perhaps I can find a suitable place for her to sleep," Bodvild interjected calmly, rising from her seat. She had already noted the paleness of the young woman's delicate features and the dark smudges under her eyes. "The lass looks ready to drop from sheer exhaustion." Her gray eyes caught the expression of concern on Hakon's face. "Do not fear, brother. I am sure a good night's rest will bring the glow back to her fair cheeks."

Hakon flashed her a warm look of gratitude. "Anora, go with Bodvild," he said, though not too gently. It would not do for the clan to think him weak when it came to women, no matter how beautiful. "She will show you to a place where you can sleep." Too tired to protest, Anora merely nodded.

"But what of the lad, Hakon?" Bodvild asked. "If you wish, I could find a place for him, also."

Hakon's eyes flitted over Gwendolyn, and he chuckled to himself. It was obvious the lad was exhausted, though he was trying to mask it with his defiant stance. "Egil, escort Garric to the slave house and see that a guard is posted outside the door. Then you may return here for the feast."

"Yea, my lord." Egil nodded, gripping Gwendolyn's shoulder once again.

Taking Anora by the hand, Bodvild felt a rush of pity for the girl as she led her from the hall. Was she a slave to Hakon . . . or concubine? As a Christian, she abhorred the cruel treatment of slaves, and had done everything in her power to improve their lot at the settlement. She had also done much over the years to influence her husband in his dealings with them, despite the deep-seated belief held by the Vikings that slaves were merely a commodity to be bought and sold.

Bodvild glanced over her shoulder to see if Egil and the lad were following her. *'Tis strange how much the girl and her brother resemble each other*, she thought, marveling at the similarity of their features. Why, if she had not known better, she would surely swear that the lad was nearly as feminine in appearance as his sister, except for his short, unruly hair and clothing. Nay, it couldn't be. She shrugged, dismissing the odd thought. With Hakon's keen eye for beautiful women, surely he would be the last person to be deceived by such trickery, even if it were possible.

The women's sleeping house was not far from the great hall, and it wasn't long before Anora was settled into a narrow bed in a private room. Her head had scarcely touched the eiderdown pillow when she was fast asleep. Bodvild clucked her tongue sympathetically. Such a sea voyage was hard enough on a man, let alone a delicate creature such as this girl. She brought the soft fur coverlet up to Anora's chin, then quietly left the room.

"The slave house is just a ways up the hill," she said softly to Egil, who was waiting at the door with his charge. She frowned, her forehead creasing in thought. "This lad hardly looks so dangerous that he would need a guard."

"He has already tried to escape once, my lady, and he makes no secret of his hate for his captors," Egil replied, his large hand gripping Gwendolyn's shoulder. She winced painfully, a fierce debate raging in her mind over whether she would elbow him in the stomach or stomp on his big foot with her booted heel.

Bodvild shook her head. "There is no place for the lad to escape to, Egil. Besides, there are so many people in the settlement tonight that any attempt the lad might make would surely be thwarted." She pointed out the slave house to him. "I must return to the hall to be with my husband," she murmured softly. "If you think 'tis truly necessary, you will find a trusted slave there, Ansgar, who would be more than happy to watch the lad for you." Ignoring his startled look, she turned and walked quickly down the hill toward the great hall, her fur-trimmed cloak flowing out behind her.

Egil nodded in assent, though inwardly he could not have disagreed more. Slaves watching slaves! He had never heard of such a thing. Shaking his shaggy head with disapproval, he pushed Gwendolyn along in front of him until they came to the slave house. Several older men were sitting on benches along the outside wall.

"Who is Ansgar?" he blustered, glaring at them.

"I am called by that name," a thin voice answered him. A short, owlish-looking man dressed in rough woolen clothing rose to his feet and stepped forward. He smiled amiably, despite the Viking's forbidding stance.

Egil's eyes widened in disbelief as he looked the small man up and down. *Thor's teeth, this slave must be more than fifty winters!* he thought incredulously. *Why, he could no more guard the lad than a newborn pup!* But then he shrugged. Who was he to argue with the orders of a chieftain's wife?

"This lad is the slave of Hakon Jarl," he said gruffly. "See that he has a place to sleep this night, and watch him closely by orders of your mistress. He is wont to escape if given the slightest chance." With a grunt he roughly shoved Gwendolyn toward the door, then turned on his heel and strode down the hill. Such trouble over a mere slave! His mouth began to water at the thought of roasted meat and ale, and before long he was running toward the hall.

"May you choke on your next meal, Viking dog!" Gwendolyn called out after him, picking herself up off the ground. She bent to brush the dust from her trousers, though they were so dirty it really made no difference.

"So, you are English," Ansgar said gently, speaking her tongue. "Come, I will show you to where you can get some rest."

Gwendolyn gaped at him in astonishment, almost tripping over the threshold as she followed him into the dimly lit hall. The little man led her over to a fairly private corner of the large room, where a thick pallet was spread on the floor. "You may sleep here for the night," he said, then began to walk away.

"Wait!" Gwendolyn cried, her voice echoing throughout the hall. Her loud cry disturbed several slaves who were trying to get some rest after a long day's toil. Their disgruntled groans and sighs could be heard about the room. "Please!" she whispered desperately. Ansgar turned and looked quizzically at her. "Do you not wish to know how I came to be here?" she asked.

A faint smile stirred his thin lips. "It is not my habit to ask questions of strangers," he murmured. "Usually questions, and demands, are only asked of *me*."

"Very well," Gwendolyn said softly. "How is it that you speak my language?"

"I am English like yourself"—he shrugged—"though it has been six and two score years since I have seen my homeland in Wessex."

"But how did you come to be in this place?" she queried, startled by his revelation.

"I and several of my brother priests were captured by Viking marauders from our monastery near the sea, and sold into slavery when they reached the trading town of Hedeby in the land of the Danes." He paused, his voice almost a monotone as he related his story. " 'Twas only through divine providence that I eventually was sold to Magnus Haardrad, the father of Hakon Jarl. He was a rough man, with a violent temper, but he had a thirst for knowledge that I had not seen in other men like him. I taught both him and his sons our language, and much of other matters of the mind as well."

So, that is how the Viking came to speak our language, Gwendolyn thought fleetingly. "But tell me, Ansgar, who is the man lying on the bier in the great hall?"

Ansgar sighed deeply, his wizened face grave. " 'Tis our lord, Eirik Jarl, and Lork Hakon's brother, who died only yester morn," he replied, shaking his head sadly. "He was struck down by a strange illness, and alas, the healer could find no cure. But all is not lost, for Hakon Jarl has come to us from the emerald isle far across the sea, and shall now take his brother's place as chieftain of the Sogn."

"And the beautiful lady?" Gwendolyn asked, almost breathlessly. Perhaps she was wife to Lord Hakon, she thought hopefully. Then, Anora would have naught to fear with such a one as that to warm the Viking's bed.

"She is Bodvild, wife to Eirik," Ansgar replied almost reverently, his high esteem for her showing in his eyes. Gwendolyn's face fell at this news and Ansgar misread it, thinking she was tired. "Enough questions, lad. Now is the time for you to sleep. There will be many tasks awaiting you in the morn, I have no doubt." He walked away with slow, shuffling steps.

Gwendolyn sat down cross-legged on her pallet, her forehead creased in thought. Hakon a chieftain, and from what she could tell, a very powerful one. Yet her mind raced with so many unanswered questions. She rubbed her aching temples, then shrugged. The old man was right. She should get some rest.

Suddenly feeling very tired, she stretched out on the pallet. It was surprisingly soft, despite the fact that it lay on the dirt-packed floor. She had not slept well at all on the ship, what with the waves constantly rocking and jarring her all night long. She yearned for nothing more at that moment than a good night's rest.

Reaching for the woolen blanket folded neatly at the foot of the pallet, Gwendolyn pulled it up over her shoulders. Aye, on the morrow she would ask more questions, she decided, yawning sleepily. The more she knew about this Viking chieftain, the better she could plan the escape for herself and her sister.

Chapter Nineteen

Gwendolyn tossed and turned on her pallet, caught in a vivid, tortured dream. She could hear drums beating in the distance, and the sound of a horn carried high upon the shrieking wind. She was running along the banks of the fjord, but from what she did now know. Her heart was pounding furiously in her breast, her gasping breaths tearing at her throat. She could hear the thundering of hooves behind her, drawing closer and closer. Looking over her shoulder, she saw a horseman dressed all in black astride a mighty steed, his silver helmet flashing in the moonlight. Suddenly he reached down and caught her about the waist, his deep laughter ringing in her ears as he lifted her to his saddle and crushed her to his broad chest. His lips captured her own in a searing kiss of fire, plundering . . . all-possessing . . . drawing the very breath and soul from her body.

Gwendolyn awoke with a start, her hand to her mouth. She was trembling uncontrollably, but she knew it was not from the cold. This was the second time that dream had come to her in her sleep. The first time had been aboard the ship, right before the awful storm. She had thought it only a nightmare then, but now she was not so sure. It seemed so real . . . why, it was almost as if she could still hear the drums pounding and the deep sound of the horn echoing along the valley.

Along the valley! Gwendolyn sat up, her heart racing. Nay, it wasn't a dream! The sound of the drums was growing louder and louder. She jumped to her feet and ran to the door, almost knocking into Ansgar, who stood outside the threshold.

"Whoa! Lad, where would you be running off to?" he queried, catching her gently by the arm.

"The drums . . . they woke me," she said breathlessly, her eyes scanning the valley. The dawn was just breaking over the horizon, its faint rays skimming off the crest of the hills to the east. In the dim light she could see other slaves gathered in front of the house, their eyes trained on the long torchlit procession making its way from the great hall down to the sea. "What is it?"

" 'Tis time for the burial of Eirik Jarl," Ansgar told her, his voice near a whisper. Putting a finger to his lips, he bade her to be silent.

Gwendolyn's eyes widened at the wild scene before her. The Vikings were pouring from the hall and joining in the procession, some beating on drums, while others were shouting and waving their blazing torches in the air. She could see Hakon near the front of the fearsome horde, his tall figure dressed in a dark green tunic trimmed with gold, his broadsword in his right hand. Directly behind him, the body of Eirik was being carried on a litter draped in scarlet cloth, and borne on the shoulders of six strapping Viking warriors.

And there was Bodvild, walking proudly just to the right of the litter. Her tall, lithe form was swathed in a tunic of the finest gold silk with a marten-trimmed cloak swept off her shoulders and held in place by two large silver brooches. Her long dark hair, entwined with silken ropes, hung in a thick braid down the front of her breast.

"Where are they taking him?" Gwendolyn couldn't help asking. She did not see any grave. Nay, it looked to her as if they were carrying his body toward the sea.

"There," Ansgar said simply. He pointed to a longship that had been brought up on the land and moored at the far end of the settlement. It was supported by four corner posts of birch, and stacks of firewood had been piled underneath the hull. A large group of Viking warriors already at the ship was carrying different items on board. A bronze caldron, silver drinking horns, gaming boards, a carved sled, several battle axes—all these and many more items were being placed reverently upon the polished wooden deck.

"But why are they loading those things on the ship?" she queried, watching as a magnificently carved table was hoisted over the railing and carried over to the stern.

"The Viking dead are never sent away empty-handed," Ansgar murmured. "Eirik Jarl shall need food and ale, fine clothing and furnishings, and, most important, his weapons to carry with him to Valhalla."

The winding procession had finally reached the longship. Eirik's litter was carried solemnly on board and placed on a raised platform near the ornately carved prow. The Vikings then surrounded the platform with a wall of gold-painted shields, the tallest at Eirik's head.

As Bodvild walked up the gangplank the clan suddenly grew still, hushed, and their drums and horns fell silent. She knelt down by her husband's side for a long moment, her head bowed, her hands folded in front of her. Then she bent and placed a last tender kiss upon his ashen cheek.

Gwendolyn heard a ragged sigh escape from Ansgar's throat. She turned to look at the old man and was touched by the tears that coursed down his wrinkled face. His eyes were locked on Bodvild's lone figure as she bade her beloved husband farewell before his final journey.

At last Bodvild rose to her feet. She swayed unsteadily, and for a moment it seemed that she might fall. But Hakon rushed up the gangplank and gently took her arm. She leaned heavily on him as they disembarked, but then left his side and walked proudly back up the path to the longhouse she and Eirik had shared. The clan remained silent until she disappeared through the entrance.

"Will she not stay 'til the end?" Gwendolyn asked, though she had no idea what might still be coming in the ceremonies. A stirring of pity welled up in her heart for the beautiful woman.

"Nay. What follows is against her Christian belief," Ansgar said softly, crossing himself. He bent his head in fervent prayer.

The shouting began anew, louder and more fierce than before, as a high-spirited stallion was led into the crowd. Clearly a favored mount from its bejeweled bridle and harness, the horse reared in fright at the noise, its hooves frantically pawing the air.

" 'Tis Eirik Jarl's mighty steed," Ansgar whispered, looking up once again.

Several Vikings grabbed the reins and pulled the frightened animal up the wide gangplank. It stood snorting on the deck, tossing its proud head from side to side, its nostrils flaring. Suddenly the glint of a sword flashed through the air, followed by a loud crash as the stallion's carcass fell to the deck.

"Odin! Odin!" the Vikings exhorted, raising the bloodied sword to the heavens.

Gwendolyn gasped in horror. She could not believe what she had just witnessed. They had killed that magnificent animal! She gripped Ansgar's arm tightly, her eyes ablaze. "W-why?"

" 'Tis their belief," Ansgar said simply. "Eirik Jarl shall need his stallion as he rides beside Odin, their powerful war god, who wages a never-ending battle against the Titans." His gaze suddenly grew hard. "Perhaps you should not stay, lad. There is worse to come."

Gwendolyn swallowed. *What could be worse than this?* she wondered. "Nay, I will remain," she said, though her brave words belied the revulsion she felt.

"So be it," Ansgar said, sighing. He shrugged. The lad had been warned.

But in the next few moments Gwendolyn deeply regretted her decision to stay. She nearly retched as four oxen and several yelping dogs met the same fate as the stallion, though this time the carcasses were hacked to pieces and tossed about the deck. The Vikings then did the same with a cock and a hen. Soon it seemed that the entire deck was awash in blood and offal.

Gwendolyn sank to her knees, her hands held limply in her lap. She had never been so shocked and revolted. What manner of place was this? she wondered despondently, shaking her head. For the first time in her life, she felt abject despair.

Ansgar clucked his tongue sympathetically at the shock reflected in Gwendolyn's eyes. *'Tis a wretched sight for one so young*, he thought grimly. *But better the lad knows now what a harsh place the world can be.*

Gwendolyn watched numbly as the Viking warriors held their weapons high above their heads in a final salute to their dead chieftain. Then Hakon stepped forward with a huge bow in his hand. Lighting the oil-soaked arrow from a nearby torch, he took careful aim, then pulled back on the bow and released it. The arrow soared through the air in a flaming arc and pierced the billowing scarlet sail.

Soon it seemed as if the early morning sky was raining hundreds of burning arrows down upon the ship from at least as many bows. Leaping tongues of flame quickly swept up the sail and enveloped the carved mast. Other warriors hurled their blazing torches at the wood and straw piled high beneath the curved hull.

" 'Twill not take long to burn," Ansgar muttered. Sure enough, the dry wood caught fire quickly, the vivid orange flames fanned by the strong northern wind blowing off the fjord. Soon the entire longship was engulfed by the force of the raging fire. Great billowing clouds of black smoke soared into the dawning sky.

Ansgar placed his hand on Gwendolyn's shoulder. His grim face was illuminated by the orange glow of the fire. "At least there were no concubines," he murmured, sighing raggedly. "We can be thankful for that."

"Concubines?" Gwendolyn asked, noting the strained tone of his voice.

"Aye. 'Tis fortunate that Eirik Jarl's affection was so great for his wife that he had no concubines. I have seen one other burial such as this, of a great Viking chieftain in Vestfold." He shuddered visibly, remembering. "This chieftain had two concubines, both of them foreign slave women, who were burned alive upon his funeral ship. They were told right before they died that 'twas an honor to accompany their master into Valhalla." He shook his head, his eyes vacant, staring. "I shall never, never forget their awful screams. . . ."

"Nay!" Gwendolyn cried suddenly, the horrified expression on her face reflecting the revulsion she felt. Nay, she had heard and seen enough!

Jumping to her feet, she ran back into the slave house and threw herself on her pallet. She had tried to be strong . . . oh, how she had tried to be strong . . . not only for Anora, but for herself as well. But this night's events had finally broken down her defenses.

Gwendolyn's shoulders heaved as hot tears of frustration and bitter despair coursed down her flushed face, her small, clenched fists beating futilely against the hard dirt floor. She covered her mouth with the woolen blanket to stifle her anguished cries. *Sweet Jesu! Protect us*, she sobbed silently, until at last her agonized tears were spent.

Chapter Twenty

Anora pounded the rye dough with her small fists. A long tendril of silver-blond hair loosed itself from the knot at the nape of her neck, and she paused to swipe it from her face with her floured hand. She had been in the cooking house since early that morning, kneading innumerable lumps of dough that had to be baked into loaves for the midday meal. For more than a month now, the routine had been the same. Wiping her hands on the front of her plain linen shift, she went over to the heavy iron caldron hanging in the central hearth and stirred the bubbling contents. The wonderful aroma of the venison and barley stew made her stomach growl hungrily.

"That's a lass, stir it well now," a woman's voice called to her from across the room. Anora looked up, a faint smile on her lips as the older woman bustled over to her side.

Barely five feet tall, Berta's wide girth more than made up for her lack of height. She crossed her fat arms over the massive breasts that hung low almost to her waist. " 'Twill be many a hungry man to enjoy that stew today," she chuckled, "including your Lord Hakon!"

"He is not my Lord Hakon!" Anora retorted, though not too harshly. Berta had been kind to her, in a gruff sort of way, since she had come to work in the cooking house. She had even taught her some of the Norse language during their long hours together. Yet the woman's endless teasing disturbed her greatly.

"Yea, well, then, if he isn't yet, he will be before too long," she muttered, nodding her gray head knowingly. She had seen Lord Hakon's eyes following Anora's slender figure when they served the food in the great hall. It seemed he would rather devour the wench than the steaming food placed before him!

Berta clucked her tongue disapprovingly. For the life of her she could not understand why the girl was not pleased at Hakon Jarl's attentions. Why, any other wench would welcome the chance to frolic in his bed! He was more than enough man for many women, let alone one, what with his strapping good looks and those stirring blue eyes! A shiver ran through her, and she chuckled lustily.

It was well known among the slaves that Lord Hakon had not yet taken anyone to his bed, at least during the few nights he had been at the settlement. Some of the other slave women, beauties in their own right, had virtually thrown themselves at his feet while serving at meals, each vying with the other to win his affection. One bold wench, a fiery-haired woman who had been sold into slavery by her destitute father, had even gone to his hall and waited for him in his bed, no less! He had merely thrown her out on her well-cushioned bottom, amid much shrieking and crying.

Yea, he has eyes only for this one here, Berta thought, glancing appraisingly at Anora. The wench was a pretty one, she had to admit, with her flowing silver hair and those deep emerald eyes that mirrored the color of the sea. But she was much too thin, and had hardly any breasts at all! She chuckled to herself, looking down at her own ample figure. Now, there was a bosom a man could lose himself in!

Berta shrugged. Nay, she just could not understand it. It was clear to all that Lord Hakon wanted Anora. He had even warned his men to stay away from her or feel the sting of his sword! Yet for some reason he had not taken her by force. She sighed, shaking her head. Whatever happened to the days when a Viking chieftain took a wench if he wanted her, and that was that! She closed her heavy-lidded eyes, a secret smile on her face, as she remembered her youth.

"Do you think the stew is ready, Berta?" Anora asked, leaning over the steaming caldron.

Berta's eyes flew open. *Enough daydreaming!* she chided herself. There was work to be done! She took a long ladle from a hook on the wall and dipped it into the thick, meaty stew, stirring it around and around. Breathing in the hearty aroma, a broad smile of satisfaction spread across her face. She ladled a good amount into a soapstone bowl, then eased herself down on a nearby bench and set the bowl in her wide lap.

" 'Tis always a cook's right to sample the stew. Only then can it be served!" she stated emphatically.

Anora watched hungrily, her eyes wide, as Berta spooned a goodly portion into her mouth. The woman's happy grin caused her to smile.

"Well, go on, lass, try some for yourself," Berta invited warmly, nodding toward the steaming caldron.

Anora did just that. Helping herself, she sat down on a low stool and quickly devoured the contents of her bowl, along with a good hunk of bread to sop up the savoury juices. Her stomach now satisfied, she felt much better. Perhaps, if she asked nicely, Berta would allow her to take a bowl of the stew and some bread to Gwendolyn in the stable. She had not seen her sister since yester morn, and she longed to hear the news of her journey to the trading settlement.

Berta seemed to have read her mind. "There is still much

to be done this morn, lass. If you are thinkin' that perhaps you might visit that brother of yours, well . . ." Her voice trailed off as she shook her head. But the look of abject disappointment on Anora's face changed her mind. Her tone softened considerably. "Very well, then, but don't you be too long!" she warned, her kindly eyes belying the stern look on her broad face.

Anora smiled her thanks. She wrapped a heavy cloak around her shoulders, then filled a good-sized bowl with the stew. Grabbing a loaf of rye bread from the table, she headed out the door.

"Remember, now, lass, I'll come looking for you if you don't return within the hour!" Berta shouted as the door swung shut. She smacked her lips. "I think I'll just have me a little more stew," she muttered, waddling over to the caldron.

Anora walked quickly along the path that led to the stable. Hugging her cloak more tightly about her, she was grateful for the warmth of the bowl in her hands. The morning air was frosty and cold. The night before, there had even been a little snow, the first snow of the season. The ground and the roofs of the longhouses were dusted with a blanket of soft white.

She could hardly believe how long it had been since they had arrived at Lord Hakon's settlement. The time had passed so quickly, hastened by the coming of winter. The days were much shorter now, while the nights were long and dark. Suddenly she cast down her eyes as she passed a Viking warrior on his way to the great hall.

The young man looked at her appraisingly, openly admiring her fragile beauty, but said nothing as she hurried by him. Hakon Jarl had made it very clear that this woman was not to be harassed by any of his men, and so far no one had dared. And the young warrior, for one, valued his position as one of the chieftain's resident guards too highly to lose it over a slave wench . . . even one as lovely as she. Without a backward glance, he continued on his way.

Anora breathed a sigh of relief and quickened her pace. The stable lay to the west of the settlement, a good walk from the cooking house. If she used up all her time walking, she thought worriedly, she would have little chance to sit and talk with her sister. And she did not want the stew to be cold by the time she reached the stable. She walked as fast as she could, her panting breaths hanging in fine clouds of white vapor before disappearing in the frigid air like smoke.

The door to the stable was slightly ajar, so she pushed it open with her shoulder and stepped inside. Leaning against the inside wall for a moment, she paused to catch her breath. The stable smelled of dung and straw, but to her it was a comforting smell. It was in the stable that she could always find her sister if she needed her. The dusty air was warm, heated by the many animals huddled together in their stalls. Lord Hakon had not only a thriving herd of sheep, but many cattle and horses as well.

A movement near the far wall of the stable caught her eye. She walked toward it tentatively, carefully avoiding the piles of dung. "Garric?" she called out. She knew she did not dare use her sister's name until she was certain they were alone. But she was answered instead by the lowing of several cattle and the nervous rustling of the sheep. "Garric?" she tried again, louder this time.

A tousled head looked out over the rim of a stall. "Over here!" Gwendolyn replied, throwing one last handful of hay into the great stallion's feed bin. She gently rubbed its black velvet-soft nose. "That's my boy," she murmured. She had just finished rubbing him down after Hakon's morning ride. The stallion was indeed a beauty. She had not seen a finer one even in her father's stables. Too bad she would not get the chance to ride him, she thought, then shrugged. Nay, she and Anora would not be here long enough for that! She stepped out of the stall just as Anora reached her side.

"I brought you some stew and fresh-baked bread." Anora said, smiling. Gwendolyn took it from her hands gratefully. Her morning meal had been interrupted by Hakon's men, who brought the last herd of sheep down from the mountains where they had been grazing through the summer and fall. She had helped them chase the skittish sheep into the stable, and by the time she had returned to her meal it had congealed into a cold, unappetizing lump at the bottom of the bowl.

"Come, let us sit over there." Gwendolyn nodded to a bench set against the wall near the door. They sat down, and Anora watched with approval as Gwendolyn hungrily devoured the still steaming stew and crusty bread. In only a few moments she was done.

Anora laughed, something she did only too rarely. She brushed some crumbs from the side of her sister's mouth. "Your manners have gotten no better since we left . . ." Sobering, she could not finish her sentence. The smile faded from her lips.

"Aye, say it, Anora—since we left our home," Gwendolyn finished for her. "It has been more than a month since we were abducted. Ansgar has told me they will celebrate Yuletide here within the fortnight. He says the Vikings feast for twelve days and nights to welcome the winter solstice." She paused and leaned closer to Anora, her voice a whisper. "But perhaps we will be on a ship before then, and on our way back to our homeland!"

Anora's eyes grew wide. "Were you able to speak with that merchant again yesterday, the one you told me about?" she asked breathlessly, her heart pounding.

"Aye, I spoke with him, and 'tis all arranged!" Gwendolyn replied excitedly.

"Oh, Gwendolyn! I can hardly believe it!" Anora exclaimed. She leaned her head back against the timbered wall, her hands clasped to her breast.

No doubt she is thinking of Wulfgar's embrace, Gwendolyn thought happily. Truly, their escape had been easier to arrange than she had thought it would be!

She had accompanied Hakon several weeks ago to a trading settlement only a short distance south along the fjord for winter supplies. While he had been busy with an oil merchant, she stopped to admire another merchant's wares at one of the large open-air stalls, and had unwittingly asked him the price for a small knife, not in Norse, but in her own tongue. Much to her surprise, the man answered her in English. Hakon had called her away before she could strike up a conversation, but during another trading visit the previous day she had been able to talk to the man for almost a quarter hour.

Hakon had been overseeing the loading of supplies onto his longship, so his attention had been diverted while she spoke to the merchant. At first the man had been a bit wary of her, wondering why a slave who obviously had no money would so strongly wish to talk with him. When she asked how he had come to know their language, he had muttered reluctantly that he was a Frankish merchant, but often traded in London, where it helped to speak the native tongue. He then tried to dismiss her with a curt nod, and turned to wait on two cloaked men standing at the far end of the stall. But she had pressed on. She had not known if she could trust him, but she decided it was worth a chance. Hurriedly she told him of how she and her sister had been abducted from their homeland.

"But what is this to me, lad?" the merchant asked impatiently. "So there are many slaves in this land who were taken from their homes in England."

"Our father is the Earl of Cheshire, kind sir," she had

whispered, her tone almost pleading. "He would most certainly pay a king's ransom for our return to England, as would my sister's betrothed, Wulfgar Ragnarson, a prince of the Danelaw!" The merchant's shrewd eyes had suddenly glittered at this bit of news, knowing an opportunity when he heard one. He rubbed his hands together, thinking hard.

"Aye, so I see," he muttered, his raspy voice now no more than a whisper. "But what is it you want me to do, lad? I had planned to sail on the morn, before the heavy snows start to fly. Truly, I have no love for these Viking barbarians. I only journeyed this far inland along the Sogn because their love of trade in this region is unsurpassed." He pointed to the stacks of fine furs piled high along the back of his wooden stall, luxurious proof of his words. "It will be a rough sea crossing as it is, lad. I cannot afford to tarry here much longer."

At that moment Hakon suddenly called out to her from his longship, gesturing for her to climb aboard. Gwendolyn noted his stormy expression, and hoped fleetingly that she had not raised his suspicion.

"Please, sir, if you would only wait one more day," she had said hurriedly, her eyes desperate. "Lord Hakon and most of his men will be leaving the settlement on the morrow after the midday meal to journey inland. Your trading vessel is much too large to pass unnoticed along the fjord, but if you could bring a small boat to just south of the settlement after it grows dark, near the high waterfall, my sister and I could meet you there! Then we could row back here, board your ship, and be off!"

"Aye, 'tis a good plan. But how do I know you speak the truth, and that you are who you say?" he had asked, his narrowed eyes searching hers.

"All I have to give you is my word," she replied simply, "and my promise that your reward will be great. Are we agreed, then?"

The wily merchant had shaken his head in assent. After

all, he had naught to lose from this venture. If indeed, it was a lie, he had no doubt he could find plenty of traders interested in buying so striking a lad. And if his sister was near as pretty, well . . . "Aye, I will be there," he had rasped, his eyes glinting with greed.

Gwendolyn had barely enough time to flash him a look of thanks. Then she had run swiftly back to the ship.

Hakon glared at her as she jumped onto the deck from the wooden dock. "What was so important that you held up our journey home, Garric?" he asked, his voice low.

" 'Twas naught, my lord. That ridiculous merchant wanted me to buy a knife, of all things! I told him first I had no use for any weapons, and second, that I had no money with which to buy it." She shrugged, then quickly made her way to her bench, hoping he had believed her. He said nothing to her all the way back to the settlement, so she considered the matter dropped.

"So when do we leave? What should I do?" Anora asked, interrupting Gwendolyn's thoughts. Her eyes were ablaze with excitement.

"We shall leave tonight, though I think it best you do not know all the details," Gwendolyn whispered. "As soon as Hakon and his men finish their meal later today, they will be leaving for a council meeting across the valley. Ansgar has said they will be gone for several days, which will give the merchant's ship plenty of lead time, should Hakon try to follow us once he returns and finds us gone. If he does, by the time his longship reaches the mouth of the Sogn we will be sailing across the seas toward England!"

Anora hugged her sister tightly. "Oh, Gwendolyn, you promised we would escape, and tonight we will!" Suddenly she realized she had been gone overlong from the cooking house. "I must get back before Berta comes looking for me. Where shall I meet you?"

"As soon as the Vikings ride out of the settlement, meet

me here. There will be guards scattered about, but I know of a way we can avoid them."

Anora nodded, then hurried to the door of the stable. "Tonight, then," she murmured, her eyes shining. She slipped through the door.

"Aye, tonight!" Gwendolyn watched her sister walk quickly down the path until she disappeared from view around the corner of a nearby longhouse. Turning back into the stable, she could not suppress a joyful leap into a pile of hay. Frightened chickens scattered in every direction, their squawking and cackling drowning out her happy laughter.

Anora smiled to herself as she hurried along the outer wall of the longhouse. Soon she would feel Wulfgar's strong arms around her again! She was so engrossed in her thoughts that she did not see the tall, cloaked figure waiting for her under the gabled entrance until she almost ran into him. Startled, she looked up into a pair of startling blue eyes.

"M-my lord," she stammered, her heart suddenly pounding in her chest. How long had he been waiting for her? Sweet Jesu! Had he perhaps overheard their conversation in the stable?

Hakon's hands gripped her arms tightly, pulling her to him. "I went to the cooking house in search of you, and Berta said you had gone to the stable with some food for your brother. I was only just now on my way there."

Anora relaxed visibly in his arms. So, he had not heard. Relieved, she tried to pull away, but he only drew her closer, hugging her to him beneath his fur cloak. She could feel the heat of his muscled body through her thin shift. His breath was warm against her cheek. "You seem to grow more beautiful to me every day, Anora, though perhaps it is because I have been gone from the settlement overmuch."

Indeed, he had been gone overmuch, Hakon thought wearily. His duties as Jarl had kept him busy from the day of Eirik's burial until now, and even today he had to leave on nother journey to a meeting of the council at his uncle's ettlement across the valley. He had only just returned from he Hardanger, where he had taken Bodvild and her small laughter, Erika, to live with her family. It had been her vish to do so, though he wanted her to stay on with him at he settlement. He smiled faintly, remembering their con-ersation a week past.

"But I know nothing of running a household," he had roaned, shrugging his broad shoulders in exasperation. 'Tis women's work, Bodvild. Stay on here at the settlement is the honored wife of my brother, and help me!"

But she had only laughed at him, her gray eyes full of nirth. "Nay, 'tis not seemly for me to stay, Hakon, and well ou know that. The settlement is now your responsibility, in-luding the household, though I will miss it. . . ." Her voice railed off, a hint of sadness in her expression. "Nay, I wish o return to my homeland. Erika and I will be happy there. This place holds too many memories for me."

It had pained him to see the haunted look on her beau-iful face. Kneeling on one knee, Hakon mock-pleaded for ier to stay, though in his heart he had known she was right. His antics had served to enliven her spirits, for her laughter iad rung out once again in the great hall.

" 'Tis time for you to take a wife, Hakon Jarl," she ad-nonished him, her face sobering. Taking the bunch of keys rom the belt at her waist, she had laid them in his hand. 'For the new mistress of Sogn, whoever and wherever she nay be!"

A wife, Hakon groaned inwardly, breathing in the heady ragrance of Anora's silky hair. Nay, that was not what he ieeded, nor wanted, at this moment. He already held in his irms the one woman he desired most of all.

He held Anora's slender body tightly against his, reveling n her softness. Bending his head, he suddenly brought his lips down upon hers in a crushing kiss. He would drive her fear away, he thought wildly, savoring the sweetness of her mouth, deepening his kiss. He had to. . . .

Summoning all her strength, Anora pushed away from him so abruptly that he was almost knocked backward against the timbered wall of the longhouse. Before he could reach out and grab her, she was running down the path, her long hair flowing out behind her, as if Gorm, the hellhound of the gods, was snapping at her heels.

Hakon cursed vehemently under his breath. *You are a fool to think she will ever come to you willingly!* he raged at himself. Truly, his patience was wearing thin. He had tried everything he knew to gain her trust: he had spoken to her with gentleness, but she had spurned his every advance; he had given her beautiful silken clothes, but she had refused to wear them, preferring instead the simple linen shifts that the rest of the slave women wore; he had given her freedom of movement, but she had confined herself to the cooking house and the solitude of her own chamber in the women's slave house—all this and much more he had allowed her, but still the expression of fear had not left her emerald eyes.

Hakon strode angrily toward the great hall, firmly resolved that after his return from his uncle's settlement, he would wait no longer. She would come to him, willing or not!

Anora dashed into the cooking house and slammed the wooden door behind her. She leaned against the roughhewn wall for a moment and closed her eyes, her chest rising and falling rapidly as she tried to catch her breath. She felt as if her heart were in her throat. The Viking's kiss still burned upon her lips, and the skin on her arms had red imprints from where his hands had held her so tightly. She took off her cloak, her hands trembling uncontrollably, and hung it upon its hook near the door.

Berta, hearing the slam of the door, called out to her

from the hearth, where she was turning some loaves of bread on an iron griddle. "Did Garric enjoy my stew?" she asked pleasantly, knocking the crusty top of one of the loaves with her third finger and thumb. *Yea, these are done*, she thought, straightening up. She lifted the heavy griddle to the table near the hearth where other loaves were cooling. "Anora?" Receiving no answer, Berta looked toward the door.

Anora was sitting silently upon a stool, her eyes downcast, her face pale and drawn.

"What is it, lass?" she queried, bustling over to Anora's side and putting a fat arm about her shoulders. Yet she already knew the answer. Her keen eyes noted well the red marks on the young woman's slim, white arms. *Yea, 'twill not be long now*, she shook her head knowingly, *before Lord Hakon will have his way with her*.

"Why don't you go to your room, lass, and lie down for a while?" she said gently. "All is in readiness for the midday meal, and if I need aught else I will get one of the others to help me. Go on with you, now."

Anora looked up gratefully. "Thank you, Berta," she murmured. Aye, a rest was what she needed, she thought numbly, wrapping her cloak about her once again. It would hasten away the hours 'til it grew dark. Then soon enough she and Gwendolyn would be gone from this cursed place forever.

Berta shook her head as Anora closed the door behind her. "Someday the lass will surely look back on this and realize her fears were for naught," she muttered under her breath, walking over to the hearth. To her mind, there could be no greater honor than being the concubine of a great chieftain . . . especially one so handsome and powerful as Hakon Jarl!

Chapter Twenty-one

"If rumors are to be believed, it seems Rhoar Bloodaxe continues to strengthen his forces against you, my lord," Olav said, his voice low. "Perhaps 'twould be best to postpone this meeting of the council across the valley for another time. Even a few days' absence from the settlement could prove too tempting an invitation for that bastard!" Olav leaned forward in his chair, the concern evident on his swarthy face. He took his new role as adviser to Hakon Jarl very seriously, as he had taken his former position as helmsman on his longship. It was his belief that though Rhoar had not attacked the settlement upon Eirik's death, his threat was still very real . . . and possibly imminent. He was merely waiting for the right opportunity.

Hakon shook his head. "The council meeting at my uncle's settlement will help to solidify my control in that region. It cannot be delayed," he said tersely. He took a long draft of ale from his goblet. "There will be more than enough guards left here to protect the settlement. 'Twould be different if we were to be more than a few hours' ride away, but Rhoar would be a fool to attack while we were only in the next valley . . . and with plenty of reinforcements close at hand."

Hakon's eyes scanned the great hall, unable to keep his mind on the conversation. By the blood of Odin, where was she? He pushed his plate away, his food barely touched. Settling back in his chair, he toyed absently with the ale in his goblet, swirling the amber liquid around and around. The black scowl deepened on his face, warning those who sat near him that their chieftain was indeed in a foul mood.

"More ale, my lord?" a buxom servingwoman ventured, rubbing her thigh seductively against his knee as she leaned over to refill his goblet.

"Be gone, wench!" he roared, shattering the brooding silence in the hall. The woman backed away in fear, then hurried away. Hakon caught the furtive glances of his men, who then quickly looked back to their plates of food, and he cursed again. What spell had Anora cast over him? he wondered, his ire rising with each moment she did not enter the hall.

"Was the food not to your liking, my lord?" Berta asked quietly, removing his plate from the table.

"Nay, 'twas fine, Berta," Hakon replied, his tone softening as he looked at the rotund woman who had served his family for so many years. "Where is Anora?" he asked, trying to appear nonchalant, though hardly succeeding. "Why is she not here serving with the others?"

Berta was not fooled by his seeming indifference. *He is indeed a proud one*, she thought sagely, stifling a smile that would force itself to her lips. His face was inscrutable, yet his eyes bespoke the hold the wench had over him.

"Anora is resting, my lord," she replied. "She seemed well enough earlier this morning when she took some food to her brother in the stable, but upon her return she was quite overwrought." Her eyes watched the play of emotions across Hakon's face. "From the looks of her, I'd say she had quite a shock."

Hakon slammed his goblet down upon the table, his blue eyes flaring dangerously. The set of his jaw was grim, determined. "We ride within the half hour," he stated evenly to his men, hiding the anger that raged within him. So, his kiss disturbed her so greatly that she had sought the comfort of her bed! Thor's teeth, but he was a fool! He almost felt like overturning the table, but thought better of it. It would not do for his men to see him behave like a besotted youth whose love had been spurned by the object of his affection. Rising from the high seat, he strode angrily out of the great hall.

The men at the surrounding tables sat in stunned silence for a moment. Then suddenly the hall was filled with the scraping of benches as they jumped to their feet. Tossing down the ale in their goblets, they hurried out after their chieftain.

Olav was the only one to rise slowly from his chair. He turned to Berta, who stood by the table. "I have known Hakon for many years, but I have never seen him so taken by any one wench." He sighed. " 'Twas your words, woman, that brought on this rage. I know naught of what took place that could explain their meaning, but my warning to you is this: See that the wench is well protected while we are gone. Hakon has laid claim to her, and there would be hell to pay if aught is amiss when we return." With that, he turned and walked out of the hall.

Berta shook her head slowly. Yea, she would see that Anora moved only from the cooking house to her chamber, and back again. She did not want it upon her head if aught happened to the girl while Lord Hakon was away. She snapped at the servingwomen standing near the door, "Why do you stand there gaping while there is work to be done?"

The women quickly moved about the hall, picking up the

debris from the meal. Berta ambled over to a chair and sat down heavily. *So much trouble over one wench*, she thought, draining the ale from a half-empty goblet.

Hakon looked over his shoulder to see his men rushing out of the great hall. Then he turned back around, his voice roaring out loudly as he strode toward the stables. "Garric! Saddle my horse!"

Gwendolyn jumped up from her pallet, where she had been resting just as he pushed open the door. She backed away slightly, for she could see he was in a black mood.

"Did you not hear me, lad? Saddle my horse, and be quick about it. The sky is already growing dark," Hakon stated sternly. "I wish for you to accompany me on this journey as well, to care for my stallion, so you had best hurry. I am sure my uncle does not have a groom at his settlement who comes close to your skill with horses."

Gwendolyn felt a sudden sense of panic at his words, but quickly regained her composure, her mind working fast. She suddenly clutched her stomach, a look of intense pain on her face. "Oh, b-but, my lord," she stammered, "I have b-been lying here on my pallet since this morning. I fear I have t-taken sick . . . probably from that stew Arona brought me this morning." She moaned convincingly, doubling over as if in intense misery.

Hakon looked at her doubtfully. He could not very well take the lad if he was sick, he decided. Garric would then be more of a hindrance than a help. "Very well, lad. Lie back down on your pallet. I will send the healer to you with some herbs for your stomach." Pulling the saddle from the wall, he strode over to his stallion and hoisted it onto its back. He then tightened the girths beneath the horse's belly, and drew the harness over its proud head.

Gwendolyn watched from the corner of her eye as Hakon led the high-spirited animal by the reins from its stall. She clutched her stomach again and groaned several times for good measure. Hakon paused for a moment by her pallet, and she looked up at him as he towered above her. "My lord?" she asked weakly.

Hakon studied her face, a niggling sense of doubt pricking at his mind. The lad was somewhat pale, he admitted, though his groans seemed a bit too convincing. "Egil will remain here to keep an eye on things while I am gone," he warned. "In other words, Garric, do not try anything foolish. I have given him permission to mete out punishment if any is necessary." He was answered with a small nod as Gwendolyn rolled over onto her side.

Aye, that Viking dog Egil would no doubt relish every minute of it if given half the chance, she thought fiercely, watching through half-closed eyes as Hakon led the stallion through the door of the stable. Too bad he would never get the opportunity!

She lay on the pallet listening to the commotion as the Vikings prepared to ride out of the settlement. She could hear the clanking of swords against wooden shields slung from saddles, and knew that they were well armed. This came as no surprise to her. She had heard all about Rhoar Bloodaxe, Hakon's bastard brother, and his threat of blood vengeance from Ansgar.

At last came the command she had been waiting for, as Hakon shouted to his men to prepare to ride. Jumping up from her pallet, she flew to the door of the stable and peeked outside. Hakon made a commanding figure astride his mighty stallion, dressed all in black except for the white-blond of his hair. *That's how I will remember him*, Gwendolyn thought, fully appreciating for the first time his handsome looks. After all, she allowed herself, she was a woman, too!

The ground thundered from the many flashing hooves as the Vikings rode out of the settlement. Indeed, the hour was growing late. The moon had already risen in the darkening sky to just above the jagged slopes of the mountains towering above the fjord. Gwendolyn could not believe how quickly it grew dark in this northern land. Why, it could not be more than four hours past the noon hour!

She turned back into the stable. There were just a few things to be done, but she wanted to be ready when Anora came to meet her. She hurried over to a far corner of the stable, shooing away the frightened sheep that got in her way. Kneeling near the wall, she felt around with her hands until she found what she was looking for. A smile lighted her face as she pulled out a narrow-bladed knife from beneath the straw. Anora had stolen it for her one day from the cooking house. It was not nearly as fine as the hunting knife she had lost to Svein, but it was a sorely needed weapon nonetheless.

Fitting the knife into her belt, she ran over to her pallet and pulled together what little clothing she possessed that was not already on her back. Hakon had given her several woolen tunics in the style of the Vikings, and another pair of loose-fitting breeches. But she still preferred the clothing she had worn on the day of their capture. Pulling her fur-lined jerkin about her, she was ready at last. She sat down on her pallet while she waited for Anora.

It could not have been more than an hour when she finally heard a small rap at the door of the stable. Gwendolyn hopped up, her heart in her throat. "Anora?"

"Aye, 'tis me," Anora replied, slipping furtively through the door, her fur cloak swirling about her. She grabbed Gwendolyn's wrist. "I fear someone has followed me," she whispered tremulously, her eyes wide. "Shh! I hear him coming now!"

"Stand over there, behind the stall!" Gwendolyn hissed. Grabbing a wooden plank nearly as tall as she, she leaned up close against the wall near the door.

It opened slowly, creaking eerily. A man, his face hidden

in the shadows, eased carefully inside. Gwendolyn did not wait to discover who it was. She lifted the plank, then brought it down with all her strength upon the man's head. He fell heavily to his knees, groaning and holding his head. She hit him again. This time he fell forward with a heavy thud.

"Quick, Anora, you take one leg, I'll take the other!" Gwendolyn whispered. Together they dragged him to the back wall of the stable, though he was a big man and very heavy.

" 'Tis Egil!" Anora cried out softly, as a shaft of moonlight hit the man's face through an opening in the wall. Blood trickled down his forehead, pooling on the ground behind his ear.

"So, he has finally gotten what he deserves!" Gwendolyn muttered fiercely, covering him up with heaps of straw. She did not feel even a twinge of remorse. "Come on!" Taking Anora by the hand, she dragged her sister across the stable to the entrance, where she gathered up her few belongings. Nudging the door open with her booted toe, she peered outside.

There were several Viking guards posted down the hill near the great hall, and some were walking about near the docks; otherwise, the settlement appeared quiet. Gwendolyn eased open the door, then looked over her shoulder at Anora. "We will have to run up into the woods behind the stable, then follow along the crest of those hills for a ways," she explained in a whisper. "Ready?"

Anora nodded, her eyes bright in the moonlight. "I am ready."

"Aye, then, to freedom!" Gwendolyn dashed out alongside the stable with Anora close on her heels. Pausing for a moment after they rounded the corner, they broke out in a run up the hill until they reached the cover of the thick trees surrounding the settlement. Anora was hindered somewhat by the skirt of her shift, but she quickly hoisted it above her knees and soon caught up with Gwendolyn. They slowed their pace a bit as they disappeared into the trees, for they knew they could no longer be seen.

It seemed as if they had been walking for at least an hour when Gwendolyn gestured to Anora to start down the side of the hill. Leaving the cover of the trees, they began the steep descent to the fjord. Gwendolyn could hear the loud roar of the waterfall not far in the distance, and she knew they were almost there. With every step, her heart grew lighter. She could have laughed out loud with joy.

"Is it much farther, Gwendolyn?" Anora asked, leaning for a moment against a large rock outcropping to catch her breath.

"Nay," she replied. Then she whispered excitedly "Look, Anora, I can see the boat!"

Anora's heart leaped in her breast at the sight of the small boat bobbing along the shoreline of the fjord. They quickened their pace, half sliding down the steep slope of the hill that was slippery from the wet snow. Almost to the bottom, Gwendolyn suddenly lost her footing and rolled down the rest of the way.

"Gwendolyn!" Anora called out sharply, her hand to her throat. Relief surged through her body at the sound of her sister's uproarious giggle.

"Go on! You should try it, Anora!" Gwendolyn called out softly.

Though she smiled, Anora shook her head. "I think I would prefer to walk the rest of the way down." When she reached her sister at last, they embraced each other tightly.

"There it is!" Gwendolyn cried, turning around. The boat was yet a few hundred feet away from them, anchored just off the shoreline. They carefully picked their way in the dark along the rocky beach, for the full moon was now hidden behind a dense bank of clouds.

Gwendolyn was the first to reach the boat. To her surprise, it was empty. A strange feeling of foreboding settled over her, and she turned and looked about them. It was so dark that she could barely make out the details of the shoreline. Anora reached her side, and her hand clutched Gwendolyn's arm.

"Where is the merchant?" she asked.

Gwendolyn could tell her sister was frightened by the tone of her voice. She was, too, but she was loath to admit it.

" 'Tis quite a shame, really, but the merchant decided he had other plans," a low voice growled in the dark.

Gwendolyn whirled around and pulled her knife from her belt, but she saw no one. She knew that awful voice, God help them, she knew it!

"Run, Anora, run!" Gwendolyn yelled, giving her sister a shove. Anora began to run back along the shoreline, but her efforts were hampered by the sharp, jagged rocks.

"The lass is all yours, Torvald!" the evil voice cried. "At least for now!"

Suddenly Anora felt herself lifted up into the air and hugged tightly against a broad chest. She screamed once, a loud, shrill sound, before a large hand was clapped over her mouth. She struggled futilely in the Viking's huge arms for several moments, then gave up in despair.

Gwendolyn heard Anora's muffled cries and her heart sank. It was all so horribly familiar. At that moment her knife was suddenly knocked from her hand. It fell clattering to the rocks several feet away, and she knew she would not be able to find it in time.

" 'Twas so good of you to share your plans with us in the marketplace, lad," Svein muttered, stepping out from behind a huge rock. He walked up to Gwendolyn, a long knife held in his hand. "Of course, it would have meant our deaths to allow Lord Hakon to see us there. So we stood just behind the merchant's stall as you told him your life's story."

He laughed cruelly. "What good fortune, or should I say strange coincidence? Torvald and I had been at the tradin' settlement only two days, and who should we see? 'Twas then we decided to fetch you for ourselves." He clucked his tongue in mock sympathy. "The good merchant kindly allowed us to borrow his boat. It seems he will na' be needing it any longer!"

At that moment the moon broke away from the clouds, illuminating Svein's scarred face. He walked toward her menacingly, brandishing the knife. "And do na' think to sway me with talk of your father's gold, lad. 'Tis not gold we want now, but revenge!"

Gwendolyn had barely heard him, her mind working quickly. But before she could make any move, Svein lunged at her and brought his arm about her neck. She elbowed him fiercely in the ribs, and was rewarded with a sharp slap across the face that knocked her reeling to the ground.

"Come on, Torvald, let's get them on the boat," Svein ordered gruffly. He bent down and grabbed her by the thick lining of her fur jerkin, pulling her roughly to her feet.

Nay, she would not give up that easily, she thought desperately, flailing her legs and arms. One of her legs caught him hard in the groin and he doubled over in pain, cursing vehemently. She pulled away from him, free. Catching sight of a glint of steel in the moonlight, she grabbed the long knife from his hand. Without a thought, she plunged it deep into his chest. Svein screamed in agony, trying to cover the wound with his hand, while warm blood spurted between his fingers.

Gwendolyn quickly ran over to where Torvald stood holding Anora. She knew this huge Viking would be a far more formidable foe. Her fears were confirmed when he dropped Anora to the ground and pulled his broadsword from the scabbard at his belt. Anora tried to crawl away from him on her hands and knees, but he caught her by the hair and dragged her back again, all the while keeping his eyes upon Gwendolyn.

Torvald towered above her, grinning wolfishly in the moonlight. He swung his sword once, barely missing her as she dodged just in time, though she tripped on a sharp rock and fell heavily to the ground. Seeing his chance, he raised his sword high above his head, an awful, blood curdling scream wrenching from his throat.

Suddenly Gwendolyn heard a high-pitched whistling sound in the air, then a strangled, gurgling noise from Torvald as his whole body jerked spasmodically. He seemed to sway for a moment, his arms still high above his head. Then he fell forward with a crash onto the rocky beach.

Gwendolyn gasped at the long spear protruding from Torvald's broad back. Looking up, she saw several riders fast approaching them from the direction of the settlement. Their leader, dressed all in black, was riding far ahead of the others. She could hear the snorting of his mighty steed, and the pounding of its hooves as it galloped along the rocky shoreline. Rushing over to Anora's side, she held her sobbing sister in her arms as the rider bore down upon them. His bronzed face was barely discernible in the moonlight, but she could sense the cold fury flashing dangerously from his eyes.

Chapter Twenty-two

The full moon was high over the fjord by the time the silent party returned to the settlement. Hakon brought his great stallion to a halt in the stable yard and dismounted, his expression grim. He reached up, encircling Anora's slender waist with his hands, then lifted her from the saddle to the ground. She avoided his eyes and immediately ran over to her sister, who had sunk to her knees in exhaustion, her head slumped to her chest.

Gwendolyn had been forced to follow on foot all the way back to the settlement, her hands tied together with a long piece of rope that had been attached to the pommel of Hakon's saddle. Hakon had walked his stallion all the way back, but she had still been forced to run to keep up with them or else be dragged along the shore.

Hakon looked at them coldly, a mixture of anger and relief raging within him. He had been almost an hour's ride from the settlement when he had suddenly decided to turn back, a growing suspicion burning in his mind. He had bidden most of his men to continue on without him, saying only that he would meet them on the morrow at his uncle's settlement. Olav and three other warriors had returned with him, their horses galloping hard to keep pace with Hakon's powerful stallion.

He had reined in first at the women's slave house, not even bothering to announce his entrance. He had strode in amid the women, his eyes scanning the room for Anora. Berta had rushed forward at that moment, her round, anxious face telling him all he needed to know.

"She is not here, my lord!" Berta had lamented, wringing her hands. "I have only just returned from the cooking house after finishing my work for the next day's meals, and when I looked in her chamber, 'twas empty!"

This news had brought forth a blistering curse from Hakon. He entertained only one thought as he mounted his steed and rode over to the stable—Garric! He angrily recalled the events of the past few days—Garric's lingering overlong at the foreign merchant's stall at the trading settlement; his eagerness to please, so unlike him, just that morning when Hakon had taken his stallion out for a ride; his illness in the stable, and now as Hakon thought back, most likely feigned—and he could not believe he had failed to recognize these signs for what they had been . . . a prelude to escape. Grim-faced, he only hoped he would not be too late.

He had rushed into the stable, knowing in his heart that it, too, would be empty. A loud groan from along the back wall had led him to Egil, who was sitting in the middle of a pile of straw holding his head in his hands. Surrounded by cackling chickens and nervous sheep, with pieces of hay sticking to his thick hair and beard, the robust Viking made a comical sight. Hakon might have laughed had the situation been different, but laughter had been the last thing on his mind.

"Tell me quickly, Egil, did you see aught of the lad and

Anora?" Hakon asked him, noting that he was none the worse for his mishap save the angry welt on his forehead.

"Yea, my lord," he murmured, groaning. "I followed the wench here from the women's slave house. She was acting a bit strangely, what with looking over her shoulder, peering around corners and such, so I thought I had better have a look. When I walked in the door . . ." He shook his head in disbelief. "There was a loud crack, and then I remember naught else."

Hakon helped Egil shakily to his feet, then bade one of the other men to care for him. Just as he was rushing from the stable, his keen eyes scanning the waters of the fjord, he heard the scream. Loud and high-pitched, it carried out over the water, echoing among the hills surrounding the settlement.

He had wasted no time in mounting his stallion, though a sense of dread settled over him as he rode like the wind down the hill and along the rocky shoreline. Just barely able to make out several battling figures in the darkness, he had sent a fervent prayer to Odin that he would not be too late. He had drawn his winged spear from his saddle, holding it poised and ready in hand until he could be sure of his target.

The wild Viking war cry carried high upon the wind had been all Hakon needed. The deadly weapon had sailed through the air, finding its mark, the awful scream cut off as abruptly as the life of the man who had uttered it.

Dismounting from his stallion with sword in hand, Hakon had quickly taken in the scene before him. Relief had surged through his body once he knew Anora was unharmed, but it had soon been replaced by cold, restrained fury at the look of hateful defiance that had burned in the lad's eyes.

"My lord!" Olav's shout interrupted Hakon's dark thoughts, as he rode up into the stable yard and dismounted from his sweating horse. "The bodies of Svein and Torvald have been thrown into the fjord, as you commanded, and may Hel, goddess of the underworld, enjoy their foul company!" he spat fiercely.

Hakon only nodded, his face grim, his chiseled lips a tight line. Anora still huddled beside Gwendolyn, her arms tightly hugging her sister's shoulders. Truly, they made a pathetic pair, he thought. But right now he had no time for pity.

Walking up to Anora, he bent down and pulled her away from Gwendolyn's side. She struggled, but in vain. Her protests were no match for his muscled strength. "Hold her fast," he bid Olav, who grabbed her and held her arms tightly.

"Stand up, Garric!" Hakon ordered.

Gwendolyn raised her eyes to meet his. Angry rebellion shone from the emerald depths, hitting Hakon with an almost physical force as she rose unsteadily to her feet.

Even now the lad shows his hate, he marveled, impressed by Garric's courage despite the severe punishment that was sure to come. A Viking guard approached the small group carrying a studded lash and handed it to Hakon. He took it, wrapping it about his right hand.

"Tie him to the post!" Hakon commanded. Two warriors rushed to obey, seizing Gwendolyn by the arms and dragging her up against the thick timbered post. She offered no resistance as they tied her securely. Her face was expressionless, though her eyes glittered defiantly.

Hakon stood back several feet from the post as he tested the lash. The cruel piece of leather cut through the air like a slithering serpent, the metal studs cutting small gouges in the snow-covered dirt as it hit the ground.

"I have warned you from the start, Garric, not to force my hand, but in this last instance you have pressed me too far. Though you are but a mere boy, I can no longer tolerate such blatant defiance on your part. You must be punished."

Gwendolyn closed her eyes tightly and leaned against the

post as she heard the lash sing through the air. She jerked as it cut across her back, though the pain was slight due to the thickness of her fur-lined jerkin. Again the lash sailed through the air, this time hitting her across the legs. The woolen breeches were no match for the biting sting of the studded lash. She cried out in pain.

"Nay . . . please stop . . . please!" begged Anora, suddenly wrenching free from Olav's arms. She ran over to Hakon and threw herself at his feet, her beautiful face streaked with tears as she looked up at him beseechingly. "Please, strike him no more!" she pleaded, her slender body wracked by sobs. "If you will only stop, my lord Hakon, I promise that I will come to your bed this night. You have made known your desire for me many times. If it is still your wish, I . . . I am yours."

Hakon's face was inscrutable as he looked down at Anora, a cold, empty feeling inside him. So, he had won at last, he thought bitterly, though his victory was indeed a hollow one. He bent down and gently lifted Anora to her feet, his blue eyes searching her face. For the first time she met his gaze evenly and without fear, despite her trembling.

Only her love for her brother and her desire to protect him has brought her to this, he thought ironically. His punishment of Garric had accomplished so easily what his patience and gentle words had failed to do. He noted well the set determination of her delicate chin, and the hint of defiance in her eyes that now matched that of her brother's. Hakon sighed. This was not how he had imagined it would be. But, if he could not have her heart . . . he would no longer deny himself her body.

"You are mine, Anora, by your consent or not," he murmured possessively, drawing her close. "Garric will be spared not because you have given yourself to me at last, but only if I wish it to be so." With that, he held her away from him, one hand gripping her arm, while the other still toyed with the lash. He stared at Gwendolyn for several moments, not saying a word. Truly the lad deserved to be punished further for the escape attempt, for he had no doubt that Garric had been the one to plan it. But Hakon had spent his wrath. His mind had turned to other things. . . .

"Cut him down!" he ordered tersely. One of the Viking guards drew his sword and quickly severed the ropes binding Gwendolyn. She did not fall, but stood leaning on the post. Anora gasped in relief and tried to run to her sister's side. But Hakon held her fast.

"Please, my lord, allow me a few moments to help Garric to his pallet in the stable, and to see to his wounds," she entreated, her eyes pleading with him.

"Nay, Anora." Hakon shook his head. "You will hold to your promise this night, and accompany me to my hall."

But Anora stood fast, awakened to the power she had over him. She looked at him with a newfound boldness that she had not known she possessed. "I cannot come to you knowing my brother is hurt. If you will allow me only a few moments to care for him, I will be most grateful, my lord Hakon." She gazed up at him unabashed, her meaning reflected in her eyes.

Hakon looked confounded for a moment. Loki's mischief, he would never understand women! For the past month Anora had avoided him at every turn, spurning his advances, and now she had gifted him with such a look that made his blood boil! He glanced over at Gwendolyn, who was leaning her head against the post. *The lad does indeed look pale*, he admitted, *and she has asked for only a few moments. . . .*

"Very well," he said gruffly, letting go of her arm. "But do not linger overlong. My patience has already been sorely tried this day." She nodded, then ran over to Gwendolyn's side. His eyes hungrily followed her lithe form. Yea, he would not wait long. "Olav, see that Anora is escorted to my hall after she has seen to her brother," he ordered.

"Yea, my lord," he answered, watching as Hakon threw the lash to the ground and strode off in the direction of his hall. He sighed, grateful for how the night had ended. Hakon's wrath would have turned on them all if aught had happened to the wench.

"Come on, Gwen— . . . Garric," Anora whispered in her sister's ear. Gwendolyn let go of the post and leaned on her for support, testing the strength in her legs. She gritted her teeth at the pain.

"I am fine now, Anora," she murmured, limping as she walked toward the stable. Her sister held her arm, despite her weak protests, until they had walked through the stable door.

Anora's delicate features were etched with concern. "Here, let me help you to your palle—"

"Shut the door behind us!" Gwendolyn suddenly hissed, interrupting her. She feigned a collapse on the pallet for the benefit of Olav, who stood watching them from the stable-yard. Anora looked dubiously at her sister, then hurried back to the entrance and quietly closed the wooden door.

"We must work fast, Anora!" Gwendolyn whispered urgently. She jumped up from her pallet, ignoring the ache in her legs, and ran to the far wall of the stable, where the farming implements and metal tools were kept. Her eyes quickly scanned the varied assortment until she found the one she was looking for—a long metal blade that was used to shear sheep. She yanked it from its hook and tested the blade's sharpness with her finger. Aye, it would do, she thought, hurrying back to her sister.

Anora looked at her incredulously. "What are you going to do?"

"I will not have you give yourself to that Viking!" Gwendolyn blurted angrily, a fierce light burning in her eyes. "I made a promise to you on that ship, and I mean to keep it! We will escape from here, but it will take more time." She paused, her voice low. "I will go to Lord Hakon tonight in your place!"

Anora could not believe her ears. *Sweet Jesu! Gwendolyn has gone mad!* she thought frantically, tears rushing to her eyes. It was more than she could bear. She fell to her knees, her shoulders shaking from the despair that wracked her body. Would that Svein had killed her rather than see her sister like this!

Gwendolyn dropped to her knees and shook Anora roughly. "Listen to me," she pleaded desperately, "for we have little time left! No doubt Olav will soon call for you." She held Anora's face in her hands. "I cannot bear the thought of you sacrificing yourself for me. You belong to Wulfgar . . . he is the only man who should ever touch you!"

Anora nodded numbly. Her eyes stared into the distance as she remembered those long days spent in the tent on Hakon's ship during the sea crossing. She had never told Gwendolyn that she had considered ending her life then, that she would rather have died knowing one night with Wulfgar than feel another man's hands upon her. It was only Gwendolyn's vow to her that had restored her will to live and given her hope.

Gwendolyn rushed on anxiously. "I had thought all was lost until you begged Hakon to allow you a few moments to care for me. It gave me the time I needed to think." She stood and pulled off her jerkin. "Here, quickly! Exchange your clothes with mine. Then I will have to cut your hair, Anora. 'Tis really the only thing that sets us apart. You must now play the part of Garric, while I will go to Lord Hakon in your place. He will never know the difference, for we look so much alike. If I have managed to deceive him this long as a boy, surely this plan cannot fail!" She hurriedly stripped off her shirt and bent down to pull off her leather boots. "Now, Anora! Give me your clothes!"

Anora stared dumbfounded, her mind racing. "You would do this for me?" she asked, searching Gwendolyn's face.

"Aye," Gwendolyn replied simply. She straightened up and embraced her sister tightly. "I would do aught to protect you, Anora."

Her eyes shining with grateful tears, Anora hesitated no longer. She quickly slipped her plain woolen mantle, then the linen shift, over her head. She had lost her fur cloak during the awful encounter along the shoreline, though she had scarcely noticed the cold until now. She stood shivering while Gwendolyn finished undressing. Then she quickly donned the clothes tossed over to her.

"You always wished you had the daring to wear men's clothing, Anora," Gwendolyn whispered, a faint smile on her lips as she pulled the shift down over her head, then the mantle. "Now is your chance." At any other time she would have laughed. But a strange fear was beginning to gnaw at her, chasing all thoughts from her mind and threatening to weaken her resolve. Nay, she could not change her mind now, she chided herself. There would be no turning back. . . .

Anora's worried voice interrupted her dark thoughts. "But I know naught of horses and such, Gwendolyn. What shall I do—"

"I will teach you what I can whenever Lord Hakon is away from the settlement, though you will have to learn fast," she replied. "And if there is need, I can always become Garric again!" She winked reassuringly. "Now, kneel down, Anora, so I may cut your hair," she murmured, picking up the blade from the ground.

It did not take long before the stable floor around them was strewn with Anora's long, silver-blond tresses. Gwendolyn stepped back to survey her handiwork. Aye, it would have to do, she thought grimly, noting with satisfaction how her sister's newly shorn hair curled softly about her face much the same as her own.

" 'Tis a small price to pay for such a cost," Anora murmured. She quickly gathered her hair in a pile and was about to hide it under the straw when Gwendolyn stopped her.

"Nay, Anora, I wish to take it with me to the Viking's hall," Gwendolyn whispered. She bent down and scooped up the silky mass.

Suddenly Olav's voice boomed out from the stable yard. "Enough, wench! If the lad needs further help, I will fetch the healer to minister to him. Come out from the stable!"

Gwendolyn wheeled around, her hand to her throat, the other clutching the long strands of silver-blond hair. Suddenly she did not feel so brave.

Anora threw her arms about her sister's neck, her face wet with tears. "I shall never forget what you have done for me this night, Gwendolyn," she said softly.

Gwendolyn nodded, though her eyes were distant. "Lie down on the pallet . . . quickly!" She covered her sister with the woolen blanket. "You are now Garric, slave and stable hand to Hakon Jarl!" she whispered vehemently. "We will play this out as long as we can, and hopefully find a way to escape before our guise is discovered!"

And if God wills it, she thought, crossing herself. She turned away abruptly, knowing that if she lingered any longer she might lose her courage. At that moment Olav pushed open the stable door.

"Come on, wench, before Lord Hakon returns himself to carry you back to his hall!" he blustered. He stepped back in surprise. *What has the wench done to her hair?* he wondered, his mouth gaping as he looked at the long strands dangling from her hand. Truly the short curls did little to lessen her beauty, but he could not help but think Lord Hakon would be extremely displeased. He shook his head, his eyes flickering over the huddled figure lying on the pallet. He bent down to pull back the woolen blanket, but Gwendolyn stopped him.

"Please, do not disturb him," she murmured quietly, her hand on his arm. "My brother is sleeping at last."

Olav stood up, shifting uncomfortably under her steady, emerald gaze. He was not immune to the charms of a beautiful woman, and this one was truly bewitching. He found himself nodding, then followed her from the stable as she stepped out into the cold night air. She shivered visibly. Olav took his heavy hooded cloak from his shoulders and wrapped it around her.

"Come, lass, I will show you the way," he muttered, holding her arm gently. Two other guards walked before them, their blazing torches held high to light the path leading to Lord Hakon's hall.

Chapter Twenty-three

Gwendolyn entered the dimly lit hall, still wrapped in Olav's hooded cloak. Her heart was pounding madly, and try as she would, she could not still her trembling. She could see a glowing light from the central fireplace within the main room, but she did not see any sign of Hakon. For a moment she stood as if rooted to the floor, overwhelmed by fear of what was to come.

Hakon's deep voice suddenly called out to her from across the hall. "Come forward into the light, Anora," he commanded.

Gwendolyn raised her chin defiantly, the fear chased from her mind by the burning hate that flared within her at the sound of his voice. Aye, she hated him . . . for bringing them to this cursed land, for condemning them to a life of slavery, and, most of all, for what he was about to do to her. And it was this hate that gave her the strength she needed. She squared her delicate shoulders and began to walk slowly into the main room.

Her eyes widened in astonishment as she noted the richness of the furnishings and the fine woven tapestries gracing the timbered walls. She had never seen such luxury before! Everywhere she looked were new and strange sights: delicately glazed pottery; blue-tinted vessels that one could see through; silver goblets and bowls of every size and shape; a bronze urn resting on the floor from which scented smoke was wafting. All this and much more attested to the great wealth the Viking had acquired as a merchant trader. Ansgar had told her Lord Hakon was as wealthy as he was powerful, but such richness was beyond belief!

Why, he even has fine furs upon the wooden floor! Gwendolyn marveled. She had never heard of such a thing. She stepped gingerly around a thick black fur placed in the middle of the hall.

"The furs are laid on the floor to walk upon." Hakon laughed easily, rising from an ornately carved chair set near the fireplace. "There is no need to step around them."

Gwendolyn looked up, a sudden blush warming her skin. She was no stranger to men's bodies, having grown up surrounded by her father's thanes, but she had never seen a man built so powerfully as Hakon. She wondered why she had never thought so before, but then she decided it was probably because she had never seen him so scantily clothed.

He had changed from his black riding garb into a sleeveless tunic, open down the front, that only too well revealed his muscled arms and the bronzed expanse of his chest. The tunic was tucked loosely into snug-fitting trousers that were molded to his tapered hips and sinewy thighs, while soft leather boots came just to his knees. He had no belt, but only a silken drawstring tied at his waist. His white-blond hair, brushed back from his wide forehead, tumbled about his neck in soft waves.

Her wide-eyed perusal pleased Hakon, for he smiled, his teeth a flash of white against the bronzed planes of his face.

He crossed the remaining distance between them in only two strides, and gathered her into his arms.

"Anora . . . my Anora," he said huskily, crushing her to him. Gwendolyn stiffened in his arms. He was so tall that he seemed to tower over her, her head barely coming to his shoulder. Suddenly he bent his head and lifted her chin to him, capturing her soft lips with his own.

Gwendolyn started in surprise, her breath caught in her throat. She had never been kissed by a man before. Hakon's lips were warm upon hers, even tender, and she found herself thinking the new sensation was not altogether unpleasant. Unconsciously she leaned toward him, closing her eyes, an odd stirring awakening deep within her.

Sensing her unexpected acquiescence, Hakon deepened his kiss, his tongue forcing open her lips as he sought to taste the hidden sweetness of her mouth. Gwendolyn's eyes flew open in shock at this new demand, reality once again flooding her mind. She tried to pull away from him but he held her fast, one strong arm encircling her waist, while his other hand caressed the small of her back and her slender hips. Suddenly she twisted her head to the side, tearing her lips from his. The hood of the cloak slipped from her head.

Hakon stared in disbelief for a moment, holding her away from him. "What have you done?" he asked finally, his voice low. His eyes glittered dangerously in the orange, glowing light of the fireplace.

Gwendolyn stepped back, frightened, and shakily held out her hand. The silver-blond tresses tumbled to the floor like finely spun gossamer and landed at his feet, a stark contrast to the black fur rug. Hakon looked from her to the floor, then bent down on one knee and picked up a silken tendril.

"Your beautiful hair . . . why?" he murmured softly after several minutes, deceiving Gwendolyn into thinking his rage was past.

"It matters naught," she replied simply, though her heart was pounding hard against her chest. " 'Tis done, my lord, and cannot be undone." Strangely, she found she could not say what she had planned—that she had denied him at least a part of her.

Hakon slowly rose to his feet, his blue eyes raking her with heated intensity. "Nay, little one, it matters a great deal to me," he whispered huskily. "You are mine, Anora, and have been since the moment I found you on my ship. Everything you are, and everything you possess, is of great importance to me." He took a step toward her. "I have long awaited those words you spoke earlier this night . . . too long. I should have taken you in the bathing house at Sumburgh Voe, but I had hoped one day you would come to me willingly. What a fool I have been! Even tonight I had thought your heart had softened toward me, but again I have been deceived!" He held out the shining lock of silver-blond hair. "By doing this, you have taken what belongs to me. Now, I shall take what is mine!"

Hakon swept Gwendolyn so suddenly into his arms that it seemed the room spun around her. Holding her tightly against his broad chest, he carried her from the main hall into a large adjoining room that was softly lit by small oil-burning lamps. She struggled wildly in his arms, her mind reeling from the force of his words. But before she could even begin to grasp fully their meaning, she found herself flung upon a wide, fur-laden bed. Desperately she tried to crawl to the far end, but he caught her by one leg and dragged her back.

Her emerald eyes met his, and it was then that she realized any further attempts to escape him would be useless. Hakon's eyes, burning with desire, seemed to devour her as he easily ripped her mantle and linen shift in two, exposing her slender beauty to his gaze. Gwendolyn tried frantically to gather the remnants of her clothing about her, but suddenly he was upon her. He caught her wrists over her head with one hand, while he pulled her body against his hard length with his other arm.

Gwendolyn closed her eyes tightly, awaiting the rape she knew she did not have the strength to fight. Her only thought was to resist in the one way she had left to her. Aye, she thought defiantly, the Viking could have his way with her, but she would be damned if she would respond to his hated touch. She suddenly went limp in his arms and turned her face away.

Hakon was not surprised when Gwendolyn ceased her struggles and lay still. A faint smile crossed his face as he gazed down upon her delicate features. By the blood of Odin, she was by far the loveliest woman he had ever held in his arms, he thought appreciatively. He had no intention of raping her, though he knew he had given her that impression from his rough treatment. His anger had cooled now that she was beside him, and in its place was a growing desire to savor every inch of her.

Hakon gently traced his finger along the determined line of her chin, trying to stifle a chuckle. He was well enough versed in the ways of women to know she had issued him a challenge he could not refuse. She might lie limply in his arms now, but he was sure that before the night was through she would want him as much as he wanted her . . . and cry out for his touch.

His eyes wandered down the delicate length of her, his hand pulling aside the torn clothing to reveal fully her form to his heated gaze. She was so fair, from the silver-blond curls that framed her face to the silky blond mound between her slender thighs. Her creamy skin, shining like alabaster in the soft glow of the oil lamps, was a sharp contrast to the burnished bronze of his own. Her breasts, though small, were high and perfectly rounded, the pale pink nipples taut from the cool air in the room.

Hakon drew in his breath sharply. The very sight of her made his blood hot, yet he knew he would have to take his time with her. He could tell Anora was no common wench to be bedded and then forgotten. Her dignity and proud bearing alone bespoke a high birth and genteel upbringing. She was like a fine, high-spirited filly that had not yet been broken. He had no doubt that she was yet a virgin. Her shock at his kiss had attested to that.

Nay, he would go slowly with her, not only because he longed to see passionate desire for him burning in her emerald eyes . . . and perhaps one day, something more . . . but because he wanted her to find pleasure in his arms. Too much rested on this one night for it to be otherwise. Perhaps she would not be so hesitant to share his bed in the days and nights to follow. He bent his head, his lips tracing a feather-light path down the long column of her throat, while his hand caressed the taut hollow of her belly.

Gwendolyn shivered suddenly. A strange sensation was building within her unlike anything she had ever felt before. She fought to lie still in Hakon's arms, but it was becoming impossible. It seemed his hands were everywhere at once, caressing, teasing . . . yet ever so gently. This was not the cruel assault she had expected. Nay, this was almost worse, a lingeringly slow torture that heated her skin wherever he touched her. His lips once again captured hers, seeming to draw the very breath from her body, demanding a response.

Hakon was rewarded as a soft moan broke from Gwendolyn's throat. He lifted his head to gaze down upon her. Thor, but she was beautiful! A triumphant smile played about his lips, but he knew it was yet too soon. She was still fighting him with her spirit, though her tantalizing body was beginning to betray her.

"Open your eyes, Anora, and look at me," Hakon whispered huskily, his breath warm against her ear. Shaken by his last kiss, Gwendolyn felt almost drugged as her eyes flickered open, but her resolve to resist him still burned within her mind. She gasped as he began to remove his clothing, but for some strange reason she could not tear her eyes away. He easily shrugged off his silken vest, fully baring his sculpted chest with its mat of golden curls to her view. He kicked the leather boots off his feet, then pulled the drawstring at his waist, loosening his trousers, and slid them from his long legs.

At the sight of his erect manhood Gwendolyn quickly looked away, a burning blush firing her cheeks. Hakon ignored the look of shock in her eyes and drew her to him again, cradling her in his strong arms. *So, she has never seen a man before*, he thought. Yea, it pleased him mightily that he would be the first. He reveled in the silken feel of her body against his muscled length, and once again he began his gentle assault.

His hands stroked the narrow indentation of her waist and the slender curve of her hips, while his lips gradually became more demanding, plundering her mouth. He then trailed a molten path of fiery kisses down one delicately boned shoulder to the crest of her breast, his tongue tentatively flicking the pale nipple. Cupping the perfect mound with his hand, he suckled hungrily.

Gwendolyn arched her back at this new sensation, her fingers unconsciously entwining in Hakon's blond hair. Sweet Jesu! How could she fight what he was doing to her! She could feel his strong fingers stroking the silken skin of her inner thigh ever so lightly. Then his hand strayed purposefully to the moist core of her, probing, searching.

"So beautiful . . ." Hakon murmured thickly, kissing her breasts, her throat, her love-bruised lips.

A ragged sigh tore from her as his expert fingers found the sensitive point he had been seeking. She arched against his hand, her body no longer in her control as wave after wave of heady sensation rippled through her, all resistance forgotten.

Exulting in her passionate abandon, Hakon was no longer able to contain his own burning desire. The sight of her writhing wantonly beneath him was more than he could withstand. He quickly shifted his weight until he was poised over her. Then he gently parted her legs with his knee. His throbbing shaft nudged the final barrier of her maidenhead at the heart of the satiny folds, rubbing against the pearl of her desire.

Gwendolyn cried out again as another wave of pleasure surged through her body, her slender hips moving instinctively against him as she reached out to pull him to her. At the height of her ecstasy Hakon brought his mouth down upon hers in a crushing kiss and plunged himself into her.

A sudden, tearing pain caught Gwendolyn by surprise. "Oh!" she gasped against his lips, her passion-dimmed eyes flying open.

"Now there will be no more pain, little one . . . only pleasure," Hakon whispered soothingly, moving ever so slowly within her.

It was true, she thought fleetingly. The pain passed quickly, and she was overwhelmed by a surging crescendo of heated passion building within her. All conscious thought fled her mind as she wrapped her arms about Hakon's muscled back, matching the thrusting movements of his body perfectly with her own. His stroke was gentle at first, but then it increased in intensity as he delved within her, deeper and deeper.

Her lips clung to his, drawing from them, breathing with him as one, as they soared together on a tidal wave of raging desire. Their bodies moved in a rhythm as old as time itself, merging, writhing, the hot tension mounting higher and higher until it broke over them both in an exploding shower of searing, throbbing delight.

Gwendolyn did not know how long they had been lying there, clasped tightly in each other's arms, when she finally opened her eyes. She felt dazed, yet strangely at peace. A numbing sense of contentment had settled over her, like nothing she had ever felt before. Hakon's tousled head was resting on her shoulder, and she unwittingly ran her tapered fingers through his thick, white-blond curls. His rumbling deep voice startled her and she stopped, suddenly aware of what she was doing.

"You have hidden your passion well from me, little one," he murmured huskily. "Until now." He raised his head from her shoulder and gazed down upon her with tenderness, his hand gently stroking the side of her face. His lips brushed lightly against hers, his breath warm upon her skin. "You have pleased me greatly this night, Anora."

A twinge of anger flared within Gwendolyn at his soft-spoken words, the sense of contentment fleeing from her mind as quickly as it had come. Aye, so her body had betrayed her, she thought with some chagrin. At least her defiant spirit still remained intact, if naught else! She tried to shift her weight from beneath him, but it was of no use. His powerful body seemed molded to her slender form.

Hakon groaned audibly at her movement, feeling himself grow hard deep within her. Thor, this woman fired his blood like no other! Suddenly he rolled over onto his back, carrying Gwendolyn with him. Her emerald eyes widened in astonishment as she found herself astride him now, her silky thighs hugging his tapered hips. He laughed deeply, a wicked glint of desire lighting his blue eyes.

"It seems I have not yet had enough of you, little one," he murmured thickly, his large hands grasping her narrow waist as he began to move slowly within her.

"Oh . . .!" Gwendolyn cried, trembling uncontrollably, her hands resting on his broad chest. Her fingers entwined themselves in the dense golden curls as a heated rush of pleasure surged through her body. Her eyes, half-closed with passion, followed the fine line of hair trailing down his taut abdomen to where they were joined as one. She blushed bright pink.

" 'Tis how man and woman were meant to be." Hakon

chuckled easily. Then he pulled her to him, his warm mouth nuzzling her high, firm breasts. Gwendolyn moaned as his tongue traced a moist circle of fire around one taut nipple, while his hand caressed and teased the silky smooth skin of the other. There was a fierceness to his movements this time, possessive, demanding, as he took her with a burning urgency he knew only she could fulfill.

Their melded bodies, bathed in a fine sheen of perspiration, were one in a wild dance of passion, swirling ever upward on a wave of rapture so intense that Gwendolyn thought she would surely die from the surging sensations. Hakon's lips captured hers at the very pinnacle of their release, stifling the cry that tore from her throat. For a moment it seemed as if time stood still, and there was nothing save the tumultuous ecstasy they both shared.

Sated at last, Hakon gently lifted her from him and cradled her in his arms as he rolled over onto his side. He kissed away the tears of passion that streaked her lovely face. Then, reaching behind him with one hand, he pulled a thick fur blanket over them both.

Too exhausted to offer any resistance, Gwendolyn lay her head against his chest. Lulled by the steady beating of his heart, she slipped into a dreamless sleep.

Hakon smiled, his eyes drinking in every delicate feature of her upturned face. He marveled at the dark length of her gold-tipped lashes, fluttering ever so slightly as she slept, and the rose-tinted translucence of her creamy skin. Gathering her closer to him, he was amazed at the strength of his feelings for her. He had never felt so drawn to any woman before, but in her he believed he had finally met his match.

"Before Odin I swear this woman is mine!" he whispered fiercely. "And woe to any who try to wrest her from me!" He lay his head back against the eiderdown pillow, but it was a long time before he slept.

Chapter Twenty-four

Gwendolyn snuggled deeper under the lush fur blanket covering the wide bed. It was so soft and warm . . . so much nicer than her straw pallet in the stable. Suddenly her eyes flew open, remembering where she was. Hakon! She blushed heatedly, vivid memories of the night before flooding back to her. Turning her head, she looked furtively over her shoulder expecting to find him lying by her side. But he was not there, and after a quick glance around the room she saw that she was alone. She felt an odd twinge of disappointment, then shook her head angrily. *What was coming over her?* she wondered, chiding herself. She sat up, her eyes darting curiously about the room.

The late-morning sun was pouring in through two narrow windows on the far wall, casting myriad patterns on the wooden floor. The room was a large one, and its furnishings clearly bespoke a masculine influence. Several massive, ornately carved chests rested against the walls, while a low table and sturdy leather-backed chair were placed near one of the windows. Four heavy posts, intricately carved with writhing serpents and grinning beasts, supported each corner of the wide bed, which took up nearly a quarter of the space alone.

The room had little decoration except for the many brightly polished weapons hanging from the timbered walls. There were long pointed spears with lavishly ornamented sockets, fierce, triple-edged broadaxes, and several iron swords, though none was as fine as the one she knew Hakon carried in a leather scabbard hanging at his belt. His sword had fascinated her from the moment she had seen it aboard his ship, with its hilt of contrasting precious metals and the hand guard carved from polished ivory. A conical, silver helmet with nose and eye guards was laid on a roughhewn bench near the bed, along with a thick chain of mail that glinted brightly in the sunlight.

So, this is what Ansgar meant when he said a Viking warrior was never far from his weapons! To think that Hakon kept such an arsenal in his private chamber. Why, no doubt he had left his sword within arm's reach last night while they . . .! She blushed again. She could still feel the heat of his caress upon her skin. Trembling suddenly, she quickly pulled the fur blanket up over her shoulders.

A pile of crumpled clothing that had been lying on top of the blanket tumbled off the side of the bed. Gwendolyn gasped as she recognized what little remained of her linen shift and mantle, noting well the jagged tears from collar to hem. *There will be no hope of mending these garments*, she thought wryly, even if she could sew! But what was she to clothe herself with now?

"Perhaps one of the chests might have something that would fit me," she muttered. It was worth a try. She stepped gingerly from the bed, her teeth chattering from the cold. Grabbing the ends of the fur blanket, she whisked it off the bed and wrapped it quickly about her shoulders.

Gwendolyn gasped at the blood-red stains that stood out

glaringly against the white of the linen sheet. She cursed under her breath, wondering if the Viking had yet seen the proof of her innocence . . . the innocence that he had so wantonly taken from her. She was about to pull the offending sheet from the bed when a soft knock was heard at the door. She turned around, her slender back straight and her head held proudly, though her eyes were wide with apprehension.

A jovial face peeked from around the corner of the door. "So, you are finally awake, lass," Berta said, clucking her tongue approvingly. She bustled into the room carrying a steaming tray of food and set it down on a beautifully carved table near the bed. Straightening up, she was about to say something about the young woman's shortened hair when another knock echoed through the room. "Yea, come on in with ye!" she called out. Two young servingwomen hurried in, one carrying an armload of what appeared to be fine silken clothing, while the other carried a small carved casket.

"Set them down over there. Then be off with ye," Berta commanded in a severe tone, pointing to the chair by the window. The women hastily complied, but not without first casting several envious glances in Gwendolyn's direction. Their eyes widened at the vivid bloodstains on the sheets. . . . So the favored wench had been a virgin after all! They giggled behind their hands as they fled the room.

"Don't mind them, lass." Berta shook her head, promising herself to deal with them later. " 'Tis only jealousy at your good fortune." She closed the door firmly behind them.

Gwendolyn had not moved since Berta and the two women had come into the room, but she had relaxed visibly. If it had been Hakon, she did not know what she would have done. She had heard much about the cook from Anora, and knew she had naught to fear from her. Anora had said she was a kindly woman, despite her gruff manner.

Berta ambled over to the bed and stood with her hands on

her waist. "If you're wondering where Lord Hakon has gone, lass, he left early this morn with Olav and some guards for his uncle's settlement across the valley." She shook her head in sympathy. " 'Tis a pity he had to leave you. From the looks of him I'd say he would rather have stayed!"

"He is not missed," Gwendolyn muttered, plopping down on the bed. She ran her fingers through her short curls, obviously annoyed.

Berta gaped in astonishment. She could not believe her ears! Here the wench had been bedded by a Viking chieftain—nay, *well* bedded from the looks of the sheets—and she had naught but cross words to say about him! She made a disapproving sound in her throat. Perhaps the wench was tired, she thought. Slave or not, Anora was obviously highborn. Perhaps her delicate nature had not taken kindly to Lord Hakon's lovemaking. Nay, Berta shook her head, she could hardly fathom that to be true! Well, whatever the reason, it was none of her affair. Lord Hakon had given her specific orders before he had left, and it was her job to see them through.

" 'Tis Lord Hakon's wish that you no longer work in the cooking house," she said, walking over to the window. She picked up one of the silken garments draped over the back of the chair: a delicate chemise in shimmering hues of gold-trimmed sapphire. "You are now the favored one, Anora, concubine to Hakon Jarl. 'Tis his command that you learn the workings of this household and serve as mistress over it. These clothes and jewels are for your pleasure alone, as befits the honored position you now hold."

Ignoring Gwendolyn's gasp of surprise, Berta opened the lid of the small casket and drew out a long beaded necklace. She held it up to the light, a smile spreading across her round face. The necklace was truly the finest she had ever seen, its richly colored glass beads alternating with small, gold filigree pendants that glittered brightly in the sun.

She turned to Gwendolyn, sobering, her eyes full of caution. "Now perhaps you will think no more of escape, eh? You have been blessed with good fortune, lass. There are many broken hearts in the settlement this day, many women who envy what fate has bestowed upon you. It is now for you to use it wisely." She returned the necklace to the casket, then hurried to the door. "But first you must bathe," she said over her shoulder.

At the clap of her hands, two male slaves carried in a large wooden tub and set it on the floor near the bed. Neither dared to look up from his task; both scurried quickly out of the room, only to return time after time with steaming buckets of water until the tub was filled.

Gwendolyn succumbed quietly to Berta's ministrations, her mind too preoccupied with what the older woman had said to offer any resistance. The water in the tub did feel wonderful; it was the first real bath she had enjoyed since the day of Anora's betrothal feast. She leaned her head against the rim and breathed in the fragrant steam.

Mistress of the household! Aye, those had been Berta's words, though she could hardly believe it. That Hakon could trust her enough to give her free rein within the settlement, even after the escape attempt of last night . . . nay, she could not believe it!

But a short while later, after she had been dressed in the most beautiful clothing she had ever seen and bedecked with fine jewelry, she was beginning to believe it was indeed true. The sapphire blue chemise, long and pleated with narrow, delicate sleeves, felt deliciously cool against her freshly scrubbed skin. A scarlet satin tunic went over the chemise, the embroidered shoulder straps held up by a pair of oval, gold filigree brooches, while a belt of finely twisted strips of gold and silver encircled her narrow waist. She was given a pair of soft leather shoes, fur-lined for warmth, and at the last, Berta carried into the room the most luxurious gray fur cloak Gwendolyn had ever seen.

"The air grows colder with each passing day," Berta said

simply, wrapping the cloak about Gwendolyn's fine-boned shoulders. "You will need this." She gathered the two ends of the cloak together and bound them with a richly ornamented gold brooch inlaid with precious stones. Standing back, she rested her hands on her wide hips and surveyed her handiwork.

Yea, the lass was truly a beauty, she thought appreciatively, despite the loss of her long hair. Her short silver-blond locks had dried into soft, gleaming curls that delicately framed her fair features. Berta still did not know why the lass had cut her hair, but she surmised it had been meant as another way to defy Lord Hakon. Well, it was none of her affair, she reminded herself. She whisked her own cloak about her huge form, then started toward the door. Suddenly she stopped in her tracks and threw her hands up in the air.

"Ah, we have forgotten your meal," she said. "No doubt 'tis cold by now."

"It matters naught," Gwendolyn replied. "I am not hungry this morn." Truly she was not. Her mind was racing with the opportunities that had now presented themselves to her, and she longed to see Anora. Her head was filled with plans, and she was too excited to eat.

"Come, then, lass. There is much to be done before Lord Hakon returns," Berta said. "We shall first visit the brewing house."

"Nay, Berta," Gwendolyn disagreed firmly. "I wish to visit my brother first, in the stable."

Berta drew herself up, a disgruntled look upon her face. But the glint of determination in Gwendolyn's eyes squelched any protest she would offer. *Yea, Lord Hakon will have his hands full with this one*, she thought indignantly. "Very well, lass, but mind you do not linger overlong. Lord Hakon expects you to be well taught by the time he returns!"

Gwendolyn nodded, then swept hurriedly out of the

room, her fine cloak flowing out behind her. She did not bother to wait for Berta, knowing the portly cook would catch up to her at the stable. Besides, what she had to say to Anora was for her sister's ears alone. She quickly made her way through the hall, not even glancing at the treasures that had so intrigued her the night before, and pushed open the great wooden door leading outside. She blinked from the bright sunlight and gathered the cloak about her. Berta was right, the air had grown much colder. She walked quickly along the path to the stable, unaware that she was being closely followed by a Viking guard.

Gwendolyn spied Anora near the door of the stable, struggling to lift a bale of hay. Her back was turned, so Gwendolyn was able to walk up quietly behind her. " 'Twould help if you bent your knees a bit, Garric," she murmured softly.

Anora wheeled around, her eyes wide with surprise. "Gw——Anora!" she exclaimed, though not too loudly, noting the guard who stood watching them several paces away. She took her sister's arm and led her quickly into the stable. They embraced each other tightly for several moments. Then Anora drew away to look searchingly at her sister's face. "Are you well?" she asked, though she felt somehow ill at ease. Her question, though heartfelt, seemed hardly appropriate.

Gwendolyn caught the fleeting look of embarrassment in Anora's eyes. "There can be no regrets, Anora, not now, not ever," she replied simply. " 'Tis done."

Anora looked away, sudden tears rushing to her eyes, but she did not allow herself to cry. Swallowing hard, she pulled Gwendolyn down beside her on the bench by the door. "Lord Hakon came here early this morn, but he did not disturb me. I heard him walking toward the stable, and I pulled the blanket up over my head. He was whistling, Gwendolyn—a strange, lilting tune!"

Gwendolyn blushed at these words, but quickly looked

down in her lap so Anora would not see it. *Aye, so the man whistled. That matters naught to me*, she thought angrily. Perhaps his morning meal had pleased him!

Not noticing her sister's discomfort, Anora rushed on. "He stood by the pallet for several moments, looking at me. Then he went and saddled his own horse. All the while he was whistling away, as if he did not mind in the least that I had not jumped up to help him." She sighed heavily. "I have never said so many prayers before in my life! If he had asked me to saddle his stallion—"

"You will have to learn, Anora," Gwendolyn interrupted. "If our guise is to succeed, you must know how to care for his stallion." She clasped her sister's hand reassuringly, feeling perhaps she had been a bit too abrupt with her. " 'Tis not hard, I promise. I will teach you later today. Just think of how surprised Wulfgar will be when you one day saddle his great stallion!" They both giggled at the thought, then fell silent, their hands clapped over their mouths as Berta called to them from just outside the door.

"Come out with ye, lass, before I die of frostbite!" she shouted through chattering teeth. She was breathing in great gasps of the frigid air, cursing all the while the steepness of the path leading to the stable. "What are you laughing at?" she snapped at the Viking guard, who was fighting to keep a grin off his bearded face. He shook his head and looked away, chuckling to himself.

Gwendolyn and Anora could barely suppress their laughter. The thought of Berta, as well padded as she was, suffering overmuch from the cold was truly impossible!

"I must go, Anora, but I will try to return as soon as I can," Gwendolyn murmured at last, rising to her feet. But Anora caught her arm.

"Is it true what they have been saying, Ansgar and the others, that you are to be the mistress of the household?" she asked. She had taken her morning meal in the slave's cooking house; the talk had been of nothing else.

"Aye, 'tis true. You can see how richly Lord Hakon rewards those who please him," she replied bitterly, fingering the beaded necklace around her throat. The sudden pain in her sister's eyes caused her to regret her words, and she sought to reassure her. "Please, Anora, do not fear for me. Hakon is a hard man . . . you and I have both felt his anger. But he is not cruel." Gwendolyn suddenly recalled the tenderness she had seen in his eyes the night before, and the gentleness of his touch, but she angrily dismissed the thought. Nay, he was their enemy above all else . . . a cursed Viking!

She walked quickly to the door, then turned and looked back at Anora, a fierce light in her emerald eyes. "I will learn much as mistress of this settlement, Anora. And the more I know of the Viking and his ways, the better I can plan our escape." A faint smile crossed her lips. "Until later, then, Garric." As soon as she stepped through the door, Berta hastened to her side.

"I'm half frozen, lass! What kept you so long?" Berta asked, hugging her cloak tightly about her wide bulk. She did not wait for an answer, but grabbed Gwendolyn by the arm. "Come on with ye, now! There is much to be done!"

The rest of the day passed in a dizzying whirl. Gwendolyn was led first to the brewing house, where male slaves were busy making the strong mead and ale so favored by the Vikings. The heavy fragrance of barley spiced with aromatic herbs hung in the air, making it difficult to breathe, but Berta refused to leave until she had sampled a hearty mug of the brew.

" 'Tis nectar of the gods." She smacked her lips, after a long draft of the foaming mead. "Here, have a try," she offered kindly. But Gwendolyn shook her head. She wanted to keep her wits about her this day.

Next was the weaving house, where Gwendolyn was informed she would be spending much of her time. This news irked her greatly. She had never been one for the womanly arts of weaving and needlework, and had balked whenever her mother had subtly suggested she learn to use the loom. She decided then and there that she would try to avoid the weaving house as much as possible.

Berta did not bother to show Gwendolyn the cooking house, for she thought she was familiar enough with it already. She did show her the large building where they kept the dried and smoked meat, salted fish, and the large vats of curdled milk that had been salted, soured, and stored to last through the long winter. Dried berries, apples, and nuts were also stored in abundance, as well as great quantities of onions, leeks, and field peas.

Gwendolyn felt her stomach rumble as she looked at all the stored food, reminding herself that she had not yet eaten. It was way past midday, and the sky had already begun to darken. Suddenly she was feeling strangely tired. She tried, unsuccessfully, to stifle a yawn.

"Come, lass, let us return to Lord Hakon's hall," Berta said kindly, noting the paleness of Gwendolyn's cheeks. There was so much to learn yet, but perhaps she had been pushing her young mistress too hard. It would not do for Lord Hakon to return to find Anora completely exhausted from her new duties.

Gwendolyn nodded her head. It had indeed been a long day. As they walked together to the hall, Berta chattered on and on about the myriad duties that accompanied managing a chieftain's household, especially one as large as this. She did not stop talking until they had reached the door of Hakon's chamber.

"Go on in with ye, lass," Berta said, pushing open the carved door, "whilst I see to your meal." She turned and bustled off.

Gwendolyn sighed in relief. She knew Berta meant well, but her ceaseless chatter had given her a throbbing headache. Rubbing her temples, she walked over to the wide bed and sat down. Everything was happening so fast. One minute she was a slave. Then after one night of passion she had become not only Hakon's concubine, but the mistress of his household! Her forehead crinkled in thought. He had no reason to trust her. She had given him last night only what he had taken, and no more. Perhaps he was testing her, but for what purpose she could not imagine. Could it be that he felt more for her than lust . . . perhaps something even closer to affection?

Nay, it was not possible. Gwendolyn shook her head fiercely. From what she had heard of the Vikings—the gruesome tales of their bloodthirsty brutality, their single-minded devotion to valor and heroic deeds, their cold hearts thought to be as hard as the steel of the swords they wielded—nay, Hakon could not possibly be capable of anything more than lust.

She sighed raggedly. Why was she being tormented by such thoughts? She cared naught if the Viking had any affection for her! Glancing furtively behind her at the sheets on the bed, she was relieved to see that the stained ones were gone, replaced by fresh linen. She lay down, pulling her fur cloak about her, and closed her eyes.

Berta entered the room a short while later, only to find Gwendolyn fast asleep. *Ah, well, 'tis probably best*, she thought. *At least the lass will be well rested for the morrow.* She set the tray of food on the table near the bed, then lit the bronze brazier in the corner to lend some warmth to the room. With a last backward glance over her shoulder, she shut the door quietly behind her.

Chapter Twenty-five

It was almost dusk several days later when Hakon and his men finally returned to the settlement. The flashing hooves of their horses thundered upon the hard, snow-covered ground as they rode into the stable yard.

"Garric!" Hakon shouted. He threw his long leg over the side of his saddle and dismounted. "Garric!"

Starting at the sound of his voice, Anora dropped the chunk of bread she had been eating, the last remnant of her evening meal. Several stray chickens immediately set upon it, but she had no time to kick them away. She quickly pulled a woolen cap over her head, her fingers shaking nervously, and hastened out the door of the stable. She almost could not swallow the bite she still had in her mouth, her throat was so constricted in fear.

"Ah, there you are, lad," Hakon said good-naturedly. He handed her the reins to his stallion, his eyes flicking over her. Garric seemed strangely ill at ease this day, almost cowering in his presence. He shrugged. Perhaps the lad was still suffering from the lash, he thought, though he surmised it was probably more a case of hurt pride than anything else. "See that he is rubbed down well, and given an extra measure of oats," he stated. Then he turned on his heel and began to walk down the hill.

"Aye, my lord," Anora murmured softly, barely loud enough for him to hear.

Startled, Hakon stopped in his tracks and wheeled around. "What? No retorts for me this day, Garric?"

But Anora seemed not to hear him as she led the spirited stallion into the stable. Her mind was on the instructions Gwendolyn had given her. She guided the horse into its stall, then gently patted the velvety softness of its nose. The horse snorted loudly, then crunched contentedly on the dried apples she pulled from her pocket and held out to him. This might not be so bad after all, she thought, relieved.

Hakon shrugged again. As he walked hurriedly down the path to his hall, he chuckled to himself. Perhaps Garric's defiant spirit has been tamed at last, though Hakon was not ready by any means to let down his guard just yet. The lad might still be plotting a rebellion against him.

"Lord Hakon!" Berta cried out, her short legs carrying her up the hill from the cooking house. She met him at the entrance to his hall, her great breasts heaving with exertion beneath her woolen shawl. "Welcome . . . back, my lord." She panted, trying to catch her breath. A pleased grin lit her broad face.

"Thank you, Berta," Hakon replied warmly. "I fear the council meeting kept me longer at my uncle's than I had intended. Has all gone smoothly during my absence?"

"Oh, yea, my lord!" she answered happily. "Anora has taken very well to her new duties, though at first I must say she seemed a bit surprised at her good fortune. Already she has been seeing to the preparations for the Yuletide feast—with my help, of course."

Hakon smiled. "I appreciate your efforts, Berta. But now, my only wish is for a hot bath. We can talk of these things later."

"Very well, my lord. Shall I summon her to you?"

"She is not in my hall?" he asked, stepping away from the door. "I had thought I would find her there, taking her evening meal."

"Nay, she is still in the weaving house, my lord. She has not taken kindly to the loom, though I have insisted that she spend some time there each day." Berta frowned, shaking her head. Indeed, it had been a struggle to get the wench to pick up a needle. "I have never seen the like before, my lord. The lass is obviously well bred, but she doesn't even know the difference between warp and filling threads!" she exclaimed with obvious exasperation.

Hakon threw back his head and laughed, a hearty, rich sound. "Do not fret, Berta. Give her some time, she will learn." He was striding up the hill before she had a chance to reply. "See that a bath is prepared in the bathing house," he called out over his broad shoulder, "and that there is a vessel of wine placed near the tub with two goblets!"

Berta nodded, then smiled as he walked away. Ah, would that she were a young wench again, when her blood ran hot and she had her pick of lusty, young Viking warriors! She sighed wistfully, then hurried away to do his bidding.

Hakon's heart was pounding in his chest as he reached the weaving house and slowly pushed open the door. Thor, he felt more like a green youth than a man full-grown! During the days at his uncle's settlement he had been busy enough so that he was not tormented by thoughts of Anora, but during the nights . . . yea, that had been different. She had come to him in his dreams when he had finally been able to sleep, taunting him with her slender, curved body, always almost in his grasp, but then suddenly disappearing like a wisp of smoke.

He stepped inside the door, his eyes searching for her. Many women were still working busily at their looms, both slaves and wives of his men alike, their happy chatter echoing about the large room. But they fell silent when they saw Hakon standing at the threshold—all save for one.

"God's blood!" Gwendolyn cried out, her finger catching on a sharp hook holding the threads to the loom. She brought her pierced finger to her mouth, her eyes suddenly meeting Hakon's as he gazed heatedly at her from across the room. She gasped in surprise.

Hakon strode quickly to her side and took her hand in his. He raised the injured finger to his lips and kissed it gently. "Come with me," he murmured, his voice low.

Gwendolyn shivered, the touch of his hand sending strange tremors of excitement through her body that, try as she might, she could not suppress. She rose to her feet and followed closely behind him. The envious stares of some of the women were burning into her, but for some odd reason she did not seem to care.

"Where is your cloak?" he asked softly. She pointed to where it hung near the door. He pulled it off the hook and wrapped it about her shoulders, then held her against his side as they walked from the weaving house. Once outside the door, Hakon gathered her into his arms and crushed her to him. He seized her lips with his own, trying to slake the desperate, aching thirst for her that had built up inside him.

Gwendolyn had rehearsed this moment so many times in her mind over the past few days—how, when he returned, she would meet his gaze with defiance, how she would hold herself rigidly in his arms, angering him by her lack of response to his kiss—but now that he was there, holding her against his powerful body, the male scent of him enveloping her senses, she felt her firm resolve to defy him melt within her. With his lips, warm and possessive, upon hers, she no longer understood her feelings. Everything was jumbled in her mind. It was as if her will was no longer her own.

Releasing her at last, Hakon held her hand while he led her along the path to the bathing house. He ignored all the curious glances cast their way by his men, though he returned Olav's grin from across the way where he was talking with Berta.

Gwendolyn blushed when she realized where Hakon was taking her. What could he be thinking? Did he perhaps want her to bathe him? Surprisingly, the thought gave her an undeniable rush of pleasure.

As Hakon opened the door, warm steam rushed out of the small stone building, melding with the brisk air in dense clouds of white vapor. Once inside, he shut the door firmly behind them and bolted it. "So we will not be disturbed," he murmured, drawing her into the small anteroom, where there were two benches lining the walls. Without hesitation he began to strip off his clothing.

Gwendolyn's first instinct was to look away, but she could not, her eyes widening as his muscular form was revealed to her. She drank in the sight of his powerful body, slender where it should be slender, and broad where it should be broad, from his head to his feet a perfectly beautiful man. Shocked by her bold thoughts, she closed her eyes, trying to regain a shred of her resolve to hate him. Suddenly she heard a loud splash.

Her emerald eyes flew open. Hakon had stepped into the huge tub in the center of the room and had sat down, the steaming water rising to the middle of his bronzed chest. He reached over the rim to a small table set nearby and poured a red, clear liquid from a pottery vessel into two silver goblets. He brought one of the goblets to his lips and took a long draft, though his eyes never left hers.

"Shall you disrobe, my lady, or will I have the honor?" he asked, smiling rakishly. Gwendolyn looked at him incredulously, hesitating a moment too long. In a flash Hakon set down his goblet and was out of the tub, his bronzed body glistening with tiny droplets of water. He whirled the fur cloak from her shoulders and tossed it onto one of the benches, then picked her up in his arms and carried her over to the tub. He stepped over the rim, then slid into the steaming water with her, a wicked gleam in his eye.

"B-but the clothes . . . they are silk, my lord!" Gwendolyn blurted, the soaked garments molding to her body like a second skin.

" 'Tis no matter, little one," he replied huskily, his blue eyes raking the curved outline of her breasts, her raised nipples tantalizingly taut against the wet fabric. "I have bolts of silk enough in my storerooms to make you a thousand more just like them." He pulled her to him, holding her tightly against his broad chest. His lips, warm and sensuous, kissed her eyelids, her white throat, her lush mouth.

Gwendolyn could taste the wine on his lips, sweet and fragrant. Hakon suddenly drew away from her, reaching for one of the silver goblets. " 'Tis Frankish wine from my last trading voyage," he said, offering it to her. She took the goblet from him and drank deeply, savoring the heady liquid. She had never tasted anything so wonderful. She licked her lips, reddened from the wine, then drained the goblet. A delicious sensation of warmth coursed through her body, easing whatever tensions she still possessed.

Hakon took the goblet from her and set it on the table. He then unfastened the brooches holding up the straps of her tunic and dropped them over the side of the tub to the wooden floor. His hands roamed over her at will, stroking, caressing, as he eased the wet fabric from her body, until only her thin chemise remained.

Gwendolyn sighed with pleasure. Everything felt so delightfully warm to her—the steaming bath, the red wine coursing through her blood, Hakon's breath against her throat. She moaned softly as he nibbled at a tender earlobe, sending piercing shivers of passion through her body, while his strong fingers teased between the softness of her thighs.

Suddenly he lifted her and drew the clinging garment up above her hips, then set her down ever so slowly upon his lap.

Gwendolyn's eyes widened in surprise as she felt Hakon enter her, impaling her, yet ever so gently, on his erect shaft. But he did not begin to move within her. Instead, he drew the wet silk of the chemise over her head, his warm mouth capturing a rose-tipped breast as her arms were stretched high above her. He lingered there, suckling, nipping her playfully until she moaned in ecstasy. At last he freed her arms and flung the garment aside.

Hakon moved slightly away from the side of the tub, wrapping Gwendolyn's slender legs about his waist, his large hands grasping her hips. He nuzzled her firm breasts, but he remained still within her. His patience was soon rewarded as she began to move instinctively against him, slowly at first, but then faster and faster.

Gwendolyn felt as if she were on fire. An intense need was burning within her, surging, all-consuming, driving her onward to completion. Hakon's lips captured hers, and she met him passionately, measure for measure, with a raging abandon that both awed and delighted him. He could no longer remain still within her, as she demanded from him everything he had to give.

Matching her movements with his own, they strove together to that highest point, until at the moment of her greatest pleasure Gwendolyn arched her back and cried out, her nails raking his broad, muscled back. Hakon pulled her to him as he shuddered deep within her, his loins surging powerfully from the blazing heat of their passion.

They held each other for a long while, the small room quiet but for the sound of their breathing and the lapping of the water against the sides of the wooden tub. Hakon leaned back, his hand caressing Gwendolyn's damp curls as she lay with her head resting on his wide shoulder. "We have yet to bathe, my lady," he teased softly, relishing the thought of the lovemaking that would carry them through the night.

Aye, Gwendolyn smiled faintly, they had yet to bathe.

Chapter Twenty-six

Under Berta's watchful eye, Gwendolyn straightened the linen tablecloth on the wide table set before the high seat.

"Nay, lass, 'tis done like so," Berta said patiently, running her hand over the cloth until it lay perfectly flat against the surface of the table. "There, now," she muttered, a pleased look on her face. She looked up just as Gwendolyn plopped herself on one of the ornately carved chairs next to the high seat, her slim arms hanging limply over the sides.

"I am exhausted, Berta," she murmured, closing her eyes. Truly, she didn't think she had ever felt more tired. She had been up since the first light of dawn, assisting with the final preparations for the Yuletide feast that would be held in the great hall that evening.

Berta nodded her head in agreement. Yea, the lass had done more than her fair share during these last two weeks to help prepare for the celebration of the winter solstice. And, she chuckled, one also had to take into account the pleasurable demands placed upon her by Hakon Jarl!

"Very well, Anora," she said kindly, for truly she had grown quite fond of the lass. She may have caused her a bit of trouble at the start, Berta thought, but she had more than made up for that in her eagerness to learn everything she could about running the household. "Rest here for a moment, whilst I have a bath sent over to Lord Hakon's hall for you."

"My thanks, Berta," Gwendolyn replied, opening her eyes as the older woman bustled away. She looked about the great hall. Aye, everything was in order, she thought, noting the beautifully embroidered linen cloths that graced the tables, the thin wafer-like wheat breads set at every place that would serve as plates, and the sacred banqueting table in the very center of the hall, upon which sat an enormous caldron that would be filled later with foaming mead. Why, there was even a special table prepared for the dead. Berta had told her that on this night Hakon's ancestors would be honored, their great deeds recited and sung in poetic verse by the skalds.

She had learned that to the Vikings, the Yuletide feast of midwinter was one of the most important celebrations of the year. There would be many invited guests at the settlement this night, some traveling from quite a distance. As Jarl of the region, Hakon was expected to present an elaborate table for his guests, as testimony to his great wealth and power. No doubt at this very moment he was probably overseeing the slaughter of the Yule boar, the traditional meal for such an occasion, which would then be roasted to perfection in a large outdoor pit near the cooking house.

Gwendolyn sighed shakily. Why was it that whenever she thought of Hakon she felt a strange stirring sensation deep within her? This feeling constantly plagued her, tearing at her defenses, giving her no peace during those times when she was away from him. And then when she was with him, his strong arms wrapped about her, it was almost like a sharp, physical pain, a longing so intense that it would overwhelm her completely.

She shook her head fiercely, trying to dispel the image of him from her mind, but she could not. In utter frustration she pounded the wooden arm of the chair with her fist, but that did little more than to hurt her hand. Damn the Viking and his hold over her! she cursed vehemently under her breath. These feelings disturbed her greatly, for they were at cross purposes with her sworn intent to hate him . . . and to one day escape from him. Yet now it seemed that not only her body, but her heart as well, was beginning to betray her. Though she tried to deny it to herself, and to fight against it, she knew that her hate was melting away in the searing heat of the passion they shared.

Gwendolyn could hardly believe that this change in her feelings had come about in the two short weeks since Hakon had returned from his uncle's settlement. The time had passed so quickly.

During the days she had been busy with Berta, learning the many responsibilities of overseeing Hakon's household. She had also managed to visit Anora often in the stable, but that was becoming increasingly more difficult. She knew she was still being watched, followed everywhere she went by a stern-faced Viking guard. She feared her frequent visits were drawing too much attention to them, perhaps threatening their guise, so she had not been to the stable in several days.

But another reason had kept her away from the stable. She also feared that Anora might perceive the change in her feelings for Hakon and despair of their plans for escape. That fear alone had served to strengthen her resolve to fight the changing tide of her feelings, aye, that and the vivid memory of the vow she had made to Anora the day of their capture.

But it was during the nights—those long, northern nights

—that she felt the most threatened by her emotions. Hakon's lovemaking drew from her a wild, passionate abandon she had not known she possessed, leaving her shaken from its intensity. Then afterward, cradling her in his arms, he would tell her stories of his youth, and strange, exciting tales of his travels as a Viking merchant to mysterious, distant lands, until she was lulled to sleep by the rich tones of his deep voice and his gentle caresses. That he would share such personal knowledge with her had taken her by surprise, leading her to wonder about the depths of his own feelings for her.

It was this awakening curiosity about Hakon's emotions that frightened her the most. Nay, she did not want to know! His words might steal away the last shreds of resistance she needed to make good her vow to Anora!

"Your bath should be ready shortly, lass," Berta said, gently shaking Gwendolyn's shoulder. " 'Twill be waiting for you in Lord Hakon's chamber."

"Nay!" Gwendolyn's cry echoed through the large, silent hall, startling both herself and Berta, who stepped back in fright. Her thoughts had so overwhelmed her that she was breathless, her heart beating rapidly against her chest. She shook her head, dazed. Looking up, she finally noticed the older woman standing beside her, staring at her with widened eyes, her hand to her throat.

"I . . . I am sorry, Berta. Did you say something?" she asked, rubbing her aching temples.

" 'Tis only your bath, Anora, not a trial by fire!" Berta replied, clearly shaken. "What mischief of Loki is this, lass?" She put her hand on Gwendolyn's flushed cheek. "Are you not feeling well?" Thor, it would be all she needed this day, for Anora to take sick!

Gwendolyn smiled faintly, rising to her feet. "I am fine, Berta, though I think the bath and a short rest would serve me well right now." She declined Berta's proffered arm with a nod, then walked quickly from the hall.

Berta watched her until she disappeared through the massive entrance doors. Yea, she would mention this to Lord Hakon, as soon as she saw him, she decided firmly. She turned back to her work, her round face etched with concern.

Indeed, a few hours later Gwendolyn felt much more like herself. She was almost finished dressing after her bath and a rest when Hakon entered the room. Her fingers shook nervously at the sight of him, but somehow she managed to close the gold clasp on the brooch at her shoulder.

Hakon stood staring at her for a moment, his eyes taking in every detail of her appearance. Thor, but she was a vision! She was wearing a chemise of dove gray silk that clung to her slender curves, while over it an emerald tunic shimmered in the light of the lamps, its silken hues matching perfectly the color of her eyes. He dismissed the servingwoman with a nod, but did not speak until she had scurried out the door.

"I had hoped to find you still at your bath," he murmured softly, "but I see I shall have to wait 'til another day for that pleasure." He walked up to her and drew her into his arms, but she turned her head away from him. "Is aught amiss, little one?" he asked, drawing her back to face him. He did not say that Berta had spoken with him right before he had returned to his hall, telling him of her concern. He wondered what could have upset her so.

"Nay, my lord, all is as it should be," Gwendolyn replied steadily, despite the rapid beating of her heart. She avoided his gaze, though she could feel his eyes burning into her, searching. She pulled away from his arms and went to stand by the window. She was determined to fight the feelings stirring within her. She would not give in to them this time!

Hakon's heavy brows knitted in thought, his eyes clouding with frustration. Thor, one minute she was warm and willing, and the next . . .! He shook his head, perplexed. Then a slow smile spread over his face. Walking over to one of the massive chests, he lifted the heavy lid and drew out a small bundle wrapped in silk cloth. He unwrapped it carefully, holding up a delicate necklace made of interwoven strands of silver and gold that was studded with glittering emerald stones. Yea, perhaps this would bring the light back to her eyes, he thought hopefully.

He walked over to where she stood with her back to him and gently drew the necklace about the alabaster column of her throat. Closing the delicate clasp, he bent and tenderly kissed the nape of her neck. " 'Tis from Byzantium, Anora," he murmured, his lips brushing against the softness of her cheek. "I had it made for that one day when I would find a woman who could equal its fire. I see now that you far surpass it with your beauty."

Suddenly Gwendolyn wheeled around to face him, anger flaring from her eyes. "If you think that your rich gifts will buy my affection, you are sadly mistaken, my lord!" she railed at him. She felt a twinge of remorse at the pain and confusion she saw reflected in his eyes, but she hardened her heart. Biting words were the only defense she had left against the feelings within her that even now threatened to overwhelm her resolve. She brushed by him, but before she had gone three steps he grabbed her by the waist. With one easy movement she was in his arms, his mouth crushing cruelly down upon hers.

She tried to break free of him, but her struggling was to no avail. His lips ravaged hers, his arms like tight bands of steel around her. Suddenly he tore his mouth from hers and looked down at her. His blue eyes were darkened with rage. "If I choose to give you gifts, you will wear them, and gladly," he said gratingly. His voice was low, implacable. "Remember this above aught else, Anora. You are mine. I will have you . . . with or without your affection."

With that he pulled her toward the door. "We are expected in the great hall. You have a choice, Anora. Either walk by my side, or I shall carry you in my arms. I am sure the assembled guests would find that most amusing."

Gwendolyn's thick lashes glistened with unshed tears, though she did her best to fight them back. At that moment, she knew she was lost. It seemed there was no defeating him. And from this last exchange, she was no longer sure she wanted to. "I shall walk, my lord," she stated evenly, belying the storm of emotions that raged within her. She held her head proudly as he wrapped her fur cloak about her delicate shoulders, then took his proffered arm.

Chapter Twenty-seven

Hakon did not speak to her again until they reached the massive wooden doors at the entrance to the great hall, though Gwendolyn could tell he was no longer angry by the gentle pressure of his hand on her arm. He turned to face her beneath the gabled entrance and drew her to him. " 'Tis a festive night, Anora, and meant to be enjoyed," he murmured in her ear, loud enough so only she could hear his words. "Let us do so, and forget what passed between us in my chamber." His lips brushed lightly against her own. Then he nodded to one of the Viking guards, who pushed open the heavy doors.

Warmed by his words, Gwendolyn felt her spirits rise as they stepped into the hall. Aye, she could forget . . . *for now*, she thought, her eyes widening at the merry scene that greeted them.

The long main room was ablaze with light. At least a hundred torches burned brightly from polished wall sconces, casting everything in a golden glow. Green pine

boughs were festooned around the thick, carved pillars
their fresh, spicy fragrance melding with the mouthwaterin
aromas of roasted meat turning on the spits above the cen
tral fireplaces.

The Vikings' love of fine clothes and elaborate jewelr
was much in evidence this night, as warriors and their wive
milled about dressed in their very best. Servants carryin
brimming vessels of foaming mead moved among the crow
of guests, hurrying to fill and refill the goblets so quickl
emptied. The merry conversation and uproarious bursts o
laughter seemed to echo from every corner of the hall, punc
tuated every so often by a wild Viking cry to Odin.

A great roar of greeting went up as Hakon and Gwen
dolyn stepped from the dark entranceway into the mai
room. The crowd of guests moved aside quickly, making
path for them. Gwendolyn tried to ignore the appraising
curious glances cast her way as they walked together to th
high seat, but she could not help but overhear several loudl
whispered comments.

"Is that the foreign wench? Thor, I have never before see
such beauty! 'Tis as if she was fashioned by the hands o
Odin himself to tempt us all!"

"Yea, her eyes alone could bewitch the strongest man . .
and from the looks of it, she already has!"

" 'Tis a pity she is but a slave. . . ."

Gwendolyn blushed heatedly at this last remark. Ob
viously her position as their chieftain's concubine seemed t
be common knowledge, and most likely the favored topic o
conversation. She was surprised when Hakon squeezed he
arm reassuringly. So, he had heard them, too. With he
slender back straight and her head held high, she took he
place in the carved chair to the left of the high seat.

Hakon stood before the crowd, looking truly magnificen
in his dark blue tunic embroidered with gold-braided edg
ing, and his matching cloak trimmed in fine fur. "I bid yo
welcome!" he shouted warmly, gesturing for everyone to b

seated. Ordinarily men and women took their meals apart. But on this festive night they sat together, the women occupying the inner end of the hall, while the men were seated at the outer end, toward the main entrance. Benches creaked as all took their places. Then the hall fell silent.

Hakon picked up the ceremonial silver drinking horn set before him, then strode over to the sacred banquet table in the middle of the room. With one motion he dipped the horn into the huge caldron filled with mead, then held it up high, the amber liquid spilling out over the rim and onto the rush-strewn floor. Though his expression was solemn, his eyes sparkled with laughter. "I salute you all, in the name of Odin!" he stated loudly. Bringing the horn to his lips, he drained it with one draft, then wiped his hand across his mouth. A great smile lit his handsome face. "Drink and be merry, for 'tis Yule!"

The guests roared their approval, pounding their fists, spoons, goblets, and whatever else was handy upon the tables. As Hakon returned to the high seat, servants rushed in with steaming bowls of water and towels, so that everyone could wash their hands before the meal.

Gwendolyn furtively glanced up at Hakon as he took his seat, but then hastily looked down again, blushing. She had not missed the desirous intensity burning in his eyes. She busied herself with washing her hands, then took a hasty sip from her goblet, hoping the frothy mead would cool the warming sensation his gaze had fanned within her.

Suddenly a chorus of loud screams soared above the din of the crowd, seeming to come from the entrance of the hall. Startled, Gwendolyn gasped as the great doors swung open. A large group of men, masked as horses and rams and wearing furred clothing, rushed into the room, banging their spears upon their wooden shields. Yelling fiercely, they ran among the tables of delighted guests, stopping every so often to drink from an offered cup of mead.

Berta had not told her about this, Gwendolyn thought

fleetingly, as a tall, broad-shouldered man, larger than the others and masked fearsomely as a grinning ram, broke away from the screaming hoard and approached their table. He did not go near Hakon, but came directly to her. She could see his eyes, hard and glittering, through holes in the mask, and the fringes of a thick red beard flowing from beneath it.

Her breath caught in her throat as he took the silver goblet from her hand and lifted the mask only high enough to drain its contents, though never uncovering his face. "Good Yule, my lady," he murmured, his voice low and menacing as he set the empty goblet on the table. Gwendolyn felt a cold, inexplicable chill course through her body, though she could not understand why. Then, in a flash he was gone, melding into the crowd of masked revelers that was converging upon the sacred banquet table.

Seeing the frightened look on her face, Hakon leaned toward her. His warm hand took hers. "There is nothing to fear, Anora," he said soothingly. " 'Tis good fortune to share your cup with the masked ones."

But Gwendolyn was not reassured. Her eyes searched for the tall man among the writhing figures, but he was no longer there. It was as if he had disappeared from the hall.

The masked men, joined by several Viking warriors caught up in the frenzied spirit of the moment, danced around the sacred banquet table three times shouting "Yule! Yule!" Soon everyone in the hall had joined in, until it seemed the very walls would burst from the sound. Gwendolyn covered her ears with her hands as even Hakon lent his voice to the melee. The hall resounded with the deafening cries, until at the very moment when it seemed they could yell no louder, the men ripped off their masks and tossed them high in the air.

Great peals of laughter greeted them as their identities were revealed. Gwendolyn recognized Egil and Olav among them, as well as many of Hakon's guards, but she did not see the tall, red-bearded man who had worn the ram's mask. How strange, she thought, perplexed. But she knew she had not dreamed it. Her attention was diverted at that moment by the procession of the Yule boar into the hall, set on a great platter and borne on the shoulders of six male slaves.

The unmasked revelers, laughing and roughly jostling one another, quickly took their seats among the other guests as the roasted boar was paraded around the room for all to see. One Viking warrior, apparently so hungry he could not wait for the meal to begin, drew out his sword and lopped off a great hunk, just barely missing one of the slaves. Holding the browned meat in his hand, he bit off a succulent mouthful, much to the roaring delight of the guests. The savory juices from the roasted boar dripped down his chin and into his beard, but he did not seem to mind in the least. Grinning from ear to ear, he bowed to Hakon.

"I've ne'er tasted a finer Yule boar, my lord!" he shouted, taking his seat amid uproarious laughter. Hakon raised his drinking horn in acknowledgment, smiling broadly.

After the Yule boar was loudly dedicated to Frey, the god of pleasure and fertility, the feast began in earnest. Countless steaming platters of spit-roasted meats and fowl were paraded before the ravenous guests and set upon the linen-clothed tables. Baskets of crusty, flat barley loaves, warm ground pea porridge with leeks and onions, and smoked fish accompanied the meal, along with baked apples drizzled with precious golden honey.

Gwendolyn smiled at Berta, who passed by her table with a platter of roast lamb. " 'Tis a magnificent feast," she said warmly. She was rewarded with a pleased nod from the portly woman. Aye, Berta had truly outdone herself this night. She noted that the loud din in the hall had not abated, even though the guests were busily devouring the well-prepared food. Countless toasts were being offered to every Norse god imaginable; some names, like Odin and Thor, were heard over and over again.

She looked over at Hakon, who was engrossed in conversation with the Viking warriors to his right. Her eyes roamed over the bronzed profile of his face: the straight nose, his chiseled lips, the strong, square cut of his jaw, the cleft in his chin. Aye, she had to admit, she had never seen a more handsome man.

A sensation of intense longing suddenly flared within her as she recalled their last bout of lovemaking the night before. Once again, her mind seemed to have a will of its own when it came to Hakon. She sat back in her chair and closed her eyes. She could almost feel his burning caresses upon her skin, and she flushed with warmth. A curved smile played about her lips. She did not know that Hakon had turned and was watching her intently.

"I take it everything is to your liking, little one," he said softly, so low she almost did not hear him. "But I must warn you. Your secret smile is firing my blood. I believe your thoughts right now and mine are the same." He chuckled lustily. "We shall have to keep our minds upon the feast, Anora, else I will be forced to retire with you early from the hall and let the guests celebrate Yuletide without us!"

Gwendolyn's eyes flew open and she looked away, embarrassed. God's blood, his very words could send shivers of desire coursing through her body! Shakily, she took another sip of mead. The fiery liquid burned her throat, but it seemed to help her regain her sense of composure. Throwing caution to the wind, she took a long draft.

"Nay, my love," Hakon murmured, staying her hand. He gently took the goblet from her. " 'Twill be a long night, and the mead is much stronger than what you are accustomed to. You must drink it slowly." He raised the goblet, touching his lips to where hers had been only a moment before.

"Lord Hakon, I must speak to you!" Olav whispered anxiously. He had walked up to their table so suddenly and quietly that neither of them had heard him.

Annoyed at the interruption, Hakon's voice was gruff. He did not take his eyes from Gwendolyn's face. "Yea, Olav, tell me your news, but be quick about it."

Olav leaned close to the high seat. He kept his voice low, so the guests nearest Lord Hakon's table would not hear him. "A great bonfire has been sighted atop the tallest mountain peak that rises above the Sogn, and others have been lit all along the fjord leading to the settlement," he said urgently. " 'Tis the Jarl of Lade's signal, my lord!"

Hakon set the goblet down abruptly, the contents splashing out upon the linen tablecloth. Grim-faced, he rose to his feet. "Stay here and enjoy the feast, Anora. I will return shortly," he murmured, brushing a light kiss against her cheek. He then strode quickly out of the hall with Olav close behind him. Several guests noticed his hasty departure, but they quickly returned to their revelry. The skald, a singing poet, had begun to recite the heroic deeds of long-dead warriors, capturing everyone's attention with his lilting, high-pitched voice.

What could Olav have meant? Gwendolyn wondered. Surely it must have been something important, or Hakon would not have left the feast. She sat there listening with the others to the skald for what seemed a long time, her mind racing with unanswered questions. And when he had finished his songs at last and the drinking had begun again in earnest, Hakon still had not returned.

As the night wore on, it was obvious tempers were beginning to flare from the copious quantities of mead that had been consumed. Two Viking warriors suddenly fell over one of the tables, fiercely grappling with each other. Several women screamed, but no one moved to break them apart. There was so much laughing and loud boasting going on that it seemed very few of the guests were paying any attention to the battle being waged in the center of the hall.

Gwendolyn watched wide-eyed as the two men drew their swords, the cold steel of their blades ringing out from the mighty blows. Still no one intervened. Berta had told her that Viking warriors tried to get themselves into what they considered a godlike state of total drunkenness several times a year, believing it was a foretaste of the endless drinking, fighting, and feasting in Valhalla. But she had not believed it until now. She suddenly recalled a story Ansgar had told her of one Yuletide feast during the reign of Magnus, Hakon's father, when, after hours of drinking, the mead-soaked hall had been strewn not only with the bodies of guests who had passed out peacefully, but those of the dead and wounded.

She sighed with relief. At least this battle had ended without bloodshed. One of the Vikings had collapsed in a drunken heap on the floor, unharmed, and the other warrior had sat down on top of him, laughing uproariously, another full goblet of mead in his hand. Aye, they were barbarians, she thought heatedly.

The air in the hall was becoming increasingly warm and stuffy, dense with smoke from the blazing fireplaces and the sputtering torches. Gwendolyn coughed, her eyes smarting. Where was Hakon? It had been at least two hours since he had left with Olav. Rising to her feet, she wrapped her cloak about her and walked quickly to a side door leading out of the hall. She had to get some fresh air, else she would surely faint.

Gwendolyn pushed open the door and stepped outside. The air was cold and frosty, but it felt wonderful. She drank it in with deep breaths, immediately feeling refreshed. Leaning against the rough-timbered wall, she looked up at the night sky. Countless winking stars glittered like so many jeweled stones, covering the heavens as far as she could see. It was a clear night, with a half-crescent moon that shone in a long sliver of light across the surface of the fjord. The ground was lightly dusted with snow that had fallen earlier that day, glowing white in the moonlight.

A bright orange glow burning atop a distant mountain caught her eye. *So, that must be the bonfire*, she thought. And there were others dotting the rugged peaks all along the fjord as well. She could see a large group of men gathered near the docks, and from what she could tell, they were loading casks and other supplies aboard Hakon's longship. Suddenly she heard his voice carry out across the hillside.

"Yea, and we will need plenty of fresh water and food for the journey. I leave that to you, Olav. Egil, see to it that the men who sail with me on the morrow are not too far gone in their cups to pull the oars. 'Twill be a long, hard row in front of them. Now, it is time I returned to the feast."

Hakon, sailing in the morn? Gwendolyn's forehead creased in thought. What could be of such urgency that he would leave in the middle of Yuletide celebrations? Well, whatever it was, she would find out soon. At least he was finally returning to the hall.

Aye, it was time she also went back inside, she thought. Shivering, she reached for the door. She was beginning to feel cold, and she knew that Hakon would no doubt be displeased if she was not in the hall to greet him. She had almost opened the door wide enough for her to slip through when it was suddenly slammed back into place.

Gwendolyn gasped as two large hands gripped her about the waist, spinning her around. Her breath caught in her throat and her eyes widened in horror at the grinning ram's mask that loomed above her. She heard low, throaty laughter as the tall man wearing the mask captured her in his arms, drawing her slender body crudely against his own. He clapped a hand over her mouth.

"What a fair prize I have found this night," he murmured huskily. "Odin could not have blessed me with better fortune!"

Gwendolyn struggled wildly, but he pressed her back up against the timbered wall, pinning her arms cruelly between their bodies. She could not move. Suddenly he tore the mask from his face.

She blinked in astonishment at the resemblance the man had to Hakon. He was taller and of broader build, with a ruddy complexion and long, flowing red hair and beard, but his startling blue eyes gazed at her with a heated intensity that was achingly familiar.

"Would that I might see the expression on my brother's face when he finds I have taken his favored wench," the man muttered fiercely, "but we shall be far from here by then."

Sweet Jesu! 'Tis Rhoar Bloodaxe! Gwendolyn thought, her mind racing. *It must be!* Hakon had told her much of his bastard brother during one of their nights together; how he had hated and despised his younger brothers, almost drowning Hakon one day in the fjord when he was just a lad, and of the oath of blood vengeance he had sworn against them when he had learned he would not inherit the wealth and power of their father, Magnus Haardrad.

Rhoar brought his face close to hers, his warm breath fanning against her flushed cheek. "Come now, wench, don't look so frightened. I'm sure my caresses will please you far more than those of my brother," he sneered, putting special emphasis on the last word. The depth of his venomous hate for Hakon flashed from his eyes.

Nay, this cannot be happening! Gwendolyn once again tried to twist free of his grasp, but he was so big, so powerful, that it was impossible. Suddenly she sank her teeth into the palm of his hand, drawing blood. He grunted in pain, moving his hand from her mouth just long enough that she could scream. And scream she did, with all the force she could muster.

Hakon stopped in his tracks along the path to the great hall, then broke into a run. That was not the pleasured scream of a serving wench enjoying a tumble with one of his men, but an anguished cry for help. He ran swiftly up the hill, drawing his broadsword from the scabbard at his belt as his keen eyes searched the darkness. The scream was cut off abruptly, though it still echoed eerily about the surrounding mountainsides.

Rhoar had clapped his huge hand back over Gwendolyn's mouth, but he knew it was too late. Looking over his shoulder, he cursed violently. He could see Hakon's form rushing toward the great hall. Thor's teeth, he was not prepared to take on his brother this night!

He had only sneaked into the settlement to see for himself the strength of Hakon's forces, joining in the Yuletide festivities as part of his guise. He had almost been ready to ride out to meet some of his men, who were waiting for him in the dense trees surrounding the settlement, when he spied the wench leaving the hall through the side door. It had been a temptation he could not refuse. He had desired her from the first moment he had seen her in the hall, swearing to himself that she, too, would one day be his. But now he knew that he would have to leave her behind if he was to make good his escape. Her kicking and struggling would only slow him down.

"Your scream has saved you from me this day, wench, but soon you will be mine!" Rhoar whispered fiercely. "Give my brother this message. Tell him the days are few before I will seek my revenge!" He crushed her to him, seizing her lips savagely with his own, plundering her mouth with his tongue.

Gwendolyn could not breathe. Choking from the force of his kiss, she tried to fight against the blackness that was beginning to overwhelm her. With one last effort she brought her hand up and raked her nails down the side of his face.

Rhoar started and drew back, though he still held her

tightly with one strong arm. He rubbed his stinging cheek. A wolfish grin spread across his bearded face as he looked at the red blood staining his fingers. "I prefer bedding a wench with fire and spirit, and shall consider these scratches only a promise of the pleasure you will give me!" He released her suddenly, laughing. She fell back heavily against the timbered wall, then slipped to the cold ground. When she looked up he had disappeared into the night, though she could still hear his crude laughter growing fainter and fainter.

Hakon felt a cold chill course through his body at the sound of the laughter. It was vaguely familiar, but he could not place it. Yet he could swear he had heard it somewhere before. Dashing around the corner of the great hall with several of his guards now accompanying him, he saw a huddled figure struggling to rise from the ground. He held his sword in front of him, his eyes darting about warily as he and his men approached what now appeared to be the cloaked form of a woman. A flash of terror seized him. Thor, it couldn't be! His heart jumped to his throat. Anora! He quickly slid his broadsword into the scabbard at his belt, then bent down and gathered Gwendolyn up into his arms.

Chapter Twenty-eight

" 'Twas Rhoar, my lord!" Gwendolyn moaned softly. She felt suddenly safe as he held her tightly against his broad chest.

Rhoar! Hakon's face set in hard lines, his mouth grim. He turned to his men. "Search the grounds. If you find him, bring him to me," he commanded, his voice low. The Viking guards rushed to obey.

So, he *had* known the laughter, Hakon thought fiercely, though he had not heard it in more than ten years. He looked down at Gwendolyn, alarmed by the ashen pallor of her skin. He felt shaken to the depths of his being. Thor, if he had not heard her scream . . . if he had lost her . . . He could not bear to finish the thought. Yea, by the blood of Odin, for this Rhoar would surely die! He strode angrily toward his hall, clutching Gwendolyn to his breast.

She looked up at him. His handsome face was inscrutable in the faint moonlight. "But what of the Yuletide celebration?" she asked faintly, listening as the raucous sounds from the great hall faded away into the distance.

" 'Twill go on without us, my love," Hakon replied, brushing a gentle kiss upon her forehead. He kicked open the door to his hall and strode quickly across the main room into his chamber. The room was dark except for the reddish glow from the large bronze brazier in the corner. He lay Gwendolyn gently upon the wide bed and covered her with the thick fur blanket, then went and lit several of the small oil lamps about the room.

Crossing back over to the bed, he sat down and gathered her into his arms, resting her tousled head against his shoulder. His strong fingers gently stroked her silver-blond curls. "Tell me what happened, little one."

Gwendolyn sighed raggedly. Even now she could not believe how close she had come to being abducted by the renegade Viking. "I saw him first in the hall this night, though I did not know then who he was. He wore the mask of a ram, and drank from my goblet."

Hakon started in surprise. Thor, the bastard had walked to within three feet of him, and he had not known it! How he must have gloated! Rage swelled within him, yet it was tempered by his own humility. He recalled an old saying that Ansgar had taught him once: Let whoever opens a door make certain there are no enemies hiding behind it. Yea, he had learned an awful lesson this night. And it could have been far worse. . . .

"It grew so warm in the hall, and the smoke from the fireplaces was burning my eyes," she murmured, shaking her head. "There was so much yelling and fighting, I had to get some fresh air."

"So you disobeyed my orders, Anora," Hakon said softly, though he knew he could not blame her. He had not planned to be gone so long, but there were so many preparations to be made. If he had been there with her, he could have accompanied her outside, and perhaps none of this would have happened. "Why did you not call a guard to accompany you?"

"I planned to be outside for only a few moments," she replied. "I did not see any harm in going alone." She continued, relating her story, while Hakon listened grimly. He did not say another word until she had finished.

The thought of Rhoar's hands roaming at will over her body, his mouth upon hers . . . kissing her . . . ravaging what belonged to him, filled Hakon with jealous rage. He had come so close to losing her. Surely Rhoar would have raped her before the night was through, then possibly might even have killed her as another act of his blood vengeance. Yea, if that had happened, a part of him would have died with her. Hakon knew he could no longer deny to himself how much she meant to him.

"I heard you speak of sailing on the morrow," Gwendolyn said softly. "Does this have aught to do with the bonfires Olav mentioned in the great hall? I saw them myself, burning brightly atop the mountains."

"Yea, my love. In the morn I must sail for Trondheim, to the north. The bonfires are a summons by my liege lord, the Jarl of Lade. It is a signal for all the Jarls under his rule to gather at his estate, and I am one of them. It must be a matter of great importance, for travel at this time of year is treacherous at best."

Hakon sighed deeply. The Jarl's signal could not have come at a more inopportune time. Yet he had already made provisions so that the settlement would be well protected while he was gone. As soon as he had seen the bonfires, messengers had been sent out, seeking reinforcements from many of the petty chieftains under his own rule. The added strength would be needed, especially now that he knew Rhoar's threat of revenge was close at hand. It would serve to hold his bastard brother at bay, discouraging an attack until he could return. But when that would be, he did not know. He only hoped it would not be too long.

"Shall I accompany you, my lord?" Gwendolyn did not know why she asked, but it seemed natural that she would go with him.

"Nay, I cannot take you with me, Anora. The rough winter seas are a trial for even the most seasoned crew, and I will not subject you to such a dangerous voyage. You will be well protected here, and far safer, despite Rhoar's threat. There will be twice as many men here to guard the settlement until I return. I shall have only enough men to row my longship, and Garric will accompany me to serve as my page at the Jarl's court."

He paused, noticing that Gwendolyn had stiffened in his arms. He drew her closer. "Do not fear, little one," he murmured. "Would that I might remain here with you, but I cannot. It is my duty to answer the Jarl's summons. As for Rhoar, he would be a fool to attack the settlement while I am gone, for he would be far outnumbered. Nay, I believe that he will wait until he can meet me in battle face to face."

But Gwendolyn had not even heard his last words. Her mind was racing at the news that he would be taking Garric with him on the voyage. Nay, it would not be possible for Anora to accompany him as Garric!

It was true Anora had done well so far in the guise of a boy. Her sister had quickly learned the skills she needed to work in the stable, and had discovered in herself a natural ability with horses. Yet she had not been able to match the boyish mannerisms Gwendolyn had displayed as Garric, or the same swagger and biting tongue. Fortunately, this had not posed a problem, for there had been very little contact between her and Hakon during the past few weeks. But to serve as his page, to be in his presence constantly . . . nay, it was not possible! Gwendolyn was sure it would not be long before her sister's guise would be discovered. All that was needed was one misstated word, one highly feminine expression, and all would be lost.

"Will you sail at dawn, my lord?" she asked, fearful of his answer. If they left that early, she would have no hope of venturing unnoticed to the stable to exchange places with Anora once again.

"Nay, though I had hoped we might," he answered, somewhat surprised by her question. "I shall wait until the reinforcements from the surrounding settlements have arrived before we sail." He put his finger gently to her lips. "Enough talk, little one. It will be many nights before I shall hold you in my arms again. All that matters now is that you are safe, and here with me."

Aye, then, there would be time, Gwendolyn thought, a surge of relief coursing through her body. But it was quickly replaced by the kindling of desire as Hakon lifted her chin and brought his lips down upon her own. His mouth moved against hers, warm, tender, in a breathless kiss that caused her to tremble uncontrollably. She could feel her body yielding to him, relaxing in his arms. All thoughts of the Yuletide feast, Rhoar, and even Anora flew from her mind as she returned his kiss, her delicate fingers entwining in the soft waves of his hair as she held his face in her hands.

Hakon drew away from her and gazed into the emerald depths of her eyes, dark with passion. He exulted in the desire he saw reflected there. An intense wave of emotion suddenly welled up within him that was so strong he could have cried out, his heart pounding madly against his chest. Yea, he knew now that he loved her, more than life itself. . . .

Perhaps he had all along, Hakon thought with a sense of wonder, since he had first found her aboard his ship. Perhaps that was why he could not take her against her will that night in the bathing house, though his body had ached to possess her. This beautiful woman, like a goddess in the perfection of her face and form, had so captivated his soul with her passionate spirit that he knew he was lost to her forever.

Hakon lay her back gently on the bed and began to draw the silken garments from her one by one. Murmuring soft words of love, his strong hands caressed her satiny-smooth skin as her lithe body was slowly revealed to him. She writhed luxuriously from his touch, arching her back as his mouth briefly teased her pert nipples. His lips burned a molten path between her breasts to a delicate shoulder, then along the alabaster column of her throat until he once again captured her mouth with his. She wrapped her slender arms about his neck, pulling him to her.

Hakon chuckled from deep in his throat. Her wild response never ceased to delight him. "One moment, my love." Suddenly he moved away from the bed. Gwendolyn opened her eyes in surprise. Then a faint smile curved her lips. He was quickly stripping away his own garments, until his powerful body was bared to her gaze. Truly, he was a magnificent sight!

Delighted by her admiring and lusty perusal, Hakon did not tarry from her side for long. Before she could blink she was once again wrapped in his strong arms as he drew her against him.

He traced his finger slowly down the side of her face, his hand stroking the small of her back and her slender, curved hips. "I want you to touch me, Anora," he whispered huskily, brushing his lips against her long, gold-tipped lashes.

She blushed heatedly at his request. He had never asked this of her before!

" 'Twould please me," he murmured, sensing her obvious embarrassment by the flushed rose color of her cheeks. Still she hesitated, unsure of herself, so he gently took her hand and guided it down his taut, sculpted belly to between his sinewy thighs.

Gwendolyn gasped as his manhood seemed to leap into her hand. Then, emboldened by her desire, she tentatively caressed the tip. It was smooth to her touch. She wound her fingers around his growing hardness, not knowing quite what to do. Slowly she began to caress him.

Hakon groaned with pleasure, the pressure of her hand stoking the burning fire that was raging in his loins. Suddenly he drew her hand away and pressed her back against the eiderdown pillows. Nay, he could endure her sweet torture no longer!

"Have I displeased—"

Hakon cut off her whispered question with his kiss, determined to erase the memory of Rhoar's touch from her lips, her body, her mind. "Nay, my love, never . . . never," he replied, his voice low, emphatic, as his kisses seared like wildfire across her slender body.

His strong hands were everywhere, teasing, stroking, until her skin felt warm and tingling from head to toe. His fingers explored the moist core of her, while his mouth, hot, insistent, suckled hungrily at her breast, occasionally nipping her gently with his teeth. She moaned in ecstasy, overwhelmed by the heated torrent of his desire, as he trailed a fiery path of kisses down the curved indent of her belly to the soft silver-blond mound of curls between her silky thighs.

Gwendolyn gasped in surprise as his mouth found the bud of her desire where his fingers had been only moments before. She tried to pull away from him, but he held her fast, his hands supporting her hips. Thrilling to this new sensation, she gave in to the heady waves of passion that coursed through her body like flickering tongues of flame. She moaned with wild delight, arching her back.

Suddenly Hakon drew himself up over her, his startling blue eyes ablaze with desire as he slowly entered her. Supporting his weight with his arms, he held back for a moment, watching in fascination as she writhed beneath him. She reached up and wrapped her arms about his waist, then pulled him to her.

Hakon could wait no longer. Inflamed with an urgency borne of the burning need to possess her completely, he plunged himself into the warmth and softness of her body. She cried out his name, over and over, her legs gripping him tightly, as he thrust deep within her to the hilt of his manhood.

Gwendolyn met him with a passionate fury that equaled his own. Panting, breathless, they raced together to that apex of desire. For one blinding moment it seemed that the world had stopped but for the fusion of their bodies into a throbbing, shuddering whole.

Hakon collapsed against her, nuzzling her neck with gentle kisses as their breathing returned to normal. Afraid that he might crush her with his weight, he gently rolled over to one side and pulled her to him, cradling her head against his shoulder. Holding her close with his strong arms, he felt a numbing sense of contentment wash over him. He knew this was how it was meant to be between them . . . forever. He chuckled deeply as her fingers played absently with the golden curls on his broad chest.

"Yea, I believe 'tis time I took a wife," he stated softly.

Gwendolyn started in surprise. "My . . . my lord?"

"Perhaps a wench with silver-blond curls and emerald eyes the color of the sea." He smiled, his teeth a flash of white as she looked up at him in astonishment. He suddenly brought himself up on one elbow, his hand tenderly caressing the silky skin of her cheek. His eyes burned into hers with piercing intensity.

"I love you, Anora."

Gwendolyn gasped, but he gently touched his finger to her tender lips.

"Yea, and when I came so close to losing you this night, I finally realized that my life would be naught without you.

Never again shall it be said during a feast that 'tis a pity you are a slave. When I return from Trondheim, you shall become a free woman, and my wife."

Bending his head, he pressed his lips to hers in a breathtaking kiss that seemed to echo his words over and over . . . *I love you . . . I love you.*

Tearing his lips away from hers at last, Hakon gathered her into his arms. "We must rest now, my love. The morn will come only too soon." Sighing contentedly, he lay his head back against the eiderdown pillows and closed his eyes. He knew his revelation had startled her, and, he hoped, had pleased her. She had given him no response, though he had not really expected one. He knew such a fragile thing as love could not be forced. Yet he felt sure that one day Anora would return his love. Why, even tonight there had been more than passion and desire reflected in those deep, emerald depths. Yea, something more . . . perhaps a smoldering ember of affection that could one day flare into a raging love that would match his own.

It was not long before the steady rhythm of Hakon's breathing told Gwendolyn he was asleep. She looked up at him, her heart in her throat. Slowly, and ever so softly, she traced her finger down the high-boned planes of his face and across the sensuous curve of his mouth. Suddenly she shuddered from deep within her, and would have cried out but for fear that she would wake him. She felt as if she were being torn in two, her soul ripped asunder by the conflicting emotions that warred within her. The feeling that had plagued her, tearing her apart and destroying her resolve, had at last found a name . . . love.

Aye, she loved him, more than she wished to admit to herself. Hakon, the Viking warrior she had sworn to hate and defy until that one day when she and Anora would escape from him forever.

Gwendolyn's agonized thoughts swirled about in her

mind. What could she do? Tell Hakon the truth, that she had adopted the guise first of a boy, then of Anora, to protect her sister's virtue? He was in love with the women he thought was Anora, not her! Would he release her sister, and allow her to return to their homeland if she stayed with him in Norge? Nay, she could not be sure. Perhaps he would have them both! She knew that many Vikings had more than one wife!

She shook her head fiercely. Nay, their love could never be! She would play the part, whether it be of Garric, or wife to Hakon Jarl, until that day when she would make good her vow to Anora, and escape from the Viking and the love that would capture her heart forever.

Unable to keep her eyes open any longer, Gwendolyn at last fell into a tormented sleep.

Chapter Twenty-nine

Gwendolyn awoke with a start to find she was alone in the wide bed. She sat up, rubbing the sleep from her eyes, and looked about the room. It was clear that many of Hakon's things were gone—his silver coat of mail, the conical helmet, several weapons—and the lids to the heavy, carved chests were open, as if he had not wanted to disturb her slumber by closing them shut.

Sweet Jesu! What if they have already left! Gwendolyn bounded out of the bed and ran to the nearest window. She tore aside the leather shade and peered outside. The sky was overcast, laden with gray clouds that foretold a coming snowstorm. It was so dark that she could not tell what time of morning it was, though she had an awful feeling it was late. She could see many Viking guards walking about the nearby longhouses, but this side of Hakon's hall faced away from the fjord. She would have no way of knowing if his longship was still moored at the docks until she walked from the main entrance.

Turning back into the room, she hurried over to the ornately carved chest that held her clothing and threw back the lid. Hastily she donned a plain linen chemise of pale yellow and a mantle made of gray fustian, a strong cotton cloth. Her fingers shook as she quickly fastened two silver filigree brooches to the shoulder straps of the mantle. Her eyes darted about the room in search of her leather, fur-lined slippers.

"God's blood! Where are they?" she cursed impatiently, her heart pounding against her chest. Finally she spied them near the bed. She ran and picked them up, hurriedly slipping them on. Grabbing her fur cloak from the hook, she wrapped it about her shoulders and ran from the room.

The main hall was dark and cold. Even the glowing embers in the central fireplace lent little warmth to the large room. Gwendolyn hurried across the hall, gathering her cloak about her, and pushed open the massive wooden door. She could scarcely breathe, dreading what she might find. If Hakon's longship was gone, all was lost.

Relief flooded her body as she caught sight of the longship, still moored at the dock. Already some of the crewmen were taking their seats at the oars, and she could see Hakon on the deck, directing what appeared to be the last load of supplies into the cargo well. His voice, deep and resonant, carried out over the din of commotion that surged around him.

"Yea, put that over there, man! Olav, if all is ready we will sail shortly. The wind is picking up, and from the looks of the sky it does not bode well for good weather. We must sail soon if there is any hope of reaching the mouth of the Sogn by nightfall."

"Yea, my lord!" Olav replied heartily from his place at the helm of the longship.

Gwendolyn felt a tingling sensation at the sound of Hakon's voice, remembering the words he had said to her the night before. But she shook her head. Nay, there would be plenty of time to think of that later, she chided herself. Now, she had to find Anora.

Anxiously she hurried along the path toward the stable. What if Anora was no longer there? She had not seen her aboard the ship, but perhaps Hakon had sent her on some errand elsewhere in the settlement. She shivered, her cold lips mumbling a quick prayer that she would find her sister yet in the stable. Her eyes darted about, noting the swelling numbers of Viking guards now manning various posts at each of the longhouses. No doubt many of them had arrived during the night, while others even now were riding in from various settlements across the valley.

She was not surprised that none of the Vikings harassed her or even tried to speak to her as she made her way to the stable. She could see several of them watching her closely, their heated glances frank and appraising. Yet she suspected that they had already been warned to stay away from her. Berta had told her that Hakon made it known he would kill any man who touched her.

The door of the stable was ajar. With her heart in her throat, Gwendolyn stepped into the dark, musty building, her eyes peering all about. She saw no one. The only sound was the baaing of the sheep and the cackling of chickens. She felt a sinking feeling in the pit of her stomach as she turned and walked back to the door. God's blood! She was too late! A sudden wind blew in through the open door, swirling the dust from the hay into the air. It tickled her nose, and she sneezed violently, startling Anora, who was just returning from the storerooms with a small bag of dried corn for the chickens.

"Gwen— —Anora!" she exclaimed, dropping the bag of corn, her eyes wide. She picked it up quickly, looking furtively about her, then pushed Gwendolyn back inside the stable and pulled the wooden door shut firmly behind them. Her voice was almost frantic.

"I hoped you would come, Gwendolyn, but when it grew

so late I was beginning to think I would not see you before I left with Lord Hakon!" She gripped her sister's arm. "What am I to do? I know naught of serving as a page . . . I shall be found out! I do not want to sail with him, Gwendolyn!"

"And so you shall not," Gwendolyn replied hastily. "Quick, hand me your clothes, Anora. We shall exchange places once again!"

Anora quickly obeyed, her hands shaking as she pulled at the leather belt at her waist, while she kicked off the boots on her feet. Shrugging off the fur-lined jerkin that had so successfully camouflaged her small breasts, she stripped the woolen shirt and breeches from her slender body and threw them toward Gwendolyn, who was pulling the pale yellow chemise over her head. It was just a few more moments before they were once again dressed in each other's clothes.

A faint smile curved Gwendolyn's lips as she adjusted the leather belt about her waist. It felt so good to be dressed in breeches again! Though the silken garments had been a delight to her skin, she had missed the freedom of movement only a man's clothes could afford.

"These are so much finer than the plain shifts I wore in the cooking house," Anora murmured, rubbing the soft linen sleeve of the chemise against her cheek.

"Aye, so they are," Gwendolyn agreed, "as befits the favored concubine of Hakon Jarl."

Anora gasped. She had been so caught up in admiring the garments that she had forgotten how they had come about. She blushed, her eyes downcast.

"Listen to me, Anora," Gwendolyn whispered, ignoring her sister's discomfort. Her eyes were intent, searching. "You must remember to act the part of mistress of Lord Hakon's household while I am gone. I have told you of many of the duties Berta has taught me. You must do them just as I would, and give her no cause to think that aught is amiss." She smiled reassuringly. "I am sure you will have no trouble with the loom. Just mind that you do not appear too proficient. You know how I am when it comes to such tasks!"

"Aye, Gwendolyn, I will not forget." Anora nodded.

"And one other thing," Gwendolyn murmured, then hesitated. She had to tell her about the night before with Hakon, so she would know how to respond to him this morning. If she were too cold, too aloof, surely he would think something was strangely different about her. But how could she tell her of the passion they had shared, and his words of love, without giving her own feelings away?

Gwendolyn shook her head. Nay, she would not think of her own feelings now. If their guise was to succeed, Anora had to know that Hakon planned to take her as his wife. She took her sister's hand in her own.

"Anora, I do not know if you have heard any talk of this yet, but last night Hakon's brother, Rhoar Bloodaxe, stole into the settlement during the Yuletide feast. There is not time to tell you all of what happened, but I was nearly abducted by him when I left the hall for a short while to get some fresh air."

Anora gasped, her eyes wide with concern. "Did he hurt you?"

"Nay, but he could have. Rhoar is a fearsome man," Gwendolyn replied. She shuddered, remembering the cold look of hate in his eyes. "Fortunately, Hakon heard me scream, and Rhoar released me, but not before he swore that one day I would be his. I tell you this only because you must know, Anora. Last night, after Hakon and I . . ." She paused, blushing under her sister's gaze. Then she continued: "When we lay in each other's arms, he told me that he—"

"Garric!" Hakon pushed open the door of the stable. "Come on, lad, 'tis time to sail. Leave the rest of your chores for—" He stopped in mid-sentence, gazing in surprise at Gwendolyn and Anora.

Gwendolyn's heart leaped at the sight of him, standing so tall and powerful just within the door. But she quickly looked at her feet, shifting uncomfortably. It would not do for Garric to gaze so upon Hakon Jarl! She cursed under her breath. Now, Anora would have no way of knowing the intensity of Hakon's feelings for her. Well, there was aught she could do now, only hope that Anora would not spurn him too harshly.

"I was about to return to my hall to bid you farewell, Anora," Hakon said softly, walking to her side, "but I see you had the same thought for your brother."

"Aye, my lord," Anora replied, her gaze steady as she looked up at him. "I shall not see him for many days. I only wanted to wish him godspeed."

"I, too, will be gone for many days," Hakon murmured. "Come, I will walk with you back to the hall." He took her arm and led her from the stable. "Garric, gather your things and see that you are aboard the ship before me!" he called out over his broad shoulder, with scarcely a backward glance.

Gwendolyn shook her head in disbelief. Hakon was jealous of her . . . of Garric, that was! Aye, there had been no mistaking the angry flash in his blue eyes when he saw her and Anora together. For some reason the thought gave her a rush of pleasure, but she quickly shrugged it off. If she was to be Garric again, she would have to act the part. She only hoped her eyes would not betray her. She bent down and picked up the roll of clothing Anora had prepared for the journey, then hurried from the stable. With the wind at her heels, she ran down the hill toward the longship.

Hakon did not say a word to Anora as they walked down the path to his hall. He did not know why it angered him so to see the two of them together . . . after all, Garric was her brother. He shrugged. Perhaps he did not want to share her with anyone! Suddenly he noticed that she was shivering despite her fur cloak. He drew her closer to his side, his arm about her waist.

Anora stiffened, then forced herself to relax. It would not do to anger him further before he left, she thought, at least for Gwendolyn's sake. He might vent his feelings upon her once he was aboard the ship. She ventured a look up at him, and found him regarding her with heated intensity. She turned her head away, blushing, and did not look at him again until they had reached the entrance to his hall.

Hakon paused at the door, then drew her into his arms and crushed her to him. "I must leave you here, my love, though I would like nothing more than to carry you into my chamber and repeat what we shared last night!" His lips brushed against her forehead, then sought her mouth. He started. Her lips were so cold. He kissed her deeply, warming her mouth with his own, but the passionate response he had expected was not there. Drawing back from her for a moment, he gazed into her eyes. He did not see desire reflected in those emerald depths, only a hint of fearful resignation.

How strange, he thought. It was as if he held a different woman in his arms. Olav's hurried approach suddenly interrupted his dark thoughts.

"My lord Hakon, we must sail at once if we are to escape the storm that is approaching from the north! If the snow begins to fly too heavily, we will be forced to wait another day." Olav looked away, embarrassed that he had disturbed his lord in the midst of such a private moment. But there was no help for it. What was now a gentle snowfall could turn into a blinding squall in only a moment's time.

"Yea, Olav, you are right." Hakon sighed, his eyes never leaving Anora's face. He bent and whispered in her ear, his breath warm against her neck. "Remember my words from last night, Anora. As soon as I return from Trondheim . . ." He kissed her again, but lightly this time. Already his mind was on the voyage ahead. "If you would like to begin preparations early, Berta will help you with anything you need. Farewell, my love." With a last fervent embrace he was gone, striding quickly down the path to the dock with Olav at his side.

Anora watched as they boarded the ship. She could see Gwendolyn's small form sitting at one of the rowing benches and she waved her hand, a smile lighting her face as her sister quickly did the same. But she could also feel Hakon's eyes upon her. The smile faded from her lips, and she looked away.

"Oars down!" Hakon's sharp command echoed about the settlement. The oars on the starboard side of the ship hit the water with a resounding smack, while the crewmen on the port side used their oars to push away from the wooden dock. Soon the longship had cleared its moorings, sliding like a serpent over the calm surface of the fjord.

Anora's eyes followed the longship until it disappeared around the bend in the fjord. She shivered, gathering the luxurious fur cloak closer about her body. What had the Viking meant, *preparations?* Shaking her head, she stepped into the hall.

Chapter Thirty

"Garric, you must wait out here. Only freemen may enter the great hall of Haarek Sigurdson, the Jarl of Lade," Hakon said firmly.

"Very well, my lord," Gwendolyn murmured, her eyes following Hakon's tall form as he disappeared through the massive carved doors leading into the main room of the hall. A twinge of disappointment coursed through her. She had hoped to learn the reason for this sudden journey, but now it was clear she would have to wait.

She took a seat on one of the benches lining the timbered wall in the large anteroom, then drew her leg up and rested her head on her knee. She watched as other Viking chieftains—fierce-looking warriors every one—passed by her on their way to join the meeting. Soon the anteroom was crowded with the retainers and slaves of these men, the air abuzz with speculation as to the important discussions taking place within the hall. But Gwendolyn paid little attention to their talk. She closed her eyes in an effort to ease the clashing thoughts waging a battle in her mind.

The voyage north to Trondheim had taken two days once the longship had reached the mouth of the Sogn fjord and sailed into open waters. The seas were extremely rough, with dark, angry waves that buffeted the planked hull of the longship, so they had never strayed far from the rugged coastline. Gwendolyn had been plagued with seasickness once again, and spent much of her time with her head over the side, spilling the contents of her stomach into the sea. Hakon had berated her on the second day, though not too unkindly. She grimaced, recalling his words.

"If I had known you would be of such little use to me, Garric, I would have left you at the settlement!" he had shouted over the roar of the waves. Yet after each bout of seasickness he had helped her back to her pallet near the cargo well, and seen to it that she drank plenty of fresh-water and was covered with a woolen blanket to keep out the cold north wind. She had not felt better until they sailed into the calmer waters of the Trondheimsfjord late last night.

When they had at last reached the estate of Lade, near the city of Trondheim, the longship was met at the main docks by an emissary sent from Haarek Jarl. Hakon and his tired crew were escorted to a well-furnished longhouse where they first ate a sumptuous meal, then slept for the night.

Aye, if only he had left me behind, Gwendolyn thought grimly. As it was, his very presence served to remind her of the words he had spoken several nights past. *I love you . . . you shall be my wife . . .* They echoed like whispering phantoms over and over in her mind, haunting her. And even though she swore to herself time and time again that their love could never be, and that she would hold fast to her vow to Anora, she found her resolve constantly shaken every time she looked in his eyes.

She shook her head, then ran her fingers through her short curls. Why, even this morning she had almost given herself away! She had been in the main hall with the rest of the crew, eating her morning meal, when Hakon called out to her from his private chamber. He had just stepped from the bath that had been brought in for him, his powerful, muscled body wet and glistening from head to toe, when she hurriedly entered the room. She had stopped abruptly in her tracks, her heart pounding rapidly against her chest, not so much at the sight of him but at the young slave woman standing close by his side.

A comely wench with long, dark hair and hazel eyes, the slave woman was wearing an almost transparent shift that barely concealed the curved lines of her lush body. And her pleated bodice was cut low enough to reveal provocatively her generous breasts to Hakon's view. Gwendolyn's emerald eyes had narrowed dangerously at this woman, her small hands clenching into fists. It had taken a sharp reprimand from Hakon to bring her around finally. She had started visibly at the sound of his raised voice.

"What are you gawking at, lad? Have you not seen a naked man before?" he shouted, looking at her oddly. "Fetch me my tunic."

Blushing heatedly, she had rushed to do his bidding. Yet she was not able to tear her eyes away from the pretty slave. She had watched angrily, experiencing jealousy for the first time in her life, as the woman slowly dried Hakon's bronzed body with a thick towel. Aye, Gwendolyn had no doubts that the slave woman had been sent to him with special compliments from Haarek Jarl to see to his every need! Her only consolation was that Hakon paid little heed to the woman's lingering ministrations and desirous glances. He had even grown impatient with her at one point and grabbed the towel from her hand, sending her squealing from the room with a loud slap on her well-proportioned backside.

Barely able to conceal her pleased smile, Gwendolyn had kept her face low and her eyes downcast as she helped Hakon dress in his finest clothes. He had spoken little to her, his mind on the meeting that morning with his liege lord. It was only when she held his heavy broadsword out to him and he took it from her, sliding it into the fine leather scabbard at his belt, that he had broken the silence between them.

"Why do your hands shake so, Garric? Do you still suffer from the sickness that plagued you during the journey?" Hakon asked with some concern.

"Nay . . . nay, m-my lord," she stammered. She had hoped that he would not notice how her hands were trembling. She quickly clasped them behind her back.

"Well, what is it, then?" he queried impatiently. "You hardly seem like yourself this day." He shrugged when she did not answer him. Then a slow smile spread across his handsome face. "Perhaps it was the fetching sight of the wench, eh, lad?"

She had nearly choked at his words, but then decided it was best to go along with him. "Aye, 't-'twas the wench, my lord," she replied, biting her lower lip.

Chuckling, Hakon had slapped Gwendolyn on her shoulder, knocking her forward. With a hearty laugh he strode from the room, leaving her standing there alone. She would have been standing there still, trying to regain her composure, if Olav had not called out to her from the outer hall.

"Come on, lad! You are to accompany Lord Hakon to the Jarl's great hall!"

Aye, and so there she sat in Haarek Jarl's hall, for what had already seemed like hours. But what could they possibly be discussing for so long? she wondered irritably. Suddenly a tall man who looked to be a wealthy merchant entered the anteroom, escorted by an entourage of armed Viking guards. The slaves and retainers standing in the way were roughly brushed aside as the great doors were opened wide to admit these newcomers.

Gwendolyn darted from the bench in hopes of catching a

glimpse of the main hall. Her eyes widened at the length and breadth of the well-lighted room. Why, it was at least twice the size of Hakon's hall! There were many Viking warriors sitting on benches lining the tapestry-covered walls, though others were standing in small groups here and there. All were facing a raised high seat at the center of the room, on which sat a rather small man with black hair, pale skin, and blazing dark eyes. She hopped up and down, trying to catch a glimpse of Hakon, but the massive doors were once again slammed shut.

"Begone, lad!" a burly guard near the door shouted, shoving her away. Rubbing her arm, she turned to walk back to the bench, but someone had already taken her seat. Grumbling and cursing under her breath, she slid her back down the side of the wall and sat down upon the wooden floor.

Hakon chuckled to himself, though he hid his smile with his hand. He had seen Gwendolyn's antics beyond the massive doors. Her awkward attempts to see into the hall had lent a bit of humor to the grave scene about him. Yet his thoughts focused once again on the proceedings as the merchant, surrounded by Viking guards, passed close by his chair.

Hakon leaned toward Olav, his voice almost a whisper. "I recognize that man, Olav. Did he not trade with us several years back in Dublin?"

"Yea, my lord, that he did," Olav replied, nodding his head. "He is a shrewd man, as I recall, but honest and fair in his dealings." But their conversation, as well as that of others buzzing in the hall, was silenced as Haarek Jarl raised his hand.

"I now present the man I spoke of earlier," Haarek announced, gesturing toward the merchant. "He is Tryggve Graafeld, a Danish merchant, but nonetheless loyal to our cause. He arrived in Trondheim two weeks past with news from the court of Harald Gormsson Bluetooth, the king of

Denmark and overking of much of our land. You have been summoned to hear this news!" He turned to the merchant, who was now standing in front of the assembly just to the right of the high seat, and motioned for him to speak.

Tryggve Graafeld bowed his head first to Haarek Jarl, then to the gathered chieftains. "My lords, I stand before you with grim tidings," he stated steadily, his voice carrying out over the hall so all could hear. "Several months past I traded for goods in the town of York, England, in the heart of the region known as the Danelaw. While there, I heard much talk of a powerful prince, Wulfgar Ragnarson, who plans to sail on Norge in the spring with a fleet of warships that is rumored to rival any fleet ever seen before!"

This announcement elicited loud, angry rumblings and vehement curses from the chieftains, until Haarek Jarl once again raised his hand for order.

"Let him speak!" he commanded fiercely. The hall finally grew silent, all eyes turned to the merchant.

Tryggve cleared his throat, then continued. "It seems this prince's betrothed, a young woman of legendary beauty, and her sister were captured by Viking marauders and abducted from their homeland on the eve of the marriage. Wulfgar Ragnarson has sworn blood vengeance against these captors, and believes them to be Norse. He has gained the assistance of Edgar, the king of England, who will supply him with ships and supplies. I learned that King Edgar had arranged the marriage to foster unity between the Danes and the Anglo-Saxons within his own country, and that he has taken the abduction of these women as a personal affront."

"But what is this to us?" a Viking chieftain shouted out. "Surely we have forces enough to stave off an attack from this Danish prince, with or without the aid from his English king!"

Tryggve shook his head gravely. "Wulfgar Ragnarson has

also received a promise of aid from his cousin, none other than Harald Gormsson, the king of Denmark!"

Haarek Jarl jumped up from the high seat, his face livid with rage. "Now do you see?" he thundered heatedly, his words resounding throughout the hall. " 'Tis the perfect excuse, the one for which Harald has long awaited. He will try to win back the control that we have wrested from him inch by inch! Though he is yet overlord of the eastern half of our country, he is not content with that. Nay, he now seeks once again to bring all of Norge under his rule! And he will have the forces to accomplish it, once his are combined with that of this prince of the Danelaw!" He lowered his voice, his dark eyes focusing on the hushed warriors. "Those two women must be found and returned to this Wulfgar Ragnarson before he sails upon our land!"

"Yea, 'tis true!" Tryggve replied. "I have just come from Harald's court, where I went to confirm this news under the guise of trading. He shall join his forces with Wulfgar Ragnarson's, and together they will sail upon Norge's western shores in the spring!"

The great hall once again erupted in angry cries. Hakon leaned over to Olav. "At least we are safe from Haarek's wrath, my friend. 'Twas a woman and her brother found aboard my ship . . . and not two wenches!"

Olav nodded, though his face was grim. "But 'tis strange, my lord. We were in England at nearly the same time. Could it be possible—"

"Nay, Olav, 'tis a coincidence and nothing more," Hakon interrupted, shaking his head. He could have laughed out loud. "Do you think I could be so deceived, my friend? 'Tis not possible! I know a wench when I see one!"

Olav chuckled. "Yea, my lord. 'Twas only a passing thought," he said, sitting back in his chair. Truly, with Lord Hakon's eye for beautiful women . . . He shrugged.

Hakon settled back in his chair. Yea, the situation was

indeed a serious one, he thought, sobering. He had no love for Haarek Jarl, though he was his liege lord, for he had heard much of how the man had earned his position through avarice and unscrupulous deceit. Yet he could not help but admire him for keeping the Danes at bay all these years. Truly, he would rather have Haarek Jarl as his overlord than be ruled by a Danish king!

Eight years before, when Haarek Sigurdson had taken refuge in Denmark after losing his lands to his father's murderers, he had fought on the side of King Harald during the conquest of Norge. Yet after the victory, Haarek had shrewdly devised a way to regain his lands along the western coast. He persuaded the Danish king to allow him to rule a large part of the vanquished country in his stead as a faithful vassal. Since he could not aspire to kingship in Norge or Denmark, being of no direct lineage to either throne, he convinced Harald that there was no danger of his ever becoming a rival. An agreement was struck between the two men, with Haarek promising to pay the Danish king a tax amounting to half of the incomes from the lands which he received.

Yet once back in Norge, Haarek had gradually reduced this tax to the nominal sum of twenty falcons a year, and had eventually declared himself and his territories in the west independent of Denmark. King Harald had made several attempts to reconquer these lands, but so far he had been unsuccessful, always lacking the numbers of men needed to regain control. But now, with this new development, it seemed the tides were turning against the wily Jarl . . . unless he could quickly prevent it.

Hakon's thoughts were interrupted by Haarek Jarl's thin, raspy voice. "Two mere women are not worth the loss of our independence!" he shouted angrily, standing before his high seat. His eyes moved about the room, burning like two glowing coals. "I have sent messengers out to the rulers in Haalogaland in the far north, to Viken near the Foldenfjord, and even to the regions ruled still by Harald Gormsson, seeking news of the whereabouts of these two women." He raised his arm suddenly, pointing one by one at the gathered chieftains, who were now all standing.

"Send out messengers within your own lands! The women must be found!" he admonished fiercely. "If the one is as beautiful as they say, surely there must be those who would remember such a face. And if you find them, or learn any news of their fate, send word to me at once! Now begone, all of you! Sail this very day! And may Odin grant you safe passage as you return to your lands!" He paused, his barrel chest heaving, then warned, "Meanwhile, my lords, until you hear otherwise, prepare for war!"

The Viking chieftains quickly opened a wide path for Haarek Jarl and his retinue as he strode among them toward the massive doors at the entrance to the great hall. His pale face was grim, his mouth a tight line as he acknowledged their clenched fists raised in homage, while other warriors pounded their brightly painted shields with their spears. His glittering eyes searched every face that lined the path, and he paused occasionally to mutter a greeting to a favored chieftain. He had almost reached the doors when he spied Hakon standing back from the others with Olav at his side. He stopped abruptly.

"You must be Hakon, Jarl of Sogn," he stated loudly. The chieftains in front of Hakon quickly moved aside.

"Yea, my lord," Hakon said, stepping forward. He met the smaller man's penetrating gaze evenly.

"I much admired your elder brother, Eirik," Haarek said simply. "You greatly resemble him, though I believe you are taller and of broader build than he." He paused for a moment, then murmured, "I am greatly comforted that 'tis you who shall carry on as Jarl in his stead . . . and no other."

Hakon bowed his head, not missing Haarek's unspoken

reference to Rhoar Bloodaxe. "You have my oath of allegiance, my lord."

"Of that I had no doubt," Haarek replied, his gaze never wavering from Hakon's face. A fleeting smile touched his stern features, then was gone as he turned on his heel. The great doors swung open, immediately silencing the loud din in the anteroom as the Jarl swept through.

Gwendolyn leaped to her feet to avoid being crushed by the mob of Viking guards that surrounded the small, stocky man with the blazing eyes. She watched in fascination as he passed by her. So this was the great Haarek Jarl! She had heard much about him from Ansgar, who had taught her some of the history of the Norse people. He had said the man was as feared as he was respected, and though he was of small stature, he ruled his vast holdings with a will of iron.

Her eyes scanned the faces of the Viking chieftains who were now pouring from the great hall, but she did not see Hakon. It was several moments before he finally walked through the doors, at least a full head taller than those around him. She felt a thrill of excitement course through her body at the sight of him. Aye, he was by far the most splendid warrior of them all!

"Lord Hakon!" Gwendolyn called out, for the crush of the crowd was so great she could not break through to get to his side. She watched as he easily made his way over to the timbered wall where she stood. Without a word, he took her arm and led her through the surging crowd. Olav followed not far behind.

"Where do we go from here, my lord?" she asked, shouting over the swell of raised voices. "Will there be a feast?" She hoped so. Her stomach was growling hungrily.

"Nay, lad. You will have to settle for salted fish. We must sail at once," he replied, the bronzed planes of his face inscrutable.

"But we have only just arriv—"

"Ask me no further questions, Garric!" he cut her off sharply.

Gwendolyn felt as if she had been struck. Aye, very well, she thought, angered and hurt by his abrupt manner. Then she shook her head, chiding herself for her foolishness. What more could she expect? She was not playing the part of the beloved Anora now, but of Garric, the stable hand. She was worthy of no more consideration than what she had just received! She sighed raggedly, following close behind Hakon as he walked from the great hall into the bright afternoon sun.

Chapter Thirty-one

Gwendolyn pulled halfheartedly on her oar, her mind working quickly as the longship cut across the surface of the icy water. Hakon's settlement was just around the bend of the fjord.

Soon the charade will begin again, she thought miserably, her eyes upon Hakon as he stood beside the dragon-headed prow, his legs spread wide, his muscled arms folded across his broad chest. Aye, she loved him, that she knew. But like a double-edged sword, she also knew that she could not betray Anora's trust in her. She sighed heavily. Never before had she been faced with such an awful dilemma. She now dreaded the role she must play for her sister's sake, fearful that at any time she might give herself away. Yet she could not deny that she longed for the feel of Hakon's strong arms about her, the scorching heat of his touch, and the warmth of his lips upon her own.

She shivered suddenly. Aye, there was nothing left of the serenity she had felt the last two days. The homeward journey had been a welcome respite from the inner turmoil that plagued her; but it had, too, quickly passed.

It had taken less than two days for the longship to sail southward along the rocky coast to the mouth of the great Sogn fjord. The entire journey had been blessed with a steady north wind, calm seas, and clear blue skies during the day, while at night the longship was guided by the light of a half-crescent moon and thousands of winking stars.

Gwendolyn had actually enjoyed herself during much of the return voyage. Thankfully she had been spared the seasickness that had wracked her body on the way to Trondheim. The brisk wind in her hair and the golden rays of the sun on her face had enlivened her senses, giving her some peace and allowing her to forget, even for a short time, the disquieting thoughts that had been tormenting her so.

She had spoken little during the voyage, preferring instead to sit quietly at her bench to watch the ever-changing scenery of the rugged Norse coastline. But it had also given her a chance to observe silently the easy camaraderie Hakon had with his crewmen. It was obvious that the good weather had buoyed everyone's spirits. Outrageous jests and ribald stories had flown through the air, and hearty laughter had rung out across the waves. A couple of times Hakon had even goaded her with a few good-natured taunts, especially about the slave wench in Trondheim. But she had done her best to ignore him, until he finally shrugged and left her alone.

She noticed that Hakon had said nothing, not even to his trusted crewmen, about the matter of grave importance that had summoned him to Trondheim. And she had not ventured to ask, fearing another sharp rebuttal like the one she'd received in Haarek Jarl's hall. She had also caught him staring at her rather strangely several times, but he had always looked away quickly, avoiding her eyes. She shrugged it off, thinking that perhaps he was puzzled that she had not joined in the merriment of the others.

It was best that way, she decided. If she did not speak, and stayed away from him, something not so easily achieved on so narrow a ship, she would have no fear of giving her emotions away, and perhaps threatening her guise as well.

It was only when they reached the mouth of the Sogn and left the open seas behind them that she noticed Hakon had grown increasingly impatient to reach the settlement. He had been standing alone at the prow for the past hour, his eyes intent on the landscape before him. The sun was sinking behind the surrounding mountainsides in a glowing ball of orange fire when the longship finally rounded the last bend in the fjord.

Hakon whooped with delight as he caught sight of the settlement. His wild cry startled Gwendolyn, though Olav and the crew laughed uproariously. Aye, she knew why he was so elated. Soon he would once again hold Anora in his arms.

"Up with your oars, men!" he shouted to the crew, a broad smile playing across his handsome features.

Gwendolyn shook her head grimly as she complied with his order. No doubt Hakon would rush to find her sister as soon as the ship was moored. If his greeting were anything like the one she had received in his bathing house . . . She blushed hotly, remembering. Nay, she had to find Anora first, and exchange places with her before . . .

The longship suddenly scraped against the wooden dock, jarring her thoughts. There was an instant commotion as the Viking guards onshore rushed to grab the lines tossed to them. With their sinewy muscles heaving and straining, the men tied the ship securely to the dock.

"Welcome, my lord!" Egil called out, jumping down onto the wooden deck. He had been left behind to oversee the settlement and the extra men while Hakon was in Trondheim.

Hakon greeted him with a hearty slap on the back. "Was there any trouble during my absence?" he asked.

"Nay, my lord," Egil replied, shaking his shaggy head. "It has been very quiet these past few days . . . perhaps too quiet."

"How so?" Hakon queried, lowering his voice.

Seeing Egil and Hakon engrossed in conversation, Gwendolyn seized her chance. She knew there was not a moment to lose. Without hesitation, she jumped up from her bench with her roll of clothing clutched in one hand and bounded over the side of the ship onto the dock. Running up the hill as if the very hounds of hell were snapping at her heels, she did not stop even when she heard Hakon's voice calling out after her. *Perhaps Egil will keep him occupied for a few moments*, she thought wildly. That Viking was known to be long-winded even at his best moments. Aye, she could only hope he would be the same this day.

Hakon cursed aloud, interrupting Egil's detailed account of the last few days. Where was Garric off to, and in such a hurry? Then he shrugged. No matter. He would see to the lad's impudence later. Now he had other things on his mind. A slow smile spread over his face as he thought of Anora. "We can talk of this later, Egil. From what you have said so far, I see no cause for alarm."

"Very well, my lord," Egil said, noting his impatience. His eyes glinted knowingly. Yea, if he had a wench as beautiful as Lord Hakon's, he would not wish to tarry overlong from her side!

With a nod to Olav, Hakon jumped from the ship to the dock with one agile movement. Whistling, he strode quickly along the path to his hall, his blood beginning to race with excitement.

Gwendolyn said a quick prayer of thanks when she saw there were no guards at the entrance to Hakon's private hall. She pushed open the heavy door and hurried across the main room. Bursting in the door to his chamber, she startled Anora, who was sitting in the leather-backed chair facing the window. Her sister stood up and whirled around, dropping to the floor the fine needlework she was stitching.

"Gwendolyn, you frightened me!" Anora cried out. The look on Gwendolyn's face sent a surge of fear through her body. "How long have you been here? Where is Hakon?"

"I think he is still at the docks! Quickly, Anora, there is no time to talk. We must change clothes . . . *now!*" Gwendolyn whispered fiercely, pulling off her leather jerkin. But at that moment she heard the door at the entrance to the hall grate open. A familiar, lilting whistle echoed about the main room. *God's blood! 'Tis Hakon!* she thought wildly. Her heart flew to her throat. Nay, their guise could not end like this! There had to be another way!

Suddenly her eyes flew to the window, and back again to Anora. She rushed over to her sister's side and shoved the roll of clothing into her hand. "Climb out the window, Anora, and do not stop until you get to the stable!" she hissed urgently. "You can change into some of my other clothes once you get there . . . then hide the ones you are wearing under a pile of straw! Now go!"

Anora nodded numbly. She did not hesitate, though her eyes were wide with apprehension. Gripping the roll of clothing tightly under her arm, she hoisted her silken chemise and mantle over her knees and climbed through the window as Gwendolyn held back the leather shade. "But what of you?" she whispered urgently, peering over the wooden ledge of the window, her face pale and drawn.

"I will be fine. Now go, quickly!" Gwendolyn dropped the shade as Anora hurried off. Stepping away from the window, she pulled frantically at her woolen clothes. Truly, she had never undressed with greater speed as she did in those few moments, all the while hurrying to the ornate chest that held her fine clothing. She flung back the lid and dumped her fur-lined jerkin, shirt, breeches, and leather belt into a far corner and covered them quickly with silken garments.

Drawing out a fine, almost transparent chemise of emerald green silk gauze, she pulled it over her head, then quietly closed the lid of the chest. She could hear heavy footsteps approaching the door. With a last look around the room, she dashed over to the wide bed and jumped under the covers.

"God's blood!" she suddenly cursed under her breath. Throwing back the fur coverlet, she yanked off her fur-trimmed leather boots and tossed them under the bed. She ran her fingers through her short curls, then gathered the thick coverlet up about her shoulders and rolled over onto her side. She forced herself to take several deep breaths until she felt somewhat relaxed, though her heart still pounded madly against her breast. No more than a moment had passed when she heard the door to the chamber open slowly.

Hakon looked about the room, his eyes coming to rest on the slender form lying beneath the fur coverlet. He drew in his breath sharply. He had thought of little else since he left Trondheim but to hold Anora once again in his arms. But if she was resting soundly, he did not want to disturb her. Nay, not yet. First he would have a warm bath and rid himself of the grime and smell of the voyage. Then he would have Berta bring wine and a sumptuous meal to his hall. Only then would he wake her.

Yea, it will be a long night. He chuckled lustily, a gleam of desire flaring in his eyes. *Let her rest while she may. . . .* Smiling to himself, he turned and walked quietly back across the threshold and shut the door softly behind him.

Gwendolyn's eyes flew open in surprise. She sat up in the wide bed, then kicked away the fur coverlet and threw her slender legs over the side of the down mattress. Running to the door, she listened until the sound of Hakon's footsteps had died away. Only then did she open the door a crack and peer out, just in time to see his broad back as he stepped from the hall and closed the heavy door behind him.

She shut the door and slumped limply against it. Suddenly she started to laugh, not only from relief, but from the sheer ridiculousness of it all. It started as a snicker, but quickly grew into hearty peals of laughter that, try as she might, she could not suppress. She ran to the bed and buried her face in one of the eiderdown pillows, and still she laughed until the tears were rolling down her flushed cheeks and she was almost choking.

But the tears of laughter soon gave way to hot, wrenching tears of frustration as the tension of the past few days suddenly overwhelmed her. Gwendolyn doubled over, her slender body wracked by silent sobs. Confusion, pain, fear, and intense longing all seemed to erupt within her. Hugging a pillow tightly to her chest, she cried until her tears were spent. And when she could cry no more she lay on the bed for a long time, until she at last fell asleep from sheer exhaustion.

Chapter Thirty-two

"Wake up, my love," Hakon murmured, nuzzling the silky skin at the nape of Gwendolyn's neck. He trailed a path of kisses down the top of her spine.

Gwendolyn's eyelids flickered open, a delicious shiver running through her body. She stretched her slender limbs languidly, unable to suppress a wide yawn. Suddenly she felt herself lifted from the bed by a pair of strong arms.

"Oh!" She gasped in surprise. Her startled gaze met Hakon's.

"If you do not awaken, little one, you shall miss the fine dinner Berta has prepared for us." Hakon chuckled. Holding her close against his bare chest, he strode out of the chamber with her and into the main room of the hall.

Gwendolyn shielded her eyes with her hand until she grew accustomed to the light of the blazing fire burning brightly in the central fireplace. But her eyes widened with astonishment when she finally looked about her.

It seemed as if the far end of the hall near Hakon's chamber had been transformed. The luxurious rug that had been in the center of the room was now stretched out before the fireplace, the flames reflecting off the glistening sheen of the black fur. Pillows swathed in silken fabrics were scattered about the rug, while a low table was set at one end. There were two fine ceramic goblets and a matching vessel upon a silver tray set atop the table. Resting beside the tray was a large covered platter, still steaming hot from the cooking house.

A flush of embarrassment reddened Gwendolyn's cheeks as her stomach growled hungrily and loudly. It had been such a long time since she had last eaten! Hakon threw back his head and laughed.

"Did you not eat while I was gone?" He shook his head in mock anger. "I will have to chastise Berta when I see her for not taking proper care of you!" He grinned wickedly as he set her down gently with her back against a large pillow. "Yea, the food does smell wonderful. I think Berta might have outdone herself this night." He dropped down beside her and gathered her into his arms. "But the meal will have to wait for a few moments, my love."

His blue eyes heatedly raked her slender body. Yea, the emerald silk of her chemise did little to conceal her charms from his gaze. Her silky skin shone like alabaster through the almost transparent fabric, the clinging bodice stretched taut across her firm breasts and pink-crested nipples. Hakon groaned inwardly. It was all he could do not to take her this very moment, but he cooled his growing ardor. Nay, he wanted to savor their evening together . . . slowly.

"I have missed you, Anora," Hakon murmured, his lips warm against her throat. His mouth, searching, insistent, moved to her delicate earlobe. He lingered there, nibbling ever so gently.

Gwendolyn closed her eyes, her body tingling with the sensations that swept through her. She could not fight him, nor did she want to. When they were together like this, it was so easy to forget the awful dilemma that tormented her . . . and to think only of love. Her hand strayed to his broad chest, her tapered fingers entwining in the thick golden curls. When he at last kissed her, parting her lips and tasting the honeyed sweetness of her mouth, she surprised him by flicking the tip of her tongue against his.

Hakon drew away suddenly, his breath ragged. He was almost trembling with desire. By the blood of Odin, what this woman could do to him! "Perhaps we had better eat," he muttered thickly. "It seems I have taught you too well, my love. One more kiss like that and the food will be long cold before we even look to see what lies beneath the cover!"

Gwendolyn smiled, strangely pleased at the power she had over him. "Aye, my lord, let us eat."

Hakon almost could not tear his eyes away from her face. He saw her smile so rarely, and when she did he never ceased to be stunned by her exquisite beauty. He said a silent prayer of thanks to Odin as he got up from the rug and walked over to the low table.

Gwendolyn's eyes moved appreciatively over his body as he bent to pour some red wine into the ceramic goblets. She watched the play of rippling muscles across the broad span of his shoulders and back, and admired the burnished bronze of his skin. His silken trousers barely concealed the tapered lines of his hips and his taut buttocks. Every sculpted inch of his body bespoke power and strength. He was so magnificent . . . so virile. . . .

She could not believe the wantonness of her thoughts. Why, only a few hours ago she had cried agonized tears into her pillow, cursing the cruel fates that had brought them together. Yet at this moment for the first time she was truly glad—glad for the wild delight they found in each other's arms, glad that she belonged to him, and, most of all, glad that he loved her and would make her his wife. She shook her head, perplexed. When would she ever understand her feelings? How could this one man so completely overwhelm and conquer her sense of reason, just by his touch? He was unwittingly enticing her to betray her sense of duty to Anora, the sister she also loved with all her heart!

Hakon handed her a goblet, interrupting her jumbled thoughts. "Why do you frown so, little one?" he asked softly. She started at the sound of his voice. She had not even noticed he had returned.

" 'Twas naught, my lord," she murmured, blushing warmly. She reached up and took the other goblet of wine from him. He then walked quickly back to the table and returned with the large covered platter. He set it gingerly in front of her, then sat down cross-legged close by her side, his hard, muscled thigh brushing against her leg.

"Nay, 'twas something, I know it," he insisted gently. "I have seen you frown so before, when you were deep in thought." He smiled rakishly, his blue eyes burning into hers with heated desire. "I forbid you to think of aught else but me this night," he said huskily. "Now drink with me, Anora."

Taking one of the goblets from her hand, he raised it to his lips and drank deeply. Gwendolyn did the same, her eyes not leaving his. It was more of the same red wine they had shared in the bathing house, she thought, savoring the heady sweetness. Memories of that long night flooded back to her, and she hoped that tonight would be as passionately fulfilling.

Hakon set down his goblet and lifted the cover from the wooden platter. As the steam escaped from under the dripping lid, the mouth-watering aroma of roasted pheasant filled the air. There were four of the delectable birds arranged on the platter, surrounded by pit-roasted small potatoes and steamed figs.

He smiled at Gwendolyn's gasp of pleasure. Breaking off a well-browned leg, he handed it to her, then tore another off for himself. Berta had even provided a crusty loaf of rye bread slathered with golden butter, and several moistened towels for their hands.

They ate in contented silence, Hakon handing Gwendolyn choice pieces of roast pheasant and the plumpest figs. One ripe fig burst when she bit into it. The sweet juice ran down her chin and on to the bodice of her chemise, soaking through to her skin, before she could wipe it away. She giggled as Hakon drew her to him and kissed the nectar from her mouth.

"I will savor the rest of it later." He grinned lustily, his eyes on her breasts. The thought sent shivers of anticipation racing through her. He was about to rise to fetch more wine, but Gwendolyn stopped him. Rising to her feet, she walked to the low table, very much aware that his gaze was following her every movement. She picked up the tall vessel and turned around, a faint smile on her lips.

Hakon almost choked. Her silken garment was so sheer, it was as if she were standing before him with no clothes on at all! The leaping flames in the fireplace cast a glowing aura about her slender form, accentuating her delicate curves. She seemed bathed in light, from her head to her toes. The delicate beauty of her features shone with ethereal radiance, the soft curls of her silver-blond hair glinting with shimmering highlights. If Hakon had not known she was a flesh-and-blood woman, he would have thought for sure she was a goddess sent down from the high throne of Odin himself! Overwhelmed by raging desire, he knew he could wait no longer.

He rose swiftly to his feet. Hastily stripping off his silken trousers, he stood before her in all his masculine glory, his manhood erect and throbbing. Walking over to her, he took the vessel of wine from her hand and set it down on the table.

Gwendolyn gasped, awed by his male beauty. Taking both her hands in his own, Hakon stepped back, gently drawing her with him to the center of the thick rug. As his strong arms encircled her narrow waist, she gazed up at him with an impassioned look of love that took his breath away.

Thor, it was true . . . at last! Hakon's heart raced at the raw emotion he saw reflected in the emerald depths of her eyes. He had known if he waited long enough, one day she would return his love. Bending his head, he captured her parted lips fiercely with his own. Their arms wrapped tightly about each other in a timeless embrace. They stood there for a long moment in the light of the fire, oblivious to all but the love they shared.

"Anora . . . my only love," Hakon murmured huskily, finally tearing his lips from hers. He slowly sank to his knees, his hands caressing the silky length of her body. As he gently cupped her breasts, his tongue flickered around and around the pale pink nipples in a ring of fire, tasting the nectar of the fig upon her warmed skin.

Gwendolyn moaned softly, wrapping her fingers in his long white-blond hair as his mouth moved down her abdomen, caressing her navel, to the mound of silver-blond curls below. He held her against him, reveling in the taste and feel of her, while his strong fingers teased and stroked the soft cleft between her silky thighs.

Wantonly writhing within his grasp, Gwendolyn felt lost in a passion-numbed daze. Everything was so sweet, so wonderful. . . . Throwing back her head, she exulted in the exquisite sensations that caused her to tremble uncontrollably.

Hakon at last drew her down beside him on the luxurious black fur until his hard length was poised above her. Thor, she was beautiful . . . so soft, so willing. . . . He knew she was ready for him. Ever so gently he parted her legs with his knee, then entered her, but not too far. She reached up to pull him to her, but he tenderly stretched her slender arms above her head, holding her wrists with one strong hand. Suddenly he brought his lips down upon her own at the same time he entered her completely.

Gwendolyn gasped with pleasure, arching her back as he lunged deep inside her. She struggled to free her arms so she could wrap them about his neck, but he would not let her loose.

"Nay, Anora, do not struggle," he whispered in her ear, his warm breath sending shivers racing through her. "Do not move." She tried to do as he bade her, though it was difficult at first, her hips instinctively moving in rhythm against his slow, measured thrusts. "Nay, nay, lie still, my love," he said softly. "Let me move within you."

Gwendolyn relaxed beneath him, closing her eyes as the most delicious sensations washed over her. This was different from the times before. Just as intense . . . but so achingly, so wonderfully different. She felt as if her body were adrift in a warm sea, as wave after wave of the purest pleasure radiated within her, crescendoing, yet ever so languorously. She could feel his warm kisses on her throat, her eyelids, her lips. His fingers teased at her breast, stroking, caressing. Suddenly her breath caught in her throat, all conscious thought driven from her mind, as the sweetest, most exquisite wave of bliss broke over her.

Watching her beautiful face for the moment of her release, Hakon smiled as she writhed beneath him. He could hold back no longer. He groaned as he shuddered deep within her, overwhelmed by the tumultuous sensations that seared through his loins.

They lay together so, merged as one and entwined in each other's arms, long after the logs blazing brightly in the fireplace had been reduced to glowing embers.

Chapter Thirty-three

A fierce pounding on the heavy door to his hall roused Hakon enough to raise his head. He opened his eyes and looked about him. Only a dull glow remained in the central fireplace, telling him that the fire must have died out hours ago. Most likely it was near dawn, he thought, shaking his head. The pounding at the door grew louder.

"Lord Hakon, I must speak with you at once!"

The warrior in Hakon became instantly alert as he recognized Olav's voice. His men knew well enough not to disturb him at night unless it was a matter of the greatest urgency. Pulling gently away from Gwendolyn's arms, he swiftly covered her with one end of the fur rug and hurriedly slipped on his silken trousers.

"What is it, my lord?" Gwendolyn asked drowsily, opening her eyes. She, too, had been awakened by the pounding. She brought herself up on one elbow.

"Stay there, little one," Hakon admonished softly. He grabbed his broadsword from beneath some nearby pillows and held it at his side as he strode to the door.

At that moment Olav burst into the hall and rushed into the main room, almost running into Hakon. Several Viking guards were also with him, but they stayed just outside the door, their great torches shedding light into the darkened hall.

"Forgive me, Lord Hakon," he said hastily, averting his eyes from the fetching sight of Gwendolyn lying barely covered beneath the fur rug. " 'Tis Rhoar Bloodaxe! He and his forces, numbering several hundred strong, have been sighted just over the valley. I fear this is the day he shall seek his vengeance, my lord!"

"Thor's blood!" Hakon cursed loudly, his voice echoing about the hall. "Who has brought this news?"

"A messenger from your uncle's settlement was on his way here when he almost rode into the very midst of Rhoar's camp. He arrived only a few moments ago. Shall I send for him, my lord?"

"Nay, Olav. I will speak with him shortly." Hakon's face was grim in the bright light of the torches, his mind working fast. "See that the men are alerted and ready for battle," he ordered. "Post a third of the guards around the perimeter of the settlement, and see that several men are stationed at each longhouse . . . though I want at least ten to guard my hall." Olav nodded as Hakon continued. "We are fortunate that most of the reinforcements I summoned to guard the settlement while I was in Trondheim still remain," he said tersely.

"Yea, my lord, 'tis fortunate indeed." Olav shook his head in assent, though he felt a slight sense of unease. Hakon had the advantage of at least two men to every one of Rhoar's, but some of them would have to remain behind to protect the settlement. No doubt Hakon's forces would meet the enemy in battle near their camp in the valley, for he was sure Hakon would do everything in his power to keep Rhoar and his men away from the settlement.

"Go, Olav, and see to it that all is in readiness," Hakon commanded, interrupting his thoughts. "I will join you in a few moments."

"Yea, my lord." Turning on his heel, Olav strode quickly from the hall.

Hakon stood for a moment, lost in thought. So, the day of Rhoar's blood vengeance had finally come! Today his hated bastard brother would make a violent play to wrest from him the right of his inheritance, or meet his death trying.

Yea, for Hakon knew it would be a fight to the death. There could be no other way. He shook his head grimly. He would meet Rhoar in battle, but now there was more to fight for than just his inheritance. He looked over to where Gwendolyn lay, her emerald eyes searching his face. Her tousled beauty took his breath away. His fist clenched tightly around the hilt of his broadsword. Nay, he would not have such happiness taken from him! By the blood of Odin, he vowed angrily, he could not, *would not*, be defeated!

He walked back to her side and held out his hand to her. She grasped his hand, the fur rug falling away from her slender body as he gently pulled her to her feet. Holding her close against his bare chest, he caressed her silken curls.

"You heard Olav's words?" he asked softly.

Gwendolyn nodded her head, though for some strange reason she could not speak. She listened to the strong, steady beating of his heart, a cold lump of apprehension in her throat. She turned suddenly and looked up at him, their eyes meeting in a gaze of longing so intense she could have cried out. But still she was silent. What would be her and Anora's fate if aught happened to him? What would her life be without him? She shook her head fiercely. Nay, she would not think of it! A solitary tear ran down the side of her face. Seeing it, Hakon gently brushed it away.

"Nay, my love, there is no time for tears," he murmured. "You must have courage . . . it will help me to do what I must. Now, come, I must prepare for battle." He led her into his chamber and sat her down on the wide bed, leaning his broadsword against one of the carved corner posts. Thankfully the room was warm from the glowing heat of the bronze brazier, but he still wrapped her within the thick coverlet.

Gwendolyn watched as he strode over to one of his massive chests and lifted the heavy lid. He stripped off his silken trousers and hastily donned a black woolen tunic that reached to mid-thigh. Then he bent and pulled on woolen trousers and protective leggings fastened at the back of his calves. Next came high leather boots that rose to just below his knees, and then he wrapped his wide leather belt with the long scabbard finely ornamented with metal mounts about his waist. A mail shirt made of linked iron rings that reached just to his belt went on over the tunic. He drew a thick black mantle trimmed in fur from the chest and wrapped it about his shoulders, attaching it to the mail shirt with two large silver brooches.

Gwendolyn was astonished at how quickly he dressed, and with such practiced efficiency. Lastly he pulled a massive wooden shield from the timbered wall where it had been hanging. It was brightly painted in black and yellow, and an iron boss glinted from the center that would serve to protect his hand.

Hakon ran his free hand through his white-blond hair and approached the bed. He bent and picked up his heavy broadsword and slid it easily into the scabbard at his belt. "You must stay here, Anora, in this room, until I return," he commanded softly. "There will be guards posted outside the hall to protect you, so you need not fear. 'Tis my hope that the battle will be fought and won before night falls once again." His voice grew hard as he thought of what lay ahead. He could tarry no longer. "I must go, my love," he said, the bronzed planes of his face determined, grim.

Gwendolyn suddenly rose from the bed, the fur coverlet falling to the floor. She flung her arms about his neck, standing on tiptoes, and kissed him with such passionate fervor that it nearly took his breath away. The iron links of his mail shirt bit cruelly into her skin, but she did not care. Nothing mattered for that one moment but the kiss they shared.

At last Hakon tore his lips from hers, chuckling deeply. "I shall look forward to many more of those, my love." He strode over to the table near the window and picked up his silver helmet. Holding it in the crook of his arm, he glanced one last time at Gwendolyn.

She stood beside the bed, her beautiful body bared to his heated gaze. Thor, he had never before seen her look so vulnerable and alone! "Do not fear, little one, Odin shall protect me," he murmured reassuringly. And with that, he was gone from the room, his footsteps echoing down the length of the hall until the heavy door slammed shut behind him.

Gwendolyn waited a moment, still and silent, until she was sure he was gone. Then, without wasting any more time, she raced over to her chest of clothing and threw back the lid. *Nay, my love, I shall be with you*, she thought resolutely, *not as Anora, but as Garric*. . . . She knew Hakon would probably need the services of his stable hand to see to his stallion, and perhaps he would even need a weapons bearer. Their guise would fail for sure if Anora went with him into battle. Her sister knew nothing of weapons and warfare. Aye, if she hurried, she would probably make it to the stable before he got there!

Gwendolyn pulled her jerkin, woolen shirt, leather belt, and breeches out from beneath the pile of silken garments, and dressed quickly. She then ran to the wide bed and peered underneath it. Her leather boots were out of reach, but after a few lunges she was able to grab them and put them on her feet. Now, all that was needed was a weapon, she thought, glancing about the room. She was not about to go onto a battlefield empty-handed!

Her eyes scanned the array of weapons hanging on the timbered walls of the chamber. Spying a long-bladed knife with an ornately carved hilt, she lifted it from the two wooden pegs it was resting on and slid it into her belt. She then ran back over to the bed and mounded several eider-down pillows up beneath the fur coverlet. At least that way if anyone came into the room, they would think she was fast asleep and not disturb her!

Gwendolyn hurried to the nearest window and lifted the leather shade. She peered outside furtively. The early morning sky was just beginning to lighten with the first golden rays of sunlight. Several inches of new snow had fallen during the night, adding to the icy covering already on the frozen ground. Relieved at seeing no one near Hakon's hall, she hoisted herself up and over the window ledge and jumped easily to the ground below.

She hugged the outside wall for a moment, getting her bearings. Suddenly two Viking guards rounded the corner of Hakon's hall, so she started walking nonchalantly in the direction of the stable. Her heart was pounding wildly against her chest. Sweet Jesu! If they had come a moment sooner . . .! She did not want to think about it. It certainly would have looked suspicious for a stable hand to be sneaking out of the window of Hakon Jarl's private chamber! She had almost reached the path to the stable not far from the hall when she heard a familiar voice call out to her.

"Garric!" She froze in her steps, looking over her shoulder. Hakon was standing near the front of his hall surrounded by Olav and about twenty Viking warriors. "Fetch my stallion, lad, and be quick about it!" he commanded in a tone that bespoke no resistance. Gwendolyn broke out in a run, her panting breath billowing out in clouds of vapor from the cold morning air.

God's blood, that was twice she had been lucky! Hakon had obviously not yet been to the stable. She only hoped now that he would not return to his chamber and find her gone! Reaching the stable door, she pushed it open and leaned against it for a moment, trying to catch her breath.

"Garric, are you here?" she called out, not daring to use Anora's name until she knew for sure her sister was alone. Her eyes searched the dim interior. There was no answer. At least it was warm, Gwendolyn thought, rubbing her cold hands together as she closed the door behind her and stepped farther into the stable. "Garric?" There was a sudden rustling from the direction of one of the stalls.

"Aye, 'tis I," Anora whispered faintly, stepping out from behind the nearest stall. There was hay stuck in her short curls, and from the rumpled appearance of the clothing Gwendolyn had given her the night before, she must have been sleeping. She rubbed her eyes, then stared in startled surprise at her sister.

"Gwendolyn, what are you doing?" she blurted, though not too loudly. "We cannot both be dressed as Garric!"

Gwendolyn shook her head and quickly explained. "Lord Hakon has received news that Rhoar Bloodaxe is planning to attack this very day!" She ignored Anora's gasp and rushed on. "I changed into these clothes and hurried here." She smiled fleetingly. "The same way you escaped last night. I have no doubts that Lord Hakon will wish for Garric to accompany him to the battlefield. As I did not think you would enjoy the task, I came as quickly as I could!"

Anora nodded fiercely in agreement, her eyes wide and frightened. "But how shall I get back to his hall? It was hard enough last night, though thankfully I had cover of darkness."

"Nay, you will have to stay here, in the stable," Gwendolyn replied. "But you must keep yourself hidden. Hakon bade me not to leave the chamber before he left this morning. If he saw you walk now from the stable . . ." She shrugged. Anora nodded in understanding.

"Aye, but what of when you return, after the battle?" she asked, then shuddered. Nay, she would not think that Gwendolyn might not return.

Gwendolyn seemed to have read her thoughts. "Do not fear, Anora, I will stay far back and well out of danger," she said reassuringly. "I am sure the Vikings do not employ mere youths to fight their battles!" She grimaced. At least, she hoped not! "And when I return to the settlement, I will simply sneak back through the window of Lord Hakon's hall and resume my guise. No one will be the wiser!"

Suddenly she heard the tramp of many feet and loud voices echoing from the stable yard. They must be getting ready to march from the settlement, she thought wildly. "Anora, hide yourself, and well!" she hissed. "I will somehow let you know when all is safe for you to come out of hiding."

"Please be careful, Gwendolyn," Anora murmured. She hugged her sister tightly, then disappeared into the dark recesses of the stable.

Gwendolyn ran to the stall where Hakon's great stallion stood tossing its proud head and neighing loudly in response to the sounds from other horses in the stable yard. With practiced hands she quickly saddled the huge animal, then grabbed the reins and led it from the stable.

"What took you so long, lad?" Hakon asked angrily, striding toward her. "Do you think the battle waits upon your pleasure?" He grabbed the reins from her hand. "Here, hold my shield while I mount." Gwendolyn almost collapsed under the heavy weight of the brightly painted shield, but somehow she managed to hold it upright until Hakon could take it from her. He hoisted it easily from her arms and fixed it to the side of his saddle. "Join the other boys back there, and be ready to assist if you are needed," he said gruffly. Pulling sharply on the reins, he brought the spirited stallion about so he could face his men.

Hakon felt a surge of excitement course through his body as several hundred pairs of eyes stared back at him with fierce, undying allegiance. Most of his warriors were on foot, some armed with spears, axes, and rude cudgels, while others had swords and bows and arrows slung over their shoulders. Only he and the petty chieftains under his rule were on horseback. All was quiet, hushed, save for the impatient nickering of the horses, and the sound of the cold wind as it whipped through the white banners painted with leering, fanged dragons that were carried by the standard-bearers.

Hakon pulled his mighty broadsword from its scabbard and lifted it high above his head. "To Odin!" he shouted loudly. "To victory!"

A great roar went up from the Viking warriors. "Odin! Odin!" they intoned, as if with one thundering voice. "Odin! Odin!" Their fierce cries echoed about the mountainsides across the fjord as they marched from the settlement behind their Jarl.

Chapter Thirty-four

Gwendolyn dropped the spears she was carrying and let the heavy quiver of arrows slip from her shoulder to the snow-covered ground. They had been marching for close to an hour. Hakon's forces had moved stealthily along the hill-sides, scattering and rejoining according to the nature of the ground, until they had reached the valley where Rhoar and his army of renegade Vikings had camped during the night.

Apparently their arrival had been anticipated, for Rhoar Bloodaxe and his forces stood ready and waiting in a massive, heavily armed line at least four men thick that stretched the entire length of the open field where they would do battle.

Gwendolyn felt a cold fear grip her as she scanned the hardened, ruthless faces of Rhoar's men. She said a quick prayer that all would go well, but she was beginning to have her doubts. Though she and the rest of the young arms bearers stood on a crest of a hill well away from where the battle would take place, they had already been told they would be used as reinforcements if needed. Apparently this news had struck great terror in the hearts of several of the youths, though they tried hard not to show it, for they had heard stories of the men in Rhoar's army.

They were outcasts, all of them. Some had defied their chieftains and had been exiled from their lands, while others were murderers and thieves. Rhoar was rumored to have enticed these men to his cause, knowing they would fight with a bloodthirsty abandon that only desperate men who had nothing to lose possessed. It was against this enraged, blinding lust for wealth and power that Hakon's men would be fighting.

Gwendolyn's eyes followed Hakon's commanding form astride his mighty black stallion as he moved about his men, his strong voice guiding them into position.

Suddenly the sun came out from behind the clouds, blinding Gwendolyn as the bright rays hit the white surface of the snow-covered field. Bloodcurdling Viking battle shrieks and terrible, wolfish howling broke from the throats of Rhoar's men at that same moment, shattering the eerie silence of the battlefield as they began their advance.

Shielding her eyes from the sun, Gwendolyn watched in horror as they rushed toward the line of Hakon's forces, wildly brandishing their flashing weapons over their heads as they screamed, some even biting upon their wooden shields like mad dogs. And though scores of arrows rained down upon them from the bows of Hakon's men, still they kept coming, a relentless, almost inhuman onslaught. Horns signaled the start of battle from each side, the haunting sound sending a chill through the very marrow of her bones. She looked on with grim fascination, unable to tear her eyes away, knowing that this battle could mean not only Hakon's doom and that of his men, but her own and Anora's as well.

Her breath caught in her throat at the fearsome sight of Rhoar Bloodaxe astride a dappled stallion. He rode fearlessly at the head of his men, his awful triple-edged axe held high. His flaming red hair and beard shone brightly in the sunlight, and she could almost hear his wicked laughter above the din of battle, carried high upon the wind. She watched in horror as he gleefully buried his axe in the back of an opponent, only to wrench it free, dripping with blood.

Patches of bright red soon stained the snow as the fierce battle raged on. To Gwendolyn it seemed everything was happening so fast! Both forces of men were now waged in hand-to-hand, man-against-man combat, a macabre dance of death. She could still see Hakon wheeling his huge stallion about in the wild melee, his black-and-yellow shield raised in front of him, while his broadsword rained deadly blows down upon his enemy.

But suddenly Gwendolyn lost sight of him as he was violently wrenched from his saddle by the arms of a huge opponent. Her heart went to her throat. Sweet Jesu! Protect him! Without thinking, she dashed down the hill. One of the other arms bearers tried to catch her about the waist, but she eluded his grasp. She ran into the thick of battle as swiftly as her legs could carry her.

All around her were the deafening sounds of combat as sword rang out against sword, the agonized screams of the injured and dying filling the air. She nimbly dodged grappling opponents and fallen bodies, her eyes frantically scanning the ever-shifting fray for a sign of Hakon.

It was the evil sound of Rhoar's laughter that caused her to turn her head. Suddenly everything stopped around her, time froze, as she caught sight of the terrible scene that greeted her. Hakon was lying on the snowy ground not more than twenty feet away, his broadsword knocked from his hand. Rhoar towered over him, laughing hideously, his bloody axe raised and glinting in the sun.

All Gwendolyn knew at that moment was that her life would mean naught without him. Acting on finely honed instincts, she pulled the knife from her belt and took swift aim, throwing it with all her strength at Rhoar's uplifted arm. He started in surprise as the long-bladed knife sank into his flesh, taking his eyes from Hakon for a split-second.

It was all the time that Hakon needed. He lunged violently for his broadsword and, grabbing the hilt, in one swift movement brought it up and impaled Rhoar on the shining blade. Rhoar's gleaming eyes widened as he watched his lifeblood spill out upon the white snow, a gruesomely pathetic expression on his bearded face. "Damn you, Hakon . . ." he whispered hoarsely. He was dead before he hit the ground, his eyes staring lifelessly at the cold winter sky.

Hakon staggered to his feet. "Odin!" he shouted with all his might, raising his clenched fists high above his head. Already he could see many of Rhoar's men running from the battlefield, knowing all was lost now that their leader had been dealt a death blow.

Gwendolyn felt a surge of overwhelming relief course through her slender body at the sound of his victory cry, but it was short-lived. Suddenly she felt shattering pain as a long spear hit her just below her left shoulder. The impact knocked her to the ground. She screamed in agony, calling out Hakon's name. Then all went black as she mercifully lost consciousness.

Hakon grimly wrenched his broadsword from Rhoar's body and wiped the blade in the snow. Then he bent and pulled the long-bladed knife from his bastard brother's upper right arm. He immediately recognized the ornately carved hilt. Why, it was one of his own—from his collection of weapons in his chamber, no less! He turned, his eyes scanning the battlefield, which was littered with the dead and wounded. But who threw the knife that had saved him? He started in surprise as he spied Gwendolyn lying crumpled and still upon the ground not far away. Nay, it couldn't have been! Not Garric!

Holding his broadsword poised in his hand, he ran swiftly to where Gwendolyn lay. His mouth drew into a tight line as he saw the spear sticking from her shoulder, and the bright red stain of blood spreading out from the wound. Her face was devoid of color, pale as death.

Sheathing his broadsword and removing his silver helmet, Hakon dropped to his knees and lay his head on her chest. At least the lad was still breathing, though it was shallow at best. Thor, if Garric should die . . . He did not care to finish the thought. He only knew that it would drive a wedge between him and Anora that might never be removed. Yea, she would never forgive him if her brother did not return alive, he thought grimly.

Hakon quickly put one hand over the wound and wrapped his other hand about the wooden handle of the spear. Gritting his teeth, he slowly drew the pointed blade from her shoulder. It came out cleanly. Tossing the spear aside, he then quickly tore off a piece of his woolen tunic to staunch the heavy flow of blood from the gaping hole. He cursed under his breath, feeling strangely helpless, knowing he could do little more. Gathering her limp form into his arms, he strode hurriedly toward the healer's tent that had been erected on the hillside overlooking the battlefield.

"My lord, the battle is won!" Olav called out excitedly, reining in his horse alongside Hakon. He was covered in grime and sweat, and there was blood on his arm where he had suffered a minor slash wound, but his eyes burned with exhilaration. "What has happened to the lad?" he asked, sobering at the hard expression on Hakon's face.

"I believe Garric has done no less than save my life this day," Hakon said, not breaking his stride. "If 'tis so, we shall have him to thank for our victory!" He called out over his broad shoulder, "See that the last of the enemy are routed, Olav. I shall not be long from the battlefield."

Hakon looked down at Gwendolyn's pale features as he

hurried along the hillside toward the healer's makeshift tent. Why did the lad look so achingly familiar? It was almost as if he held the very likeness of Anora in his arms. How could brother and sister look so much alike? He tried to shake off his disturbing thoughts, but he could not dispel the feeling of foreboding welling up inside him.

At last he reached the tent. Pushing back the leather flap at the entrance, he ducked his head and rushed in, almost knocking into the stooped figure of the healer as he bent over a wounded warrior.

"My . . . my lord!" the old man stammered, straightening and stepping back in surprise.

"This lad needs your care . . . *now*," Hakon muttered, concern etched on his face. He looked about the large tent for an empty place to lay his charge. Many of his men already lay on pallets lining the makeshift walls, and from the looks of some of their wounds, he knew there would sadly be no help for them.

A pit had been hastily dug near the center of the tent for a fire, and a steaming caldron of boiling water hung on an iron tripod above the roaring flames. The air was stifling and overwarm, smelling of pungent herb poultices and sweating bodies. Hakon noted the stone pan of cooked leeks and onions set near one of the wounded, and knew the odorous mixture was being fed to the man to aid in diagnosing a possible stomach wound. If the smell of the onions could be discerned escaping an injury, it usually meant it was fatal.

"Lay him there," the healer said abruptly. He pointed to a thick blanket stretched upon the ground near the rear of the tent. Hurrying over to the caldron, he used a wooden paddle to lift out several dripping rags from the boiling water and dropped them onto a platter held in his other hand.

Hakon gently lay Gwendolyn upon the blanket, then rose to his feet. His tall, powerful body made the tent seem very small. He strode back to where the healer was hastily preparing a thick, green herb paste for a poultice.

"I must return to the battlefield. Send for me when you have news of the lad's condition," he said, his voice low. He walked to the entrance, then stopped and turned back around. "See that he does not die," he muttered tersely. With that, he pushed aside the leather flap and was gone.

The healer sighed raggedly. Gathering together all the things he would need, he hurried over to the blanket where Gwendolyn lay. He kneeled down beside her, then took a sharp knife from his belt and carefully began to cut away first the leather jerkin, then the bloodied woolen fabric surrounding the wound just beneath her left shoulder. He shook his head. Such tender skin for a lad, he marveled, gently touching around the flaring hole. From what he could tell, though blood still flowed in a trickle from the wound, it did not appear to be fatal. He lifted her gently, checking to see if the spear had pierced through to her back. Nay, it had not. He clucked his tongue, relieved, as he set her back down upon the blanket.

Suddenly his eyes widened in astonishment; his breath caught in his throat. The cut half of the woolen shirt had fallen away, revealing to his startled gaze a high, firm breast! The healer almost choked. Swiftly cutting away the rest of the garment, he could not believe his eyes. 'Twas not a lad, but a young wench! Hastily he covered her breasts with another blanket, looking furtively about him to see if any of the other men had noticed. Thankfully none had. It would not do for anyone to know of this before Lord Hakon, he thought wildly. Then he chided himself. It was none of his affair if the lad was a wench! It was only his duty to see that she did not die!

Though still unconscious, Gwendolyn started violently as

the steaming cloths were applied to her wound. "Hakon . . ." she murmured over and over, writhing in fevered delirium.

The healer shook his head, pleased, as the flow of blood was finally halted. He took away the cloths and packed the angrily swelling hole with the foul-smelling herb poultice, then gently rubbed the paste on the damaged tissue surrounding the wound. Finally he wrapped a clean piece of cloth over her shoulder and then beneath her arm, around and around, until the entire area was bandaged. He sighed, sitting back on his haunches. There was naught else he could do but hope that the wound would not grow infected. If that happened . . . He shuddered, afraid to think of the consequences. He brought the blanket up under her chin and tucked it in around her.

Now there were others to attend to, the old man thought wearily. He rose shakily to his feet and wiped his soiled hands on his bloodied tunic. There were so many wounded. He carried the platter of rags back over to the caldron and dumped them into the boiling water.

Suddenly Hakon threw back the flap of the tent and rushed in, startling the healer once again.

"My lord, I would have sent word—"

Hakon silenced him with an abrupt wave of his hand. Once he had seen that the battle was indeed won and that those of Rhoar's men who had been captured were put swiftly to the sword, he had returned as quickly as he could, deciding not to wait any longer for news of Garric's condition.

"Will the lad live?" he asked, his eyes flying apprehensively to the far end of the tent where Gwendolyn lay. He grimaced at the ashen pallor of her skin and the shallow rise and fall of her chest beneath the woolen blanket. He quickly glanced back at the healer, dreading his answer.

"The wound is deep, my lord, and there has been a great loss of blood," the old man murmured, shifting his feet uncomfortably, "but in time, yea, in time it will heal."

Hakon's broad shoulders slumped visibly with relief. He walked over to the blanket and knelt down on one knee beside Gwendolyn. The healer walked up slowly behind him.

"Th-there is something you m-must know, my lord," he stuttered nervously.

"Yea, what is it?" Hakon asked, his voice low, not taking his eyes from Gwendolyn's face.

"The lad is a . . . I mean, he is not a . . ."

"Speak up, man!" Hakon shouted gruffly.

" 'Tis a wench, my lord, not a lad!" the healer blurted out, backing away several steps.

Hakon stood up suddenly and faced the older man, towering over him. "What did you say?"

"When I was dressing the wound, my lord, I discovered that 'twas a young woman you had brought to this tent, not a lad," he hastily explained. He stepped back a few more steps, afraid of Hakon's reaction.

Stunned, Hakon did not move for a moment. Garric . . . a wench! Nay, it could not be! Slowly he turned around, then lifted the blanket. His blue eyes narrowed, an angry scowl darkening his features. What mischief was Loki playing on him? His white-blond brows were knit in confusion.

Suddenly Gwendolyn tossed her head deliriously, moaning in pain. "Nay, my love, nay!" she cried out in heart-wrenching anguish. Though her slender body was racked by shivering spasms, she was bathed in perspiration. Her lips were parched and dry. "Hakon!" she murmured hoarsely. "Hakon . . ." Her voice died away as she lay still once again.

Hakon stared at her as if he had been struck. Falling to his knees, he gathered her into his arms, tucking the ends of the blanket about her delicate shoulders. "Anora," he murmured thickly, his voice catching on her name. He rocked her in his arms, stroking the sweat-dampened hair that curled in tendrils about her pale face. But how? he wondered frantically. Odin help him! She must have disguised herself as Garric and followed him into battle to be near him. That alone would explain the long-bladed knife from his chamber! Gwendolyn moaned softly and licked her dry lips, her muted cry breaking into his tormented thoughts.

"Fetch me some water, man!" Hakon shouted at the astonished healer, who stood wringing his hands helplessly.

"Yea, my lord!" The old man hurried to his vials of herbs, his fingers trembling as he poured fresh water from a small cask into a soapstone bowl. Had he heard right? Was she indeed the beautiful Anora, Hakon Jarl's favored concubine? His legs felt wooden as he rushed over to Hakon. He spilled half the water on the ground in his haste.

Hakon grabbed the bowl from the healer's wrinkled hand and gently raised it to Gwendolyn's lips. He gave her only a small amount for fear she might choke. She swallowed it thirstily, much to his relief. But after giving her another sip he drew the bowl away. " 'Tis enough for now," he murmured, more to himself than anyone else. He handed the bowl to the healer, then gathered Gwendolyn's limp form to his chest and rose to his feet.

"Do you have any other spare blankets?"

"Yea. Here, my lord," the old man replied hastily. He bent and picked up a thick blanket lying on the ground. He shook it roughly, then wrapped it snug and tight about Gwendolyn's shoulders.

"Good. I shall tell Olav to have litters brought here shortly for these men," Hakon said, striding toward the entrance of the tent. "See that their wounds are bandaged well enough for the journey back to the settlement." He wheeled around suddenly to face the healer, his eyes bright with the pain of his emotions. "You have my thanks," he murmured.

The old man bowed his head in acknowledgment, overwhelmed with pity at the anguished expression of concern etched on Hakon's face. "Take care not to jar her overmuch, my lord," he warned, his raspy voice almost a whisper. "It could well cause the bleeding to begin anew."

Hakon nodded. Then without another word he ducked his head and pushed aside the leather flap.

"Lord Hakon, how is it with Garric?" Olav asked, dismounting from his horse. He looked somewhat startled. Why was Hakon carrying the lad from the tent? He was even more surprised when Hakon walked up to him and gently placed Gwendolyn in his arms.

" 'Tis not Garric," Hakon muttered tersely. " 'Tis Anora. Take care of her for a moment, Olav, while I fetch my horse."

Olav stared in horrified disbelief at Gwendolyn's fair features, so deathly pale in the bright sunlight. Anora! Nay, he could not believe his eyes!

"But how did she . . . when . . .?" he gasped. A young woman on the battlefield . . . he had never heard of such a thing! And she had saved Lord Hakon's life, no less!

"We can talk of this later, Olav. My only thought now is to get her away from this cursed valley and back to the settlement," Hakon said grimly, easing his spirited stallion up beside Olav. "Hand her up to me, yea, but gently now."

Olav lifted Gwendolyn easily into Hakon's waiting arms, then held the reins for him until he had her settled in front of him, his right arm encircling her protectively.

Hakon tucked in the blankets securely around her, fearful that she might take cold from the wintry air. "My thanks, Olav. I will see to it that a hearty meal and plenty of mead await your arrival at the settlement. Pass that news along to the men as well."

"Shall I not ride with you, then?" Olav asked, his eyes lighting with concern as he handed Hakon the reins. "Surely you do not plan to ride unescorted, my lord! There may still be some of Rhoar's renegades about the valley."

"Yea, Olav, you are right, but I need to leave you in charge of the men," Hakon replied. He nodded toward several of his petty chieftains not far away. "I shall have those four men accompany me."

"Very well, then," Olav said, the expression on his swarthy face darkening as his eyes scanned the battlefield. "But what of the bodies, my lord?"

"See to it that those of our men are carried back to the settlement. They are heroes and deserve a Viking burial as befitting their bravery this day," Hakon replied. His eyes grew cold, an angry tic working in his jaw. "Leave the rest for the wolves." He clicked his tongue to his stallion and urged him into a gentle trot.

Olav watched Hakon ride over to where the four chieftains were standing alongside their horses. He spoke to them in low tones, and they quickly mounted and reined in beside him. Then the small group eased into a gallop. It was not long before they had disappeared over the crest of the hillside.

Chapter Thirty-five

"Fetch Berta to my chamber at once!" Hakon ordered grimly, taking Gwendolyn from the arms of the Viking guard who held her while he dismounted. The burly warrior nodded, then set off at a brisk run toward the cooking house. Hakon kicked in the heavy door to his hall, cursing under his breath. He had taken great care not to jostle her overmuch, but he feared the bleeding had begun again. She had lain so still in his arms during the ride back to the settlement, not once calling out his name. He strode quickly across the hall to his chamber and pushed open the door.

His eyes widened in surprise at the slender form outlined beneath the thick, fur coverlet on the wide bed. "What folly is this?" he muttered, his startled gaze moving from the bed back to Gwendolyn's pale face. He could feel his heart pounding against his chest. He crossed the floor and threw back the coverlet with one hand, his breath caught in his throat. But there were only three eiderdown pillows clumped together.

Hakon let out his breath sharply. If he had not been so concerned, he would have been livid with anger at her ploy. Yet he knew if she had not been there on the battlefield, his fate would have been far different. She must have jumped from the window, he thought fleetingly, shaking his head. There would have been no other way she could have avoided the Viking guards posted just outside his hall.

He pushed aside the pillows and lay her on the bed, then gently drew back the blankets he had wrapped around her. Hakon sighed raggedly, his worst fears confirmed by the deep red stain that was seeping through her bandages.

"You summoned me, my lord?" Berta's hearty voice rang out across the chamber. She started, aghast, as Hakon looked up from the bed. She had never seen his face so drawn and haggard! She rushed to his side, her hand flying to her heart at the pitiful sight before her. "Anora!" she gasped in disbelief, her massive breasts heaving. "But how can this be? I brought a midday meal to her earlier this day. It seemed she was sleeping, so I did not wake her. See? The meal is still there!" Her eyes flew to the table by the window. "Though it is untouched . . ." Her voice trailed off as she looked back to Hakon, her expression troubled and confused.

" 'Twas not her sleeping, Berta," Hakon murmured, nodding toward the pillows shoved to the other side of the bed. "She covered those pillows to fool anyone who might have entered the chamber while she was gone. She followed me into battle, dressed as Garric."

Berta's mouth gaped open in stunned surprise, but she quickly regained her composure, taking charge when she saw the ugly bloodstain spreading ever wider across the cloth bandages.

"Cut away the bandages, my lord! Then take this cloth and hold it tight against the wound. I will return shortly!"

She shoved a linen towel into his hand and bustled out of the room.

Hakon took the long-bladed knife from his belt and swiftly cut away the soiled bandages. He grimaced at the flaring hole, now swollen and red despite the herb poultice the healer had applied to it earlier that day. Thor, he could not lose her now! he raged silently. Wadding up the linen cloth, he pressed it against the oozing wound. He wiped the sweat from his face with his free hand, his lips murmuring a fervent prayer. "Odin, hear me!" he prayed, his voice a muted whisper. "Do not take her from me!"

It seemed that only a few moments had passed before Berta hurried back into the room, followed by a guard carrying a steaming kettle of boiling water.

"Set it over there"—she pointed to the small table near the bed—"but do not leave. I may yet need your help." The Viking guard nodded, quickly averting his gaze from Hakon Jarl's concubine lying naked from the waist up on the bed. He took his place by the door, his arms folded across his broad chest, his eyes downcast.

"Now, my lord, if you will step aside," Berta said matter-of-factly. Hakon obliged her, walking over to the other side of the bed.

Berta clucked her tongue as she lifted the towel from the wound. " 'Tis a bad one, my lord," she murmured, "though from the looks of it, the healer's herbs have given her some relief." She looked up at him, her expression grim. "I tell you this only because I must. She is strong, but already her skin burns as if on fire. If Anora survives the night, my lord, I believe she may live."

Hakon felt cold fear grip him for the first time in his life. He had braved many battles in the past, and had fought against fierce opponents—yea, the fiercest of all this very day—yet he had never known fear, not once. But now, the mere thought of losing the only woman he had ever loved was more than he could bear. For a moment he was unable to reply, his blue eyes staring off into the distance.

Suddenly he shook his head fiercely. Nay, he would not let death steal her from him! "Hear me, Hel, goddess of the underworld, you will not take her!" he yelled, his defiant voice echoing about the chamber. He snatched the long-bladed knife from the bed and drove it with all his might into the carved corner post. It sank in to the hilt, splintering the wood.

Berta's eyes were wide with awe as she looked at the carved hilt of the knife protruding from the post. Yea, if that did not serve to protect her young mistress and drive away the spirits that would wrench the life from her body, then nothing would. She looked back at Hakon, who stood tall and powerful by the bed, a blaze of heated defiance in his eyes.

"I will stay with her this night," he stated evenly. "Tell me what I must do."

Berta nodded. "The room must be kept very warm, my lord. I will see that a roaring fire is lit in the central fireplace, and a slave will tend it through the night to see that it does not go out. There will also be a caldron of boiling water for your use. You must see that the wound is cleansed often. I will leave you plenty of cloth for bandages, and more of the herb poultice. First apply hot cloths to the wound, then the poultice, then the bandages. I will also leave a cask of cool water by the bed, and some soft cloths to bathe away the fever from her body. I will cleanse the wound this time, my lord. Watch me carefully."

With practiced hands she deftly applied the hot cloths. Gwendolyn started from the searing heat. Though still unconscious, she screamed out in pain. "Pay no mind to her cries, my lord, it must be done," Berta said, rubbing the herb paste all around the wound. Then she quickly wrapped a bandage over it, tying it tightly under her arm. "There, now, that should do for a while. The bleeding has stopped, thankfully." She started to walk to the door. "I will go now and prepare a soothing broth to give her if she awakens. It will help her keep up her strength."

"My thanks, Berta," Hakon murmured. He moved back to the other side of the bed and began gently to remove the rest of Gwendolyn's clothing. Suddenly he remembered the Viking guard standing quietly by the door. "Wait outside, man," he ordered, though not too gruffly, "but leave the door open so the heat from the fireplace may warm this room."

"Yea, Lord Hakon," the guard replied, complying hastily.

Hakon threw her soiled clothing on a pile beside the bed. How had she gotten Garric's clothes? He looked about the room. The heavy lid to her chest was thrown open, and silken garments were scattered about the floor. His eyes flew to the timbered wall where he kept his weapons; the spot where the knife had rested on two pegs was bare.

He could read the scene before him almost as well as if he had been there to see it. She must have dressed in great haste, probably right after he had left the chamber, then grabbed the long-bladed knife from the wall. She had then jumped from the window to the ground below, and headed for the stable. That was when he had seen her, and had called out to her to saddle his stallion. Hakon shuddered. If only he had known it then!

Hakon wrung out one of the cloths in the hot water and gently bathed her slender body. Her alabaster skin was flushed, glowing with a fine sheen of perspiration. He almost choked with emotion. Thor, she was so beautiful! When he was finished bathing her, he pulled the fur coverlet up over her delicate shoulders.

Hakon looked down at his own sweat-soaked garments. There were several bright red splatters on his tunic . . . the blood of his enemies. He grimaced. And Anora's. He walked to the leather-backed chair by the window and unfastened the silver brooches that held his cloak. Easing it from his shoulders, he draped it over the chair, then pulled the heavy shirt of mail over his head and dropped it with a clanking thud to the floor. He kicked off his boots, then stripped off his tunic and leggings. Pulling a linen tunic and trousers from one of the massive chests, he hastily put them on. There would be no time for a bath this night.

"Hakon!" Gwendolyn's anguished cry tore from her throat, shattering the stillness of the room.

Hakon rushed over to the bed and sat down by her side. He gathered her into his strong arms, willing some of his strength into her. "I am here, love," he murmured. "I am here."

Gwendolyn's eyelids fluttered open. Her emerald eyes were glazed and overbright, her fair features flushed with fever. She clung to him, hot tears coursing down her cheeks. "It hurts so . . ." she whispered hoarsely. "Make the pain go away . . . please . . ."

Hakon felt a hard lump in his throat. *Odin, why are you trying me so?* he raged helplessly, stroking the side of her face. The sight of Berta rushing through the door flooded him with relief. "She has awakened, Berta!" he exclaimed softly.

" 'Tis a good sign," Berta replied, nodding approvingly as she hurried to the bed with a wooden tray. "Here is the soothing broth, my lord. I have mixed in some sleeping herbs that should help to calm her. If she is asleep, the pain will not plague her as much." She set the tray upon the table, then dragged the chair over to the side of the bed and sat down heavily. "Hold her head still, my lord."

Berta gently spooned some of the broth into Gwendolyn's mouth. She was pleased to see that she swallowed it readily. Before long the bowl was emptied. "Another good sign,

Lord Hakon. The more of this she drinks, the better! I shall leave the pot of broth on the hearth above the fireplace." She heaved herself out of the chair. "If you have need of aught else, send one of the guards for me and I will come at once." She smiled faintly. "Good night, my lord."

Hakon reached out and caught her hand, squeezing it gratefully. "Again, you have my thanks," he murmured. Berta reddened in embarrassment, unable to speak. Nodding, she turned abruptly and moved about the room, lighting the small oil lamps one by one. Then without a backward glance she hurried out the door. *Yea, and may Odin protect the lass*, she thought fleetingly, hugging her hand to her breast.

Hakon leaned his head back against the timbered wall. He closed his eyes, his broad shoulders slumping with exhaustion. He must have fallen asleep for a moment, but he was jerked awake as Gwendolyn cried out once again.

So began a seemingly endless night as Hakon changed the bandages on Gwendolyn's wound, bathed her feverish body, and fed her spoonfuls of broth when she was conscious enough to swallow. He held her in his arms and caressed her burning skin. He murmured her name over and over so that she would know he was there with her, never leaving her side.

At one point she screamed so loudly that the Viking guard rushed in, his eyes wide with alarm. "Shall I summon Berta?" he asked fearfully.

Hakon waved him from the room. "Nay, 'tis only the fever," he murmured, holding her tightly. She writhed deliriously in his arms, her head tossing from side to side.

"Nay, Anora, run . . . run!" she moaned. "Damn the Viking! We will escape from him, Anora, I promise you!"

Hakon sat up, listening. He had paid no heed to her wild ravings until now, for they had been mostly unintelligible. But why was she calling to Anora? *She* was Anora!

"How can you . . . how can you marry him?" Gwendolyn ranted feverishly. "Wulfgar Ragnarson . . . a Dane . . . our enemy . . . nay, Anora!" She licked her dry lips. " 'Tis all right, 'tis all right . . . she loves him . . . so much water, all around . . . he must not touch her . . . she belongs to Wulfgar Ragnarson . . . must go in her place . . ."

Hakon started, his eyes widening as she repeated the name once again. Wulfgar Ragnarson! The man Haarek Jarl had spoken of at the meeting in Trondheim! He felt a strange sense of foreboding tugging at his mind, the same feeling that had overwhelmed him on the battlefield, but he tried to ignore it.

"What can I do . . . I have no choice . . . escape, we must escape . . . the merchant . . . what has happened to the merchant!" Suddenly Gwendolyn wrenched herself free of Hakon's arms and sat up in bed, her face a mask of horror. "Nay, Rhoar . . . there is no time . . . the knife, throw the knife . . . Hakon!" she cried out, anguished tears running down her flushed cheeks. "Hakon!" Her whole body trembled as fierce sobs racked her body.

Hakon gently pulled her back down beside him and she slumped, exhausted, in his arms. The tears had scarcely dried upon her face when she fell into a deep sleep, her fever broken at last. He gathered her close and pulled the thick coverlet over them both.

But Hakon could not sleep. He felt as if the cold steel of a knife had been thrust into his heart and twisted cruelly around. Who was this woman he held in his arms? Was she Anora, or someone else? He suddenly remembered the question he had asked himself on the battlefield: How could brother and sister look so much alike? How could brother and sister . . . unless they weren't brother and sister after all!

Suddenly everything seemed clear to him, achingly, painfully clear. His powerful body trembled uncontrollably, as if he himself were racked with fever. Ever so gently he slid his arm out from beneath Gwendolyn's tousled head and got up from the bed. He briefly touched her forehead. It was cool to his touch, and her breathing had returned to normal. At least he could be grateful for that, he thought, tucking the coverlet snugly about her. He walked almost in a daze to the door.

"Find Garric, and bring him here to me!" he ordered, startling the Viking guard who was asleep on a bench just outside the door.

"G-Garric?" the guard asked, jumping to his feet.

"Yea, the stable hand. Take other guards if you must, only find him . . . and quickly. I wish to see him, now!"

The Viking guard wasted no time. He strode quickly across the main room of the hall and hurried out the door.

Hakon turned back into his chamber and walked over to the chair by the bed. He sat down, his startling blue eyes fixed upon Gwendolyn's face, and waited.

Chapter Thirty-six

The Viking guard returned a short while later, breathing hard from running back to the hall. "My lord, the lad is not in the stable!" he gasped. "I have alerted the other guards and they are out looking for him now, but so far there is no sign of him!"

Hakon slammed his fist down hard upon the wooden arm of the chair. "Garric must be in the stable," he muttered, almost to himself. He rose to his feet. "I will go with you and we will look again." He quickly pulled on his boots and grabbed a thick fur vest hanging on a wooden peg near the door. He glanced over his shoulder at the bed. Gwendolyn was still sleeping soundly. He rushed out of the room, the Viking warrior close behind him.

Hakon's voice startled the woman who was busily tending the blazing fire in the central hearth. "Go sit in my chamber and watch Anora carefully until I return," he called out, striding across the hall. "If she wakes, see that she drinks more of the broth. The herbs should help her to sleep again."

"Yea, my lord!" The woman bowed her head, wiping her hands upon her woolen tunic. She hurried into his chamber.

Hakon drew in his breath sharply as he stepped outside. Thor, but it was cold this night! Their footsteps made crunching sounds in the new snow that had fallen as they hurried along the path to the stable.

They were met at the door to the stable by several Viking warriors. Their faces were grim as they held up their torches. "We have not found the lad, my lord. We even looked in the women's slave house, thinking perhaps he might be with a wench—"

"Nay, you will not find him there," Hakon cut him off abruptly, a sardonic half smile upon his lips. He pushed open the door to the stable. "Hand me a torch," he demanded.

Hakon stepped inside the large, darkened room. He held up the torch in front of him, making a slow sweep of the shadowed recesses of the stable. The sheep and cattle rustled nervously about in their stalls, while frightened chickens dodged for cover, clucking incessantly.

"Garric!" he called out sharply. He was answered only by the snorting of his stallion, which tossed its head in greeting. "Garric!" He waited a moment, but still there was no reply. Anger flared within him. His instincts told him that Garric was in the stable, somewhere, perhaps hiding.

" 'Tis Lord Hakon, lad. You must come out at once! Anora has taken sick this night with a burning fever. Even now she is calling out your name. I promised her I would find you and bring you to her side!"

Hakon's ruse was instantly rewarded. He heard a rustling of hay from the far end of the stable, then the sound of footsteps, as a slender figure hurried forward into the light cast by the blazing torch. He started, recognizing the tunic and breeches she wore. They were the extra clothes he had given Garric, the ones the lad had always refused to wear.

But on her small feet were soft leather slippers . . . women's slippers!

"My-my lord?" Anora murmured apprehensively, shielding her eyes. Her mind was racing. Gwendolyn, taken sick? But how? When? Her face was pale and drawn, and she swayed unsteadily on her feet. She had not eaten for almost two days.

Hakon reached out and grabbed her roughly by the arm. "Come, we must waste no more time!" He pulled her from the stable, dragging her along the path to his hall, while the Viking guards watched in puzzled astonishment. He could feel her shivering from the cold, but he did not slow his pace.

Anora's heart was pounding in her chest. She panted for breath, the frigid air hurting her lungs as she tried frantically to keep up with him. Suddenly she stumbled on the slippery path. She gasped when Hakon picked her up in his arms and carried her the rest of the way, hugging her close to his broad chest. Hakon Jarl would not treat a lad so, she thought fleetingly, as he kicked open the massive door to his hall and strode across the main room. He set her down just outside his chamber and took her by the shoulders, his eyes burning into hers.

"Go in to your sister, Garric," he murmured, his voice low. His face was inscrutable, though his eyes glittered dangerously. With that, he released her abruptly, and she staggered back, almost falling. Catching herself on the timbered wall, she felt her legs grow wooden as she entered the softly lit room and crossed over to the bed. She barely noticed as the older woman sitting in the chair suddenly got up and hurried out. Her eyes were on the thick white bandages wrapped about Gwendolyn's left shoulder, and the deathly pallor of her skin.

"Gwendolyn . . ." she whispered in stunned horror, oblivious to Hakon's tall form standing near her. She sank to her knees by the bed, hot tears coursing down her cheeks as she fiercely clutched the fur coverlet. "Nay, this cannot be!" she cried out in bitter anguish, burying her face in her hands. Suddenly she looked up at Hakon. "How did this come about?" she asked, her voice ragged.

"I had hoped you might be able to answer that same question, Anora," Hakon replied grimly.

"Nay," Anora whispered fearfully at the sound of her name. Her eyes widened in awful surprise. So, he knew at last! Sweet Jesu! Help her!

Hakon bent down and lifted her easily to her feet, taking her arm as he tried to lead her from the room.

"Nay, where are you taking me?" Anora screamed, struggling to break free of his iron grip. She fought him so fiercely that he finally had to grab her and toss her over his broad shoulder, holding her slender legs tightly so she could not kick him. Even then she pummeled him with her small fists, landing a well-aimed blow just below the back of his rib cage. He grunted in pain, yet did not stop until he was out in the main room of the hall. Waving the older woman away, he plopped Anora down into a carved chair near the central fireplace, then caught her wrists with one strong hand as he leaned over her.

"Tell me about Wulfgar Ragnarson," Hakon muttered, his deep voice almost a whisper.

Anora paled visibly. Dumbfounded, she opened her mouth to speak, but she could not. She could scarcely breathe.

"Answer me, Anora," Hakon snapped, his mouth a tight line, his bronzed features hard, inscrutable.

"He . . . he is m-my betrothed," Anora stammered, fear gripping her. "H-how do you know of him?"

Hakon let go of her wrists and stood up, his heart hammering in his chest. So, the tides of fate had turned against him, he thought bitterly, and there was nothing he could do to stop them. He went over and stood by the fireplace, staring into the bright flames. The hall grew silent, except for the crackle of the logs in the fire. An orange spark suddenly flew out from under the hearth, spitting and hissing.

" 'Tis Loki, the fire spirit, beating his children," Hakon said softly, an ironic smile on his lips as he stepped on the glowing ember, crushing it. He sighed, his handsome profile illuminated by the roaring flames. It was best to have out with it. "It seems your Wulfgar is gathering together a fleet of warships to sail on Norge in the spring . . . in search of you and your sister," he said, almost dispassionately. "Unless, of course, you both are returned safely to England before he sets sail." He ignored Anora's startled gasp and continued, though he did not look at her.

"I only learned of this a few days past when I went to Trondheim under a summons from Haarek Jarl, my liege lord. It was his command to the gathered chieftains that if you and your sister were found in Norge, you must be returned as soon as the north seas can be crossed, to divert a war with Denmark."

Hakon turned, a strange look on his face. "It seems your abduction has created quite a stir, Anora. For, you see, there is more at stake now than just your freedom . . . and that of your sister. Wulfgar Ragnarson has received the support of not only King Edgar of England, but King Harald Gormsson of Denmark as well. Haarek Jarl believes it is the perfect ploy for King Harald to seize control of our land once again."

Hakon's voice grew hard. "But all of this meant naught to me until this night. Haarek Jarl had said two sisters had been abducted from their homeland, not a brother and sister, so I gave the matter no more thought. 'Twas only from your sister's fevered rantings that I heard the name Wulfgar Ragnarson, revealing your guise." He paused, his eyes cold. "I did not know until this night that I have been played the fool." He took a step toward her. "Was it you who traveled with me to Trondheim as Garric?"

Stunned by all she had heard, Anora did not answer for a moment. She could scarcely believe it! She felt a surge of incredible joy well in up inside her. They would be returned to their homeland . . . and she to Wulfgar! Then she sobered suddenly, recalling the ashen pallor of Gwendolyn's face. What if her sister did not survive her wound? She shuddered visibly. Nay, she would not think of it!

"Was it you, or your sister?" Hakon repeated his question, watching the play of emotions across Anora's fair features.

Anora met his penetrating gaze. She slowly shook her head. " 'Twas Gwendolyn, my lord," she replied softly. She could see no harm in telling him the truth now. He would not dare harm her or Gwendolyn. If he did, he would be defying the orders of his liege lord. Surely that would be a punishable crime!

Gwendolyn. So that was her name, Hakon thought. It was a beautiful name. . . . "Then who came to my hall that night you both tried to escape?" he asked, his voice low. He turned his gaze back to the leaping flames. He could already sense her answer.

"Gwendolyn, my lord. She sacrificed herself to protect me."

Hakon grimaced. So that was how she had thought of that night. She had seen herself as a sacrifice.

Anora's voice interrupted his dark thoughts. "Gwendolyn played the part of Garric from the very first day we were captured, believing it would somehow help us. It was only when you caught us trying to escape"—Anora flushed heatedly—"when you were using the whip against her and I promised to come to your . . ." She could not say it.

"When you promised to come to my *bed*," Hakon finished for her. "Yea?"

Anora's voice was almost a whisper. "Gwendolyn cut my hair so we could pass for each other. 'Twas the only thing that set us apart. Then we exchanged clothes, and I became Garric. She went to your hall in my place."

Hakon shook his head in disbelief. How could he have missed what was going on before his very eyes? He thought back to that day on his ship when he had seen Garric smile for the first time, and how he had thought he was too pretty for a lad. And the change in him after the lashing . . . he had thought he had crushed the lad's defiant spirit. Yet it had been Anora all along, too frightened even to look him full in the face!

His thoughts raced on wildly. And when they had returned from Trondheim, when Garric had jumped from the ship and raced madly up the hill? The lad had been Gwendolyn again! She must have gone directly to his hall and taken Anora's place, just barely in time before he entered the chamber. Thor's blood! How could he have been so blind?

"Was it always Gwendolyn then, in the bathing house after I returned from my uncle's settlement . . . and during the nights?" Hakon asked, a catch in his voice.

"Aye," Anora said simply. "She vowed she would bear it only until she could find a way for us to escape."

"I have heard enough!" Hakon exclaimed suddenly, pounding his clenched fist against the timbered wall next to the fireplace. "Leave me, Anora!" He strove to check the cold fury threatening to overwhelm him. "Go attend to your sister in my chamber. No doubt she will thrive under your care. This hall will be yours until we sail for England in the spring. I am sure you will find it comfortable . . . and much more suited to the style in which someone of your high birth is accustomed. Now leave me!" he shouted angrily.

Anora rose from the chair, frightened by his outburst. She

walked hurriedly toward his chamber, but turned around just before she reached the door. "You have not yet told me how Gwendolyn was wounded, my lord," she murmured. His back was to her, so she could not see his face.

"A spear hit her in the shoulder, just after she threw the knife that saved my life," Hakon replied. "Now leave me." He sighed heavily, not knowing she was still there, and leaned against the timbered wall as if for support.

Anora felt a strange wave of pity and sadness wash over her at the anguished pain in his voice. He looked so vulnerable standing there, so alone. This powerful man who had terrified her from the first moment she had seen him . . . Could it be that he felt more than lust for her sister, perhaps even some affection? Suddenly she heard a soft moan carry out into the main room of the hall. Gwendolyn! She turned and fled into his chamber, shutting the door behind her.

Hakon felt a sudden, wrenching pain within him that was sharper, more excruciating, than any wound he had ever suffered. So, the only woman he had ever loved had made a mockery of his affections! He pounded his clenched fist into the timbered wall again. But what more could he have expected? he berated himself. He had taken them from their homeland, away from the people they loved, had forced his attentions upon them, and had expected to be loved in return! Thor, what a fool he had been!

His shoulders slumped with weariness, but he shrugged it off. Nay, there was no time for that, he thought angrily. There was much to be done. He would have to sail at first light of day for Trondheim. Olav could take charge of the settlement while he was gone. Yea, he thought bitterly, no doubt Haarek Jarl would be most delighted with his news!

Hakon walked to the door of his hall, overwhelmed by utter despair, but he knew his feelings mattered naught. Come spring, Gwendolyn would be lost to him forever. It would be almost as if she had perished, yet he would know she still lived and breathed, somewhere far away from him. He pushed open the door and stepped out into the frigid air. It hit him like a fierce slap on the face.

He looked up into the night sky, just beginning to lighten along the far horizon. It seemed all his questions had been answered by Anora, save for one. Yet he did not think she knew the answer. It haunted him, tormenting his mind. Why did Gwendolyn save his life if she longed so much to escape from him? She had never said she loved him, though he could have sworn he had seen more than desire reflected in the emerald depths of her eyes. He shuddered suddenly. Her choice on the battlefield had been him . . . or Rhoar. Perhaps she had saved his life only because she feared him less!

Hakon cursed himself for a fool. Whatever the reason, it no longer mattered. Raising his clenched fists to the heavens, he raged silently against his gods for their cruel deception . . . to take from him the truest happiness he had ever known.

Chapter Thirty-seven

Gwendolyn awoke to a burning sensation in her left shoulder. She opened her eyes, heavy-lidded from sleep, and squinted in the bright golden sunlight pouring in from the two windows. Her head hurt terribly. She shaded her eyes with her hand, until she grew accustomed to the light. God's blood! Why did she feel so dizzy? She tried to sit up, hoisting herself up on her elbows. A piercing wave of pain shot through her. She gasped aloud, then fell back on the eiderdown pillows.

"Gwendolyn!" a familiar voice cried out across the chamber. She heard hurried footsteps move toward the bed. Then Anora's concerned face hovered over her. "You must lie still, else the wound will open again!" her sister chastised softly.

Gwendolyn blinked. Then her eyes widened. Was she imagining it, or was Anora dressed in a silken chemise and tunic? "Anora, what are you doing? Why are you dressed like that!" she exclaimed weakly. "Quickly, put on Garric's clothes, before Lord Hakon sees you!" She tried to sit up again, but fell back, wincing in pain. She moaned softly, biting her lower lip.

"Nay, lie still, Gwendolyn, 'tis all right," Anora said, her voice low and soothing. She brushed her small hand across her sister's forehead. There was no longer any sign of fever, she thought gratefully. And the rosy color was slowly returning to her cheeks. She lifted the fur coverlet and brought it back up about Gwendolyn's delicate shoulders.

Gwendolyn lifted her tousled head from the pillow, her emerald eyes clouded with confusion. "How can you say 'tis all right, Anora? This is Hakon Jarl's chamber, is it not? He could walk in at any moment!" Suddenly she lay back down, a ragged sigh escaping her throat. Hakon's chamber . . . But how had she gotten here? As Garric, she should be in the stable, shouldn't she? Her head was beginning to ache from the turmoil of her thoughts.

"Lord Hakon left the settlement four days ago, Gwendolyn," Anora murmured, gently plumping up the eiderdown pillows beneath her sister. She turned and drew the leather-backed chair closer to the side of the bed, then sat down. Aye, the quicker she told Gwendolyn what had happened, the better. It would do her sister little good to excite herself overmuch, especially now when she was still so weak.

"Wh-where did he go?" Gwendolyn whispered, another wave of pain shooting through her. She glanced down, her eyes widening at the thick linen bandages covering her shoulder. Suddenly everything came rushing back to her. The awful battle, the twisted, blood-soaked bodies, Rhoar standing over Hakon, his axe glinting brightly, throwing the knife . . . then the exploding pain that had shattered through her body. She shuddered, her hands trembling uncontrollably.

Anora leaned forward and took Gwendolyn's hands in her own. "He sailed for Trondheim with news for Haarek Jarl," she replied softly.

"Trondheim? But we only just returned from there. He did not say he would be sailing there again, and so soon!" Gwendolyn cried hoarsely, her mind trying to make sense of this news.

"Gwendolyn, if you would only let me speak," Anora said gently, yet insistently. "I have something to tell you that concerns us both." She squeezed her sister's hands, barely able to contain her excitement. "Much has happened during the past four days while you have been asleep. It is such wonderful news!" She paused for a moment, her voice almost breathless. "We shall be returned to our homeland as soon as the seas are safe to cross! 'Twill be only a few months from now, in the early spring!"

Stunned, Gwendolyn almost could not grasp what Anora had just said. Returned to their homeland? But how could that be? The last thing she remembered, she had been Garric, marching into battle with Hakon Jarl, and Anora had been hiding in the stable. Now, all of a sudden, they were to be returned to England!

"Aye, 'tis true," Anora said, reading the bewildered expression on Gwendolyn's face. She quickly explained what Hakon had told her a few nights before, the night he had discovered their guise.

Gwendolyn listened in dazed silence. So, that was why Hakon had been summoned to Trondheim. She could scarcely believe it. Wulfgar, gathering together a mammoth fleet, and joining forces with the King of Denmark to sail on Norge! She shook her head gravely. No wonder Haarek Jarl had been so incensed. She had learned enough about political strategy from her father to understand the awful urgency behind the Jarl's desire to avoid this war if at all possible.

And to think that she and Anora were at the center of it all! She suddenly recalled how Hakon had looked at her so strangely on the return voyage from Trondheim. Perhaps he had guessed the truth even then, but had not wanted to admit it to himself for fear of losing the woman he loved.

Gwendolyn sighed heavily. So, her own words had given them away, she thought ironically, after she had done everything in her power to preserve their guise. She wondered fleetingly what Hakon must have thought at that moment. A pained expression flitted across her face. Nay, she would not think of it! She felt no joy at Anora's news, only a mixture of relief and overwhelming sadness. She sighed heavily. At least she would no longer have to play the part of Garric . . . or Anora. She turned her face away, hot tears welling up in her eyes.

"But what is the matter, Gwendolyn?" Anora asked, her face etched with concern. She had very rarely seen her sister cry at anything, let alone something she thought would bring her great joy. "We are no longer the slaves of Lord Hakon. We are free and shall be home within a few short months! If you are frightened of when he returns from Trondheim, why, he can no longer touch you. He would not dare! You are free of him, Gwendolyn!"

Nay, my heart shall never be free of him, Gwendolyn thought desolately. She could no more have stopped her tears at that moment than she could have denied she loved him . . . aye, loved him with every fiber of her being. She turned her head and met Anora's concerned gaze.

"Do you remember that day at the grotto, right before we were captured, when I asked you if a man's kiss burned like fire or ice?" she asked, her voice almost a whisper.

"Aye, I remember," Anora replied softly. " 'Twas one of Leah's superstitious sayings. How did it go? 'If a man's kiss burns like ice, his love will bring pain and ruin, but if a man's kiss'—"

"—'burns like fire,' " Gwendolyn finished for her, " 'his love will be true.' " She hesitated, brushing the tears from her eyes. "You said that one day I, too, would know such a kiss."

"Aye, 'tis true. I remember."

Gwendolyn's voice shook with emotion. "I have found that

man whose kiss is like fire. . . . 'Tis Hakon, Anora. I love him more than life itself."

Anora was so completely stunned she could not speak for a moment. She stared wide-eyed at Gwendolyn, her heart pounding against her chest. "Sweet Jesu . . ." she said finally, almost as a whisper. Gwendolyn . . . in love, and with their Viking captor!

Gwendolyn rushed on, releasing the raging torrent of emotions she had kept welled up inside her for so long. "Hakon told me that he loved me the night that I was almost abducted by Rhoar, and that when he returned from Trondheim I would become a free woman . . . and his wife."

"His wife?"

"Aye. I tried to tell you of this after we exchanged clothes that morning the ship was to sail for Trondheim, but Hakon came into the stable before I had a chance."

"He did speak to me of making some kind of preparations for when he returned," Anora recalled, her fair brow creased in thought. "But I would never have imagined he meant wedding preparations!"

Gwendolyn caught her sister's hand. "Anora, I was afraid to tell you of my feelings for fear you would think I had betrayed my promise to you. But it was always my intent to hold to my vow, and find a way for us to escape. I swore to myself that I would fight against this love, but every time I was with him, every time he held me in his arms . . ." She sighed sorrowfully, painful tears welling up in her eyes as the torment of the past weeks overwhelmed her.

"Please, Gwendolyn, 'tis over," Anora said, trying to comfort her. "You did not betray me. You have been so brave, so strong, never thinking of yourself, but always of me." How she must have suffered, she thought, chiding herself that she had not seen the turmoil that had been tearing her sister apart.

"But 'tis not over for me, Anora." Gwendolyn shook her

head sadly. She grimaced at the pain in her shoulder. Truly, she thought, the wrenching pain in her heart was far worse. "When I saw Rhoar standing over Hakon on the battlefield, with his bloody axe poised and ready to deal him a death blow, I knew then my life would be naught without him. Now I see that I have lost him just as surely as if he had died that day."

Anora looked away for a moment, overwhelmed by the agonizing despair reflected in the depths of Gwendolyn's eyes. She had never seen her sister like this before, yet she knew what she must be feeling. She had known the same sorrow, the same hopelessness, when she had been taken from Wulfgar on the eve of their marriage. She had looked then to Gwendolyn for solace, strength, aye, and protection, these past months, and she had never failed her. Yet now her sister needed the same from her.

She gazed down at Gwendolyn's pale face. She looked so fragile, so weak. If this news had threatened her sister's will to live . . . nay, there had to be something she could say to ease Gwendolyn's terrible heartache!

Anora suddenly recalled that night when she had told Lord Hakon of their guise. There had been such terrible anguish in his voice, such pain. He seemed almost a beaten man as he stared distantly into the fire, as if he had lost the one thing that had given his life meaning. And now that she knew he had planned to make Gwendolyn his wife, and had expressed his love for her . . . A faint smile curved her lips. So, her instincts had been right, then. He had felt more than lust for her sister. Lord Hakon truly loved Gwendolyn!

"Perhaps all is not lost, Gwendolyn," Anora said softly, leaning toward her. "Have you yet told him of your feelings?"

"Nay," Gwendolyn replied. "I could not, for fear I would be betraying my promise to you."

Anora sighed. "You have kept your promise to me, Gwendolyn, so you need have no fear of betraying me any longer. Now it is time for you to think of yourself," she said gently, yet insistently. "When Lord Hakon returns to the settlement from Trondheim, tell him of your love. Perhaps there is yet a way to resolve all of this happily."

Gwendolyn felt a glimmer of hope suddenly flare within her at Anora's words. Aye, she would tell Hakon that she loved him and wanted to be his wife. Perhaps he could send word to Haarek Jarl that she did not want to return to her homeland, but instead wished to stay in Norge. Surely if Anora were returned safely, it would be enough!

Anora noted the rosy flush of color in her sister's cheeks and murmured a silent prayer of thanks. "Now, 'tis time you rested, Gwendolyn. I must go to the cooking house and fetch some more broth. I will be gone only a few moments," she said as she rose from the chair. She tucked in the fur coverlet around her sister's shoulders. "Try to sleep. 'Twould be a welcome sight for Lord Hakon if you are up and about when he returns." She walked quietly from the room and closed the door behind her.

Gwendolyn smiled faintly, the pain in her shoulder forgotten. Aye, she would run down the hill to the docks to meet him, and tell him of her love, she thought happily. She closed her eyes and fell into a peaceful sleep, his name upon her lips.

Chapter Thirty-eight

Gwendolyn sat alone in the chamber, her chair turned toward the open window. The leather shade was drawn back, and morning sunlight was pouring into the room, the bright rays warming her upturned face. She reached out, her small hand trying to catch the tiny flecks of dust whirling about in the streaming shafts of light. Smiling to herself, she dropped her hand to her lap and leaned back in the chair.

She took a deep breath of the early spring air, scented with the musky fragrance of new grass and wet earth. The soft breeze blowing through the window teased the silver-blond tendrils framing her delicate features, and carried with it the joyful melodies of birdsong. She could just barely see green tufts of grass peeking up from the drifts of melting snow.

Gwendolyn sighed, the faint smile disappearing from her lips. The sky was a vivid blue, the color of Hakon's eyes. She had not seen him for almost three months now. She shook her head sadly. Would he ever return?

She closed her eyes, trying to conjure up an image of him in her mind, but for some reason she could recall the strong lines of his powerful body . . . but not his face. She shuddered suddenly, crossing herself. She hoped it wasn't a bad omen.

The days had passed by so slowly, merging into weeks, then months, and still Hakon and his crew had not returned to the settlement. The fierce northern winter had raged all around them, wrapping everything in a thick blanket of white as the snows had flown with a blinding fury the likes of which had not been seen for many years.

Her wound had healed well under Anora's watchful and caring ministrations, but slowly. Eventually there was nothing left to remind her of that awful day but the red scar just below her left shoulder, and the infrequent tinglings of pain that plagued her still.

She had stayed in bed for the first few weeks after Hakon left for Trondheim, too weak and light-headed to sit up. But one day, despite Anora's repeated pleas to wait just a while longer, she had swung her slender legs over the side of the bed, determined that she would walk to the roughhewn table near the window. She had hoisted herself up by holding on tightly to the carved corner post. Then, with her hand on Anora's arm for support, she had taken several hesitant steps.

Gwendolyn grimaced as she recalled the awkward sensation she had felt as her knees suddenly buckled beneath her. If it hadn't been for Berta's standing so close behind her, she would have crumpled to the floor. She was hastily tucked back into bed, much to her chagrin. But on the next day's try she had succeeded, laughing with exhausted relief at her accomplishment.

As her strength returned, and along with it her sense of daring, each passing day had seen her walk a little farther from the bed. And soon she was able to walk about the hall without anyone's help. She had even begun a little daily ritual. Each morning, after she dressed, she walked to the entrance and slowly opened the great door. On some days the snow was falling so heavily that she was unable to see all the way down to the fjord. But on other days, when the sky was clear, she looked out over the sparkling, snow-covered hillside in the direction of the docks, searching for any sign of Hakon's longship. Yet she was always disappointed. The docks had remained empty, the stout posts and wooden planks glistening under a transparent sheen of thick ice.

Aye, but that ritual had soon ended, Gwendolyn thought with a secret smile. She remembered with distaste the strange queasiness that had begun to plague her each morning after she awoke, and she found herself miserably retching the contents of her stomach into a wooden bucket. She had thought perhaps it was the sleeping herbs making her ill, but her intuition was confirmed when she twice missed her monthly flow.

Thankfully the sickness was over now, Gwendolyn thought as she lay her hands gently over her stomach. It was still flat, only perhaps slightly rounded near the center. She reveled in the knowledge that she carried Hakon's child within her. It was one more link that bound them together. Yet she had made Anora swear not to say a word to anyone, and especially not to Hakon when he returned. Aye, it was her secret. Hakon would learn of it from her lips alone.

Yet despite the happiness she felt about the child, it had not served to make the days go by any faster. The settlement had become completely snowbound. And though narrow paths had been dug out between the longhouses, it had been deemed unsafe for her and Anora to venture outside.

But there had been a few bright spots to relieve the boredom of their wintry confinement. A loom was set up in Hakon's chamber for them, accompanied by sacks of fine yarns, though Gwendolyn found little pleasure in that. It was Anora who spent many contented hours working on a beautiful tapestry, and stitching delicate embroidery with silken threads of every hue.

Nay, it was Berta who had truly enlivened their days. She had spent a great deal of time with them, once she had gotten over her initial shock at their true identity. Her countless ribald stories of her past, when she had been a young serving wench in the service of Magnus Haardrad's household, Hakon's lusty father, had both embarrassed and amused them. She had also seen to it that they had plenty of well-prepared food to eat. Gwendolyn sometimes wondered if perhaps Berta had somehow guessed her secret from the constant, prying questions about her health. But she had simply smiled, assuring the kindly woman that she had never felt better.

And occasionally Olav had come to visit. At first he never stayed but a few moments, just long enough to inquire gruffly after their well-being. But eventually he had spent several afternoons in their company, seemingly delighted to sit and chat with two such lovely maidens. He told them entrancing tales of the sea, and of his boyhood home far to the north of Trondheim, where he had tamed strange, wild creatures called reindeer.

Yet, when pressed for any news of Hakon's expected return, Olav had always grown silent, saying only that perhaps the fierce winter weather had kept him from sailing homeward. Gwendolyn had not missed the worried expression in his eyes, though he had done his best to hide it. His apprehension had not helped to ease her own mind in the least.

The haunting sound of the great horns brought Gwendolyn suddenly out of her reverie. She sat forward in the chair, listening, her heart pounding furiously against her breast. The rich tones echoed about the steep hillsides surrounding the settlement, surging, crescendoing.

A thrill of excitement coursed through her slender body. Could it be the horns were a signal of greeting to an approaching longship? She stood up and quickly walked the few steps to the open window, leaning on the wide ledge as she looked outside. It was almost as if the very air was charged with anticipation. Viking guards were running by the longhouse, shouting and whooping, some pointing in the direction of the docks. She waved to one of them, a tall, black-bearded warrior, trying to get his attention.

Somewhat taken by surprise that the Jarl's concubine would wish to speak with him, the Viking stopped in his tracks, then strode over to the window. "My lady?" he asked, smiling broadly, his bold eyes raking over her.

Gwendolyn ignored his heated gaze, though a warm blush spread over her cheeks at his frank perusal. "Why have the horns been sounded?" she asked almost breathlessly. "Is there a ship approaching the settlement?"

"Yea, my lady, 'tis Hakon Jarl!" he replied excitedly. "His longship has just been sighted, rounding the bend in the fjord. 'Twill not be long now before it docks!" He looked over his shoulder, the smile disappearing from his bearded face. Several other Viking guards were standing not too far away, watching him. He shifted his feet uncomfortably, anxious to be on his way. He did not wish to be seen speaking overlong to Lord Hakon's woman. Even though it was common knowledge throughout the settlement that she and her fair sister would be soon returned to their homeland in England, they were still under his protection. He turned back to her. "If I may go, my lady?" he muttered, growing more ill at ease with each passing moment.

"Aye. My thanks," Gwendolyn murmured, sensing his obvious discomfort. She dismissed him with a nod. Without even a backward glance, the warrior hurried off down the hillside to rejoin his fellow guards assembling at the docks.

She stood at the window for a moment, staring into the

distance as her tapered fingers nervously clutched the silken tassel on her belt. Hakon, home at last! She felt a rush of relief to know that he was safe, then a tingling warmth of pleasure as she imagined herself within his strong arms once again. She could hardly wait to tell him of her love!

Anora suddenly rushed into the room, the door opening all the way and slamming against the timbered wall behind it. The loud noise startled Gwendolyn, and she whirled around in surprise.

"Gwendolyn, I have wonderful news!" Anora blurted, her fair skin flushed with excitement. " 'Tis Lord Hakon! He has returned! I had just stepped from the cooking house when I heard the horns. Come quickly!" She ran to Gwendolyn's side and grabbed her sister's arm. "The longship is still a good distance away, but if we hurry we can meet it just as it arrives at the docks!"

But Gwendolyn held back, a strange sense of apprehension welling up inside her. Then she shook her head. Nay, she would not allow any worries to plague her this day! She looked down at her clothes, her trembling hands smoothing the pleats of the silken tunic. "But surely I should change into a finer gown, Anora. This one is so plain."

Anora smiled at her sister's self-consciousness. She had never thought she would see the day when Gwendolyn would show the least bit of interest in what she wore!

" 'Tis hardly plain, dear sister!" she assured her. "You have never looked lovelier." And, indeed, Gwendolyn was a vision, Anora thought admiringly. She wore a shimmering gray silk chemise that hugged the slender curves of her body, and a vivid blue mantle embroidered with silver threads that heightened the emerald color of her eyes. Aye, her sister had truly blossomed over the past months, which in itself was remarkable, considering the length of her recovery from her awful wound. Her creamy skin glowed with renewed health, and her eyes sparkled warmly. Perhaps it was the babe, Anora thought fleetingly.

"I am sure Wulfgar will find you just as lovely when he sees you again," Gwendolyn replied, looking at her sister. Anora's lustrous hair was growing long once more, and already reached just below her shoulders. She, too, was dressed in a fine silken chemise and tunic. Truly, they had never seen such beautiful clothes as the ones they had been given to wear!

Her observation was instantly rewarded by Anora's radiant smile. "Come, Gwendolyn! 'Tis the moment you have long awaited. Now, we must hurry or we shall miss his arrival!"

"Very well. I am ready," Gwendolyn murmured. She took just a moment to run an ivory comb through her short hair, then threw a light cloak about her shoulders. Together they hurried from the hall.

Gwendolyn's heart felt as if it were in her throat as she and Anora walked side by side down the steep path toward the shoreline. Hakon's longship had not yet reached the docking area. She held up her hand, shielding her eyes from the brightness of the morning sun. The longship looked like a proud serpent as it skimmed across the glistening waters of the fjord toward them.

She gasped as she recognized Hakon's tall figure standing beside the dragon-headed prow. He looked so strong, so magnificent! The brisk wind was rippling through his hair, and his black cloak whipped out behind him. The steel of his broadsword, raised in salute, glinted brightly in the sun.

"Let us stand over there," Anora murmured, nodding her head toward a slight rise in the hill that was just beyond the docks. "We will be close enough for him to see us clearly, but not in the way."

"Aye, that will be fine," Gwendolyn agreed breathlessly,

following close behind her sister. She could hardly tear her eyes away from Hakon. She could just now make out the expression on his face. He was smiling, his teeth a flash of white against his bronzed skin. God's blood, he was handsome! More so than she remembered!

A great roar went up from the gathered warriors as the longship slid up against the dock. Their loud, boisterous cries of welcome drowned out the scraping of wooden benches as the crewmen jumped to their feet to secure their oars. Thick ropes were tossed over the side and caught by outstretched hands. It was not long before the mighty ship was moored.

Gwendolyn watched as Olav jumped onto the deck and caught Hakon in a bear hug. Hakon responded in kind, slapping his burly helmsman on the back. Their laughter rang out heartily above the din. The two men stood talking for several moments, seemingly oblivious to the raging commotion about them. The crew began unloading the ship, the muscles in their bare arms bulging as they heaved several large chests up onto the dock.

"Perhaps we should go back to the hall and wait for him to summon us," Gwendolyn murmured suddenly, the same feeling of apprehension that she had felt earlier overwhelming her once again. It was strange, she thought. Hakon had not even looked once in their direction, though they stood alone on the hill in full view of the ship.

"Buy why?" Anora asked, startled by this suggestion. "Give him a few more moments, Gwendolyn. Surely when he leaves the ship he will see you."

But Gwendolyn did not even hear her words. Her eyes widened as Hakon turned away from Olav and reached out his hand to a small cloaked figure sitting on a nearby rowing bench. She gasped in disbelief as two delicate, white hands pushed away the hood of the cloak, revealing a very pretty young woman with long, flowing hair the color of golden flax. The woman took Hakon's outstretched hand, smiling as he drew her to his side.

"Nay . . ." Gwendolyn murmured in horror. She felt numb to the very core of her being. *Nay, this cannot be!* her mind screamed, even as she watched in stunned silence. Hakon had found another love!

The young woman's bright laughter carried out across the hillside, piercing through her heart just as surely as the spear had penetrated her shoulder months before. Without another word, she turned and fled up the hill to Hakon's hall, scalding tears dimming her eyes.

Chapter Thirty-nine

"Gwendolyn, you must eat something," Anora urged softly. "Look, Berta has prepared a wonderful tray for you. There is warm rye bread, goat cheese, and even some of the wild berries you like so well. Please, if you would try just a little . . ." She waited a moment, but there was no response.

Sighing, Anora shook her head sadly. It was useless. Gwendolyn had not moved from the bed since that morning, and it was already past midday. She lay on her side huddled under the fur coverlet, clutching it tightly just below her chin. Her eyes stared fixedly at the timbered wall in front of her.

Anora set the wooden tray on the small table near the bed, then walked to the window and leaned against the ledge. She folded her arms in front of her, hugging her chest. "Damn the Viking!" she swore fiercely under her breath, surprising herself. She had always been the one to chide her sister for using coarse language, but those words truly expressed how she felt at that moment. How she longed for the day when they would be free of this cursed land!

Anora angrily recalled the scene near the docks that morning. She had never seen Gwendolyn look so crushed, as if the very light had gone out of her eyes. And when she had looked toward the longship to see what had upset her so, she hadn't a chance to utter a single word before Gwendolyn left her side, racing as fast as she could up the hill.

She had followed her sister a few moments afterward, even though she heard Lord Hakon's voice call out to them from the longship. She doubted if Gwendolyn had heard him call out her name, and doubted even more that she would have stopped. She had already been lying on the bed, just as she was now, by the time Anora rushed into the chamber.

A sudden knock at the door broke into her thoughts. "Who is there?" she said irritably, venting her frustration at whoever waited outside.

"Hakon."

Anora's hand flew to her throat. She glanced quickly over at the bed, but Gwendolyn had not stirred. She hurried to the door and opened it just a crack. "My lord?" she queried tersely, though a shiver of fear coursed through her. She had forgotten how tall and broad he was!

"I wish to speak with you both," he replied evenly, his eyes meeting hers through the narrow opening.

" 'Tis not possible, my lord. Gwendolyn is not feeling well—"

"Nay, let him enter," Gwendolyn's determined voice interrupted her. Anora whirled around, surprised to see her sister had moved silently from the bed to the chair near the window. She opened her mouth to protest, but Gwendolyn shook her head.

" 'Tis all right, Anora. Let us hear what Lord Hakon has to say," she murmured steadily, belying the turmoil raging within her.

Anora shook her head doubtfully, then moved away from the door and hurried over to Gwendolyn's side. She stood next to her chair and rested her hand on her sister's shoulder.

Hakon drew in his breath sharply as he entered the sunlit chamber. Truly, he had never seen two more radiantly beautiful women! Yet his eyes sought only Gwendolyn's. She met his gaze evenly, though he could see she was trembling. Thor, how many tortured nights had he spent dreaming of her, how many anxious days wondering if she had recovered from her wound! But he quickly caught hold of himself, remembering his sworn vow to harden his heart against her. She was lost to him, he told himself fiercely. There was naught he could do.

"You said you wished to speak to us, my lord," Gwendolyn murmured softly. Her delicate hands lay in her lap, clasped tightly so they would not shake. Hakon seemed to fill the very room with his powerful presence, overwhelming her, shattering her ability to reason.

Hakon started at the lilting sound of her voice. Yet her simple statement served to remind him of the purpose for his visit. He took a few steps toward them, his hand resting on the polished hilt of his broadsword. His voice was hard, implacable.

"I have come to tell you that we shall sail within the fortnight for England. Haarek Jarl has already sent emissaries to both your father and Wulfgar Ragnarson, informing them of your imminent . . . and safe return." He paused, noting the sudden paleness of Gwendolyn's cheeks. "If you are not feeling well, we can talk of this later, Gwendolyn."

She, too, started visibly. She had never heard him say her name before. "I am fine, my lord," she replied, though somewhat shakily. She was grateful for the reassuring pressure of Anora's hand on her shoulder.

"Very well, then. As soon as preparations are made and all is in readiness, we will set sail for your homeland. Two of Haarek Jarl's warships will meet us at the mouth of the Sogn and escort us during the journey." He looked at them pointedly, an unspoken question in his eyes. "I would have given you this news earlier this day, but it seemed you were both in a great hurry to return to the hall."

Gwendolyn turned her face away, a burning blush firing her cheeks. So, he had seen them standing there on the hill after all! She fought to keep her voice low and steady. "It seemed to us that you were well occupied, my lord. We thought perhaps our meeting should wait for another time." She looked back at him, hurt and betrayal flaring in the emerald depths of her eyes.

Hakon was taken aback by the force of her gaze. What could she possibly be referring to? he wondered, perplexed.

Gwendolyn did not wait for a response. "Is it your wish that we gather our few things together and move to another longhouse . . . to make room for your new concubine?" she asked bitterly.

"Concubine?" Hakon muttered, almost to himself. Then his eyes widened in surprise as he guessed the meaning of her question. Had he detected a hint of jealousy in her voice, or had he imagined it? Nay, it was not possible. Gwendolyn cared naught for him. He quickly dismissed the thought.

"If you speak of the young woman aboard my ship this morning, she is a sister to the wife of Haarek Jarl," Hakon explained. "She wished to return to her home, which is in this region, and I offered to escort her this far. Her kin will be here tomorrow morn to fetch her." Hakon shrugged. "She is a winsome lass, and comely as well. I have half a mind to ask her kin to consider a betrothal between her and my uncle's middle son. 'Twould be a fine match that would join our family to that of Haarek Jarl's."

"Oh!" Gwendolyn cried. She looked down at her hands,

embarrassed, as overwhelming relief surged through her body. So, all was not yet lost! A faint smile curved her lips.

Anora squeezed her shoulder, then left her side and hurried toward the door. "If you will excuse me, my lord, there is a matter I must attend to," she murmured, lowering her eyes as she passed by Hakon. "My thanks for your news." She pulled the door shut behind her, but not before she had smiled reassuringly at Gwendolyn.

The room fell silent after the sound of Anora's footsteps had died away. Hakon shifted uncomfortably. He had not planned to be alone with Gwendolyn, fearing it could prove too much of a temptation for him. His resolve to remain distant had already been tried enough during this short visit!

His eyes roamed about the chamber and he noted the decidedly feminine trappings here and there. His weapons had been removed from the timbered walls, and a loom had been set in the far corner. A half-worked tapestry was stretched across the wooden frame.

"I see you have kept busy these past months," he said, turning back to her, breaking the awkward silence between them.

" 'Tis Anora's work, not mine," Gwendolyn replied softly. "I do not care much for the loom and such things."

Hakon tried to suppress a smile, though unsuccessfully. He suddenly remembered what Berta had said so long ago about Anora's reluctance to spend much time in the weaving house. But that had not been Anora, he reminded himself grimly, his smile disappearing as quickly as it had come. The wrenching pain of discovering their guise gripped him as if it had been only yesterday.

"I am glad you have returned, my lord," Gwendolyn said simply, watching the rapid play of emotions across his handsome face. " 'Twas my fear that perhaps the sea had claimed you."

Her gently spoken words stunned him. Why would she

care if aught had happened to him? She had gotten what she wanted, hadn't she? "The winter was such that we could not sail until a few weeks ago," Hakon said tersely.

"Aye, that is what Olav told me," she replied, "though I think he was worried, too."

"Olav has been known to fret overmuch," Hakon muttered. He turned his head away, pretending to look about the room once again. Yea, the brutal winter had been part of the reason, he thought grimly, but not all. He had stayed in Trondheim as long as he possibly could, dreading to return to the settlement. The thought of seeing Gwendolyn there, knowing that she would never be his, had been more than he could bear.

Haarek Jarl had generously provided lodging to him and his crew during the past three months, but eventually he had been angered at Hakon's reluctance to return to his lands. Finally he had commanded him to sail at once for Sogn, berating him for tarrying overlong when so much was at stake. And though the shrewd Jarl had never asked for an explanation, Hakon believed he had surmised the truth for his delay. He vividly recalled Haarek's parting words.

"There are many women in the world," Haarek Jarl had said grimly, his dark eyes boring into Hakon's with heated intensity. "But one woman, no matter how beautiful, is surely not worth the betrayal of an entire people. Think well on this, Lord Hakon. I have entrusted to you the task of returning these women to their homeland. Do not fail me."

Hakon had resigned himself to the inevitable, and had set sail that very day. Yet even so, Haarek Jarl had ordered two well-armed warships to accompany him, no doubt to ensure he followed through with his orders.

"My lord," Gwendolyn murmured, "there is something I must tell you."

Hakon started, his eyes meeting hers. He had been so engrossed in his thoughts that he had not even noticed she had left the chair and was now standing only a few feet from him. As ever, he was struck by her incredible beauty. Yet he looked at her warily. What could she possibly want to say to him? When she had played the part of Garric, there had always been biting words upon her tongue. Perhaps it was not enough that she had won her freedom. Perhaps now she wished to flaunt it at him, exulting in the fact that she and her sister had played him for a fool.

Nay, he shook his head fiercely. He did not care to hear her words, whatever they might be. His male pride had been hurt enough already. "There is nothing left to say between us, Gwendolyn. You have heard the news which you no doubt have long awaited. Now it is time I returned to the great hall." He turned on his heel and strode toward the door.

"Hakon . . . please, wait!" Gwendolyn cried out desperately. She ran over to him and caught his arm. What had she done to make him so angry?

He stopped and looked down at her, his expression cold, inscrutable. Yet he could not deny her touch sent a surge of longing through his body.

Gwendolyn stepped back, her emerald eyes bright with unshed tears at his sudden indifference. "Hakon . . . I have longed so for your return. I wanted to t-tell you . . . I . . . I love you," she almost whispered.

Hakon's breath caught in his throat. He felt the strangest sensation, as if time suddenly stood still around him. All he could hear was the beating of his heart, pounding furiously against his chest. It grew louder and louder in his ears, almost drowning out Gwendolyn's voice as she repeated the words.

"I love you, Hakon."

Yet his expression did not change. Only his eyes betrayed the terrible chaos of emotions raging within him. He could feel the anger of his hurt pride melting away, only to be replaced by an inner agony that was so great he could have cried out from the crushing pain.

Odin, help him! Hakon felt as if he were being ripped apart by the overwhelming desire to take Gwendolyn in his arms and never let her go . . . and his fierce loyalty to his homeland. Wildly he wished that she had never said the words he had long ago despaired of ever hearing from her lips. It would have been far easier for him to return her to her homeland thinking she had made a mockery of his love.

For Hakon knew he had no choice. Once a Viking warrior had sworn allegiance to his lord, it was inviolable, a sacred vow that could never be broken. He had to obey the command of Haarek Jarl. To do otherwise would bring lifelong contempt upon his entire clan, and possibly their deaths as well.

Hakon swallowed hard, his eyes locking with hers. She looked so vulnerable, so hopeful. Yet he knew their love could never be. He sighed raggedly. There was only one way he could answer her. It would be better for her—for them both—to endure what was to come, he tried to tell himself. Yet Hakon knew his next words would haunt him the rest of his life.

His deep voice echoed about the chamber. "Your love matters naught to me, Gwendolyn," he said harshly. " 'Tis better if you save it for an Anglo-Saxon." The stricken look on her beautiful face was more than he could bear. He turned abruptly and left the room.

Gwendolyn stood for a moment, unable to move. She did not feel the hot, bitter tears streaking her face, nor the nails biting so cruelly into her clenched hands that they drew blood. Numbed to the very core of her being, she felt as if her heart were shattering within her breast.

Then, slowly, defiantly, she lifted up her trembling chin. In the silence of the room, she cursed Hakon's name, and the unhappy fates that had ever brought them together.

Chapter Forty

Gwendolyn leaned on the ledge of the window and gazed up at the morning sky. The eve of their homeward journey to England had dawned bright and clear, boding well for the weather they could expect during the voyage. Small white clouds dotted the endless expanse of blue. The settlement still lay in shadows, though golden shafts of light from the rising sun were peeking above the surrounding mountains.

She took a deep breath of the pristine air, filling her lungs. Everything smelled so fresh and new. During the past two weeks the last of the snows had melted, the icy moisture feeding the thick grasses that now carpeted the curving slopes surrounding the settlement. Truly, she had never seen such rugged beauty as this in her own land.

Gwendolyn sighed heavily and turned back into the darkened chamber. She glanced over at the wide bed. Anora was still sound asleep, her silver-blond hair spread out like fine gossamer across the eiderdown pillow. Gwendolyn shrugged. At least her sister would be well rested for the journey, which was more than she could say for herself. She had been unable to sleep well at all since Hakon had . . .

Nay, she would not think of it, Gwendolyn told herself fiercely. She stood at the bedside for a moment, wondering what she could do to pass the time until the morning meal. A slow smile spread across her delicate features. Perhaps a walk would take her mind off the memories that continually plagued her. Aye, that was what she would do!

She walked quickly to the ornately carved chest that held her clothes, her bare feet padding across the wooden floor. She quietly lifted the lid, then bent down and rummaged around for a moment. With a satisfied smile, she pulled out a pair of soft linen trousers and a matching tunic. Hastily she whisked the silken shift she was wearing over her head, and tossed it aside with some distaste. She was sick and tired of the confining nature of women's clothing. Luckily Berta had secured for her this one pair of trousers and tunic, albeit with much cajoling. The kindly woman's initial reluctance had reminded Gwendolyn of her mother, and their constant battle over what was appropriate for her to wear.

Gwendolyn quickly donned the trousers, pulling tight the leather drawstring at her still-narrow waist. She gently touched her stomach. Even though she was nearing her fourth month, her slender form had changed little but for the subtle rounding of her belly, and an increasing tenderness in her breasts. Yet she knew it would not be long before her body would betray her secret. She shook her head. Nay, she would not think of that either, at least not now!

She drew the linen tunic down over her head, sighing with pleasure at the freedom of movement men's clothing afforded her. She planned to wear this during the voyage to England, whether anyone protested or not.

Hopping first on one foot, then the other, she quickly slipped into a pair of hard-soled leather slippers. She did not know what had happened to her favorite pair of boots. Perhaps Hakon had given them to one of his other slaves, she thought. She shrugged, then ran her fingers through her tousled hair. At least that had not changed! Anora had refused to cut her sister's hair during the weeks she lay on her sickbed, but as soon as Gwendolyn was up and about she had seen to it that it was trimmed every month. That was how she liked it!

"Gwendolyn, what are you doing?" Anora's drowsy voice suddenly called out to her from the bed. She brought herself up on one elbow, rubbing her hand over her eyes.

"I am going out for a walk along the fjord," Gwendolyn said softly, wrapping a light cloak about her shoulders. " 'Tis a beautiful morning, and I am weary of being confined to this chamber."

"Would you like some company?" Anora asked, though she knew she would far prefer to sleep a while longer.

"Nay, I think I would like to be alone," Gwendolyn replied. "I will be back before the morning meal." She eased open the door. "Go back to sleep."

Anora sank back down upon the soft pillows and snuggled under the warm coverlet. "Very well, Gwendolyn," she whispered, her heavy eyelids closing once again. "Just be careful . . ." Yet as she drifted back to sleep, Anora knew she did not have to worry. The Viking guards who followed them everywhere they went would see that her sister was well protected.

Gwendolyn closed the door quietly behind her. She hurried across the main room of the hall, her cloak swirling about her trousered legs. She pushed on the heavy wooden door at the entrance, ever so slowly so it would not creak, and peered outside.

She could not believe her good fortune! The Viking warriors who usually guarded the hall were nowhere in sight. Yet that surprised her. Hakon had demanded that she and Anora be kept under constant guard to prevent any possible mishaps before they sailed. Perhaps they had thought it was safe to step away for a few moments, she surmised. She had never ventured out this early before, so they would have had no reason to be concerned. Aye, that was probably it.

Gwendolyn shrugged. Whatever the reason, she was determined to seize her unexpected opportunity. If she were truly lucky, she might be able to sneak away from the settlement unnoticed and enjoy her walk in blissful solitude. She slipped through the door, her eyes watchful and wary. She felt a heightened sense of adventure that enlivened her long-numbed spirits.

Suddenly her stomach growled hungrily, startling her. God's blood! she thought, exasperated. Then she giggled nervously. Her own stomach had frightened her! She looked longingly toward the cooking house. A thin column of white smoke was wafting from the opening in the roof, and she could smell the mouth-watering aroma of fresh-baked bread carried upon the light breeze. No doubt Berta had been up and about for several hours already, preparing the morning meal that would be served in the great hall to dozens of ravenous warriors.

Gwendolyn's appetite had suffered during the past few weeks, but she had forced herself to eat because of the babe she carried within her. But today, for the first time in a long while, she felt truly hungry. She doubted whether she could wait any longer to eat!

Thinking fast, she drew the hood of the cloak over her tousled hair and hurried down the hill. If she kept her head down, she thought hopefully, no one would recognize her in these clothes. She held her breath as two Viking guards passed by her, but they took little notice of her. She did not stop until she had reached the back door of the cooking house. It was ajar. Gwendolyn knew that Berta kept it that way to allow some fresh air into the main room, which was usually warm due to the raging hearth fires.

She peeked inside. Berta was bent over a caldron of bubbling stew, humming to herself, her back turned to the door. Gwendolyn wasted no time. She tiptoed into the room and over to a nearby table, then grabbed one of the crusty loaves of bread that was still warm from the clay oven. She spied a small round of goat cheese, and grabbed that, too. Then she turned and hurried from the cooking house, just as Berta straightened up.

"Who's there?" the stout cook called out, whirling around, her eyes sweeping about the room. The wooden door was swinging slightly on its hinges, creaking eerily. " 'Tis Loki and his children, up to some mischief," she muttered under her breath, shaking her head. She shrugged, then turned back to her stew.

Gwendolyn could not help but smile at her success. Clutching the loaf of bread and the round of cheese in the crook of her arm, she hurried alongside the timbered wall of the cooking house until she got to the far end. It was some distance to the thick line of trees that surrounded the settlement, but if she ran, it would take her only a few moments to reach them. She looked furtively about her. She could see a few guards here and there, but none was close enough to see her from this angle of the building. She took a deep breath, then raced swiftly across the grassy slope to the nearest trees.

She dodged behind a massive tree trunk, panting, and listened for any calls of alarm. There were none. Gwendolyn breathed a sigh of relief, exulting in her newfound freedom. Now, if she remembered correctly, she could follow the tree line down to the fjord. By then she would be way past the settlement, and she could enjoy her walk out in the open without fear of being seen.

She set out happily. Occasionally she gazed up into the trees as she walked, admiring the shimmering green leaves that seemed to dance and sway in the cool morning breeze.

She loved the rustling sound they made. There was a freshness in the air that invigorated her, renewing her senses. Her step was light, buoyant. It did not take her long to reach the bank of the fjord.

Gwendolyn walked for quite a while, paying no heed to the distance she was covering, until she came to a narrow peninsula that jutted out a short way into the fjord. The grassy knoll overlooking the peninsula looked soft and inviting, and she was feeling a little tired and quite hungry. She took off her cloak and spread it out upon the ground, then sat down. From here she could just barely make out the settlement, set in among the steep, rolling hillsides at the end of the fjord.

After tearing a generous hunk from the loaf of crusty bread, Gwendolyn crumbled some of the pungent goat cheese on top of it. She took a bite, savoring the simple flavors. The bright sunlight warmed her skin through her clothes, and she kicked off her leather slippers, stretching her toes. She looked out across the glistening expanse of water, marveling at the reflection of the snow-capped mountains on its tranquil surface. The stunning beauty of the land made it so easy to forget the numbing pain that had plagued her heart these last two weeks. Yet try as she would, she could not forget it completely.

She had seen little of Hakon since that awful day he had returned from Trondheim, and that was how she wanted it. After she told Anora what had happened, she had insisted that they never speak of it again. She and Anora had taken all of their meals in their chamber, preferring each other's company over that of a teeming hall full of Viking warriors and their wives. Only Berta had been welcome to visit them. The kindly woman had seen to it that they ate well, and they had never wanted for anything.

Gwendolyn sighed unhappily. It was those few times when she had seen Hakon that haunted her, tormenting her mind.

One morning only a few days past, she had been returning from the bathing house when he suddenly rounded the corner in front of her. She had been looking down, and had run right into him. His strong arms had encircled her, instinctively drawing her close. She looked up in startled surprise, her eyes locking with his for one breathless moment. His handsome face was strangely gaunt, almost pale, despite the bronzed tint of his skin, the blue depths of his eyes full of turmoil. She felt him shudder. Then he had suddenly released her and had hurried away.

And then only the night before she had ventured from the hall for a breath of fresh air. It was almost dusk. She had stretched her arms high above her head for a moment, then had leaned against the timbered wall, looking up at the stars just beginning to appear in the night sky. She had suddenly sensed that someone was watching her. Turning her head, she spied Hakon only a few feet away. He had started to walk toward her, then wheeled around and strode almost angrily down the hill toward the great hall.

Gwendolyn shook her head fiercely. If she thought of this any longer, it would surely spoil the day for her. Whatever had been between them was over, finished. Hakon no longer loved her, if he ever had at all. Yet even as she tried to wrest him from her mind, she could not forget.

She quickly ate the rest of her simple meal, then rose to her feet. It was probably time she headed back to the settlement. The sun had already crept up high in the sky, telling her it was almost midday. She must have missed the morning meal entirely. No doubt Anora would worry if she did not return soon. She stepped into her leather slippers, then shook out her cloak and whisked it about her delicate shoulders. A slight twinge of pain shot through her. Aye, she grimaced, even her healed wound would not let her forget him.

She left the grassy knoll overlooking the peninsula and

walked back down to the bank of the fjord. The sound of a rushing waterfall was suddenly carried to her on the breeze. A cool drink of fresh water would taste so wonderful, she thought, realizing how thirsty she was. Surely it could not be very far from where she was.

Instead of walking back toward the settlement, she hurried farther along the fjord. With each step the sound of the waterfall grew more thunderous, more powerful, until at last, after rounding a steep hillside, she was greeted by a sight that took her breath away. A sheer wall of rock towered high above her, and spilling over its glistening crags and hollows was the most majestic waterfall she had ever seen. Swollen by the melting mountain snows, the waterfall plummeted with deafening fury into the fjord below, sending up a dense white spray of cold mist into the air.

Gwendolyn gathered her cloak more tightly about her, for it was much cooler near the waterfall. She could see several small pools of water worn into the rocks not far from the surging cascade. She walked over to the nearest one and knelt down. Cupping her hand, she dipped it into the icy water, then brought it to her lips. She felt instantly refreshed as she drank thirstily. Some of the water spilled from her hand onto the front of her tunic, but she did not mind. She filled her cupped hand, again and again, until she was sated.

The sun-warmed rock she was kneeling on reminded Gwendolyn of her favorite grotto back in her homeland, and that fateful day that now seemed so long ago. She leaned over the side, gazing at her reflection on the placid surface of the pool. She did not look any different, yet she knew she had changed. Aye, how she had changed . . .

She touched her wet fingers to her lips, as she had done those many months past. A wave of incredible sadness washed over her, and she felt hot tears streak her face. One by one they tumbled into the clear water, distorting her reflection as tiny ripples radiated out to the edges of the pool.

Suddenly Gwendolyn's eyes widened in horror as she noticed another broken reflection staring up at her from the surface of the pool. She gasped in disbelief as she recognized the leering, evil grin. *Nay, it cannot be!* her mind screamed, as she plunged her hand into the icy water to dispel the horrible image. But she heard cruel laughter behind her, and she knew it was real. She wheeled around just as two clawlike hands bit into her shoulders. She winced in pain as the gnarled fingers dug into the skin just above her scar. She tried to scream, but fear had constricted her throat. Like a hideous apparition back from the grave, Svein's scarred face loomed above hers.

"At last I have my revenge," he snarled, his fetid breath assailing her, causing her to gag. He shoved her to the ground with unbelievable force, then kneeled astride her, grinning madly as he pulled a long knife from his belt. His pale eyes were red-rimmed and bulging. "I'll wager you did na' think you'd be seeing the likes o' me again, eh, lad?" he rasped hoarsely. He brought the knife down to within inches of her face. "I could na' believe my good fortune when I saw 'twas you, Garric."

"But how . . . I st-stabbed you . . . Hakon's men threw you into the fjord . . ." Gwendolyn gasped, her frantic thoughts rushing back to the night she and Anora had tried to escape. Aye, it was her knife that had felled him, she thought wildly.

Svein threw back his head and laughed, a high-pitched, wheezing sound. Then he stopped just as suddenly and looked down at her with boiling hatred in his eyes. "Aye, your knife almost finished me, lad. And if I hadn't lain so still, not even breathin' while Hakon's men stood over me, they would have run me through with their swords as well. But when they threw me into the fjord, I just drifted a ways along the shore 'til I could see 'twas safe to crawl out again. Fools!" he spat vehemently.

He shifted his weight above her, his tongue licking his cracked lips. " 'If na' for the old woman who found me, I would have died for sure. But I did na' die. I have been waitin' these many months, waitin' for the right moment to have my revenge!" He laid the cold steel of his blade across her throat. "When you taste the kiss of my knife, when I twist it into your heart, only then will you know half the torment I've suffered because o' you, Garric."

Gwendolyn felt a cold chill course through her at his words, but she did not allow herself to panic. God's blood! If she could only get the knife away from him, she thought, her mind working fast, at least then she might have a chance. She could see he was mad beyond all reason. Perhaps if she could confuse him, even for a moment . . .

She found her voice once again. "B-but, Svein, you are mistaken. My name is not Garric—'tis Anora!"

"Anora?" he repeated, his pale eyes widening. "Nay, you lie!" he hissed. "She has long, beautiful hair, like spun silver—"

"I c-cut it off!" Gwendolyn stammered, trying to stay calm despite the fierce beating of her heart. "S-see for yourself, Svein . . . tear my tunic if you must . . ." *Sweet Jesu!* she prayed fiercely. *Protect me!* She watched breathlessly as Svein's eyes moved from her face to her heaving chest. He laid his knife on the ground beside her, then took the linen fabric of her tunic in both his hands and ripped it easily from collar to hem. He gasped in surprise as her rounded breasts were bared to his stunned gaze.

Gwendolyn waited no longer. With every ounce of her strength she brought her knee up and drove it into his groin. Svein screamed in pain and doubled over on top of her, but she shoved him off roughly and scrambled to her feet. He lunged for her, but only managed to wrench the cloak from her shoulders before she was off and running along the bank of the fjord as fast as her legs would carry her. She breathed in great gulps of air that hurt her lungs, and her sides ached horribly, but she did not stop.

"Anora!" Svein shrieked, as he dragged himself to his feet. He snatched his knife from the ground and set out after her. His enraged cries could be heard even above the surging roar of the waterfall. They echoed off the steep sides of the mountains, over and over again. "Anora!"

Gwendolyn glanced over her shoulder, cold fear gripping her as she saw that he was narrowing the distance between them. Suddenly she slipped on the grass, wet from the mist of the waterfall, and fell heavily to the ground. For a moment she was stunned. She did not hear the thundering hooves fast approaching her from the direction of the settlement, nor the spirited snorting of a horse as it was reined in not far from her. She tried to get up, then felt herself lifted to her feet by strong arms.

"Nay!" she screamed, struggling wildly, thinking Svein had caught up with her. But she gasped in surprise, her breath caught in her throat, as she looked up into a pair of vivid blue eyes.

Chapter Forty-one

"Stand behind me," Hakon muttered tersely, pushing her away as Svein ran swiftly toward them, brandishing his long knife in his hand.

Gwendolyn quickly did as she was told. Clutching her torn garment about her, she took several stumbling steps backward until she was well out of the way. She watched, wide-eyed, as Hakon drew his broadsword from the scabbard at his belt, then gripped it in front of him with both hands on the polished hilt. He stood tall and straight, his keen eyes never wavering from the grotesque figure approaching him.

Svein slowed his pace, then pulled up short a good twenty feet from Hakon. Sweat had stained his tattered clothes, and his dark hair and beard were matted and damp. His red-rimmed eyes looked from Hakon to Gwendolyn, then back again. He smiled, an evil, lopsided grin that was distorted into a grimace by the red scar that slashed down the left side of his face.

"So, I see you have your protector here, Anora," Svein sneered. He bowed mockingly. "A good day to you, Lord Hakon." He spat out those last words with obvious loathing. "Well, 'tis fine wi' me. When I finish with him, the outcome will be the same." His crazed eyes raked heatedly over Gwendolyn while he slowly walked forward. "I have waited a long time to savor what is mine. If your fine lord had na' seen fit to steal you from me, I would have felt your body writhe beneath me a long time ago!"

Gwendolyn shuddered visibly and backed up a few more steps. Even his voice made her flesh crawl. Try as she might, she could not still her trembling.

"Save your wild ravings, man," Hakon growled, his blue eyes glittering dangerously. "Come, your death awaits you."

Hakon's words infuriated Svein. Suddenly he rushed forward, bellowing madly, his long knife poised in front of him. He lunged fiercely at Hakon, but he found only empty air as Hakon stepped swiftly out of his way. He charged once again, deadly intent in his pale eyes, only to be met by a swipe of Hakon's broadsword across his middle. He screamed in pain and fell to his knees, his eyes rolling as he clutched his stomach. Blood spurted from beneath his gnarled fingers.

"Mercy, Lord Hakon, mercy!" Svein shrieked in terrible fear. But there was to be no mercy. Hakon raised his broadsword above his head, his expression cold, implacable.

Svein's pale eyes widened in horror. Then he laughed, a bone-chilling, maniacal sound. "May the gods curse the rest of your day—"

The flashing blade of Hakon's broadsword sang through the air as it came down, severing Svein's head from his body in a spray of blood.

Gwendolyn gasped, closing her eyes to the gruesome sight. Nay, she could take no more of this brutal land! Repulsed and sickened by the awful carnage, her only thought was to flee from the savagery she had just witnessed, from Hakon and his blood-red sword . . . from *everything!*

She turned on her heel and took off running along the bank of the fjord, ignoring Hakon's repeated shouts for her to stop. Raging tears blinded her eyes and streaked her ashen cheeks. She stumbled and fell, crawling on her hands and knees until she could summon the strength to pick herself up and continue her mad dash along the grassy slope. Her chest heaved painfully, her labored breathing tore at her throat.

Hakon's face was grim as he quickly wiped the bloodied blade of his sword on the ragged shirt of Svein's beheaded corpse, then slipped it into his scabbard. He ran to his mighty black stallion and hoisted himself up into the saddle. Pulling tightly on the reins, he wheeled the horse about and dug his booted heels into its glistening flanks. The stallion neighed loudly, tossing its proud head, then set off across the bank at a gallop.

Gwendolyn heard the pounding of hooves hitting the earth behind her, but she did not slow her pace. She raced on desperately, her heart beating fiercely against her chest. Suddenly Hakon reined in his stallion in front of her, startling her. She turned and ran back the other way. He caught up with her again, this time throwing his leg over the saddle and sliding to the ground. She turned abruptly, but not quickly enough. As she tried to run in the opposite direction, he took a flying leap and caught her about the waist

"Nay, leave me be!" Gwendolyn screamed, pommeling him with her clenched fists as she tried to break free of his hold. But it was too late. They tumbled on the ground together in a wild frenzy of flailing arms and legs, rolling over and over down a steep incline to the very edge of the grassy bank. Hakon caught her just before she went over the side into the icy waters of the fjord and pinned her arms above her head with one strong hand. She struggled mightily against him, kicking her slender legs and tossing her head from side to side. But he caught her chin with his other hand so that she faced him, then brought his lips down upon hers with crushing fury.

Gwendolyn gasped in breathless surprise. She ceased her struggles and suddenly lay still in his arms, overwhelmed by the fiery passion of his kiss. All thought of resisting him fled from her mind, and she met him measure for measure with bittersweet abandon. It seemed as if there was nothing else in the world but Hakon, herself, and the raging kiss they shared.

Hakon tore his mouth away and looked down at her, his blue eyes searching her face as if he were seeing her for the first time. "Gwendolyn," he murmured huskily, savoring the sound of her name upon his tongue. "Gwendolyn." He traced a finger gently down her cheek and across the soft curve of her lips. "You seem determined to try me, little one. I had gone to the hall to tell you all was in readiness for the voyage, and I learned from your sister that you had not yet returned from your walk. When I found that you had eluded your guards, and had gone out alone . . ." He shuddered, a tortured sigh escaping his throat. "To think I might have been too late!"

He bent his head and kissed her, tenderly at first, but then growing more possessive. "Nay, I cannot let you go," he whispered vehemently. "I love you, Gwendolyn . . . love you . . ." Gently he kissed away the tears that streaked her face, then released her arms and crushed her to him in an impassioned embrace.

Stunned, Gwendolyn exulted in her heart at his fervent words of love. Yet she could not help wondering why he had so cruelly denied her own admission those two weeks past. She sighed, wrapping her arms tightly about him. Whatever the reason, at least there was no longer any deception or pretense between them. All thoughts were soon chased from her mind, replaced by delicious sensation as Hakon's mouth blazed a trail of molten kisses down her creamy throat. His strong hands pulled aside the torn edges of her tunic, baring her perfectly rounded breasts to his scorching touch.

"It has been so long," he murmured thickly, breathing in the heavenly fragrance of her silver-blond hair, savoring the silky feel of her skin. "Too long . . ." His fingers found a nipple, taut and hardened by the cool breeze. He plied the pink-crested nub with deft, featherlight strokes, while his teeth nibbled at a delicate earlobe.

Gwendolyn moaned softly, writhing under his touch. It seemed her breasts were so much more sensitive now than before. She gasped in surprise as his hot mouth replaced his fingers, his tongue flicking a moist circle of flame around her raised nipple. "M-my lord!" she exclaimed softly, pulling away. "Surely someone will see us here! We are so close to the settlement!"

Hakon lifted his head, a smile lighting his handsome features, a wicked gleam in his eyes. He chuckled lustily. "So what if they do? No one will question the Jarl of Sogn!" At the shocked expression on her beautiful face, he laughed and rose to his feet, holding out his hands to her. "Come with me, Gwendolyn. I will find us a soft, secluded bed for our pleasure."

Her emerald eyes locked with his as she took his outstretched hands, a curved smile upon her lips. He lifted her gently to her feet, then easily swung her up in his strong arms and hugged her to his broad chest. A bright blush fired her cheeks as her tunic fell away, revealing once again her swollen breasts to his heated gaze. She saw his eyes cloud for a moment, and realized he was looking at the scar just below her left shoulder. She gasped in embarrassment and tried to cover it with the torn edge of her tunic.

"Nay, my love, 'tis a badge of honor," Hakon said, his deep voice catching from emotion. "Through it, you gave me life." His eyes burned into hers with unequaled intensity. "We are bound together for eternity, our lives entwined forever, as ordained by the gods."

Gwendolyn breathed a silent prayer to her own God, willing it to be so. She wrapped her slim arms about his neck as he walked up the steep slope toward a copse of trees not far from the glistening fjord. The low branches made a shaded shelter, while underneath the thick green grass looked soft and inviting.

"Our bed, my lady," Hakon murmured, kneeling down. He reached behind him with one hand and tore his scarlet cloak from his shoulders, then quickly spread it out upon the grass. He held her close within his arms and kissed her for a long, breathless moment, then laid her gently upon the silken cloak. Rising to his feet, he loosened his belt and dropped it to the ground. Then he pulled his dark blue tunic over his head, baring the great, muscled expanse of his bronzed chest to her admiring gaze. It took him but a few more seconds to kick off his leather boots and strip off his tight-fitting trousers.

"I take it my body pleases you," Hakon stated, a rakish smile of pleasure on his face.

"Aye, my lord, it pleases me very much," Gwendolyn admitted. Truly, Hakon was such a beautiful man! She longed to run her fingers through the thick mat of golden curls on his chest, and follow the golden line of hair down his taut, sculpted belly to his . . . God's blood! She could not believe how bold she had become!

Hakon threw back his head and laughed delightedly at her wanton perusal, seeming to read her mind. Before she knew it, he was lying beside her once again, drawing her slender body against his well-muscled length. "You are a temptress," he whispered huskily, his breath warm upon the skin of her throat as he traced a tender line of kisses upon her scar.

Gwendolyn trembled in his arms, overwhelmed with love for this man. She put her hands alongside his face and gently lifted his head from her shoulder. "I love you, Hakon. You are my life," she said softly. She touched his lips with her own in a sweet kiss.

Hakon could hold back the torrent of his raging desire no longer. Her kiss had unleashed in him the driving need to possess her completely, to find the aching release that only her soft, yielding body could afford him. His strong hands began to caress her silky skin, but he stopped when they came up against the linen material of her trousers.

"These must go." He grinned wickedly. His warm mouth moved lingeringly from the rapidly beating pulse point at her neck to between her breasts, then down the center of her ribs to her navel. He tickled the small hollow with his tongue, then grabbed the leather drawstring with his teeth and slowly pulled it loose. He easily slid the trousers from her slender hips and cast them aside.

Hakon groaned at the sight of her beautiful body, now fully bared to his gaze. She seemed slightly more rounded, more curved than he remembered. No matter, it only made her all the more lovely in his eyes. He covered her with his massive body, taking care not to crush her with his weight. His lips captured hers as his fingers found her most sensitive point, and he was not surpised to find she was ready for him.

Gwendolyn arched her back at the tempestuous waves of liquid passion coursing through her. She moved instinctively against his hand, moaning, pleading for him to take her, but he stifled her cries with the fierceness of his kiss. Suddenly he rolled over onto his back and pulled her along with him. She gasped in surprise to find herself astride him.

Hakon gently caressed her breasts, teasing first one, then the other with his tongue. "I want to watch you, Gwendolyn," he said hoarsely, his eyes burning with hungry desire. His hands encircled the narrow span of her waist and lifted her up, then eased her down on the pulsating shaft of his erect manhood.

Gwendolyn cried out as he entered her and began to move within her, slowly at first, but then with greater urgency. She stretched her arms above her head with unbridled ecstasy, closing her eyes, then leaned far back, her hands grabbing the sinewy sides of his legs as he held her hips. Matching his sensuous movements with her own, she cried out when his expert fingers found the swelling bud of her womanhood. She trembled uncontrollably, her body racked by such incredibly delightful sensations that she did not think she could take much more.

"Come with me . . . now, Gwendolyn, now," Hakon murmured thickly, pulling her to him, seizing her mouth with his own. His tongue thrust into her mouth, delving, searching, even as his throbbing manhood surged powerfully within her. She arched against him, driving him deeper and deeper within her. She felt as if she were spinning toward an unbelievable height of piercing, exploding sensation, until at last she shuddered against him, wave after molten wave of blinding ecstasy washing over her.

"Hakon!" she cried out, collapsing upon his chest in utter exhaustion, her head on his broad shoulder. He wrapped his arms about her and held her tenderly, stroking her silken, tousled curls as their breathing slowly returned to normal.

They lay there together for a long time, joined as one. Gwendolyn sighed contentedly. How she wished she could stay like that forever. It was so peaceful under the leafy shade of the rustling trees. The spring breezes wafted over her, cooling her skin. She stretched luxuriously, smiling, and looked at Hakon. But her smile quickly faded, a puzzled frown creasing her forehead. His head was turned to the side and he was staring far off into the distance, his expression grim.

"What is the matter, Hakon?" she asked softly, alarmed.

He seemed not to hear her. "I shall defy him," he whispered fiercely under his breath.

"Defy who?" Gwendolyn queried, but still he did not answer her. Why did she have this strange, unsettled feeling? She reached up and gently turned his head so he was facing her. He started at her touch, his blue eyes meeting hers. "Defy who, Hakon? Who are you speaking of?"

"Haarek Jarl," he replied, his voice low, determined. He suddenly lifted her from him and rolled over onto his side, holding her close within his arms. He then raised himself on one elbow and looked down at her, his eyes reflecting his serious intent. Though he had tried during the past two weeks to convince himself otherwise, Hakon knew now he could not live without her. But before he acted on his plan, he had to know for sure that it was her desire to stay with him.

"But why must you defy him?" Gwendolyn whispered.

Hakon lay a finger across her lips. "First answer me this, Gwendolyn," he murmured. "Is it your wish to forsake your homeland, and remain with me . . . as my wife?"

Gwendolyn gasped, but her emerald gaze was unflinching. "Aye," she said simply.

Hakon let out his breath, unaware that he had been holding it. A flood of joyful relief surged through him. "Now I shall answer your question. I must defy Haarek Jarl, for 'tis the only way that you and I may remain together." He drew her closer, his strong arm encircling her possessively. "I have sworn to him that I will return both you and Anora to England. But I must have given him reason to doubt me while I was in Trondheim, for he has sent two warships to accompany us on this journey to see that I do not disobey his orders. Even now they await us at the mouth of the Sogn."

He paused, a flash of defiance in his eyes. "But I do not intend to carry out those orders," he said vehemently. "We shall sail on the morrow as planned, and give Haarek's men the impression that all is as it should be. But only Anora will disembark from my ship when we reach your homeland. You will stay on board with me. Perhaps once Wulfgar Ragnarson sees that she is safe, it will dissuade him from any thoughts of war." His brows knitted with concern. "Do you think your sister would be willing to explain to Wulfgar and your father that you have decided to stay with me . . . that it is by your own free choice?"

Gwendolyn nodded, a smile curving her lips. "Aye, she would. She knows already of my love for you. I cannot wait to tell her of my happiness!"

Hakon stared in awe at her radiant beauty. Thor, to think that she was to be his, at last! "Perhaps one day we will be able to return to England, and make amends to your family for our hasty departure," he said softly. Then his expression darkened. "If we can outsail the two warships Haarek Jarl has sent to accompany us on this journey, we will head for Dublin, or perhaps Normandy."

Gwendolyn's smile faded, her eyes clouding with confusion. "We would not sail for Norge? But you are the Jarl of Sogn, Hakon!"

"Nay," Hakon replied grimly. "If I break my vow to Haarek, I shall be Jarl of Sogn no longer. I shall never be able to return to my homeland again. To do so would be the cruelest folly. I would bring his vengeful wrath upon not only myself, but also upon my clan. I cannot risk their lives for the sake of my own happiness. If I do not return, they will be safe." He bent his head and brushed his lips against hers. "Yet I would not mind my exile so much knowing you were by my side."

So, that was why Hakon had denied her love, Gwendolyn thought. Suddenly it was all becoming very clear to her, horribly clear. Berta had once told her that a Viking's vow to his liege lord could not be broken without facing the fiercest consequences. Now Hakon was willing to do just that . . . and all because he loved her!

An awful thought struck Gwendolyn. "But what will happen if we cannot outsail the warships?"

"That is unlikely, for my longship is far more seaworthy than those larger vessels," Hakon tried to reassure her. Indeed, it was unlikely, he thought, but there was a chance that it could happen. He had hoped she would not ask him this, but he decided it was best she knew the truth. "If we were caught and we could not fight off Haarek's warriors, we would be taken prisoner. You, of course, would be returned to your family in England."

"And you, my lord?" Gwendolyn whispered fearfully, though she could already sense his answer. "What would happen to you?"

"I would be taken back to Norge, and tried at Haarek Jarl's court as a traitor to my people. There is only one sentence for that crime: death."

Gwendolyn shuddered in his arms. The thought that there was the slightest chance that he might die was more than she could bear. "Nay, Hakon, surely there must be another way!" she cried out, her mind racing.

But Hakon shook his head. "I can think of no other, little one," he said softly. He traced a finger tenderly down the side of her face, entwining it in a silken curl. "I have almost lost you too many times already. Do not try to spare me from what may happen by insisting I return you to your homeland. I will not do it. I cannot live without you, Gwendolyn, nor can I believe the gods have brought us through so much only to tear us apart again. If I must face the possibility of death, then so be it." He sealed his words with a searing kiss that took Gwendolyn's breath away.

Hakon lifted his head, a rakish grin on his handsome face. All seriousness was forgotten, at least for a while. "I would that we remain in this shady bower, my love. If I had known there were such beautiful forest nymphs running about half clothed, I would have made this my bed every night! But we must make our way back to the settlement. If we linger any longer, no doubt they will sound an alarm and come looking for us." He laughed as he thought of the look on Olav's face if his helmsman found them beneath this tree! He rose to his feet and held out his hand to her.

Gwendolyn could not help but smile at his teasing, yet her heart ached at the thought of what was to come. "Aye, my lord," she replied, as lightly as she could. She took his hand and he pulled her gently to her feet, then drew her into his arms. She rubbed her cheek against the soft golden hairs on his chest, breathing in the warm, male scent of him. They stood together for a long moment, looking out across the mirrored surface of the fjord, each lost in thought.

Hakon at last broke the silence between them. "We must go," he murmured, brushing a light kiss against her fair forehead. They drew on their clothes, and he wrapped his scarlet cloak about her delicate shoulders. He then strode over to his stallion, which was munching contentedly on some wild grasses not far away, and led it to where Gwendolyn was waiting.

Lifting her easily onto the saddle, Hakon put his foot in the stirrup and hoisted himself up behind her. Holding one arm protectively about her, he took the reins in his hands. He made a clicking noise to his stallion and they were off, galloping like the wind across the grassy bank of the fjord toward the settlement.

Chapter Forty-two

Gwendolyn stared out across the sparkling waters of the fjord, watching as the settlement receded farther into the distance with every stroke of the oars. Most of the Viking warriors who had gathered near the docks to see them off had already gone back to their longhouses, but she could still see Berta's stout figure standing alone on the shore. "I will truly miss her," she said softly to Anora, who stood beside her on the rear deck of the longship.

"Aye." Anora nodded, wiping away the tears that dimmed her eyes. "She was good to us."

Gwendolyn gently squeezed her sister's arm as both of them fell silent once again. She found it hard to believe this would be the last time she would ever see the settlement. It had become a part of her life, women into the very fabric of her relationship with Hakon. She had experienced not only the greatest sorrow and heartache there, but also the greatest joy she had ever known.

She did not tear her eyes away until the longship had rounded the bend in the fjord, hiding the cluster of logged buildings from her view. She sighed, then squared her delicate shoulders. Nay, now was the time to look ahead to the future she and Hakon would share. She left Anora's side and sat down on a vacant rowing bench nearby, her hands absently smoothing the wrinkled pleats of her silken tunic. She smiled to herself when she realized what she was doing, then shrugged. For some reason she had not minded donning women's clothing that morning. Suddenly she chuckled.

"What is so amusing, little one?" Hakon asked, walking up behind her. Gwendolyn started at the sound of his voice, her emerald eyes wide as she looked up at him. He laughed and sat down beside her. Now that the longship was well under way and the crew members were working hard at their oars, he could afford a free moment. He took her small hand in his own large one and brought it to his lips.

Gwendolyn felt a thrill course through her body at his touch. He looked so handsome this morning with the bright sun glinting off his white-blond hair, the long, thick waves tied back with a leather thong. The snug-fitting, sleeveless tunic he was wearing was molded perfectly to his broad, sculpted chest. His bronzed arms were bared and rippling with muscles.

She smiled and looked into his tender eyes. "I was only thinking 'tis my first time on this ship that I am not rowing with the others." She laughed gaily as he grimaced, though his eyes were full of mirth.

"Aye, 'tis true, my love. But at least I know that if I lose a crewman, there is someone who can ably take his place!" he tossed out playfully. He brushed a quick kiss against her smiling lips, then stood up from the bench and strode over to the helm to speak with Olav.

God's teeth, the very sight of him could take her breath away! she marveled. And to think she was to become his wife as soon as they reached Dublin! But suddenly her smile faded, a twinge of apprehension prickling at her mind. Nay, she shook her head defiantly. She would not allow herself to consider the possibility that all would not go well for them. She had to believe that Hakon's plan would work!

She knew that he had informed Olav and his hand-picked crew during a secret meeting the night before of his plan to defy Haarek Jarl. He had decided it was only fair to give them a choice. They could either stay on in Norge and serve under his uncle, who would take over his settlement, or man his longship and help him carry out his plan, with full knowledge that any who followed him would also be branded as traitors. But down to the last crewman, they had all sworn to remain with their chieftain, fierce loyalty blazing in their eyes.

Hakon had then seen to it that extra provisions were loaded onto the ship—food, fresh water, and most important, his own private hoard of gold and silver to use for trade. It had been done under the cover of darkness in the early hours of the morning so as not to alert any of the other warriors in the settlement to his plan. He had not rested until he was satisfied that all was securely loaded and in readiness for their departure later that morning, with enough supplies stocking the cargo well to see their way to Dublin . . . and even farther if need be.

Only then had Hakon made his way back to his hall. Anora had subtly offered earlier that evening to sleep on a pallet in the main room, so he and Gwendolyn could share his chamber during their last night at the settlement. Gwendolyn had lain awake in the wide bed for what seemed like hours, waiting for him. But when at last he had walked into the room, they had both been so exhausted that they were content simply to lie in each other's arms until the morning dawned.

Yet perhaps last night had been the sweetest of all their

nights together, Gwendolyn thought warmly. Hakon had cradled her in his arms, softly stroking her silky hair and murmuring tender words of love, until she had been lulled into a deep sleep by the steady beating of his heart.

A great flock of white sea birds suddenly startled Gwendolyn as they flew over the longship, their shrill cries breaking into her thoughts. She shielded her eyes from the sun and looked up at them, watching as they soared high into the endless expanse of blue sky, then one by one dove back down to the surface of the fjord in search of fish for their morning meal. Some of the birds carried their wriggling catch to their nests along the rocky slopes towering above the fjord, where hungry mouths were waiting to be fed.

Gwendolyn sighed. So much had changed since that first journey along the Sogn late last year. Yet it really did not seem so long ago that she had envied the soaring freedom of the sea birds. She shook her head, smiling. Nay, she did not have to envy them any longer.

She looked over at Anora. Her beautiful sister was still leaning on the railing of the ship, breezes blowing through her shining hair. Her emerald eyes were dancing with excitement, her cheeks blushing rosily with exhilaration. No doubt Anora was thinking of Wulfgar, and their long-awaited reunion.

Aye, so far their prayers had been answered, Gwendolyn thought gratefully. She smiled as she recalled Anora's expression of stunned surprise the day before, when she and Hakon had ridden together into the settlement on his spirited stallion. Her sister must have guessed at once the reason for the vibrant happiness in her eyes, for as soon as she had dismounted, Anora embraced her warmly. And after hearing about Hakon's plan, she had wholeheartedly agreed to give Gwendolyn's message to their father, assuring him that all was well and that it was her choice to stay with Hakon.

Gwendolyn leaned back against the curved side of the longship and closed her eyes. She basked in the warmth of the golden rays of sunshine heating the wooden deck. The rhythmic sound of the oars slicing through the water and the gentle slapping of the waves against the hull were soothing. A wave of relaxed contentment washed over her.

"Two warships off the port bow!"

Gwendolyn's eyes flew open at the sound of Hakon's voice. She leaned forward, stretching her slim arms above her head. Surely they had not reached the mouth of the Sogn already, she thought dazedly. She jumped up and ran over to the railing, gasping in surprise. The vast ocean was stretched out before them, as far as the eye could see.

Stunned, Gwendolyn realized she must have slept for several hours. She looked around her. Obviously Anora had decided to take a nap, too, for she could see her sister's leather slippers peeking out from the opening of the tent Hakon had erected for them near the cargo well. She ran over to the tent and tugged at one small foot.

"Anora, wake up! We have reached the ocean!" she exclaimed excitedly.

Anora sat up in the tent, yawning and rubbing her eyes sleepily. "The ocean?" she murmured, taking Gwendolyn's proffered hand as she was helped to her feet. "I must not have slept very well last night on that pallet, for when I saw you dozing off, I could not resist lying down myself."

But Gwendolyn did not hear her sister's words. Her eyes were fixed on the two warships fast approaching them from the direction of a green stretch of land jutting out from the mouth of the fjord. She gazed at them, a tremor of fear coursing through her. Were these the two warships Hakon had spoken of, the ones they would attempt to outsail when they reached England? She had never seen anything like them before! They were huge vessels, both at least ninety feet long; they were wider and lower in the water than Hakon's longship. Yet they cut swiftly through the choppy waves, their purple sails billowing in the stiff breeze.

Without thinking, Gwendolyn suddenly left Anora's side and hurried toward the dragon-headed prow of the ship, where Hakon stood. She quickly made her way along the narrow aisle between the rowing benches with practiced ease, nimbly dodging the coiled ropes lying here and there on the deck.

"My lord, are those Haarek Jarl's warships?" she called out breathlessly.

Hakon whirled around and looked down at her with surprise. His startling blue eyes narrowed angrily. He had been so engrossed in watching the ships that he had not heard her walk up behind him.

"Go back to your sister, Gwendolyn, and get inside the tent until I tell you both to come out. Now go, at once! Haarek Jarl's men must not see us standing here together!" he said tersely. His grim expression boded no resistance. "Go!"

Stunned and hurt by his tone, Gwendolyn nonetheless realized the folly of her rash action. She turned on her heel and quickly made her way back along the aisle, avoiding the disapproving glances from Hakon's men. Grabbing her sister's arm, she pulled her back into the tent. Anora opened her mouth to protest at this rough treatment, but Gwendolyn silenced her with a finger raised to her lips.

"Shh! Anora, be still! Hakon bade us to wait inside the tent," Gwendolyn whispered, her heart beating fast. God's blood! If she had ruined the plan . . . She shook her tousled head fiercely. Nay, she would not even think of it!

Suddenly a man's gruff voice could be heard shouting out something to Hakon from one of the warships. Gwendolyn lifted up the leather flap covering the entrance so they could hear better. "Listen!" she hissed. "They must be right off the port side!"

Gwendolyn leaned out just a little from the tent so she could catch the man's words. "He says his name is Thorolf Skallgrimsson . . . and that he has been charged by Haarek Jarl to accompany Hakon's longship to England." She leaned forward again, listening. "It sounds like he wants to see we are both aboard the ship!"

Her words were confirmed as heavy footsteps sounded across the wooden deck, moving swiftly toward the tent. Hakon suddenly threw back the flap, and crouched down, facing them.

" 'Tis as I feared," he muttered, looking from one to the other. His expression was grim. "Haarek Jarl has sent one of his most ruthless warriors to see that his orders are obeyed. But we shall proceed as planned. Come out now, both of you. Though I have told Thorolf that you are safe, he wants to see for himself."

Hakon first helped Anora from the tent, then Gwendolyn. He kept his voice low as he addressed her. "You must stay away from me for the rest of the journey, my love, though I would wish it otherwise. Try to appear as aloof as possible. Do not give this Thorolf the impression that you are anything but elated to be returning to your homeland." A wry smile briefly touched his face. "At least I have no worries that Anora will be anything less than convincing." With that he strode over to the port side of the ship and motioned for them to follow him.

Gwendolyn trembled at the sight of the great warship looming beside them not more than thirty feet away. She could see at least fifty armed men staring back at her, dressed in full battle gear. Suddenly several of the warriors stepped aside as a fierce-looking man, tall and swarthy, walked up to the side of the warship.

"Are those the wenches?" he yelled out, his shrewd eyes moving over them.

"Yea, Lord Thorolf. They are Anora and Gwendolyn, daughters to Earl Godric of Cheshire," Hakon called back.

He pointed to Anora. "This one is the betrothed of the Dane, Wulfgar Ragnarson."

Thorolf nodded. "They are as beautiful as the merchant said, if not more so!" He laughed crudely, but quickly sobered. "Very well, then, Hakon Jarl. Let us sail for England!"

"Yea," Hakon muttered, meeting Gwendolyn's gaze. "Let us sail for England."

Chapter Forty-three

Gwendolyn drew in a deep breath of the salty air, staring out at the lush coastline stretching out before them. England! It had taken little more than six days of sailing to reach their homeland, what with the clear skies to guide them both day and night and the strong winds filling the large sail.

She sighed. Haarek Jarl's warships had dogged them the entire journey, one flanking each side of Hakon's longship. She had stepped from the tent each morning, hoping to find that one or both of them had strayed off course during the night, but she was always disappointed. Even now they were cutting through the waves not far behind them, unswerving, like two guardian watchdogs.

"Such seriousness does not suit you, my love," Hakon said softly, walking up beside her. He stood a few feet away from her, his hands resting on the railing, knowing he could move no closer. He seemed to have read her thoughts. "Yea, they have followed us this far, Gwendolyn. But do not fear. I have no doubts that we shall be able to evade them. Soon it will be dusk and we will have the cover of night to aid us."

He paused, his eyes raking over her. Thor, how he longed to take her in his arms! But he knew that would have to wait, at least for a few more hours. He spoke to her in low, measured tones. "Thorolf does not know it yet, but his warships will be unable to follow us past the mouth of the river that runs alongside your father's lands. The water is much too shallow for their deeper hulls. He will have to content himself to wait for our return, though I am sure that will not sit well with him."

Hakon chuckled lightly at her look of amazement. "Yea, my love, I have thought of every detail." But then he sobered. "Once we are inland, you will have to show me where to moor the ship so it is as close as possible to your father's stronghold. Then I will take several of my men and escort Anora through the woods to within sight of the stronghold, where we will have to leave her. Do you think your sister will be able to find the rest of the way by herself?"

Gwendolyn nodded. "Aye, my lord. We know those woods well."

"Good," Hakon murmured. "By then it will be dark. Once we return to the longship and are under way again, 'tis my hope that we can ease past the two warships waiting for us at the mouth of the river and be well out to sea before they are able to turn about and follow us." He smiled reassuringly. "Go and tell Anora of the plan. It will not be long now before we reach the coast."

Gwendolyn nodded, watching as he strode back along the deck toward the prow. A surge of hope flared within her heart. It all sounded so simple. Surely it would not fail! She hurried to the tent, where Anora had spent much of her time during the voyage. This time it had been her sister who suffered miserably from seasickness. She was about to lift the leather flap when a bright glint caught her eye just off the starboard side of the ship, then another, then several glinting reflections all at once. She looked out across the rolling seas, shielding her eyes from the late-afternoon rays of the sun. Suddenly her breath caught in her throat.

"Hakon!" she shouted, oblivious to the fact that her voice was probably carrying out to the warships not far behind them. "Hakon!" She raced to the prow of the ship, ignoring the stunned glances of his crewmen.

"Gwendolyn, have you forgotten what I said about staying away—"

"Look there, my lord!" She cut him off breathlessly, pointing out across the water.

"Damn!" Hakon swore loudly, his eyes narrowing at the large fleet of ships, now fully discernible, approaching them from the south. Thor, he had not anticipated a welcoming party, and such a well-armed one. He knew very well that the bright glints were caused by sunlight reflecting off polished shields and weapons.

Hakon cursed himself for a fool. Why had he not considered that perhaps Wulfgar Ragnarson and his fleet might be waiting for them? Wouldn't he have done the same, had it been his betrothed? He shook his head grimly, his mind working fast. Maybe there was yet a chance they could leave Anora on the shore, then head back out to sea before the fleet caught up with them. There would still be Haarek Jarl's two warships to contend with, but he felt sure his longship could outsail them.

But Olav's shout crushed his last hope. "English warships, my lord, just off the port bow!"

Hakon wheeled around. There were at least twenty ships fast approaching them from the north. So, they were surrounded, he thought with despair, pounding his tightly clenched fist into his other hand. Truly, his gods had finally deserted him. "Head for the nearest shore, Olav!" he commanded tersely.

"Yea, my lord!" Holding fast to the helm, Olav brought it hard about and changed the course of the longship. It skimmed across the glistening waves, straight for a wide, sandy beach only a few hundred yards away.

Gwendolyn stood by Hakon's side, not uttering a word. Her face was pale, her emerald eyes filled with apprehension as she looked up at him.

"There is naught we can do, Gwendolyn," he murmured raggedly. "Soon the matter will be in Wulfgar's hands." He nodded toward Anora, who had stepped shakily from the tent. "Go to your sister."

She obeyed numbly, his sharp orders to his crew ringing in her ears. She hurried to Anora's side, watching silently as the men lowered and furled the sail and readied their oars.

"What is happening?" Anora asked weakly, holding on to the side of the tent. She had been sleeping, but the sudden commotion on board had awakened her with a start. She looked out over the waves, her eyes widening with surprise at the dozens of ships following close behind them in heated pursuit. Suddenly she gasped as she recognized the tall, dark-haired man standing at the prow of the lead ship. " 'Tis Wulfgar, Gwendolyn, and look! Father is with him!"

But Gwendolyn's eyes were on the beach ahead. Several of the English warships had already landed, and a line of armed men was standing there in grim formation, their weapons poised, waiting. God's blood, everything was happening so fast!

Suddenly she and Anora were pitched forward onto the deck as the hull of the longship grated against the sandy beach. The sound of oars splintering in two from the force of their landing rent the air. Gwendolyn lifted her head dazedly. All was in confusion as Hakon's crew threw down the broken handles of their oars and grabbed their weapons lying beneath their rowing benches. Wincing from the pain of her scraped hands and knees, Gwendolyn quickly pulled herself to her feet, then bent down to help her sister.

"Are you all right?" she asked breathlessly, looking at Anora's pale face with concern.

"Aye," Anora murmured as she stood, leaning on Gwendolyn's shoulder for support. Her eyes widened in fear as Hakon's longship was immediately surrounded by dozens of well-armed thanes.

"Hold your weapons, men!" Hakon ordered tersely. He could see they were outnumbered by at least three to one, and still more warriors were hastily disembarking from the many ships along the beach. Thorolf's two warships had also landed not far from them, and were surrounded as well.

A wooden gangplank was brought to the side of the longship and set roughly against the railing. Hakon watched in silence as the line of men moved back, forming a path for a tall, broad-shouldered warrior striding purposefully toward the longship. So, this was Wulfgar Ragnarson, Hakon thought fleetingly, shrewdly appraising the other man as he walked swiftly up the gangplank and jumped to the wooden deck, followed by several of his warriors.

"Are you Hakon Magnuson?" Wulfgar demanded, his hand resting on the polished hilt of his sword. Hakon nodded grimly. For a long moment the two men eyed each other coldly. Though one was Norwegian and the other a Dane, the same fierce Viking blood ran in their veins. Yet on this day they could have been no further apart. The tension in the air was thick and palpable.

"Wulfgar!" Anora's joyful cry broke the brooding silence. She rushed across the deck and threw herself in his arms. He embraced her tightly, though his steel blue eyes never left Hakon's face.

"You are well?" he asked her, his softly spoken words belying the near-blinding rage and hatred that were tearing at him, threatening to overwhelm him. He knew he was facing the man who had abducted her, the Viking dog who had wrenched her from him on the eve of their marriage. The emissaries sent from Haarek Jarl had told him as much before they had been put to death. Wulfgar wanted nothing more than to run his sword through this blond Viking's heart, but he stayed his hand . . . for the moment.

"Aye, my lord," Anora murmured, lifting her face to look at him. His grim expression frightened her. She had never seen him like this before. He was not the Wulfgar she remembered from their one night of passion, but a battle-hardened warrior, resolute, unflinching, determined to exact his measure of blood vengeance. "Wulfgar . . . please, there is something I must tell—"

"Karl will take you to your father, Anora," Wulfgar interrupted her abruptly. "I will be with you shortly." He led her to a huge warrior, who gently took her arm. Before she could utter another word, she was hustled down the gangplank.

Wulfgar turned back to face Hakon. His eyes flickered over to where Gwendolyn stood by the rear deck. Good, she was well out of the way, he thought fleetingly, as his voice rang out across the beach. "Seize them!"

At his command, dozens of screaming warriors suddenly rushed the longship, their battle cries shattering the eerie stillness that had settled over the beach. Some of them ran swiftly up the gangplank, their glinting swords poised in front of them, while others used crude wooden ladders propped against the hull to climb over the sides of the ship.

Stunned, Gwendolyn watched in horror as Hakon was overwhelmed by four of Wulfgar's men before he could draw his broadsword. He struggled mightily and managed to knock three of them aside, but others were quick to take the places of those who had fallen. Suddenly a cudgel flew through the air, hitting Hakon on the side of the head. He fell heavily to his knees, but still he fought on, his powerful fists hitting home time and time again. But another heavy blow sent him sprawling to the deck. Seizing their chance,

Wulfgar's men grabbed his arms and legs and began to drag him from the ship.

"Nay, please stop!" Gwendolyn cried out, tears streaking her face. But her anguished cries were drowned out as bloodthirsty shouts of "Death to the Vikings!" tore through the air.

Gwendolyn looked wildly about her, cold terror striking her heart at the vengeful bloodlust written on the faces of Wulfgar's warriors and her father's thanes. She knew there was not a moment to lose before they would wreak their own brand of justice upon the captured Vikings. She caught a fleeting glimpse of her father standing on a nearby hill. She knew he was her only hope.

Nay, they will not take Hakon from me! she thought defiantly, wiping her useless tears away with the back of her hand. Drawing courage from the power of her love, she ran to the side of the ship and climbed onto the railing. Without hesitation she jumped into the cold water below, sinking almost up to her waist. She hoisted her soaked chemise and tunic above her knees and waded quickly to shore. Dodging the arms of the warriors who sought only to protect her from the dangerous melee, she rushed along the beach and up the hill, straight into her father's arms.

"Gwendolyn!" Earl Godric cried out, a catch in his voice as he embraced her. But she pulled away from him.

"Please, Father, you must stop them!" Gwendolyn shouted breathlessly, struggling to be heard above the deafening din. "Stay their hands . . . you must . . . you must!"

At that moment Anora broke free of Karl's protective grasp and ran the rest of the way up the hill until she stood side by side with Gwendolyn. Her chest was heaving, and desperate tears streaked her face. "I-I tried to tell Wulfgar t-to stop . . . but he would not hear me!" She choked, trying to catch her breath. "Spare the Vikings, Father . . . please!"

Earl Godric stared in total confusion at his twin daughters. This indeed was not the welcome he had expected! Suddenly he raised his arm for silence. It took a few moments, but gradually the vengeful shouting died out across the beach as all eyes turned toward him.

Gwendolyn looked down the hill, frantically searching for a sign of Hakon. Then she saw him, dangling limply between two burly thanes. He had clearly been beaten, but he was alive. She felt a surge of overwhelming relief as he weakly raised his head, meeting her tear-dimmed gaze over the distance that separated them. She turned back to her father just as Wulfgar quickly strode over to them with his sword in his hand.

"What is the meaning of this, Earl Godric?" he demanded. "I thought 'twas agreed between us that the Vikings were to be put to death at once!"

Earl Godric waved his hand for silence. His expression was hard as he studied his daughters. "Why do you ask me to spare the men who abducted you?" he queried harshly. Truly, he had never been more perplexed!

Anora squeezed Gwendolyn's arm reassuringly, then walked over and stood beside Wulfgar. She looked up at him, a plaintive plea in her eyes. "Please, my lord, if you will only listen." A surge of relief coursed through her when he nodded, though his expression remained grim.

Gwendolyn stepped forward, her emerald eyes flashing with impassioned defiance. She stood straight and proud before her father. Her voice rang out boldly for all to hear. "If you have these men killed, Father, then you will have the blood of the man I love on your hands!"

Earl Godric almost choked, his piercing eyes widening in surprise. Angry mutterings of disbelief rippled through the assembled warriors, threatening to erupt once again into shouts for violence. But Godric raised his arm and they fell silent, albeit begrudgingly. Was this his Gwendolyn? he wondered, bewildered. His rebellious Gwendolyn, who had never granted a suitor a second glance?

"Show me this man," Earl Godric ordered tersely.

Gwendolyn turned and pointed at Hakon. "That is him, there!"

Earl Godric's eyes raked shrewdly over the tall, blond Viking, noting well his proud bearing, even though he had been badly abused by Wulfgar's men. "Bring him to me!" he commanded.

Wincing painfully, Hakon tried to shrug off the two burly warriors and walk up the hill on his own, but he could not. He had to limp between them, leaning on them for support. Gwendolyn met them near the top, and insisted on taking the place of one of the warriors. The tallest one grunted, then stepped aside as she gladly shouldered Hakon's weight.

"You are a brave one," Hakon murmured, a faint smile curving his lips. Then he groaned, a flicker of pain crossing his handsome features.

Earl Godric watched all this without a word. It was only when they were standing before him that he spoke again. "What is your name, man?"

"Hakon Magnuson, my lord."

It was the very man who had abducted them, Earl Godric thought in horror. He turned to Gwendolyn, his eyes registering his disbelief. "How can you say you love this man, Gwendolyn? He has committed a grave crime, not only against yourself, but against your sister as well." His expression was as cold as the tone of his voice. "The punishment he deserves is death."

Gwendolyn's eyes flared indignantly. "Then you punish me as well, Father, for I cannot live without him. It is true that he and his men abducted us, but they have also brought us back to our homeland. Anora has been returned, safe and unharmed. 'Tis a long story, and one I would prefer to tell you at leisure. But I fear that now is neither the time nor the place."

Wulfgar turned to Anora, his face inscrutable. Only his eyes betrayed the depth of the gut-wrenching turmoil raging inside him. "This Viking did not touch you?" he demanded tersely. "Any Viking?" The arm holding his sword was tense, and sweat broke out upon his wide brow. Surely if this man had touched her, he swore vehemently to himself, even Gwendolyn's love would not save him.

"Nay, my lord," Anora replied simply, the truth in her gaze adding credence to her words. She watched the incredible play of emotions across his handsome face, as the vengeful facade of the battle-hardened warrior relaxed into the face of the man she knew and loved.

Wulfgar let out his breath sharply, the white-knuckled grip on his sword slowly relaxing. It was so hard to let go of the bitter rage that had fueled him these long months, yet gradually he could feel the gripping tension, the awful torment, subsiding within him. What he had feared most had not taken place. Anora had not been harmed. He shook his head gravely. Nay, he could no longer justify taking this Viking's life. Suddenly he sheathed his sword, then looked at Earl Godric. "I would not object to sparing this man and his crew, my lord," he said evenly. With that, he gathered Anora into his arms, hugging her fiercely.

Gwendolyn sighed with relief. If Wulfgar was appeased, surely her father would not deny her.

"But what of you, daughter?" Earl Godric asked, his eyes studying her expression carefully. "Do you return the same as you left us?"

Gwendolyn swallowed hard, but she met his gaze evenly. "Nay, Father, I do not." Her eyes widened in alarm as his hand went to the hilt of his sword. "Stay your hand . . . please, hear me out," she said steadily. " 'Tis true I am not the same. But that cannot be undone, nor would I wish it to be so. I was taken from my homeland as a selfish, spoiled child-woman whose most fervent regret was that I had been born a female. Though I stand before you now as a woman who has known the love of a man, I could never wish for it to be otherwise. I love Hakon, Father, more than life itself. 'Tis his child I carry proudly within me."

"Why did you not tell me?" Hakon gasped in astonishment, his eyes searching hers.

"I had not found the right time," she murmured, a faint smile curving her lips, "until this day." She turned back to her father. "You gave Anora the right to choose, Father, and now I demand the same right. It is my wish to remain with Hakon as his wife."

Earl Godric stood for a long moment, his eyes moving from his beloved Gwendolyn's face to Hakon's, then to Wulfgar and Anora and back again. Aye, it was true, he thought. The Gwendolyn he had known was gone, and in her place was a young woman fiercely protecting the life of the man she loved. He knew he could no more deny the hopeful plea burning in her emerald eyes than he could deny the tender look of love that had passed between her and Hakon when she mentioned the child.

"Well, and what say you to this, Lord Hakon?" Earl Godric queried loudly. His expression was inscrutable, though his gaze was not unkind.

"It is as Gwendolyn has said, my lord," Hakon answered, summoning all of his strength to stand proudly before him. "I love her . . . and would have your daughter as my wife."

Satisfied with the Viking's bold answer, a slow smile spread over Earl Godric's face. "Very well. So be it."

Epilogue

Gwendolyn glanced over her shoulder. Hakon was waiting for her aboard his longship, his blue gaze meeting hers across the sandy stretch of beach, beckoning to her. She turned back to Anora and hastily wiped the tears from her eyes.

"I must go," she murmured, her lips trembling as she attempted a smile.

Overcome, Anora could manage only a nod. Her emerald eyes also glistened with tears, joy and sadness all melded into one. She reached out and hugged her sister fiercely for a long, long moment. "You have my thanks, Gwendolyn," she whispered.

Gwendolyn pulled away from Anora's arms, shaking her head. "Nay, I played only a small part," she murmured fervently. "All that has happened was meant to be." She clasped Anora's hand. "Now, I must go." She stepped back, her emerald eyes locking with her sister's in an unspoken message that only the two of them could share. They had been through so much together, yet she knew they had both found their happiness at last. She flashed a tearful smile, then turned and hurried along the beach toward the longship.

Lifting her face to the sun, she felt the warm, morning breeze dry the tears streaking her cheeks. A flood of excitement coursed through her. She and Hakon were going home . . . to Norge!

The past two weeks had gone by so quickly. So many wonderful things had happened. The very day after they arrived in England, Thorolf and his two warships had sailed at once for Trondheim, in his possession a signed charter from Wulfgar Ragnarson forswearing his intent to bring war upon Haarek Jarl. And he had also carried a charter from Earl Godric, stating that he had given his consent to the union between Hakon Magnuson, Jarl of Sogn, and his daughter, Gwendolyn.

Gwendolyn smiled as she remembered the joyful reunion with her parents at the stronghold, then the flurried preparations for the marriage of Anora and Wulfgar. The candlelit ceremony in their family chapel just a few nights past had been one of poignant beauty. She knew she would never forget Anora's radiant look of happiness when she at last became Wulfgar's wife. But the evening had become even more memorable when Father Leofwine, their family priest, had blessed her own union with Hakon after he had sworn he would forsake his heathen Norse gods and adopt the Christian faith.

"Welcome, mistress of Sogn!" Hakon laughed as she approached the longship, breaking into her happy thoughts. He held out his hand to her as she hurried up the gangplank, then drew her into his strong arms and lifted her to the deck. He crushed her to him, breathing in the familiar fragrance of her silver-blond hair. "Are you ready to sail, my love?" he asked softly, his warm lips brushing against hers.

"Aye, my lord," Gwendolyn replied, a wave of intense happiness surging through her as she looked up into his handsome face.

Hakon kissed her smiling lips once again, then drew her with him over to the dragon-headed prow. "Oars to water!" he shouted, his deep voice ringing out above the crashing of the waves on the shore.

Gwendolyn turned around as the longship slid easily into deeper water, her eyes searching the sandy hillsides. She swallowed hard, tears glistening on her thick lashes as she spied first her beloved parents, then Wulfgar and Anora, standing not far from them. She waved her hand in farewell. She did not know if—or when—she would ever see them again.

Suddenly she felt Hakon's strong arm encircle her waist. It gave her the strength she needed. She lifted her trembling chin and looked up at this man who had so captured her heart, her love, her soul . . . with his searing kiss of fire. "Take me home, my lord . . . to Norge," she whispered fiercely, as the longship glided over the waves like a mighty serpent of the sea.

* * * *

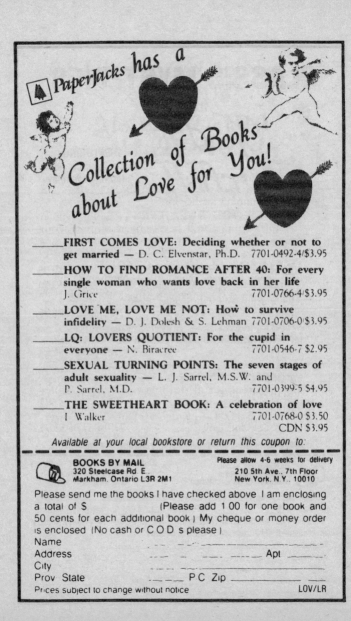

CLASSIC MYSTERIES

from

Gladys Mitchell

FEATURING
Dame Beatrice Adela Lestrange Bradley

_____ **DEATH-CAP DANCERS —** **7701-04010/$2.95**
All they wanted was a vacation in the English countryside. Until they discovered that murder never takes a holiday . . .

_____ **HERE LIES GLORIA MUNDY —** **7701-04037/$2.95**
Gloria Mundy has a nasty habit of turning up when she is least wanted — even after she's dead!

_____ **RISING OF THE MOON —** **7701-04304/$2.95**
The moon sheds light on the horrors of the night . . . and on two small boys who see too much!

_____ **SPOTTED HEMLOCK —** **7701-04835/$2.95**
College pranks turn to deadly deeds in . . . SPOTTED HEMLOCK.

_____ **UNCOFFIN'D CLAY —** **7701-04029/$2.95**
Dirty deeds in Dorset turn up secrets buried deep in . . . UNCOFFIN'D CLAY.

Available at your local bookstore or return this coupon to:

BOOKS BY MAIL
320 Steelcase Rd. E.,
Markham, Ontario L3R 2M1

Please allow 4-6 weeks for delivery
210 5th Ave., 7th Floor
New York, N.Y., 10010

Please send me the books I have checked above. I am enclosing a total of $____________ . (Please add 1.00 for one book and 50 cents for each additional book.) My cheque or money order is enclosed. (No cash or C.O.D.'s please.)

Name ____
Address ______________________________ Apt. ________
City ____
Prov. State __________________ P.C. Zip ________________

Prices subject to change without notice. (GM/1)